The portrait was different. Jim didn't appear to see it, and Andrea was not inclined to draw it to his attention, but the sheer malice of the sketch took her breath away. The subtlety of that malice was precocious and disturbing. The features were not distorted, in fact, they were those of a handsome, stately woman; but the curl of the lip, the vicious slash of the frowning brows. . . . And the cat. Jim had noted the blending of the two bodies, the identity of woman and animal, but he had not understood the implication.

Also by Barbara Michaels
published by Tor Books

The Grey Beginning

BARBARA MICHAELS

HERE I STAY

A TOM DOHERTY ASSOCIATES BOOK
NEW YORK

A TOR Book
Published by Tom Doherty Associates, Inc.
49 West 24 Street
New York, NY 10010

Cover art by Joe DeVito

ISBN: 0-812-50679-0   Can. ISBN: 0-812-50680-4

First Tor edition: June 1985

Printed in the United States of America

0 9 8 7 6 5 4 3

For Jennifer Erin, with love from Grandma
May 7, 1983

ACKNOWLEDGMENTS

I am indebted to many friends in Frederick for help and advice. Dr. Charles C. Clark helped me dispose of one of my characters, and local innkeepers answered questions while allowing me to prowl their premises. The following were particularly gracious:

M. G. (Marty) Martinez, of The Inn at Buckeystown, Maryland

Beverly and Ray Compton, of Spring Bank Farm Inn, Frederick, Maryland

Jane and Ed Rossig, of The Strawberry Inn, New Market, Maryland

It should be emphasized that the inn described in this book is not based on any of the above-mentioned establishments, or on any other actual country inn, and that the errors committed by my innkeeper were made despite the excellent advice proffered by the experts mentioned. Nor is Dr. Clark to blame for any failure to profit by his medical expertise.

Prologue

The hardest thing to bear were the ordinary, everyday sounds. Banal dialogue and canned laughter from the TV room down the hall, voices from the nursing station discussing the weather and spring fashions and how the Caps were doing. It seemed almost obscene that others could go on with the trivial business of living while in some nearby room the ultimate struggle was being waged. She had kept this vigil before, with friends and co-workers; but this time it was different. This time it was Jim. Nineteen years old, with his whole life yet to live—her only brother, her only kin.

A pale, disheveled little figure, her shabby raincoat buttoned awry over her nightgown, she sat huddled in the chair in the area the hospital had set aside for smokers. It had a grudging look; the upholstery was shabby, the magazines were six months old. She was the only one there. The ashtray beside her was overflowing. She had not moved for hours except to stub out one cigarette and light another. When the telephone roused her from sleep she had only stopped long enough to grab her coat and purse. Her short brown hair stood up in wisps around her face, which was as bare of makeup as it was of emotion. She did not look like a hero or a fighter, but she was engaged in a battle against the strongest of all antagonists, the only enemy who has never lost. "You can't have him. Not yet. I won't let him go."

Footsteps approached and slowed, before passing on. Andrea did not look up. The muscles at the corners of her mouth witched in a grotesque caricature of a smile. They were afraid she would have another fit of what *they* called hysterics, like the one she had had in the emergency room. It had not been a pretty performance—kicking, screaming, striking out—she had a vague notion she had also bitten an intern—but it had gotten her to her goal—to Jim. She had been able to touch him, to clasp his blood-streaked hand and communicate her presence and her will. She fought now to maintain that tenuous invisible bond, and to reinforce it with every ounce of strength she possessed. The alert watchers need not have concerned themselves. She would not use that method again unless she had to.

Finally they came for her. The doctor was one she had not seen before. He introduced himself, watching her warily, speaking with the hard-won dispassion of a man who cannot afford the luxury of involvement. She asked the necessary question and got the expected answer: "We're doing all we can."

Seeing Jim was even harder than she had thought it would be. The still form, bandaged and wired and rigid, bore no resemblance to the tall young athlete she loved. She fought back her tears and poured all her strength into the struggle to hold him.

When his white lips parted, the doctor gave a start of surprise. She couldn't hear what he said. The nurse bent over him. "It sounded like a name. Alice?"

"Andrea." She was certain. "He's asking for me. Let me speak to him. Please."

This time the response was stronger. His fingers, almost

the only unbandaged part of his body, were cold, but not with the icy chill of death, and his voice was louder. The word did sound like "Alice." Some girl, some unknown beloved? No. She knew all the girls, she had made a point of meeting them; she knew there was no special girl among them. Whom else would he call but her, sole sister, almost mother? She clung to the cold fingers, trying to warm them. "Hang on, Jimmie. I'm here. I'll always be here, I'll never let you leave me. Just hang on."

When they touched her shoulder she went, unprotesting. The doctor seemed pleased. "It's an encouraging sign, Miss Torgesen. Of course his condition is still critical—the extent of brain damage undeterminable as yet—but the patient's attitude is very important. The will to live."

"He won't die," Andrea said. "I won't let him die."

Chapter One

Andrea climbed down from the ladder and stood back to inspect the sign. Bold black letters, stark on a white background, proclaimed their message: SPRINGERS' GROVE INN. The sign swung gently from wrought-iron brackets atop the stone gatepost. Andrea nodded, pleased with her work. The sign was legible, it was eyecatching and—at last—it hung straight. She dropped onto the bench inside the gate and sat looking at the house.

Every muscle in her body ached, but as she studied the results of months of back-breaking work, the sweet satisfaction of success made fatigue seem unimportant. The summer had been hot and wet. The green lawn sloping down from the house looked like velvet and the old trees shading the porch flaunted leaves of brilliant emerald. However, the first touch of fall was in the air—a faint wash of gold over the maple leaves, bright crimson accents among the oaks. Against a background of rolling hills and verdant meadows the house stood like a marble monument, white paint glistening in the sunlight. The exuberance of Victorian ornament was subdued by the sheer mass of the structure and the strength of the walls. Every gingerbread curlicue was in place; the wide veranda that swept in a graceful curve around the north corner of the facade had been fitted up with wicker chairs and tables and an old-fashioned porch swing. Inside, the same perfection prevailed—charm combined with unobtrusive comfort.

Andrea's hand went to the small of her back in a gesture that was now habitual. She had had a backache for weeks, and no wonder; she had painted and hammered and scrubbed, she had argued with workmen and harassed contractors and fought with inspectors. But it had been worth it. The house was not only a sign of present accomplishment, it was her future—hers and Jim's. Remembering her first view of the place, five months earlier, a smile of triumph curved her lips.

A March morning, gray, foggy, cold. Icy rain, a few degrees away from snow, drizzled down the windshield as she brought the car to a stop by the porch steps. Jim sat beside her, hunched over, knees ostentatiously drawn up; he was six feet three and still growing, but his silent protest was directed not so much against the size of the car as against the fact that she had refused to let him drive. Deeply insulted, he had sulked all the way from D.C.—thirty miles of offended silence, which Andrea blandly ignored. The sight of the house broke through his huffiness. "Jesus H. Christ," he said.

"Don't swear," Andrea said automatically. But she couldn't help thinking that he had put the case in a nutshell.

Leafless and forlorn, the trees looked like crippled giants raising rheumatic arms to threaten the house. There were three floors of it, plus an attic under the mansard roof, and a tower at one end. Acres of walls—and not a square inch of paint that wasn't flaking, chipping, or missing. The iron railing surrounding the widow's walk looked like broken teeth, red with rust. Half a dozen windows were boarded up. One of the pillars supporting the porch roof was broken; the steps sagged, inadequately propped by stones. Even on a bright day the wreck of a once proud mansion would have been depressing. On that gloomy, dreary morning, the sight was indescribable.

Too discouraged to move, Andrea sat with her hands on the wheel. It was not her first view of the place, but it was her first view as owner—owner of ruin and decay. She had paid duty visits to Cousin Bertha once or twice a year. For the last five of those years the old lady—actually her grandmother's half-sister—had been virtually senile, clinging to her home with the unreasonable determination of the old and able to do so because the small community in which she lived had a few middle-aged, unskilled women who could be hired to tend the elderly. Andrea remembered thinking disinterestedly that the house was deteriorating, but she had not paid much attention; she hadn't imagined the problem would ever be hers. Bertha had innumerable relatives. They were widely scattered, however, and Andrea was the only one who paid regular visits to the old lady. She could honestly claim that the hope of profit had never been one of her motives; the visits had been prompted in part by proximity and in part by the stern Calvinist sense of duty Jim found so funny. He teased her constantly about her New England conscience, and when the letter from the lawyer arrived he had shouted with amusement, "Now it comes out. What did you do, con the old lady into making you her sole heir?"

Andrea was not amused. "She's probably left me some ghastly trinket—a brooch with dried-up hair in it, or her collection of seashells. Maybe it's something I can sell. I hope so. We could use the money."

Jim's well-shaped mouth tightened, as it always did when she talked about finances. "Goddamn it, Andy, if we're that broke I'll get a job. A full-time job. I told you—"

"No. You'll finish college. No one knows better than I

how important that is. I wish I could do better for you than the state university, but—"

"Maryland is fine. It's a good school. I like it. But I wish to God you'd stop talking about money!"

He left the room. Andrea stared at her clenched hands. He was right; she did harp on the subject. Jim hated being dependent on her, he knew how hard she worked to keep him in school. She had refused to let him apply for student loans; she wouldn't have him burdened by debts when he entered the job market. He couldn't understand her hatred of owing money. He had only been eight years old when the accident that killed their father and stepmother left them orphaned, without kin close enough to help. Andrea didn't want help, but it had been a shock to learn that her handsome, brilliant father had lived up to every penny of his considerable income, and that he had not even carried extra insurance. Like so many men, he had refused to contemplate the possibility of dying. He was in his early forties, at the peak of his career, when the plane crash ended his career, his life, and Andrea's college aspirations.

She had gone to work as a typist in a motel office—the first job that came to hand, but it had proved a wise choice. With the help of night courses she had worked her way up to assistant manager of a good-sized hotel, and had come to enjoy the challenges of the profession. However, it was a grueling, demanding job, requiring long hours and frequent emergency calls; she hadn't been able to spend as much time with Jim as she would have liked. All her spare hours had been devoted to him, and her efforts had paid off. Except for the normal adolescent misadventures he had given her no trouble, and she never regretted the fact that her social life consisted almost entirely of school plays and Cub Scout meetings, Little League and school football games. Jim had made State All-American in high school; his first year in college he had been asked to go out for soccer as well as football. He had wanted to work part-time, but she couldn't allow that; sports and studying were hard enough. When he protested she said jokingly, "Don't knock it, kid—how much does a pro football player make? I expect to be supported in style one of these days."

When the lawyer told her Cousin Bertha had left her everything—the house, its contents, and the thirty acres of land surrounding it—her reaction was numbed disbelief. There must be a catch to it. She had struggled so long, with so many setbacks and disappointments; she had stopped believing in luck.

Jim, who had never accompanied her on her visits to Cousin Bertha, was convinced they must have inherited a fortune. Now he sat silent beside her, staring at the decaying wreck with what Andrea assumed must be her own sense of outraged disgust. Her hands clenched. The house wasn't a white elephant—it was a dirty gray rotting carcass. The lawyer had warned her it would not be easy to sell; no one wanted big old houses that cost a fortune to heat. Now she realized that he had understated the case. She would have to pay someone to take this ruin off her hands.

"Where is that damned lawyer?" she demanded angrily. "He said he'd be here. I can't take any more time off. They're charging me leave for this morning as it is."

Jim didn't reply. His big scarred hands rested lightly on his knees. Andrea nudged him.

"We may as well go in."

He followed her. The steps and the porch floor creaked as they walked. The key stuck in the lock, and Andrea had to wrestle with it. The door opened with a howl of rusting hinges.

In the gray dimness the shapes of massive pieces of furniture loomed like behemoths waiting to attack. "Well, the place hasn't been robbed yet," Andrea said grimly. "But it's only a matter of time. I must get a dealer in here right away.

Antiques are hot these days. Maybe we can salvage something after all.''

Still mumbling, she entered the room on the left of the hall. "Get some light in here. I wonder. . . . Yes, the electricity is on. Just as well, I guess, but you'd have thought that damned lawyer would turn off the utilities. They're eating up money every second.''

The chandelier was a handsome cut-glass giant, but only a few of the bulbs remained, and a number of the dangling prisms were missing. The light only increased the impression of desolation. Dust lay thick on every surface, dulling the gleam of mahogany and rosewood. A strong smell of damp warred with another equally unpleasant odor Andrea could not immediately identify. Still, her spirits rose slightly as she ran her finger across the top of the carved mantel and felt the cool smoothness of marble. "Might be worth a few bucks," she said. "Jim, do you think . . . Jim. Where are you?''

He didn't reply. She went back into the center of the room; through the curved archway she saw him standing, a shadowy form, at the foot of the stairs.

"I'm here," he said finally. His voice was dreamy and abstracted, quite unlike his normal robust tones.

"What the hell are you doing? Get in here and help me. I want to take an inventory.''

He turned his head quickly. "I thought you were upstairs. I thought you called me.''

"I did call you. Stop wool-gathering, Jim. You saw me come in here.''

"I know, but. . . ." He shook his head in bewilderment. "I could have sworn somebody was upstairs. You didn't hear a voice, calling my name?''

"Cut it out," Andrea snapped. "I agree the place looks like the set for a horror movie, but I'm in no mood for corny jokes about ghosts.''

"I wasn't. . . ." Jim shrugged. "Okay. What do you want me to do?"

Andrea handed him a notebook and pen. "Write as I dictate. We'll start in here."

They had barely begun when a bang on the door announced the arrival of the lawyer. Andrea let him in. He greeted her with a smile, brushing the rain from his shock of thick white hair. "Sure is a miserable day," he said cheerfully.

Conversation about the weather had always struck Andrea as a complete waste of time. "You're late," she said.

"Sorry 'bout that. Well, what do you think? Fine old house, isn't it?"

"It's a catastrophe," Andrea said curtly. "Mr. Bushwaller, this is my brother, Jim."

"Just call me Fred." Bushwaller extended his hand. "You're a big one, aren't you? Basketball player?"

"Football," Jim said. "Glad to meet you, sir."

"What position?"

"Cornerback."

"That right? But you look like you'd be fast, too. Helps to have a defensive back tall enough to get to the ball before the receiver. If the 'Skins had—"

Andrea broke in. She knew that once the Redskins entered the conversation, it might go on forever. "Mr. Bushwaller, I'm short on time. Could we get down to business?"

"Why, sure. Hoped I could take you folks to lunch later— we've got one of the best restaurants in the state right here in town, and—"

"Yes, I've heard of Peace and Plenty. But I don't have time today. I want to go through the house and check your inventory."

Bushwaller took off his damp raincoat, shook it out, and draped it carefully over the newel post. He had the craggy good-humored face of a farmer and his pale-blue eyes were narrowed in amusement.

"Isn't any inventory," he said coolly. "I kept nagging Miss Bertha to have one made, but you know how she was. Had enough trouble getting her to sign that will five years back. She was over eighty, but she kept sayin' she had plenty of time. . . ."

"I might have known," Andrea muttered.

"It's all yours, anyhow," the lawyer said, with unprofessional casualness. "Nobody is going to contest that will. Drew it up all right and proper, and I'll swear the old lady was of sound mind."

"Nobody in his right mind would want this," Andrea said in disgust.

"Guess that's right. Lots of stuff here, but none of it's worth much. What were you figuring on doing with it?"

"I'll sell anything I can."

The lawyer nodded. On the surface his manner did not change, but the glance with which he swept the room roused a sudden suspicion in Andrea, who was only too prone to that emotion in any case. She felt her assumption confirmed when Bushwaller went on casually, "I know a feller in town runs a secondhand shop. He'll give you a fair shake."

"Secondhand shop," Andrea repeated.

"Junk—you know." Bushwaller added in the same disinterested voice, "You want to clear the place out fast, before the local hoodlums realize nobody's living here. I could send Sam on up here when I get back to town, if you want."

"I don't intend to talk to any dealers until after I've taken the inventory."

Bushwaller met her hostile eyes, and the twinkle in his own grew stronger. He accepted defeat gracefully. "Can't help you with anything else then, I reckon," he said.

"You can go through the house with me," Andrea said.

Bushwaller glanced at his watch—an expensive-looking gold timepiece that, like his Brooks Brothers suit, jarred with the country-lawyer image he was trying to project. "'Fraid I'm a little late this morning."

"It won't take any more time than a leisurely lunch at Peace and Plenty," Andrea said, in a tone that brooked no argument. She figured she was going to get a whopping bill from good old Fred anyway; he might contribute nothing of value, but it would give her some satisfaction to inconvenience him.

Once coerced, Bushwaller decided to relax and enjoy it. He was vague about the history of the house—"Reckon it's a hundred years old, give or take a few years"—but since Andrea was no more interested than he, she did not object. It was Jim who asked that question and others of the same nature; when Bushwaller was unable to answer them, he lapsed into an abstracted silence, and Andrea finally took the notebook from him.

The house was even bigger than it appeared from the front. Twin parlors, backed on one side by a library and on the other by a dark, high-ceilinged dining room, occupied most of the ground floor. From the dining room a butler's pantry and short passageway led to a kitchen so large, so gloomy, and so dirty, that Bushwaller was moved to malicious mirth. "Those sure were the good old days. Couldn't get a woman to work in this place today."

Andrea had to agree. The black coal stove stood aggressively in its place; it probably had not been used in years. Cousin Bertha's attendants had used a small gas stove and an even smaller refrigerator, both of which were rusted and years out of date. Andrea stamped across the wooden floor, feeling the boards sag ominously, and threw open a door at the rear. A wide corridor lined with shelves led into a back wing containing three small empty rooms and a hideous bathroom, with a claw-footed tub, a washstand, and a leaky commode jammed into a space that might once have been a closet.

"Servants' quarters," said Bushwaller, now enjoying himself hugely. The more Andrea's expression hardened, the jollier he became. "Sure wish I lived back then. All the cheap darky help you wanted."

Another door led to a steep enclosed staircase, which they climbed to reach the second floor. It was only a few degrees less depressing than the first—just as crowded with furniture, just as dusty.

"This was Miss Bertha's room," Bushwaller said cheerfully, fumbling for the light switch. "She was bedridden, poor old soul. . . . Looks like the bulb's burned out," he added, chuckling.

Andrea pushed past him, meaning to pull back the velvet draperies shrouding the windows. Bertha's bedroom was worth more than a cursory glance. The old lady had kept her most cherished possessions close at hand. Lying in the big four-poster bed, she had fumbled through her treasures, muttering in senile pleasure or distress as faded photographs and yellowed clippings reminded her of her vanished youth.

There was a stir and a rustle of bedclothes and a slow, heaving movement, as something dark rose from the center of the fourposter. Andrea fell back with a shriek.

Even Bushwaller was briefly disconcerted. He let out a stifled curse and then made a dash for the nearest window. The damp gray light fell full upon the form that stood bolt upright on the bed. It was the biggest cat Andrea had ever seen—coal black without a spot of white, and fully two feet long from its whiskers to its solid rump. Round golden eyes stared at her as if in challenge, and a tail as thick as a broom handle lashed back and forth.

"Ho, ho, ho." Bushwaller let out a rich, rotund Father Christmas laugh. "Durned if I hadn't forgotten about him. Gave me quite a start. Hope you aren't superstitious, Miss Torgesen."

"How did that—that animal get in here?" Andrea demanded. The innocuous noun hardly suited the creature; he was the personification of the witch's cat of literature. "Shoo!" She advanced on the bed, waving her arms. "Get off there—scat!"

The cat yawned, displaying two rows of sharp teeth. Turning with ostentatious contempt, it began kneading the bedclothes. Ripping sounds accompanied this demonstration.

Bushwaller's mirth redoubled. "Better not tangle with old Satan, Miss Torgesen. So he's been here all the time! Annie May was asking about him—she was Miss Bertha's nurse, you know."

"How did he get in?" Andrea repeated.

"Probably has his private holes," Bushwaller said easily. "Now, Miss Torgesen, I wouldn't advise you to touch Satan; he's never been what you'd call a pet, he sort of comes and goes as he pleases."

"He'll come and go as I please," Andrea retorted. Now she knew the source of the peculiar smell in the parlor. Satan had used a corner of it as his private litter box on days when he chose not to brave rain or cold.

The cat settled down again. As Andrea advanced, he gave her a hard look over his massive plushy-black shoulder. To the surprise of everyone, including Andrea, he allowed her to scoop him up.

He weighed a good twenty pounds, all of it bone and muscle. The warm sleek weight filled her arms. But there was nothing cuddly about Satan; he simply sat there, a solid mass of indifference. Nor did he purr.

"Well, if that don't beat the devil," Bushwaller exclaimed. "Annie May got kind of attached to the old rascal—why, I don't know—but she never dared pick him up. He'd let Miss Bertha pet him now and then, but that was it. You must have a knack with animals, Miss Torgesen."

"I don't like animals," Andrea said shortly. "And I hate cats."

Satan looked up at her, a sneer curling his lip. Andrea glared back at him. "I hate cats," she repeated. "But I won't stand for wanton cruelty. I cannot believe you and—Annie May—simply abandoned this animal and left him to fend for himself."

Even as she spoke, the image struck her as absurd. Satan looked perfectly capable of fending for himself and, if necessary, of besting any number of antagonists. Jim started to laugh.

"I wish I had my camera. The expression on both your faces . . . Here, give him to me."

But when he put out his hand, a huge black paw smacked down on it. Jim backed away, sucking scratches. "Okay, okay. He likes you, Andy."

Andy dumped the cat unceremoniously onto the floor. Satan stalked out, tail erect, whiskers bristling, with the heavy tread of a man.

"Told you he wasn't a pet," said Bushwaller. "I'd have taken care of him if I could have, Miss Torgesen," he added in an injured voice. "Haven't seen hide nor hair of him since Miss Bertha passed on. He don't look abused, does he? Annie May says he's a fine mouser, kept the house cleared out."

This aspect of the matter had not occurred to Andrea. It might come down to a choice between Satan piddling in the parlor and lounging on the bed, and battalions of mice gnawing furniture, fabric and wiring. She shrugged. "I guess he can stay till we find an alternative."

"Like to see you try to evict him," Bushwaller said. "Now that I think about it, there's always been black cats around Springers' Grove, far back as I can remember. Lots of them in town, too." He chuckled in a ribald manner and winked at Jim. "Satan gets around nights, I reckon."

"Probably black is a dominant color," Andrea said.

"Huh?"

"Let's get on with it."

They saw no more of Satan as the tour proceeded. There were five large bedrooms and two baths on the second floor, six smaller rooms on the third. They had been turned into storerooms; chairs without seats, tables without legs, and other decrepit objects filled them in motley array.

After Bushwaller had led them up to the attic, Andrea took one look at the clutter and shook her head. "Not today. I can't stand looking at any more junk."

"Reckon that's all there is up here," he agreed. "Miss Bertha never threw anything away. Nor gave it away, neither."

"Where do those stairs go?" Jim asked.

He indicated a short flight of curving steps.

"Tower, I reckon," Bushwaller said. "I got to be getting back. . . ."

Jim mounted the stairs and opened the door.

Light streamed out onto the narrow landing. This topmost floor of the round tower stood free of the rest of the house; the lower floors formed bays in the library, master bedroom, and one of the third floor rooms. Windows ran around three quarters of the circumference, providing views of the surrounding countryside—winter-browned hills to the west, the roofs of the town to the south and, opposite, the muddy rushing flood of the stream bounding the property on the north. Even in that bleakest of all seasons, with mist veiling the mountaintops and rain streaking the panes, it was the most attractive view Andrea had seen in the past hour. But when Jim murmured, "Hey, what a great room," in a tone she knew only too well, she said sharply, "You mean what a great mess. Come out of there before the floor collapses."

"The floor's all right." Jim demonstrated by stamping through the fallen plaster and scraps of paper littering the floor. "This board just inside the door sags a little, but I could fix—"

"I said come out of there."

He obeyed unwillingly and Andrea closed the door. That was all she needed—that Jim should take a fancy to the place and propose some tomfool scheme for keeping it. Mercifully the house was too far from the university to make commuting feasible, otherwise Jim would probably suggest moving in, with a "bunch of the guys"—his informal and virtually ubiquitous entourage. Andrea didn't blame Jim's friends for wanting to be with him—he was wonderful company—but she had never been able to understand why they had to travel in packs like wild dogs. She hardly ever got a chance to see Jim alone, and although she rather liked "the guys" as individuals, she resented them bitterly as a collective entity. The very phrase made her see red.

When she and Jim got downstairs, Bushwaller was halfway out the front door. Andrea slammed it after him and Jim gave her a disapproving frown.

"You were pretty rude, weren't you?"

"He's a crook," Andrea said. "There must be a few valuable antiques here or he wouldn't be so eager to bring his buddy Sam in on the deal. Let's get on with the inventory."

By the time they finished with the parlor, the morning was well advanced. "I've never seen so much junk," Andrea grumbled, closing the doors of a corner cupboard whose contents of china and glassware had filled four pages of the notebook. "But I daren't omit anything; I don't know anything about antiques and collectors are crazy, they'll pay the earth for bric-a-brac. Next time I'll bring a camera and a tape recorder; that would be more efficient than writing everything down. Friday. I've got Friday off this week. I'll come out at the crack of dawn and work all day."

"Want some help? I could meet you here—"

"You have three classes on Friday."

Jim's face twisted. "Damn it, you know my schedule better than I do. It won't matter if I take—"

"You will go to class."

"Saturday, then."

"I have to work Saturday."

28

"You won't finish this in one day. I could carry on from where you left off—bring a bunch of the guys to help."

Andrea bit her lip. Help would be welcome, for time was unquestionably of the essence, but "the guys" were not the assistants she wanted. They would descend on the house like a horde of locusts, full of goodwill and good intentions—and beer. After an hour or so they would all be sprawled on the floor talking about life and getting bombed.

"I'll think about it," she said.

Jim knew what that meant. His eyes narrowed and his lips tightened. Andrea braced herself for an argument. Jim would have hooted with disbelief if she had told him she hated fighting with him, for she always kept her cool and she always won. But she did hate it. She hated being at odds with the person she loved best—the only person she really loved. Why couldn't he just take her word for things instead of disagreeing all the time?

This time, to her relief, he capitulated with a shrug, his face remote. Andrea patted him on the arm.

"I'll think about it. We'd better get going. Lunch is on me—pizza, as usual?"

Jim headed for the car. "I'm driving," he announced belligerently.

Meekly Andrea handed over the keys. She didn't have the heart to squelch him again that morning—and he knew it. He grinned at her and set the car moving with exaggerated care. It crept like a snail down the drive. Andrea turned for a final look. The fog was creeping in. The queer peaked roof of the tower pointed at the low-hanging clouds like an accusing finger.

That night, driving back to campus in the rain and fog, Jim was sideswiped by a van trying to pass on a sharp curve. His car went over an embankment and into a tree. Andrea had just dropped off to sleep when the telephone rang.

Chapter Two

The battle had not ended the night she knew Jim would live. For weeks it went on—a grim, seemingly endless fight to hold him in a world he no longer cared to inhabit. Hour after hour she sat by his bed, reading aloud, carrying on desperate one-sided conversations. Sometimes he answered in monosyllables; sometimes he didn't respond at all. Usually he didn't even look at her but lay staring at the ceiling, a frown of rejection drawing lines across his forehead and along his cheeks.

At first Dr. Blake was reassuring. "Wasn't it Bernard Shaw who said that optimism is a gift of middle age? He's only nineteen. Young people haven't had enough experience to know that there is always a tomorrow. Physically he's coming right along, considering the extent of his injuries."

One day in April Andrea managed to corner Blake in his office. He had avoided her of late, primarily because he had come to share her forebodings. The case puzzled and distressed him. His professional pride was injured by Jim's failure to respond, and despite his attempts to remain detached he had developed an unwilling interest in the boy and his sister.

"He's not trying," Andrea said. "He won't help. What can I do?"

"You must show him you depend on him," Blake suggested, somewhat desperately. "Sometimes a sense of responsibility. . . . Tell him you need him."

"Need him?" It was a cry of anguish. "Need him?"

Blake turned his head away. After a moment Andrea muttered, "I'm sorry."

She had refused to sit down. They stood side by side, and although Blake was not a tall man he had to look down on her. He knew her age—thirty-one. She looked ten years older. The strain of the past weeks might explain the lines on her face and the grim set of her mouth, but he suspected they were habitual. She was a fighter, this one. Impulsively he started to speak, and then stopped himself. He wasn't an analyst; what the hell did he know? Besides, it was unlikely that anyone could penetrate the wall of stubborn self-righteousness that was at once her most admirable and her most maddening characteristic.

He put his hand on her shoulder. "Keep trying," he said gently. "Don't give up."

The fragile bone and muscle under his hand stiffened. "I won't."

She went back to Jim's room. He wasn't expecting her. She saw his face go blank, as if a thin film of some rapidly congealing, transparent substance had spread over his features, and her heart sank. Sitting down by the bed, she reached for his hand, searching for words—the right words. She had the feeling that this was her last chance, and at first she was at a loss. Out of nowhere, seemingly, the words came.

"I wanted to ask you about something," she said.

There was no response, not even a twitch of muscle in the limp fingers she held. Groping, she went on. "It's that damned house, Jim—Bertha's house. I don't know what to do about it. Bushwaller called this morning, said the police had scared off some kids who were trying to break in last night. I put it on the market right after . . . Well, it's been a long time, and we haven't had a nibble.''

She fancied she saw the faintest flicker of interest in his hooded eyes. Then it came pouring out in a flood, the argument as well marshaled and organized as if she had been working on it for days.

''Jimmie, what would you think about turning the house into an inn—living there ourselves? Being his own boss is every laborer's dream, but I never imagined I could own my own place—you can't compete with the big chains, not these days. But the bed-and-breakfast idea, the country inn, is catching on. I've read several articles about it. The house is certainly big enough, and there's a good restaurant nearby, so I wouldn't have to serve meals. The area is full of antique shops and battlefields and historic sites. . . . Could we do it? Or would we be taking on more than we can handle?''

For a long moment, a moment that seemed to stretch into eternity, he did not reply. Then he said, in a voice rusty with disuse, ''The house is sound structurally. Needs a lot of work—mostly painting, papering. . . .''

''Is it? It is? That's what I wanted to ask you. I wasn't sure. You know about those things, you're so good with your hands. . . .'' She gabbled, her voice unsteady as she tried to weave the thin thread of interest into a stronger hold. ''We could sell the good pieces of furniture but keep enough to furnish the rooms with real antiques. . . . Bertha left a small insurance policy, only a few thousand, but with what I've saved there might be enough to cover the remodeling. . . . Jim, I'm scared. I don't know whether I can do it.''

His head turned. His hair was lank and dull and he had lost weight; the sunken cheeks and white lips were those of an old man. ''Sure you can,'' he said. ''You can do anything.''

''Not unless you help me.''

''Sure. I could get some of the guys. . . .''

The familiar, once hated phrase was too much for her. Tears flooded her eyes. Clinging to his hand, she buried her face against the sheets. After an interval she felt his other hand fumblingly stroke her hair.

II

That same afternoon Andrea gave up her apartment and her job. The latter was a desperate expedient, leaving her without income at a time when she needed money badly, but she sensed that it was necessary to risk everything on one last hope. She divided her time between the hospital and the house in Ladiesburg. She barely took time to sleep, and when she did she slept like the dead, drained by emotional strain and physical effort. Her intention was to get the house in order before Jim came home. He would insist on helping if there was work to be done, and she was determined that he should not waste his strength on manual labor.

She made a point of consulting him about everything she did, and of following his advice when it was at all practicable. His recovery was frighteningly slow, but there were no major setbacks; she came to have an almost superstitious reverence for the house, because it was the one thing that held his interest, even in his bad times. And the cat . . .

Satan was a permanent resident. He came and went at his own sweet will—"the cat who walked by himself," said one of Jim's more literary friends, quoting Kipling—but when he was in the house he was almost always to be found on the bed in Bertha's room. Andrea did not accept this arrangement without a fight. She tried everything she could think of, from locking doors to strewing the bed with tacks, to no avail. By trickiness or teleportation Satan got into the room, and tacks didn't bother him; he shoved the shredded coverlet up around them and reclined on the sheet.

The war between Andrea and Satan became the highlight of

Jim's day. His friends, home from college and rallying around like troopers, enjoyed the cat gossip as much as Jim did. Grimly and dutifully Andrea had put food out for Satan—no animal was going to die of neglect in her house—but the day Jim first laughed aloud, when she told him about the tacks on the bed, Andrea stopped at the store on her way home and bought a container of cream—whipping cream, not the thinner variety. Satan stared at it with a look of almost human astonishment before tucking up his whiskers and diving in.

After that there was no more talking of giving Satan away or delivering him to the Humane Society. And it was Jim who offered the solution to Satan's refusal to be evicted from the master bedroom.

"There's a story in here about a resident cat," he said, indicating the copy of *Country Inns and Restaurants* he had been reading. "The cat lives in Room Number Six, and the owners just tell guests that's the way it is. It lends a certain cachet, don't you think?"

" 'Cachet' is not the word," Andrea said, laughing. His vocabulary had improved considerably. Reading was something he'd never had time for, before. . . .

At least Satan provided comic relief. Very little else in Andrea's life just then was funny. However, the work proceeded far more smoothly than she realized at the time. Workmen actually showed up on the day they had promised to come, the necessary permits were obtained without debate, inspectors passed the new wiring and plumbing with unbelievable amiability.

Andrea was also up to her chapped elbows in manual labor. She stripped wallpaper, sanded floors, painted moldings and caulked windows. She confined the alterations to the first and second floors. Five guest bedrooms were all she could handle without full-time help. In her free time she studied "do it yourself" manuals, read every article she could find on country inns, and called on local innkeepers to get ideas. Her training in hotel management helped to some extent, but many aspects of the bed-and-breakfast trade were new to her. New and exciting; as she scraped and scrubbed and sanded, her mind teemed with ambitious plans. More guest rooms on the third floor and the attic, gourmet meals, tennis courts and a swimming pool, get-away weekends for antique and history buffs, with lectures and guided tours. . . . As time went on, she found an unexpected satisfaction in her work of awakening the beauty of the old house from its cobweb-encrusted sleep of years.

It wasn't until she went to the local bank to ask for a mortgage on the house that she began to wonder why matters had gone so smoothly. She didn't expect to get the money without a fight, not at the first place she tried; but the manager, who called her "Miss Andrea," practically handed her the cash.

Dazed, she left the bank and stood on the front steps to get her wits together. The bank was a branch of a state-wide institution, but it occupied a building dating to the thirties, when banks looked like banks, not like red brick bungalows. Tall stone pillars supporting a pedimented Greek gable shone in the sunlight. Straight ahead was the main street of Ladiesburg, less than a mile from Foster's Amoco at one end to the Ladiesburg Meat and Freezer Company at the other. The business district was three blocks long, and the majority of the buildings were of the eighteenth and early nineteenth centuries. In recent years there had been a concerted attempt to restore the original appearance of the gracious Federal houses, and Ladiesburg merchants nurtured Machiavellian schemes for challenging New Market as the antiques capital of Maryland.

Andrea had met a number of these merchants in the course of her enterprise; they had been helpful and friendly but she had not had time to respond to their overtures. Now, as she pondered her newfound wealth, her eyes focused on a building in the middle of the next block. It was the largest structure in town, including the bank—a low stone building with black shutters and tubs of petunias lining the facade. Andrea started walking.

It was ten-thirty, and luncheon preparations at Peace and Plenty were underway. Andrea went through the back door and into the main dining room. Peace and Plenty had started life as an inn, "the oldest continually operated tavern in Maryland," as its brochure proclaimed. Reba Miller had taken over the restaurant from her parents. Presumably there had once been a Mr. Miller, since Reba had the title of "Mrs.," but Andrea suspected that even when that ephemeral personage had been alive he had been referred to as "Mr. Reba Miller."

Reba stood in the corner of the room shouting orders at the waitresses who were setting the tables for lunch. A cigarette dangled from her mouth without impeding speech; the top of her black beehive wig brushed the ferns that filled hanging baskets attached to the low ceiling. She was almost six feet tall and correspondingly broad. She used the same type of makeup she had used when she was twenty; the slash of crimson lipstick was crooked, and the powder was caked in the wrinkles of her broad face. Andrea arrived in time to hear her bellow, "Get your ass in gear, Susie, we open in an hour."

Susie, a slim little creature who looked delicious in the mobcap and colonial gown that constituted Peace and Plenty's uniform, grinned and went calmly on with what she was doing. Hearing Andrea approach, Reba turned and waved a hand in greeting.

"Lazy little bitches," she said around her cigarette. "Want a cup of coffee?"

She was obviously expecting a refusal. Usually when they met on the street or in one of the shops, Andrea excused herself on the grounds that she was too busy to take time off.

When Andrea said, "Thanks; if it's not too much trouble," Reba smiled broadly. The cigarette fell out of her mouth. Andrea bent to pick it up, but before she could do so Reba stepped on it and ground it into the stone-flagged floor.

"Tracy, get over here and clean up this mess," she shouted.

They had their coffee in Reba's office, which adjoined the dining room so she could harass her staff. It was a large, untidy room, containing not only a desk and file cabinets, but a dining table and chairs, sofas, and bookcases. During a lull in the conversation, when Reba had rushed to the door to chastise a waitress for forgetting the napkins, Andrea glanced at the books; somehow she was not surprised to see that the selection was, to say the least, eclectic. It ranged from a worn, well-read copy of *Mother Carey's Chickens* to Proust in the original French, and included one or two volumes of the sort that Reba's generation usually hid under the mattress.

Andrea wasted no time. "Are you the one I have to thank for all the sweetness and light and cooperation I've been getting?"

Reba tried without success to look bewildered. "What do you mean?"

"I just took out a mortgage on the house." Might as well admit it; Reba knew everything that went on in town, sometimes before the participants did. "I got more than I had hoped, with no hassle. Somebody down here likes me. Or. . . ."

Reba was quick to catch her meaning. "God, you're an evilminded little cynic, aren't you?" she said admiringly. "No, kiddo, I'm not looking for any favors. Except for sending trade my way, and that's mutual. We aren't competing, since I don't rent rooms and you don't serve meals."

"Then you are the one who's been putting in a good word for me. I'd have caught on before this if I hadn't been so busy."

"I talked to a few people," Reba admitted. She lit another cigarette and tried to look casual.

"Why?"

"Why the hell not?" Reba shouted. Her cigarette fell onto the table. She picked it up, put it back in her mouth, and mumbled, "What's wrong with doing a favor for somebody you . . . well . . . for a friend? A friend who's had a hard time?"

Andrea had grown accustomed to the fact that everybody in Ladiesburg and its vicinity knew her personal history. People who were the slightest of acquaintances stopped her on the street to ask how Jim was getting along. She hated pity as much as she hated morbid curiosity, but had forced herself to respond pleasantly; she couldn't operate without the goodwill of the local shopkeepers, and mutual cooperation was to her advantage as well as theirs. But it had never occurred to her that small-town intimacy might work in her favor.

"I'm sorry," she said, realizing that she was staring and that Reba, hideously uncomfortable, had chewed the end of her cigarette to shreds. "I just don't understand. You hardly know me."

"I like your guts," Reba said. "There was a time when I . . . Well, the hell with that. Actually, it's none of your g————d business why I do anything, is it?"

"No." Andrea smiled.

The corners of Reba's clown-red mouth twitched. "Oh, get out of here. I've got to light a fire under those worthless kids, and you have work to do."

"Right." Andrea rose. "Come over for a drink sometime."

"I might at that."

The sidewalks of Ladiesburg were of brick, large sections of which had been tumbled or displaced by the roots of the miniature weeping cherries that lent the town such distinction in April. Her eyes on the ground, Andrea walked along the street, past Raider's Antiques, Antique Haven, Past and Present (antiques), the Candle and Basket Shop (also crafts), Patchwork Paradise, and Long Remembered (antiques). Reba was the last person in the world from whom she would have expected such a burst of sentimentality. "I admire your guts," indeed. Dialogue from an old film starring Spencer Tracy and Mickey Rooney. . . . But if Reba was moved by underhanded motives, Andrea could not imagine what they might be. For all Reba's tough-guy affectations, her sexual orientation was of the kind most of the world called normal; Andrea had encountered the other variety often enough to have developed instincts in such matters. Apparently Reba identified with her and her struggles, but it was hard to picture that formidable old woman as young and vulnerable.

Though she couldn't understand Reba's motives, she had no hesitation in accepting the help they provided. Discreet questioning of workmen and shopkeepers provided her with an explanation for Reba's clout; she was the biggest property owner in town, with a sizable share of stock in the bank. It's a pity she isn't my cousin, Andrea thought, as she slapped plaster into holes in the parlor wall.

It was August before Jim was ready to leave the hospital. Andrea increased her efforts and somehow the essential work got done. The most valuable of Cousin Bertha's furniture had gone to dealers, but there was enough left to furnish the reception rooms and bedrooms in Victorian splendor. The attic had proved to be a treasure trove, containing marble-topped washstands and oak tables, handmade quilts and crocheted spreads, beds and chairs and fireplace screens. Andrea was able to advertise that "each room is furnished with genuine antiques" without stretching the truth too much. She had several advance bookings weeks before she was ready to open. Here again she had Reba to thank. "Word-of-mouth advertising is what you want," Reba had said, adding, with a lip-stretching grin that proved her point, "My mouth is big enough to help quite a lot."

The inn sign was the final touch. Andrea had deliberately waited until everything else was in order before hanging it; the act was a little private ceremony not to be shared, even with Jim. She wanted .everything to be absolutely perfect when he saw it.

He would see it in only a few more hours. The doctor had, suggested she pick him up about eleven. She knew she ought to get back to the house, shower and change. But the warm sunlight felt good on her aching shoulders and she was reluctant to move.

Out in the middle of the pasture next to the house a single dark blot broke the expanse of rippling green. Satan sat like a statue carved of jet, his coat shimmering in the sunlight. Haunches and tail were concealed by the tall grass, and in his utter stillness he resembled an expensive art object in a dealer's window, with green satin swathing his pedestal. He spent hours in that position on sunny days; presumably he was lying in wait for mice or moles. Andrea preferred not to think about that. Satan's sole virtue was that so far he had not presented her with the spoils. Such a demonstration was, she had heard, a mark of affection. It was one she could well do without.

The road behind her was a county highway, narrow but well traveled. Cars passed frequently; not a few of them slowed as they approached. Prospective customers, hopefully . . . But most, she knew, were local people gaping at the transformation of the house. Some even pulled into the driveway to stare openly. I must put up a sign, she thought—Private Road, No Trespassing. When she heard the screech of tires and the crunch of gravel she turned, frowning.

Instead of retreating in embarrassment at the sight of her the car came to a stop. Andrea's freshly laid and very expensive gravel spurted up under its wheels. She recognized the car immediately; it was one of a kind. Kevin's beloved 1965 Buick convertible, rescued from a junkyard in Connecticut, stripped and refurbished by the devoted hands of "the guys." Kevin was at the wheel, and beside him sat Jim.

Anger weakened Andrea's knees. The boys were waving and grinning like idiots. . . . She took a deep breath and walked toward them.

If they noticed her scowl they ignored it. "I asked Kevin to pick me up," Jim explained.

"So I see."

"Figured we could save you the trip," Kevin added, his hands caressing the steering wheel. "Jeez, Andy, you've done a sensational job. It looks great. Wow—is that Satan? Look at the old bastard, lying in ambush. The sign is sensational. Did you put it up yourself? Should have waited for us."

He didn't stop talking long enough for her to answer, probably because the expression on her face warned him that her comment would not sustain the cheerful mood he was trying to create. "Hop in and we'll save you a walk. There's enough room in the back, even with all Jim's stuff."

Andrea looked steadily at Jim. "Hop in," he repeated. "We can all get in the front. Here—"

"No." Andrea's hand went out in an involuntary gesture of protest. "No, thanks. You go on. I'll be there in a minute."

"Right." Kevin shifted gears and off they went, the twin exhausts roaring. He's afraid I'll crack and say something, Andrea thought bitterly. Well, I won't. At least I hope I won't. . . .

From among the boxes and bags heaped promiscuously in the back seat the crutches protruded like a pair of flagpoles, boldly defiant. Jim wasn't wearing the pants she had carefully tailored to fit; his faded, tattered jeans had presumably been supplied by Kevin. The material was wadded up and fastened with two huge safety pins over the stump that had once been Jim's left leg.

Chapter Three

She wondered if she would ever get used to it. In the beginning, when the issue had been a simple one of life or death, the loss of a limb had seemed one of the lesser injuries. But now the other wounds had healed; the hair had grown back over the holes bored through skull and brain. In a few months there would be no signs except a few scars—and the emptiness where a healthy limb had been. But she would get used to it. Jim would get used to it. People could get used to anything.

By the time Andrea reached the house, the boys had vanished inside. The front door stood wide open. Cool air poured out—she could almost see it—and insects poured in.

They were upstairs. She heard the thud of Kevin's footsteps, and another sound that made her wince—the irregular thump and beat of Jim's progress on crutches. He had resisted the idea of an artificial . . . of a prosthetic device. Later, the doctor had said. Give him time.

The thumps advanced to the top of the stairs. Andrea cried out in alarm and started up, arms outstretched. "Be careful, Jimmie—not so fast! Let me help."

Jim stopped on the landing, halfway down. Light streaming

through the stained-glass window dressed him in motley and streaked his face with crimson and green. He lifted one crutch and shook it at Andrea. Gesture and words were meant to be humorous, but there was a glint in his eyes that told Andrea he meant what he said. "If you touch me I'll fall over. Probably mash you on the way down."

Mutely she stepped back. Jim finished the descent at a pace that appeared suicidal, but landed at the bottom triumphant and unscathed.

"Balance," he crowed. "That's the key—balance. Pretty good, huh?"

Kevin followed in a more leisurely fashion. "You had a lot of practice on crutches, bro. Bound to happen if you tackled hulks like Mad Dog Martin and Too-Big Mazurski."

"I'll never forget Too-Big," Andrea said viciously. "I swear that creep kicked you in the ankle on purpose."

Kevin draped a brotherly arm around her. Like Jim, he was a good head taller than Andrea, with a shock of silver-blond hair brushed back from what he obviously believed was a high scholar's brow. Kevin read books when he didn't have to, and was therefore considered the brains of the group by "the guys." He was Andrea's favorite, as he was Jim's best buddy, but today she could have done without him. She had planned Jim's homecoming so carefully—

"Jimmie, don't you think you should lie down for a while?" she asked.

"I've been lying down for six months. I want to explore. Come on, Kevin, let's see the rest of the house."

"Your room—"

"Yeah, right, I want to see that." He paused in his head-long progress to add, over his shoulder, "Kevin's staying for lunch. I promised him spaghetti."

"Hey, I don't want to butt in," Kevin said.

"It's no trouble." The response lacked graciousness, but

Kevin had never gotten much of that commodity from Andrea. With a hasty "Thanks, Andy," he was off after Jim.

Andrea ground her teeth. Sweat had trickled and dried on her body; the jeans, stiffened into rigidity by layers of paint, rubbed her sore ankle. She had wanted to look nice for Jim—to be fresh and cool and relaxed, so he wouldn't feel guilty about leaving her with so much work to do. But if she went up to change now, she would miss the chance of showing Jim his room, and the wing of the house that was their private quarters.

She had lavished an unjustified amount of money on that area, the "servants' wing" behind the kitchen—money that probably should have been spent on the income-producing parts of the house. But she wanted it to be perfect—for Jim. It was their home, the private place where they could get away from guests and be together.

Knocking out one end of the big kitchen, she had had a bay window built that opened up the room and changed its personality beyond belief. There was space for the most modern of kitchen equipment at one end—a necessary business expense, since she planned to serve breakfasts—and for a family sitting area at the other. The wall between two of the small bedrooms had also come down, creating a large bed-sitter for Jim, with twin sofa beds so he could have his friends stay overnight. Jim's cherished possessions were there—his stereo, his books, his photographic equipment. But not all his possessions, not the ones he cherished most. Hidden in the darkest corner of the attic were the skis and poles, the tennis and squash rackets, the weights, the bench press, the hockey sticks—and the football. She had bought him a new one for Christmas. It had hardly been used.

The telephone interrupted her reverie. "Andy? It's me, Reba. I see Jim got home."

"I won't ask how you know," Andrea said resignedly.

"Just happened to be looking out the window when the car

went by. Figured it had to be him—there's quite a strong resemblance.''

Reba had her own brand of tact; she hadn't mentioned the crutches. "How about bringing him here for supper?" she went on.

Another interfering outsider trying to ruin the privacy of their first day at home! Andrea said quickly, "That's sweet, Reba, but . . . But he has a buddy with him, and if I know Kevin, he'll hang around for supper."

"Bring him along. I like kids that age. They appreciate good food."

As Andrea fumbled for a more compelling excuse, she heard the slam of the back door. Damn, she thought angrily. They've gone out—God knows where, into the pasture after Satan, probably—rabbit holes and brambles—he'll fall, he'll hurt himself. . . .

Reba took her silence for acceptance. "Good, I'll see you about eight. Fact is, I'm bribing you, Andy. Got a favor to ask."

"What?"

"That guy, Martin Greenspan—the friend of mine who booked for this weekend—"

"Yes." This monosyllable was a trifle more pleasant. Andrea owed the reservation solely to Reba. Martin Greenspan was a nationally syndicated columnist and writer. If she succeeded in pleasing him, his recommendation could carry a lot of weight.

"It's a helluva thing to ask, I know, with you just open for business—but he wondered if you could take him a day early."

"A day early." Andrea's mind fumbled with dates. "Tomorrow. Tomorrow?"

"I know, I know. But he's not fussy—he's a good guy. And if there's anything I can do—"

46

"No, it's okay." It would have to be okay, she told herself.

"Get those big louts of boys to help you this afternoon," Reba advised. "I'll feed 'em tonight. See you then, Andy. And thanks."

Andrea said, "Son of a bitch!" to the silent telephone, and collapsed onto the stairs. She had looked forward to this day so long—through long nights of loneliness and long days of labor. In the refrigerator were two steaks, ready for broiling, a big tossed salad, and half a gallon of pistachio ice cream— Jim's favorite foods. After lunch he would have rested for a while, then she would have taken him on a tour of the house. She had pictured the surprise and pleasure on his face when he saw the rooms whose restoration she had described in such detail.

The guest rooms all had names. She and Jim had discussed alternatives, with "the guys" offering their suggestions—all more or less X-rated and unacceptable. Jim insisted on referring to Bertha's bedroom as "Satan's room," and it was Kevin who pointed out the consequences of the designation. "I guess you can't call a guest room 'Hell,' can you?"

The room in question was now officially "The Lincoln Room," but Andrea wondered whether her choice of decor had not been unconsciously affected by Kevin's comment. Hangings of dark-red damask draped the four-poster bed and the circular bay windows; they had cost Andrea, who was not a skilled seamstress, many profane and frustrating hours. The wallpaper was crimson and gold, a copy of a Victorian original. Comfortable overstuffed chairs flanked the black marble fireplace. The room had the dignity and warmth of its namesake, and Andrea considered it her masterpiece.

The choice of names implied that the distinguished personages mentioned had slept there, without actually stating that fabrication as fact. The Ulysses S. Grant room had brass beds, handmade quilts, and braided rugs; the Robert E. Lee room featured *Gone With the Wind* lamps, a marble-topped washstand, and a hand-crocheted bedspread. The McKinley room . . .

So much for the tour, and for all her other plans. I might have known, Andrea thought drearily. When does anything turn out the way you hoped?

An hour later, showered and changed, she stood at the stove stirring spaghetti sauce. She hadn't bothered to call the boys; they would come when they were ready, and not before.

Finally she heard them. "Close the screen door," she said automatically, and then, "Jimmie! You're all dirty and scratched up. . . . Where the hell have you been?"

"How about me?" Kevin held out his arms, now a network of interlaced, bleeding scratches. "Some are from brambles, but that one is Satan's contribution. Hey, Andy, is that vine with the hairy stem poison ivy?"

"I'd be willing to bet on it," Andrea said. "Honestly, you two . . . Use that big bar of yellow soap. It's supposed to be good for poison ivy, though I have my doubts."

Jim started toward the bathroom, remarking, "I'll cook the spaghetti. You always stew it into mush."

"Yeah, Andy, you sit down and have a beer," Kevin added. "We'll dish up."

"I hate beer."

"A genteel glass of wine, then. Put your feet up. God knows you deserve it."

To her surprise and embarrassment, Andrea felt tears springing to her eyes. Kevin tactfully departed, and she brushed the dampness away. I'm just tired and mad, that's all, she told herself. But she decided to take Kevin's advice. Let them make a mess of the kitchen; the day was a mess anyhow.

The boys ate voraciously, but Kevin managed to talk at the same time, even when his mouth was full. "I'll bet there's trout in the stream, and we saw deer tracks back in the woods—unless they were cow tracks. . . . You've even got your own private graveyard.''

"Was that where you were? How did you get over the wall? I made sure the gate was padlocked—''

"Good idea; you don't want neighborhood kids in there. Some of them have a sick attraction to graves,'' Kevin said seriously.

"*Who* has a sick attraction to graves?''

"No, listen, Andy, you ought to get that place cleaned up. I'll bet the historical society would be interested. Did you know they fought all around here in the Civil War? Maybe there are soldiers' graves—''

"If you think I'm going to let you dig, looking for relics,'' Andrea began indignantly.

"Hell, Andy, we wouldn't do that. I'd like to restore the place, you know, cut down the weeds, put the stones back in place.''

"It would be a tourist attraction, wouldn't it?'' Jim said.

The food had brought some color to his sallow cheeks, and a smear of spaghetti sauce on his chin made him look very young and boyish. Knowing she had already lost the argument, Andrea said, "It would be a terrible job, Jimmie. The enclosure is a solid mass of wild raspberry bushes and poison ivy, there are trees, some good-sized—''

"I'd like to do it,'' Jim said.

"Why, for God's sake?''

"Why not?'' Kevin asked.

"Because—because there are lots of other things that need to be done. Our first guest is arriving tomorrow—a day early.''

"Greenspan?'' Kevin dropped his fork and leaned forward. "Yes.''

"Hey, he is a really important guy, you know? Did you read his column on nuclear disarmament?''

49

"Yes, I did, and I thought it was a crock of—"

She stopped herself in time. Both boys burst out laughing. "You're a little old reactionary, Andy," Jim said.

"And Martin Greenspan is a bleeding-heart liberal—if you want to call names. But he is an important contact, and I want everything to be perfect"

"Right. We'll help." Kevin jumped to his feet. "What do you want us to do? Make the bed, scrub the john? We even do windows."

"Now, Kevin, I wouldn't want you to give up one of the last days of your vacation."

"No sweat."

"You just want an excuse to meet your idol," Andrea said.

"No point trying to kid you, Andy; you know what a low-down, underhanded character I am. Let's go, Jimbo—I'll clear the table and you put the dishes in the dishwasher."

Kevin was obviously planning to stay for a few days. It would not have occurred to either boy to mention this, much less ask permission, for that was not their custom; but when Andrea went to Jim's room to unpack for him, she found two large brown grocery bags of clothes she didn't recognize as her brother's. The life-style of the young male American never ceased to bewilder her; many of its elements reminded her of off-beat religious communities. Property was communal—they wore each other's clothes, ate each other's food, stayed at one another's houses; time was a commodity to be enjoyed, not a series of boundaries restricting activity; trust was absolute, and betrayal of a brother to parents or police the ultimate sin. Sometimes Andrea felt like an anthropologist studying an exotic tribal group. More often she simply raged.

So there was a certain malicious satisfaction in her manner when she set Kevin to the task of scrubbing toilets and scouring tubs. Jim tossed back the dustcloth she had handed him and insisted on helping his buddy. "Squatting is something I do well," he said, with a defiant grin. "Not so much to fold up anymore."

By late afternoon Andrea had worked off her spite and was ready to dismiss her helpers. They expressed their intention of lying on the grass to "catch a few rays," and Andrea gave bathroom and guest room a final check. She had decided to give Greenspan the Lincoln Room. It was her favorite, the best and the most expensive room in the house, with its bay window overlooking the stream.

Before she left the room, Andrea lifted the dust ruffle and looked under the bed. Satan was not in the room. She was determined he should not get in. She could have put Greenspan somewhere else, since only two couples were expected that weekend, but she was damned if she was going to allow a fat arrogant black cat to monopolize her best room.

The sun was dropping toward the mountaintops when she went onto the front porch with a magazine and a glass of iced tea. The wicker rocking chair was soft and comfortable—she had made sure of that—but this was the first time she had relaxed in it, swaying gently to and fro, her aching back supported by soft cushions. The magazine had an article she wanted to read, but instead of opening it she feasted her eyes on the vision she had sometimes thought she would never see again.

The boys, still recumbent, added nothing to the tone of the establishment. Empty beer cans littered the lawn, and the old blanket on which they lay looked as if it had been used to clean a car engine. Jim seemed to be asleep, one arm over his face. Kevin, flat on his belly, was reading. His bare back was a mosaic of peeling sunburn, freckles, and—if Andrea's eyes did not deceive her—the red flush of an incipient poison-ivy rash. She rocked slowly back and forth, her hands folded in her lap.

II

Dinner at the restaurant was a success. Kevin fell in love with Reba at first sight; from the fascinated gleam in his eyes Andrea could tell he was planning to use her in the novel he had been writing for three years. Instead of shaking the gnarled fist she extended, he raised it to his lips, bowing low. Reba guffawed and gave him a slap on the back that made him stagger.

The specialties of Peace and Plenty were crab cakes and fried chicken. The boys had both, accompanied by mounds of mashed potatoes, uncounted ears of corn, innumerable home-made biscuits, and quarts of milk. Elbows on the table, Reba urged them to eat more.

She thanked Andrea again for altering her plans, and added reassuringly, "The inn is going to be a hit; I can feel it. But I'm glad you're here, Jim. Good to have a man in the house. I worry about Andy out there alone."

"Do you have a lot of break-ins?" Jim asked.

"Not so many. But there are always a few kooks around."

"I've never been nervous," Andrea said honestly. "After all, Cousin Bertha was there alone for years."

"Who owned the house before Bertha?" Jim asked.

"Her daddy, I suppose. Miss Bertha was living there alone, still hale and hearty, when I married Miller. She was always kind of queer. Not exactly a recluse, but she didn't encourage visitors." Reba chuckled. "Used to have one of those electric cars—remember them? She'd drive into town once a week to do her errands. I'd see her go by, same time, same day every week—sitting bolt upright in the driver's seat, and steering smack down the middle of the street."

"What happened to the car?" Kevin asked eagerly.

"It got smashed up the day she ran into Mr. Willis's old Chevy. She must have been past seventy then, and he was another of 'em, eighty if he was a day, still thought his was the only car on the road. It's a wonder they didn't crash before. I'll never forget that—I saw her coming like she always did, straddling the center line, and him steering straight at her from the other direction—it was like one of those old-time movies, the car and the train—you know they're going to hit and there isn't a damn thing you can do about it. They crashed head-on, out there in front of the restaurant. They were both blind as bats in the daylight, but I think part of it was pure bullheadedness. Neither was going to give way.''

"Did it total the car?'' Kevin asked.

"Your concern for human life is touching,'' Reba said with a grin. "It didn't do either car any good, let me tell you. Neither of the old folks was hurt, but Mr. Willis climbed out and started screaming at Bertha, saying it was all her fault. He got so mad he had a heart attack and dropped dead at her feet. Shook the old lady up considerable.''

"I should think so!'' Andrea exclaimed in horror. She was the only member of the group who found the story tragic. Jim was grinning and Kevin was obviously making mental notes for his book.

"She gave up driving after that,'' Reba said. "High time.''

Three people spoke at once.

"How did she manage without a car?''

"Hey, maybe the car's still there, in one of the sheds. We didn't look in all of them, Jim.''

"Is she buried in the graveyard behind the house?''

Reba was accustomed to multiple conversations. "Everybody kind of pitched in, ran errands for her,'' she told Andrea. "I don't know what happened to the car, Kevin; it could be there, she never threw anything away. What graveyard?''

Jim explained. Reba shook her head. "No, Miss Bertha's decently interred in the Methodist cemetery. I didn't realize there was a graveyard at Springers' Grove. Never been used that I can remember. But there's lots of them around, or used to be. Somebody wrote a book about them, back in the thirties. I've got a copy of it, unless it's been stolen. You know those built-in bookcases in the lobby—I bought some old books at auctions, to give the place some class. Picked 'em up dirt cheap then; now they're worth money, and sometimes customers swipe them. Ready for dessert? Apple pie, cherry, raspberry, chocolate cake?"

Egged on by an enraptured Kevin and primed by countless glasses of wine, Reba told story after story, some comical, some tragic. Jim said very little. He seemed to be enjoying himself, though, and he ate enough to satisfy the most anxious of mothers, so Andrea delayed breaking up the party until midnight approached.

"We've got a busy day tomorrow," she said, rising. "I forgot to ask, Reba—what time is Mr. Greenspan arriving?"

"Afternoon, I guess. He's reserved a table for dinner."

"We'll be ready."

They went out through the dining room, where the yawning waitresses were clearing the tables. When they reached the lobby, Jim pointed. "Are these the bookshelves you meant?" he asked.

"What?" Reba turned from the door, which she had unlocked for them. "Yeah, those're the ones."

Jim scanned the shelves. "I don't see anything about graveyards."

Reba opened the door. The night air felt hot and humid after the air-conditioned chill of the restaurant; but as she stood motionless, looking out at the street, a slight shudder rippled through her massive frame.

"Let me look," she said. Selecting a volume bound in faded red cloth, she blew dust off the top before handing it to Jim. "Here it is. Got to get those lazy little bitches to dust in here."

"I'll return it in a few days," Jim promised.

Reba put a large hand gently on his shoulder. "Take your time, Jim. Take all the time you want."

III

Since she was not in a position to employ full-time help, Andrea had to settle for a few hours a week from a local girl who had dropped out of high school at sixteen. "Linnie's not worth much," Reba told her, when recommending the girl. "But she'll work if you keep on her tail, and you can get her cheap."

Linnie was early the following morning, which was unusual but, under the circumstances, not surprising. She had been struck by the photograph of Jim that Andrea kept on her bureau. "He sure is good-looking, Miz Torgesen." With not one, but two new men on the premises, she could be counted on to be prompt until the novelty wore off.

Occasionally Linnie drove herself to work, but when her father needed his pickup truck, he dropped her off. He had done so that morning; Andrea waved, and a long arm flapped back at her from the truck window as it rattled down the drive. Hochstrasser was a widower, and Andrea felt sure that the supervision of Linnie was a never-ending trial to him.

She turned a disapproving frown on the girl, who stood before the mirror fluffing her hair. "That outfit looks terrible. What happened to the skirt and blouse I bought you?"

"They're in the wash." Linnie shifted her gum from one cheek to the other. "I usually wear jeans—"

"And how you ever manage to bend over in them I don't know."

Permanently set wrinkles fanning out from the crotch of the jeans proved that Linnie could bend at the hips, but the fabric adhered to every curve. She also wore a livid chartreuse T-shirt, sleeveless and low-cut, that clung to her heavy breasts. Her features were too flat and coarse to be pretty, but makeup and billowing blond hair gave her the kind of allure television cameramen focus on when there is an out on the field during a football game.

"You'll wear one of my blouses," Andrea said. "I'm expecting our first guest today, and you look like a waitress in a cheap bar."

Linnie was ironing and Andrea was mixing muffin batter when the boys appeared, yawning and stretching. Andrea greeted them curtly. Correctly attributing her grumpiness to nerves, Jim said reassuringly, "Everything is going to be okay, Andy. The house looks great. If you want us to do anything—" He stopped, staring at Linnie, who had come in from the dining room carrying a curtain.

Andrea introduced them. The boys studied Linnie appreciatively; Linnie smirked and swayed. Andrea sent her back to the ironing board, but she refused to stay there, wandering in and out of the kitchen on one pretext or another while the boys ate breakfast. When they had finished, Jim asked again, "Do you want us to do anything?"

"The lawn needs mowing," Andrea said.

"I'll do it," Jim said. He squared his shoulders as if expecting an argument, but Andrea had already fought her private battle on this point. The riding mower she had picked up at a local sale was a necessity, but it was also a concession to Jim's passion for cars. He had to have something to drive. And he couldn't get in trouble with the mower, the lawn was a gentle slope, smooth as a table.

"I want both of you to do it," she said. "It's a four-hour job even with the riding mower, and there are places that need hand mowing. Don't hit the trees and don't run over the flowers—"

"Picky, picky," Jim said. But the smile that warmed his face smote her with shame. Was she that hard on him? She was trying not to be overprotective; she had known even before the doctor lectured her that Jim needed to feel capable and independent. But it wasn't easy to do what she knew she should do.

"Before you start," she said, "I want that square pine table in the parlor carried up to the Lincoln room. Put it between the windows."

Kevin refused her help—and Linnie's, eagerly offered—saying he could handle the table more easily alone. Andrea went up with him to make sure he placed it properly. Jim followed. Andrea was learning self-control; she didn't even turn her head as the crutches thumped from step to step.

She went ahead to open the door for Kevin. Her shriek of fury made him jump. "Look. Look! How the bloody hell did he get in here?"

Square in the middle of the bed, curled up on the crimson spread she had constructed with so much labor, was Satan. Meeting Andrea's eyes, he deliberately extended a massive black paw and poised his claws over the spread.

"All right," Andrea shouted. "All right! You know and I know that you can shred that fabric before I can stop you. But if you do, you'll never get another bowl of cat food in this house!"

Jim doubled up with laughter. "My sister, Dr. Doolittle . . . What did he say? Or would you rather not repeat it?"

"It's not funny." Andrea swung around to confront the two grinning faces. "One of you must have left the door open."

Kevin raised his hand in solemn protestation. "I haven't been in here since yesterday."

"Me neither. Relax, Andy, he's not doing anything. In fact, he looks very classy—like a picture in one of those highbrow decorating magazines of yours."

"Mr. Greenspan won't mind," Kevin said. "He's got a great sense of humor. And he likes cats. Remember the column he wrote about—"

"Oh, shut up, both of you." Andrea glowered at Satan,

who had sheathed his claws and tucked both paws under his chest. "I am decorative in the extreme," he seemed to be saying, "and only a boor would refuse to admit it."

"Well, I can't remove him by force," she said. "He'd rip that spread to tatters. Leave the door open. Maybe he'll go of his own accord."

Satan yawned.

In view of the way the day had begun, Andrea fully expected Greenspan to arrive early, before she was ready for him. However, he was still not there when the mowers stopped for a late lunch; she had evicted Linnie, and matters were well in hand. "I may even have time to shower and put on some decent clothes," she said hopefully. "Just do me one favor, you guys—one more favor. Come in the back way so you don't leave grass all over the hall. And put on shirts, please? And shoes."

She needn't have worried. Kevin went all out to impress the object of his admiration; his intellectual image was overpowering. He looked like a young Clark Kent without the muscles of Superman—bespectacled, solemn, and extremely uncomfortable in an ill-fitting shirt and bow tie.

The bow tie moved Andrea to comment. "How about a hat with a press card in the band?" she suggested. "A card that says 'Scoop' Wilson."

Kevin looked hurt. "I thought you wanted us to make a good impression."

She patted his arm. "I did, and you do. You look fine—both of you."

"So do you," Jim said.

"Thanks. Why don't you two go and—and— Oh, I don't care what you do, so long as it doesn't make a mess. He may not be here for hours, so there's no sense hanging around."

They were sitting on the porch, Andrea in the swing and the boys on the steps. The picture was one of charming domesticity, but she didn't want Greenspan to think they had nothing better to do than wait anxiously for his arrival. However, her hint fell on deaf ears.

"You don't get a chance to meet someone like Martin Greenspan every day," Kevin said seriously. "If I decide to go into journalism—"

"Don't you dare ask him to read your book."

Kevin grinned. "It's mostly in my head anyhow."

"I guess we're not wanted around here, bro." Jim shifted the crutches and prepared to rise. "We spoil the image or something."

A car turned into the driveway. Stage fright gripped Andrea, turning her hands into solid chunks of ice. "Please, Jimmie, darling, sit down—I didn't mean. . . . Oh, my God, here he is."

Jim relaxed. "I guess I'm uptight too. Stay cool, Too-Small; you can handle anything they throw at you."

"What do you know?" But she was warmed by the compliment and by the nickname, bestowed on her after she had had to be forcibly restrained from attacking Too-Big Mazurski after he broke Jim's ankle. She made herself sit still as the car chugged up the drive between the flanking rows of dogwood trees.

It was a Volkswagen Beetle, age indeterminate but obviously not in its first youth, or even its second. The ground color was yellow, of varying shades ranging from faded cream to vivid canary, and the side-view mirror hung at a drunken angle. At first she couldn't believe the famous columnist would drive such a wreck, but then she realized the car was a perfect example of the reverse snobbism she found in Greenspan's writing. "I'm just a workingman at heart, like all the rest of youse guys—look at me, I don't even own a Mercedes."

Though blurred by the dusty windshield, his features were recognizable as the ones reproduced at the head of his bi-weekly column in the Washington *Post*. Vanity was not one of his failings; the photographs had aged along with Greenspan, depicting with unflattering fidelity his receding hairline, increasing wrinkles, and sagging jowls. The car came to a stop in front of the steps. Greenspan got out. A loud pop and a cloud of smoke emerged from the rear end of the car.

Greenspan, scratching his head, contemplated this demonstration with visible distress. He didn't look like the popular image of a famous writer; he looked like a tired, unsuccessful salesman of unwanted goods. His stomach hung out over his belt, his suit was wrinkled, and his tie was loose.

Kevin bounded down the stairs. "Sounds like the thermostat."

Greenspan turned, blinking. "Is that right? It's been doing that since . . ." Catching sight of Andrea, who had advanced to the top of the steps, he raised his hand to his forehead, realized he was not wearing a hat, and made an awkward little bow. "Forgive my bad manners, Miss Torgesen. I can only plead faulty mental coordination; for the last ten miles I've been expecting that accursed vehicle to blow up."

It didn't occur to Andrea that he might be nervous. Why should he be? She thought, What a pompous speech, and replied with comparable stiffness.

"Please don't apologize. It's a pleasure to welcome you to Springers' Grove Inn, Mr. Greenspan."

Ignoring her outstretched hand, he stood looking at her with a singularly foolish expression, his mouth a trifle ajar. "This is my brother and co-host," Andrea went on.

She had grown accustomed to stares, some openly curious, some, even less acceptable, pitying. Greenspan displayed neither; he acknowledged the introduction with a nod and a smile. Of course Reba would have warned him.

Kevin had vanished under the back end of the car. Only his legs stuck out, rigid with concentration. He shot out again and beamed at Greenspan. "I can fix it for you, sir. Won't take five minutes once I get the part."

Greenspan started to laugh. It was a rich, uninhibited sound that shook his entire body and transformed his face. All the wrinkles fell into place, signs of good humor rather than age.

"That's Kevin," Jim said. "He really does know about cars, sir."

"Kevin." Greenspan took a firm grip of the grease-stained fingers Kevin was trying to wipe on his pants. "Miss Torgesen didn't mention in her brochure that car repairs are part of the service."

"I'm also the bellhop. Bags in the trunk, sir?"

"Back seat. Thanks."

The ice had been broken into a million fragments, and Greenspan's self-consciousness was gone. Smiling, he joined Andrea on the porch.

"What a sensational job you've done with this place. I've often seen it from the road and regretted that such a fine old house should be neglected."

"I hope you'll find the interior equally to your taste," Andrea said primly. "Perhaps you'll join us for cocktails before you go to dinner; you're our first guest, so we felt a little celebration was in order. Ordinarily we don't serve drinks, but—"

"I know." He took one of her brochures from his coat pocket. "I've brought my own bottle, but don't worry— alcoholism is one of the few vices I don't enjoy."

"Which ones do you enjoy?" Jim asked.

"Jim!"

Greenspan's eyes twinkled. "All of them," he said soberly. "Sloth, envy, pride, vanity. . . ."

"But you don't object to cats, do you?" asked Kevin, taking the suitcases out of the car.

Greenspan glanced at Andrea's crimson face. The corners of his mouth twitched, but he said gravely, "It depends on the cat. Am I to understand there is a resident feline?"

Since the said feline was now out of the bag, Andrea

explained. Her account was carefully expurgated, but the boys added details that started Greenspan chuckling. "I suppose Satan insists on sleeping in the precise center of the bed? Well, we'll see how we get on. No doubt some accommodation can be arrived at. I am a great believer in compromise."

"Satan isn't," Jim said.

But Satan was not in evidence, on the bed or elsewhere in the room. Greenspan let out a low whistle of appreciation as he glanced around.

"Superb. Absolutely superb."

"Thank you. The bathroom is across the hall—please let me know if there is anything you need. We'll expect you downstairs, but only when you're rested and ready. There are no schedules here except the ones you set for yourself."

The words sounded stiff and stilted, as prepared speeches usually do.

"Thank you," Greenspan said softly. "I rather think I won't be too long in coming."

It seemed an odd thing to say, but otherwise—so far, so good, Andrea thought. She shooed the boys ahead of her down the stairs and into the kitchen, knowing that if she didn't, they would haunt Greenspan's doorway.

"Isn't he great?" Kevin exclaimed.

"I can't see that he's done anything great so far," Andrea said.

"He was damned nice about Satan."

"He hasn't met Satan. Look, we're still on probation; keep it cool, will you? Jim, you can put some ice in the bucket and get the drink tray ready."

"I'll chop up some cheese," Kevin offered.

"I was afraid you'd say that. There is a tray of canapés in the fridge—canapés, not chopped-up cheese—but don't you dare touch it till he comes."

Foraging on the despised cheese, Kevin said thickly, "The

VW's not in such great shape. I could offer to drive him tonight—''

"Not unless he asks. I told you, Kevin—cool it.''

"You did good, Andy,'' Jim said. "The perfect hostess.''

"Sexism, sexism,'' howled Kevin, waving the cheese.

"The perfect innkeeper,'' Jim amended.

True to his word, Greenspan was not long in joining them. After admiring the parlor, he said diffidently, "Would it be too much trouble to move the party out onto the porch? I haven't sat in a porch swing since . . . Well, never mind when. I'll carry the cheese and crackers.''

Greenspan appeared to enjoy himself. It was seven o'clock before he excused himself, saying he was already late for dinner. In the interval he completed his conquest of the boys, listening deferentially to their views and paying them the compliment of assuming they knew as much as he did about the subjects under discussion. Though she disagreed with most of his opinions, Andrea had to admit he was a witty, fluent speaker.

Clearing away glasses and plates, she thought again, So far, so good. But tomorrow would be the true test—four more guests, and Satan still an unknown quantity in the equation of Greenspan. The boys got hamburgers for dinner and Andrea retired early. She had given Greenspan a key to the house, but she suspected the boys intended to wait up for him. Well, she thought wearily, that's his problem; he must be used to admiring acolytes dogging his footsteps and hanging on his every word. She fell asleep at once and never heard him come in.

In the dead hours of early morning she came joltingly awake with an agonized knotting of muscles. There was no period of drowsy dislocation; she could see the open window, a pale square of moonlight, and the white muslin curtains hanging limp in the still, hot air.

The darkness reverberated with the sound of beating wings. Thrashing against the bars of night, frantic to break free, they dropped and soared and sank again; the air riven by their passage struck her shrinking flesh in rhythmic beats.

By the time the boys burst into her room, Andrea's throat ached with screaming. Through the thin sheet she had pulled over her head she saw the light go on; but Jim had to wrench the fabric from her clenched fingers.

"Andy! What's the matter?"

The sight of his sleep-crumpled face, drawn with concern for her, broke the spell of horror. "Jimmie, Jimmie—oh, God—"

"Hey." He sat down on the edge of the bed and put his arm around her. "It's okay, I'm here. Did you have a bad dream?"

Andrea shuddered. "It was no dream. There was something in the room. I swear there was. A bird—trapped, trying to get out—a big bird, Jimmie . . ."

"Nothing here now," said Kevin, in the doorway. His face looked unfamiliar and undressed without the glasses.

"Look." She sat up, but did not loosen her grip on Jim. "Look. Under the bed, behind the bureau."

Kevin obeyed. "There's nothing here," he insisted. "Not even a hole in the screen. You had a nightmare. But I don't understand what's so terrifying about a bird. Have you been watching horror movies on the Late Show?"

"A bat?" Jim suggested. "They can be rabid. Was that what scared you, sis?"

Andrea forced her clutching fingers to release their grip on his arm. "It was not a bat. It had feathers. And big—big—" She measured the size with her hands.

The boys no longer bothered to hide their smiles. "That's typical of nightmares," Kevin said condescendingly. "It isn't the image itself, but the Freudian neurosis it represents, that scares you."

Andrea dropped back onto the pillow. She was drenched with perspiration and her muscles ached as if she had run for miles, but in the last analysis she preferred nightmares to Kevin's half-baked psychology.

"Go back to bed," she said gruffly. "I'm sorry I woke you."

"You okay now?" Jim asked.

"Yes, of course."

Jim lingered. "Honest, sis, there's no way anything could get in here. The screen is tight, and there isn't a chimney."

"I know. I'm all right now."

"Want me to leave the door open?"

"No! I mean, no thanks. Go back to sleep."

It was some time before she could force herself to get out of bed and reexamine the places the boys had already searched. She couldn't blame them for failing to understand the shuddering horror of the experience; in retrospect she found it hard to understand herself. Wings, trying to fight free . . . It was an obvious symbol—birds, wings, flying, freedom. But it didn't make sense. There was nothing in her life from which she wanted to escape.

Chapter Four

To Linnie's poorly concealed disappointment the boys slept late next morning. Andrea put her to work in the parlor where, it was only too apparent, a prolonged bull session had taken place the previous night. The participants had virtuously carried their beer cans and coffee cups to the kitchen, but there were crumbs and ashes scattered everywhere, and they had overlooked a plate of cheese, now curled into leathery strips.

Greenspan had requested breakfast at eight. Although she was sleepy and out of sorts, Andrea got the tray together with a minimum of blunders. She had made the muffin batter the day before; all she had to do this morning was add a cup of blueberries and spoon the mixture into the pans. Sliced peaches and cream, an assortment of dried cereal, toast and fresh-brewed coffee. . . . She gave the tray a final check. It wouldn't do to forget anything. Sugar, diet sweetener, silverware, napkin. . . . Butter in a tiny Meissen bowl. . . . With a suppressed exclamation she went to the refrigerator. She had almost forgotten the jam. More little bowls, strawberry and apple jelly, made by a local farmer's wife. The little bowls were a nice touch; Cousin Bertha had several dozen of them. Andrea had no idea what their original function had been.

Eventually she meant to have Linnie take over the drudgery of carrying trays upstairs, but on this important occasion she decided she had better do it herself. The tray was heavy and her aching calves protested as she climbed the stairs.

The idea of serving individual breakfasts had come from a cooperative innkeeper in Virginia, whose brain she had not scrupled to pick. Toilsome as the task might seem, it was no more difficult then serving everyone at once, in the dining room, and it lent a pleasant touch of personal service. "Your clientele aren't ordinary tourists," the friendly colleague had pointed out. "Most fall into two categories—newlyweds looking for a romantic ambience, and elderly people who have to have a cup of coffee before they can put their teeth in. Don't laugh! You're a lot younger than I am, but don't you find it's getting harder and harder to face the world before you have that first cup of coffee?"

Andrea lowered the tray onto the table outside Greenspan's door, gave it a final inspection, and knocked softly. The transom over the door was ajar; she heard bedsprings creak and then a muffled groan.

"It's eight o'clock, Mr. Greenspan," she announced, and at once retreated. The door didn't open until she was on the landing, out of sight, and she smiled faintly as she finished the descent. Greenspan appeared to be one of those who wanted his coffee before he got his teeth in.

She was in the parlor, putting the final touches on Linnie's somewhat casual cleaning, when Greenspan came down. He paused in the doorway to wish her good morning.

"Excellent breakfast," he said. "I suppose you baked the muffins."

His tone was so portentous that Andrea felt a stab of alarm. Rotten berries, salt instead of sugar? "Yes, I did. Weren't they edible?"

"They were superb," Greenspan said, even more gloomily. "Well. Just going out for my morning exercise."

"It's half a mile to the gate and back," Andrea said.

"Oh, is it? That's fine. Nothing like a little jogging after breakfast. I do it every day."

"Good for you. I hope you enjoy it."

"Oh, yes. Well. Thank you for the admirable breakfast."

After he had gone, Andrea went back to her dusting. She rather suspected that Martin Greenspan, famous author, was showing off. That tummy of his wouldn't be so well developed if he made a habit of jogging every morning.

II

The other guests arrived that evening—two middle-aged couples from Pennsylvania, self-proclaimed antique freaks looking for bargains in the wilds of western Maryland. Mr. Whitman (tall and stout, with gold-rimmed bifocals) patted a stomach more developed than Greenspan's and complimented her on her muffins; Mr. Johnson (short and pudgy with gold-rimmed trifocals) tried to pat her on her behind, but was not unduly persistent.

There was only one contretemps, when the foursome returned from their auction spree on Saturday evening—hot, tired and disgruntled because prices had been higher than they expected—to discover that the air conditioner in the Johnsons' room had unaccountably quit functioning. Since two of the guest rooms were unoccupied, the problem was easily solved; Andrea simply moved them to another room. But Johnson waxed loud about the inconvenience, despite the efforts of his twittering little wife to calm him.

It may have been sheer coincidence that Greenspan chose to join the other guests in the green parlor for tea. Andrea served that beverage in Cousin Bertha's fragile Haviland cups, along with a plate of skimpily but artistically arranged cookies; one day, after she had learned to make scones and clotted cream, she hoped "afternoon tea" would draw in the lady shoppers and enable her to raise her prices. Now it was in the main a euphemism for what less couth establishments referred to as Happy Hour, and most male guests preferred to mix their own drinks, using the ice and glasses she provided. She had no liquor license and did not want one; she had not needed the warnings of colleagues to know the hazards involved in that.

Mrs. Whitman took tea and nibbled delicately at the cookies. Mrs. Johnson joined the men in a scotch and soda. Johnson was still grumbling about the air conditioner when Greenspan made his appearance.

They knew who he was. His name had been the only one in the guestbook, which they had taken care to inspect when they signed in. They had been lying in wait for him. He was unquestionably a social lion, not of the highest caliber, but well up in the second rank. Smiling and urbane, he accepted a drink from Mr. Johnson and sat down, prepared to be roasted.

The political opinions of the others ranged from far right to extreme far right. Why they bothered to read Greenspan's column Andrea could not imagine, but Johnson seemed to recall every word Greenspan had ever written. He got purple in the face when he quoted some of them.

Though Greenspan was outnumbered, the contest was not one-sided. Andrea had to admire the way he held his own, without losing his temper or raising his voice. By the time Mrs. Johnson reminded her husband that they were late for their dinner reservations, Johnson's good humor had been restored. He seemed to feel that he had won the debate, though Andrea couldn't see that Greenspan had yielded an inch.

She had been too busy during the day to think of her nightmare, but when she stood outside her door it came back to her, with a vividness that made her hesitate to turn the knob. The hesitation was only momentary; she couldn't afford to yield to that sort of weakness, not now. Nor did she leave the light on, though greatly tempted to do so. Sheer exhaustion finally brought slumber, and when she woke in the morning to face another hot sticky day, her rest had been undisturbed.

The two couples left late Sunday afternoon, after a day of antiquing and a substantial dinner at Peace and Plenty. They had enjoyed themselves, they told her.

"Think I set that young fellow straight on a few things," Johnson boomed. It took Andrea a few seconds to realize he was referring to Greenspan.

Mrs. Whitman, the tea drinker, only smiled sweetly. Later, however, while the men were packing the van in which their weekend bargains had been stowed, and Mrs. Johnson had gone upstairs for an unspecified but readily comprehensible purpose, Mrs. Whitman took Andrea aside.

"We've had such a lovely time. This beautiful old house . . ." Mrs. Whitman's voice dropped to a whisper. "And the presence—so warm, so beneficent . . ."

"Presence?" Andrea repeated.

"Oh, you needn't be shy with me, my dear; I've always been sensitive to such things. I don't talk about it in front of Harry, he is too worldly to sympathize; but I felt it from the moment I walked in the door. An invisible presence, loving and welcoming. . . ."

When Andrea grasped the meaning of Mrs. Whitman's ramblings, it was all she could do not to swear. She had been warned about this too. "For God's sake, my dear, don't let the psychic nuts take over. That's always a problem with an old house, they look for spooks and phantoms and old murders. Sure, it brings in some trade, but it scares off more, and you never know when some idiot is going to have a seizure and sue you."

71

"I'm afraid I don't know what you're talking about, Mrs. Whitman," Andrea said coldly.

Mrs. Whitman was not so easily discouraged. "Not everyone can sense it; only those attuned to the spiritual world. It was not until last night that I was sure. I lay awake for a long time feeling them hover over me—angel presences, touching me with their wings. . . . Oh, dear, Harry is calling, I must run. Thank you again, Miss Torgesen."

The single harmless word hit Andrea like a blow in the diaphragm. Coincidence, she told herself. Pure coincidence. Angels and spirit forms and angelic presences—the conventional jargon of the trade.

Summoning a smile, she went to speed the parting guests.

When the van pulled away Andrea returned to the kitchen and dropped limply into a chair. Kevin, who had helped the men load the van, followed her. Grinning, he displayed his spoils.

"Half a buck. I knew that guy Johnson was a big spender."

"You should have returned it, with a lordly sneer," Andrea said. "Thanks, Kevin. I owe you."

"No, you don't. I'm collecting material for my book."

"Where's Jimmie?" She kicked off her shoes and wriggled her toes.

"Out back." Kevin gestured.

"Not in that old graveyard? Go tell him to come in. We ought to have supper. Though right now I'm too tired to care."

"We're going for pizza," Kevin said. "No cooking for you tonight, lady."

"Could you get one for me?" Greenspan's head appeared around the door. "Everything on it except anchovy. I hate anchovies."

"Me, too," Kevin exclaimed. "I hate anchovies. How about olives? Right. Great. I'll go get Jim."

Greenspan hovered uncertainly in the doorway. "Come in," Andrea said, reaching for her shoes.

"Not unless you promise to leave your shoes off and slump to your heart's content. Can I get you anything? Tea, beer, milk, champagne?"

"But you're my guest, Mr. Greenspan. I should be waiting on you."

"Make it Martin—please."

He had a very attractive smile. The austerity of lips almost too narrowly cut was warmed by a crooked tooth and overshadowed by a strong Roman nose as impressive as George Washington's.

"I didn't realize you wore glasses," she said, looking at the pair he had pushed up onto his balding head.

"Just for reading. The curse of middle age."

"Are you hungry? I expected you would have dinner at Reba's."

"I was afraid I'd run into the Moral Majority."

"But that's terrible. I can't have my guests inconvenienced because of other guests."

"For the love of heaven, woman, stop thinking you're responsible for the entire universe," Martin said forcibly. "It won't hurt me to skip a meal. I'm putting on too much weight anyhow."

Andrea wished he would go away. She sensed that he had something in mind beyond idle conversation, but it was not until the boys had come and gone, heading for the pizza parlor in nearby Frederick, that he got to the point.

"This is probably a rotten time to bring it up, when the very thought of guests makes you gag, but I've got a proposition to put to you. You can always turn it down."

"What did you have in mind?" Andrea asked warily.

"Nothing like that." He smiled.

"I didn't mean—"

"No, of course you didn't." He began folding and unfolding the stems of his glasses. "For a professional writer, I am less than glib, aren't I? It's simple enough. My apartment in D.C. is going condo. I've always hated the place anyhow—boring, jerry-built little trap. . . . So I wondered—you see, I've got a book due; I'm already behind schedule, and my publisher swears he'll boil me in oil if it isn't finished by March first. . . ."

"You don't mean you want to stay here!"

"What's so surprising about that?"

"Why—I don't know. It's just that—I don't know."

Martin continued, more fluently. "This part of the country has always appealed to me. As you can see by my girth, I enjoy regular meals; Peace and Plenty is one of my old hangouts. I hate motels. Your house has a certain atmosphere—"

"What do you mean by that?" Andrea sat up.

He gave her a startled look. "Quiet, gracious surroundings, the charm of an old house. . . . What did you think I meant?"

"You haven't seen anything—felt anything?"

"Are you trying to tell me, my dear Miss Torgesen, that the house is haunted?"

They stared at one another in mutual consternation. Andrea was already regretting her impulsive question. If she weren't so tired, and if that stupid old woman hadn't upset her. . . .

Martin smiled. "I haven't seen anything or felt anything."

"Go ahead and laugh. I don't blame you."

"Have you? Seen or felt—"

"No. I don't believe in that nonsense. And I'm sure you are too intelligent to fall for it."

"Well." Martin scratched the fringe of hair over his left ear. "I try to keep an open mind. . . ." Seeing her expression, he laughed somewhat sheepishly. "I know what you're thinking—my mind is too damned open. You can't put me off that way, Miss Torgesen. And don't forget, you won't find too many customers who are willing to sleep with a large, pushy black cat."

"Oh, my God." Andrea covered her face with her hands. "I forgot about Satan. Did he—"

"He did. He's pretty good company, as a matter of fact. The affinity between writers and cats is well documented; with his help I may be able to produce a masterpiece. You don't have to decide this minute, Miss Torgesen. Think it over. Consult your brother."

She knew what Jim would say. And she knew the advantages of the plan. Advantages? It would be a godsend, nothing less—income she could count on during the lean winter months. Not to mention the publicity value of Greenspan's patronage. The advantages were all on one side. On the other. . . . Alone with Jim, working and planning together. Long winter evenings by the fire in the kitchen while sleet hissed at the windows, reading, talking, watching television, getting to know him again. She had seen so little of him since he started college, even though campus was only an hour away. . . .

The balance dipped, but common sense sent it swinging up again. The home comforts she wanted to create for Jim depended solely on whether or not she could make a success of the business. All her savings had gone into the inn. Times were bad; if the inn failed, she might not be able to find a job that paid enough to give Jim the things he was going to need.

"I don't need to think about it," she said. "Assuming, of course, that we can agree on terms. . . ."

III

Against all her forebodings the arrangement seemed to work out. Greenspan was an ideal guest. He hardly ever left his room except for meals and his morning run. To her secret amusement he soon began to appear in regulation jogging suits, so new that the price tags still dangled from the back of the pants. Business improved; she began to get mid-week trade, from giggling housewives escaping from their families

and from grandparents who needed a peaceful night's sleep
and a leisurely breakfast before they plunged into the mael-
strom of loving family life.

Kevin stayed on—and on. Andrea knew she should be
grateful to him for keeping Jim busy and entertained. She
wasn't the best of company herself; a faint preoccupied frown
was her normal expression, replaced by a bright artificial
smile only in the presence of guests. All the same, she could
hardly wait till Kevin left for school, and she was secretly
pleased that he had picked a midwestern university instead of
a local college. There would be no weekly visits to interrupt
the idyllic companionship she looked forward to—as soon as
she got the inn running smoothly.

Some of the things the boys did would have driven her
frantic with worry if she had had time to think about them.
They explored every foot of the thirty acres surrounding the
house, and came up with endless impractical schemes—
diverting the stream to make a swimming pool, bulldozing
nature trails through the woods, laying out a nine-hole golf
course. They dragged Jim's weights out of the attic and fitted
out one of the sheds as a gym. They searched the barn and the
other outbuildings looking for Bertha's electric car—to no
avail—but found pieces of rusting farm equipment, including
a tractor, which they took to pieces and tried to repair.

Unbeknown to Andrea, a good deal of their time was spent
in the abandoned graveyard. She didn't realize how much
work they had done until, the day before Kevin was due to
leave, he and Jim invited her to view the results.

"No, thanks," she said. "If I'd known what you were up
to, I'd have forbidden it. I can't imagine what you find so
fascinating about a horrible place like that."

Martin was eating lunch with them that day. For an exorbi-
tant additional fee, Andrea had agreed to let him forage for
sandwiches and soup when he didn't feel like going out.

"Am I invited?" he asked. "I didn't know you had a cemetery on the premises. How convenient."

"Sure you're invited, Mr. Greenspan," Jim said. "I didn't think you'd be interested."

"I'm interested in practically everything. That's why I'm always behind schedule."

"You don't want to see it," Andrea protested. "It's all overgrown with weeds and poison ivy—"

"Not now," Jim said. "What it is, Mr. Greenspan, is the old Springer cemetery. That's the name of the family that owned this property in the eighteenth century. Back then there were a lot of private graveyards. Most of 'em were abandoned as the population grew and travel was easier."

His elbows on the table, Greenspan listened with the absorbed attention he always offered Jim and Kevin, even when they told him something he already knew.

"Jim's got a book that tells about the old cemeteries," Kevin explained. "Some guy made a survey, back in the thirties or forties. Must have been quite a job, because even then some of the sites were overgrown and forgotten. Since then a lot more of them have disappeared."

"But this house appears to have been built—oh, I'd guess mid-nineteenth century, give or take a few decades," Greenspan said. "Much later then the period when the cemetery was in use."

"We figure there was a house here before this one," Kevin explained. "Not necessarily on the same site, but part of the same estate."

Greenspan nodded. "That's reasonable. Have you checked it out?"

"Oh, no, we're not going in for anything resembling homework," Kevin said with a grin. "Just some honest manual labor."

From outside the graveyard looked unchanged. The brick wall was crumbling and uneven, and overhanging cedars cast a somber green shade. But the interior was almost unrecognizable. Formerly the entire enclosure had been a mass of weeds and intertwined brambles. The boys had chopped down intrusive saplings, rooted out honeysuckle and wild blackberry bushes, and cut the weeds down to an uneven stubble. It wasn't pretty, but it was less ugly, and a few stones remained in place. Others, in varying stages of decrepitude, had been lined up along the brick wall.

Kevin flung the gate open and assumed the role of guide.

"We didn't move any of the gravestones that were still in place. And we made a plan of where we found the others." He cocked an eye at Greenspan and received the nod of approval he had hoped for. "A lot of them had fallen over or been uprooted by trees. But look at this one—look at the date."

" 'John Springer,' " Greenspan read. " 'Born Apr. 17, 1712, died. . . .' When?"

"We couldn't read it either, it's all worn down. But isn't that something? Seventeen twelve!" He tugged Greenspan away to examine the other stones.

Andrea looked at her brother. His lifted face was illumined by a ray of sunlight that filtered through the cedar boughs. His expression was dreamy and remote.

"Jim!" she said sharply.

He turned toward her, using one crutch as a pivot, his dreamy smile unchanged. "I thought we could fix it up. Plant grass and some flowers. And put a bench there, under the trees.

"Jimmie, I wish you wouldn't—"

Greenspan was at her side, his hand on her arm. "It's fascinating, Jim. You guys must have busted your biceps here."

"It was one hell of a lot of work," Jim said. "But it's just the beginning. I thought we would fix it up. . . ."

He went on to repeat and expand on his plans. But for

some reason, this time they didn't sound so—so alarming? So
morbid? Yet Andrea's dislike of the place was not lessened.
She was about to suggest that they leave when Greenspan
said, in a voice sharp with excitement, "What's that?"

He moved quickly to examine it—a tangle of leafy branches
hanging over the wall at the end opposite the gate. A few
patches of color spotted the green, and as Andrea joined
Greenspan he lifted a flower onto his palm, with as much
reverence as if it had been a rare orchid. The crumpled petals,
of softest pink, gave off a strong musky scent.

"It's a wild rose," Jim said. "It was half-strangled by
honeysuckle, but we thought it was kind of pretty, so we left
it."

"Wild rose nothing," Martin said. "Unless I'm crazy, this
is *Rosa damascena bifera.*"

"Rosa what?" Kevin asked. "What's so unusual about
it?"

Martin held the flower cupped in curved fingers. "The
autumn damask—one of the oldest roses in the world. Mentioned by Ovid and Livy. It was brought to the New World by
the Spaniards, who called it Rose of Castile."

"Cousin Bertha must have planted it," Andrea said indiffer-
ently. "You certainly have a wide range of interests, Martin."

"You mean I don't look like a lover of roses. I am,
though. Some day I hope to retire to a place like this, in the
country, and cultivate my garden. You won't find old varieties like this at a neighborhood nursery; it's only obtainable
through specialized sources. You're sure your cousin never—"

"I really can't say." Andrea could not understand his
persistence, and she was anxious to get away. "Gentlemen, I
admire your effort, your wisdom, and your general amiability,
but I've got work to do. Are you coming?"

"Wait a minute. What's this?" Martin stooped, parting the
leggy stems and the rank crabgrass from which they sprang.
"Another stone?"

"It's fallen over again," Kevin said, kneeling beside Martin. "I thought we had it set pretty solidly. It's got a funny inscription," he added casually.

Martin tipped the stone back so that the sunlight fell across its surface. One line stood out amid a tangle of half-obliterated letters. Either accident had spared that single section, or the carving had been so deep, so enduring, that the ravages of weather and time had not obliterated the message. It was indeed a funny inscription.

" 'Here I stay,' " Martin read. "Good Lord—who was the belligerent atheist?"

But the rest of the writing was almost gone. "I think the first name is Mary," Martin decided finally. "There's a date in the 1800's—could be 1809 or 1889, or almost any variant thereof. One of the Springers?"

"If we cleaned it, maybe we could read more," Kevin suggested.

"Could be. I don't know that I care that much. But someone evidently cared enough to plant *Rosa damascena* on her grave. . . . I still find it hard to believe a rose could survive so long without care. Wait." He bent again to search the tangled stems. "The roots are here, several feet away from Mary's grave. Another grave? There are a few fragments of broken stone. . . ."

His voice died away, and for an interval no one spoke. Movement was suspended in a fixed instant of time; even the breeze died to a breathless hush.

"I'm leaving," Andrea said. Her voice sounded too loud, too harsh—an affront to the silence. "I have work to do."

Martin caught up with her as she slowed her headlong flight to a walk. "What's the matter? Did I do something?"

Behind them she heard the boys laughing and talking. They were heading for the shed where they had placed Jim's weight lifting equipment. Why couldn't he find something safe and harmless to do? Waving heavy weights around, and brooding like Hamlet in a moldy graveyard. . . .

"It's morbid," she said vehemently. "Sick and morbid. Why do you have to encourage him?"

"In those terms archaeology is morbid, and so is history," Martin said. "Genealogy, paleontology, anthropology—digging up the dead bones of the past. He needs something, Andrea. New interests, new hobbies, maybe a new career. I gather he was thinking of going pro."

"That was just a pipe dream, a joke we had. He's going to major in accounting. Or computers."

"Or hotel management? Okay, so tell me it's none of my business. But I can't allow people I—people I like—to make such flagrant mistakes without speaking my mind. Jim's interests can't be artificially induced by you or anybody else. The most you can do is cultivate the ones he develops himself, and thank God for them."

"You're right," Andrea said. Martin's defensive look relaxed; she waited, hatefully, cruelly, before adding, "It isn't any of your business." She let the screen door slam in his face and ran to her room.

IV

Kevin's departure, that evening, precipitated another fight, this time with Jim. Andrea couldn't understand what she had done to anger him. She wasn't sorry to see Kevin go, but she was sure she had concealed her feelings; Kevin didn't seem to see anything lacking in her farewells and thanks, but after he was gone Jim turned on her with angry accusations of a sort she hadn't heard from him for years. "You hate Kevin—you hate all the guys—you don't want me to have any friends!" He stormed off to his room and wouldn't come out, no matter how she pleaded. When she tried the knob she found, to her

81

incredulous hurt, that the door was bolted. He must have installed the bolt that afternoon, with Kevin's help.

Andrea exhausted herself cleaning objects that were already spotless. When she went to bed she would have cried herself to sleep if she had allowed herself that kind of weakness.

Wings, beating against dark bars of shadow, trying to break free. . . . She came out of an uneasy dream to feel them all around her, stirring her hair with the wind of their passage, brushing the hands she lifted to fend them off.

Lips locked and teeth set, she managed to keep from screaming, not so much from shame as from pride. She would not use that weapon against Jim. But not for any reward on earth could she have forced herself out of the frail refuge provided by mattress and sheet, not even to reach the lamp on the table by her bed.

After an endless interval she realized that there was something else in the dark room. She fancied she could see it through her closed eyelids—a tiny point of light, like the dimmest of candle flames. It fed her failing strength, and the wings fell back before it, retreating into remote realms of shadow. She slipped a shaking hand from under the sheet and found the lamp.

And, of course, there was nothing in the room. A night breeze stirred the thin curtains. It felt cold as winter, but as the sweat of terror on her body dried, warmth and courage gradually returned. This time she had won. And next time, if there was a next time, the victory would be easier.

Chapter Five

Next morning Andrea lay in wait for Martin. He had refused to let her carry a breakfast tray to his room, claiming his schedule was too erratic and that he couldn't possibly know in advance at what time he would want his coffee. It was nearly ten before he came downstairs, dressed for jogging. When he saw her he mumbled a greeting and headed for the door.

"I want to apologize," Andrea said.

"I guess I was out of line." Martin stopped, but did not turn.

"You care about Jim. I should have given you credit for good intentions."

"But not for good sense?" He faced her, smiling. Unaccountably relieved, Andrea smiled back.

"Let's make a deal. You're entitled to give me your opinion and I'm entitled to blow up if I don't like it."

His head on one side, Martin considered the suggestion. "That seems reasonable," he admitted.

Then Andrea went to make her peace with Jim.

He opened the door as soon as she knocked. "Sorry I

flipped last night,'' he said with a carefree smile. "I hated to see Kevin leave. Not fair to take it out on you. Okay?"

"Okay." The bolt was shiny, brand-new. Jim saw her looking at it.

"Don't take it personally, sis. It's just that I have to—well, I need a place where I can be by myself. My own place."

"I understand."

"Good. I'm starved—what's for breakfast?"

He headed for the kitchen. Following, Andrea stopped to check the supplies in the pantry. She needed more mixing bowls. Linnie had broken two of the big ones in the past week. Better get stainless steel next time, she thought wryly.

From the next room she heard the scrape of Jim's chair and his casual greeting. "Hi, Linnie. Hot enough for you?"

"Here's your coffee, nice and strong," Linnie murmured. "I'll make you some bacon and eggs."

"Don't bother, Linnie."

"It's no bother. I like to do it." Her voice dropped even lower, to a crooning whisper. "You need to eat more, Jim. You're too thin."

Now that really is the last straw, Andrea thought furiously. That cheap little tart! I assumed it was Kevin she was after, hanging around the kitchen till he got up in the morning, offering to work longer hours. . . . She slammed the cupboard door—a tactical error, for it warned Linnie of her approach and gave the girl time to retreat to the stove.

"I'll do that," Andrea said, taking the bacon from Linnie. "Go and clean Mr. Greenspan's room. And hurry up, he'll be back soon."

After the girl had gone, dragging her feet and pouting, Jim said mildly, "Aren't you a little hard on the kid?"

"She gets more incompetent every day. I think I'd better look for someone else."

"I guess she doesn't need the job." The indifference in

Jim's voice reassured Andrea, but she decided it wouldn't do any harm to add a warning.

"She told me she was planning to be married next spring. At seventeen—can you imagine?"

"Who's the guy?"

"He works at the gas station. He's only a year or two older, and according to Reba he's not worth a damn. They should suit one another—two high school dropouts, with no skills and no ambition."

"Any muffins left?" Jim asked.

II

By the end of the week Andrea almost wished Kevin would come back. Jim was at loose ends, restless and resentful. He spent a lot of time lying on the couch in the kitchen watching television—game shows, soap operas, old movies, anything that unrolled before his half-closed eyes—except sports. The beginning of the football season left him unmoved, and when Andrea sat down one afternoon to watch the Maryland-North Carolina game, hoping a pretense of interest on her part would shake him out of his apathy, he got up and switched channels. She racked her brain trying to think of things to amuse him. He didn't want to do any of them, and all the things he wanted to do were physically impossible, dangerous, or against the law.

"Oh, come on," Martin protested, when she expressed this opinion. "What has he proposed—knocking over the Ladiesburg bank, growing marijuana as a cash crop?"

Martin had been hard at work for several days and she had scarcely seen him. She hadn't meant to take him into her confidence; the words had come out of their own accord when she happened to run into him on his way out to dinner.

"I don't know why I'm talking to you about it," she said. "You always take his part."

"You're talking to me because you have no one else to talk to," Martin said. "Don't suppose that I am under any illusions about that. . . . Maybe it's just as well."

"What? I'm sorry, Martin, I was thinking of something else."

After a moment Martin's wry expression relaxed. He shook his head. "Never mind. I'm not taking Jim's side or opposing yours. He's got cabin fever, Andrea, and no wonder. Why won't you let him use the car?"

"You know why."

"No, I don't. He could drive with one foot—hell, a kid that age could probably manage with one arm and one leg."

"Don't you dare let him drive the Volkswagen!"

"He couldn't. It's not an automatic shift—remember? Besides, whether you believe it or not, I wouldn't deliberately flaunt your wishes, even if I think they're asinine."

"Oh, you're impossible," Andrea said rudely. "Just forget the whole thing."

Martin tried. The following evening he invited himself for supper, giving Andrea a choice between pizza, chicken, and super double cheeseburgers. When he and Jim went to pick up the food, Jim was looking more cheerful. After they had eaten, Martin said casually, "I picked up some seed catalogs the other day; didn't you say something about wanting to plant a few flowers, Jim?"

"You can't plant seeds in the fall, can you?"

"No, but it's the right time of year for planting bulbs." He opened the catalog to a picture of brilliantly tinted hyacinths and held it before Jim's indifferent face. "Pretty," he said hopefully.

"Tulips are nice," Andrea made her contribution.

"I hate tulips," Martin said, scowling. "They remind me of blowsy, overblown Toulouse Lautrec tarts. Especially the ragged types."

"These are pretty," Jim said, turning the page. "Daffodils. They last, don't they? For years."

Pleased at Jim's interest, Martin said, "Yes, they're surprisingly tough for such fragile-looking flowers. They will spread and bloom year after year, with little attention."

When the catalogs had been exhausted Jim turned on the TV, but this time Andrea didn't mind. He and Martin had made a date to shop for bulbs the following day, and the two of them joined in a vigorous critique of the views expressed on the public-affairs program they were watching.

When the program was over, Andrea rose to change channels. The trailer for the next feature had been shown, and she wasn't interested in any of the subjects to be covered— skydiving, a scheme to raise the wreck of a Spanish treasure galleon, and interviews with people who had "died and come back to life." As she reached for the dial, Jim said, "Leave it, will you? I want to see this."

"I'm passionately interested in skydiving myself," Martin said. "I've decided I need to take up an active sport."

Andrea returned to her mending. She was working on a box of linens she had found in the attic—pillowcases, dresser scarves, and doilies of beautiful time-yellowed linen, trimmed with homemade lace. Her guests had admired the ones she had put into use, and she had been persuaded to sell a dresser scarf for what seemed to her an astronomical sum. She paid little attention to what was on the screen; watching people falling through space set her teeth on edge.

The next segment started with low thrilling music, a splash of rainbow light that expanded to fill the screen, and a lugubrious voice intoning, "Back from the dead! We bring you the most thrilling discovery of the century, perhaps of all time—the true stories of people who literally, physically died— and returned to tell us about it. Man's quest for immortality— have these people found the answer?"

The story had been filmed with an eye to viewer interest

rather than scientific accuracy, and in that it succeeded. Even Andrea watched, neglecting her sewing. The stories were strikingly similar. As one embarrassed-looking electrician described it:

"Something kinda snapped, like a stretched wire breaking. Then I was hanging in the air looking down on the bed where I was lying. I was on the bed, and I was up there too; it was like the guy on the bed wasn't really me. I could see the doctor and the nurses standing around.

"Then I was moving—straight through the walls and down a long hall with bare white walls. It was like I was floating. Down at the end of the hall I could see a light, and hear something like music and peoples' voices. I couldn't wait to get there. The light got bigger and brighter—it was all colors of the rainbow. And then, just as I was almost there—I came back."

"Back to your body?" The interviewer's voice was hushed.

"Yeah. I was, like, pulled back into it—like it was a magnet and I had to go, whether I wanted to or not."

"And did you want to go back, Mr. Brown?"

"No," Brown said. "Oh, no. It hurt. It hurt real bad."

His somber face was replaced by a row of girls dressed like beer bottles kicking up their legs and singing.

"Of all the setups," Andrea said, stabbing her needle into the fabric. "The interviewer really fed him those answers."

"No, he didn't," Jim said. "That's what it's like. Exactly."

A drop of bright blood fell from Andrea's finger to the fabric, where it spread and blurred.

After a moment Martin said, "That happened to you?"

"Uh-huh."

"You never told me, Jimmie," Andrea said.

"You'd have thought I was delirious or something."

The justice of the charge and the calm, uncomplaining voice in which he stated it, rendered her incapable of defending herself. Jim went on, "I didn't tell anybody. I couldn't stand—you know—having people pick over what I said, asking questions, looking skeptical—or laughing. Besides, I didn't know it had happened to other people. I've read about it since.''

"But not before?" Martin asked alertly. "Forgive me, Jim, I'm not doubting your word—"

"You're being scientific," Jim said, smiling. "I hadn't read anything about it then, no.''

"But you might have seen references to the subject, and not remember that you'd seen them," Martin argued. "There have been articles in magazines and newspapers."

"That's always a good out," Jim said. "If I don't remember something, it's not because it never happened, it's because I've forgotten it happened.''

"You have a point," Martin admitted. "But that's why the question will never be settled.''

"It is for me," Jim said.

"But, Jimmie," Andrea exclaimed. "You had a fractured skull—brain damage—you were full of drugs—"

Martin interrupted her, deliberately raising his voice. "I'd like to believe it. Who wouldn't? What was it like, Jim?''

"Oh, it was pretty much like that last guy said. Only instead of floating down a hallway I was in the dark, moving, but not seeing anything until the light came. It was like a star at first, far away—so far. . . . I didn't hear voices, but I knew someone was there waiting for me, someone I wanted to see." Jim lay back against the cushions. "I didn't want to come back either," he said.

Martin glanced at Andrea and looked quickly away. "Did it hurt, getting back into your body?''

"Oh, yeah, it hurt. I didn't seem to fit—it was like squeezing into a suit of armor that's too small and too hard.'' A shudder ran through him, though his expression remained calm. "The worst of it wasn't the pain. The light was so beautiful. . . . It was pulling at me, but something else was pulling the other way. I felt like I was being ripped apart.''

"Fascinating," Martin murmured.

Martin's manner, interested but detached, curious but receptive, had succeeded where Andrea knew she would have failed. It was important for Jim to talk about the most critical experience of his life; she realized she ought to be grateful to Martin for helping him achieve this vital catharsis. She had never been able to bring herself to talk about those dreadful weeks; she had never told him of her battle to save him from the ultimate horror. It had never occurred to her that the dreaded, inevitable end might not be a horror, but a longed-for goal. She felt burdened down with guilt, all the more painful because it was so unfair. Why should she feel guilty? Life was a reality, life after death a drug-induced illusion.

Jim noticed her depression. "Andy's bored," he said, with a smile. "She hates this kind of talk—right, sis? Change the subject. Skydiving, now—that might be just the sport for me. I'd have to compensate for this"—casually he touched his stump—"but I'll bet I could do it."

The sidelong glance he gave Andrea told her he was teasing her. She responded automatically, "You try that, bud, and I'll tear your ears off."

He didn't know. He believed it was the pull of the flesh, of the body, that had brought him back, torn and reluctant. She was content to leave it at that—until a day came when he could give her the thanks she knew she deserved.

III

Gardening kept Jim busy for a few days. Andrea was glad he had found something to do, even when she learned that he was working, not on the long-neglected flower beds around the house, but in the graveyard. When the bulbs had all been planted and a spell of rainy weather kept Jim indoors, she

braced herself for another siege of boredom. She had promised herself she wouldn't bother Martin again. He was hard at
work; the soft patter of his typewriter went on hour after
hour.

This time Jim found his own occupation. He came clattering down the stairs one wet afternoon while Andrea was
vacuuming the parlor and cursing Satan, whose black hairs
were everywhere.

"Look what I found," he said, holding out a tattered
magazine.

Andrea turned off the vacuum cleaner and examined his
find. "*Life* magazine. Nineteen-forty-seven. That is old."

"There are stacks of them up in the attic, some even
older."

"That's something you could do for me," Andrea said,
snatching at what seemed a heaven-sent opening. "I never
inventoried the attic or the third floor—I just grabbed the
furniture I needed and left the rest."

"If I find anything we can hock, do I get a cut?" Jim
asked.

"Jimmie, you know you can have all the money you want.
It's half yours—we share and share alike."

"Yeah, I know, but . . ." Jim traced the design of the
flowers in the carpet with the tip of his crutch. "I'd like to
earn it. You know?"

"That job would certainly be worth money to me," Andrea
said.

"Minimum wage," Jim said firmly. "I'll do that, sure.
There's something else I thought I could help you with.
Those rooms on the third floor—I could clear them out, drag
some of the junk up to the attic, strip the walls and woodwork,
and like that."

A dozen objections crowded into her mind. The attic stairs
were steep and narrow, the furniture was too bulky for him to

drag. . . . He still refused to consider a prosthesis. He had flown into a rage the last time she mentioned the subject.

She saw that Jim was watching her, his body braced for rejection. "That's a wonderful idea," she said. "I want to renovate and rent those rooms eventually. You could save some expense by doing that."

His face shining, Jim gave her a quick peck on the cheek. He went flying back upstairs, moving with a speed and agility that made her hair stand on end even while she admired it. She knew she would worry about him, but it was worth it—anything was worth it to see him look so happy. And she would not ride herd on him. She wouldn't check on him every few minutes or warn him to be careful.

She stuck to this resolution even when the sound of heavy objects crashing to the floor shook the house, and Jim's curses echoed down two flights of stairs. The first time he dropped something Martin came barreling out of his room, glasses askew and eyes wide with alarm. "What the hell—"

Andrea stood at the foot of the third-floor stairs wringing her hands. "Don't let me go up there," she pleaded. "I swore I wouldn't."

"He's okay," Martin said, listening. "He couldn't cuss with such eloquence if he had done himself an injury." He started back to his room, pausing only long enough to add, "You're a hero, lady; stick to it."

In some ways the long silences that followed Jim's furniture-moving efforts were harder on Andrea's nerves than the thuds and crashes. She did yield to the temptation of seeing what he was doing from time to time, telling herself that it was only natural she should take an interest. For several days he occupied himself cleaning and clearing out the larger of the upstairs bedrooms; but one afternoon, when she went up carrying a glass of milk and a plate of cookies, he was nowhere to be found. She was about to call out when she saw that the door of the tower room was open.

There was no reason for the sudden fear that gripped her limbs. The tower room wasn't any more dangerous than the other rooms on the upper floors. But instead of calling his name she moved stealthily, tiptoeing on the stairs, and when she saw him standing safe and sound in front of the western window she felt an equally unaccountable easing of tension.

Quietly as she had approached, he had heard her. "Come over here," he said, not turning. "Look."

It had rained earlier in the day, and the air was clear as pure water. The arch of the sky enclosed them like a blue glazed bowl protecting a miniature landscape—swelling hills and amber fields, wood and pasture and stream and valley. To the west, where the mountains stood in sharp outline against the sunset, a single bank of cloud remained; the sun, behind it, edged its rim with sharpest gold, like the fringe on a king's purple mantle. As the sun dropped lower, free of the cloud bank, every color in the autumn landscape sprang into clearer focus and brighter color, as water flowing over a pebble turns it into a gleaming gem. Its beauty would change but would not diminish with the passing seasons; in winter a world of sable and ermine and crystal, and in the spring. . . . Suddenly she felt that she could hardly wait for spring, when dogwood and apple trees were white with blossom and the stream ran deep between banks sprinkled with wild flowers. And she wondered if there could be a lovelier land, in this or any other world.

"I'm going to move up here," Jim said. "Into this room."

He took the glass from her before much of the milk had spilled. "Jim, you can't possibly—" she began.

"It's always 'can't.' I didn't expect you to understand."

"I do understand. You want to get away from me."

He had braced himself for a struggle. Her stricken face softened and disarmed him. "Not you, Andy—not you personally. I mean, if you're afraid to be alone down there, or anything like that. . . ."

He had offered her a weapon, but she could not use it, not after he had given it with such touching gallantry. Memory weakened her even more—the memory of a desolate young voice saying, "I didn't want to come back."

"I'm not afraid," she said. "That's not it."

He knew he had won. His face lit up with the look she found so hard to resist. "Just look," he urged. "Look at it. It could be the best room in the house. I'll fix it up—paint and paper and everything."

He was right. The quaint, odd-shaped room had enormous charm. It would appeal to anyone with a spark of imagination or taste. She realized that he had already begun work. The litter on the floor had been swept into a pile, and one section of peeling wallpaper had been removed.

"I don't mind your moving," she lied stoutly. "But there's so much to do here! The windowsill is rotten and the plaster on the ceiling is bad. . . . And I'm worried about the floor."

She knew he had won. But she couldn't force herself to make a formal concession, not quite yet. She moved around the room, examining the cracked plaster and stamping on the floor. Maddeningly, it absorbed the punishment she gave it until she neared the door.

"Here—this board sags badly. Probably rotted."

"I saw that. I can fix it."

Andrea knelt. "But if the joist is bad. . . ." Her fingers traced the crack, and she said in surprise, "It's not even nailed down. I can lift it right up."

"Maybe a couple of nails is all it needs." Jim came to her side.

The space exposed when she lifted the board was like a long narrow box, its base the ceiling of the room below, its sides the rough joists. Dust lay thick, like rolls of dirty cotton wool, outlining the shape of something underneath.

Jim was quicker to comprehend than Andrea. His breath caught, and he exclaimed, "The board isn't rotted. It was the cover of someone's secret hiding place. Pull out the nails, cover it with a rug, and no one would suspect. What's in it?''

It appeared to be a sheaf of heavy papers tied together into a scrapbook. The ribbon that bound the sheets, now of an indeterminate gray shade, crumbled as Andrea lifted the object out and brushed the muffling dust away. The cover was of heavy cardboard bound in fabric, so filthy that its original pattern could not be discerned, but it had protected the pages inside fairly well.

They were a collection of drawings—pen-and-ink, charcoal, watercolor—and had evidently been done over an extended period of time, for the skill of the unknown artist increased with each page. Flower sketches, doll-faced women in elaborate bustled gowns, a bride in full regalia, crowned with orange blossoms, trailing yards of tulle. A soldier, far too handsome to be anything but an idealized version of an imaginary hero. Other faces, obviously sketched from life, and far less attractive. They lacked the sure touch of the trained artist, but they had a certain quality; one, of a scowling, wrinkled old man, was almost a caricature.

On the last page was the full-length portrait of a woman. The shape of her body was oddly distorted, probably owing to the artist's lack of skill, but the face was admirable. She wore a highnecked black gown with long, tight sleeves. The boned collar was pinned with a jet brooch, and sable bangles circled her wrists. Her hair, dead-black and lifeless, was pulled back into a heavy bun at the nape of her neck. Her head was turned slightly to one side. Black brows slashed across her forehead; and at her feet, half hidden by the folds of the flowing skirt, was . . . Satan. The cat's eyes had been touched in with vivid yellow, the only color on the page.

''My God,'' Jim said softly. ''The cat is part of her—you can't tell where its body stops and her dress begins. The tail could belong to either one of them.''

''Satan's great-great grandfather?'' Andrea murmured.

"And then some. . . . It's good, isn't it?"

"Yes." Faint praise for what was unquestionably a brilliant piece of portraiture, particularly for a young girl. Why did she assume the artist was young, and female? She found reasons, after the fact; sketching and painting, embroidery and the pianoforte were the proper occupations of young ladies of good family in the nineteenth century, the period suggested by the costumes. The earlier drawings were the sort of thing one might expect to find in such a sketchbook—flowers and fashions, handsome faces and pretty brides.

The portrait was different. Jim didn't appear to see it, and Andrea was not inclined to draw it to his attention, but the sheer malice of the sketch took her breath away. The subtlety of that malice was precocious and disturbing. The features were not distorted, in fact, they were those of a handsome, stately woman; but the curl of the lip, the vicious slash of the frowning brows. . . . And the cat. Jim had noted the blending of the two bodies, the identity of woman and animal, but he had not understood the implication.

Andrea turned back to the beginning of the book. Now that she was on the lookout for it, she found a small, almost inperceptible flaw in almost every sketch. Small black worms gnawed at the hearts of the roses. Ingeniously masked by the intricacies of ruffles and folds in the fashion sketches were the lines of naked bodies—in one case, the bare bones and grinning skull. The artist's not very successful attempt to understand the underlying anatomical structure was not shocking in itself, but in the late nineteenth century, female modesty was at its more prurient and unnatural. An unmarried girl was not even supposed to know what her own body looked like.

The only drawings that seemed unflawed—and, in consequence, much more vapid—were those of the young officer and the bride. Why, Andrea wondered, were they included in the sketches—the dirty pictures—the artist had hidden from parents and teacher? Slightly sickened, she closed the sketchbook. Viewed as documents of social history, the drawings were a damning indictment of the prudery and double standards that had made Victorian life such a hell for women. Viewed in another way, the girl who had lived in this room was definitely neurotic.

Neuroses weren't contagious, Andrea reminded herself. Jim was in no danger of infection, even if he did breathe the air she once had breathed.

Chapter Six

Andrea had no patience with people who believed in omens and portents. It never occurred to her to view the discovery of the strange, disturbing book as a portent of disaster; but the following days brought one problem after another. Linnie was increasingly slow and clumsy. The price of coffee rose for the second time in a month. Rain turned the ground to mud and spirits to mush. Satan, disliking dampness, returned to his favorite indoor litter box. The leather books in the library developed mold.

Going one morning to deal with this problem, Andrea found Jim and Martin in the library. Martin was another minor annoyance; he had abandoned his typewriter and was constantly underfoot, offering assistance she didn't want and engaging in long discussions with Jim, in the course of which they strewed the house with crumbs, beer cans, and ashes.

There were two overflowing ashtrays on the library table now. And they had pulled books at random from the shelves, disturbing the neat alignment.

The library was popular with male guests; its dark oak paneling and big chairs had the elegance of an old-time

London club. The decor was not seriously marred by the television set, for when this unavoidable amenity was not in use, it was discreetly concealed by a needlepoint fireplace screen. Cousin Bertha's progenitors had not been readers; their acquisitions consisted mainly of elongated sets of "Collected Works," and most of the pages had not even been cut. However, the rows of rich red and soft brown leather spines, gilt-stamped, had a luxurious look.

Andrea replaced the ashtray at Martin's elbow with a clean one. His cigarette dangling from his mouth, he glanced up. "Thanks."

"No trouble. No trouble at all." She started wiping the books.

"The rain," said Martin, responding to her tone rather than her words, "is getting on everyone's nerves."

"How is the book coming?" Andrea asked pointedly.

Martin grinned. "It isn't. I seem to have hit the well-known writer's block."

"And this is your method of breaking it?"

"It's one way," Martin said calmly. "When the imponderables of the present are too much, the pursuit of the past offers escape and a certain sense of balance."

Jim ignored this byplay. Brown head bent over the book he was examining, he said, "We're looking for stuff about the house. It's mentioned in this book."

Happy to see him absorbed in a new hobby, Andrea looked over his shoulder. "*Old Houses of Western Maryland—Minor Mansions.* That's not very flattering."

"Victoriana wasn't in favor when that was written," Martin said. "The *major* mansions of this region date from the late eighteenth or early nineteenth centuries."

A faded black-and-white photograph, further dimmed by reproduction, showed the house as it had appeared in 1925. It had not changed in essential outline, but even in the poor photo it had a fat, prosperous appearance.

"Cousin Bertha's father must have owned the place then," Andrea said. "She'd have been in her twenties."

"Was her family name Webber?" Martin asked.

"That's right."

"Here it is." Jim pointed. " 'Mr. Josiah Webber, a well-known Ladiesburg merchant, is the present owner.' He inherited from his father, and *he* bought the place from. . . . It doesn't say who, just when. Nineteen hundred."

"And, as I suspected, the house was built in 1862," Martin crowed.

"But not by the Springers," Jim added, in antiphonal chorus. "The builder was a guy named Broadhurst. Must have been rich. He owned almost three hundred acres."

"I wonder how he made his money," Martin mused. "War profiteering, perhaps? Shoes of paper disguised to look like leather, rotten food and moldy flour. . . ."

"Pinko," Andrea said amiably. "You think all millionaires get rich by trampling on the poor."

"Back in those days they did. Then they tried to assuage their consciences, and a wrathful God, by building libraries and orphan asylums."

Andrea abandoned the argument; she never won. "It's all very interesting," she said politely, picking up the dust cloth.

"Not very," Martin said. "Books like this only give the bare bones. They don't tell you about the scandals and the tragedies, the murders and the passionate love affairs."

"What a melodramatic mind you have," Andrea said.

"Life is melodramatic—hadn't you noticed? No novelist would dare invent plots as farfetched as the things that actually happen. This house must have had its share of melodrama. Every old house does."

"Well, I don't want to know about it," Andrea said. She shifted the library steps and climbed up to attack the next row of books.

"Then I don't suppose you would be interested in attending tonight's meeting of the Ladiesburg Historical Association."

"No, I wouldn't. I've got enough problems in the here and now."

"Jim and I are going."

"So that's why you're reading up on the house."

"Doing our homework," Jim agreed. "Sure you don't want to come with us?"

"No, thanks."

It was good to be alone in the house, for the first time in weeks. The men had decided to make an evening of it, dining at Peace and Plenty before going on to the meeting, which was held at the home of a local antique dealer. Wrapped in a comfortable old bathrobe covered with fuzz, Andrea spent the evening watching the worst television had to offer. Lulled into a stupor by the sheer awfulness of what she saw, she didn't even look at the lists on her lap.

Picturing the members of the historical society as doddering septuagenarians who tottered off to bed at an early hour, she expected Jim and Martin home by eleven. It was well after midnight before the front door opened and the wanderers returned.

"Still up?" Jim asked.

"You're late. The meeting must have been fascinating."

"We dropped by the Shamrock Club for a few beers," Martin explained, tossing his wet raincoat over a chair.

"Isn't that the dive on the other side of town—the one that features topless male dancers on Wednesday night?"

"This," Martin pointed out, "is Thursday night. Dive is not an inappropriate term, however."

"Shame on you."

"I was checking the pulse of the community. Want some coffee?"

"You won't find much sympathy with your bleeding-heart views in this neck of the woods," Andrea said.

"We got up a good argument." Jim grinned broadly. "Martin sure knows how to bring out the worst in people."

She hadn't seen him look so happy and relaxed in a long time. Propped on his crutches, his hair curling around his ears, he stood smiling down at her. Damp weather always made his hair wave, driving him to frantic efforts with hair creams and blow dryers.

"Did you enjoy it, darling?" she asked.

"The meeting wasn't bad," Jim admitted. "Did you know this house was a hotel once before?"

"You're kidding. It's funny that book didn't mention it."

Martin poured himself a cup of coffee and sat down. "It wasn't the type of establishment your cousin and her father would have wanted mentioned. Nobody at the meeting knew much about it, but the impression is that it wasn't a very classy joint."

"Probably the local cathouse," Jim said.

"What an awful thing to say!"

"Don't be so stuffy, Andy."

"Prostitution and other seamy occupations take on glamour after a few years," Martin said. "People are collecting those brass tokens from Old West whorehouses—mostly fakes, of course."

"I refuse to sit up half the night discussing whorehouses." Andrea stifled a yawn. "But I'm glad you had a good time. Did you meet any nice young people, Jimmie?"

"Are you putting me on, sis? I was the only person there under eighty."

"Thanks," Martin said.

"You know what I meant—"

"Uh-huh," Martin said gloomily. "I know."

Her robe wrapped around her and her stockinged feet on a stool, Andrea listened drowsily as they exchanged amiable insults and recalled the high points of the evening's varied entertainment. They were on first-name terms now, casual as old friends. And here she sat, in disheveled dishabille, acting as if Martin were one of the family.

How had it happened? She couldn't accuse Martin of being pushy. He paid well for his privileges, and she had only herself to blame for the candid criticism he occasionally leveled at her; she had been too open with him, too free to ask for help and advice. That sympathetic, concerned manner of his was only part of his professional technique; he probably behaved that way with everybody. I'll be a little more reticent from now on, she promised herself. It's ridiculous. I know almost nothing about his personal life, and he knows only too much about ours.

When the party broke up, and Jim had gone to his room, she followed Martin into the hall.

"Thank you for tonight," she said softly.

"Why should you thank me? I enjoyed myself."

"That's not the point. You did it for Jim."

"Not only for Jim."

He stood quite still, one hand on the banister, the other holding his notebook. But something in his look made Andrea step back a pace. Don't be silly, she told herself. He's never even. . . . He wouldn't. . . . Not the way I look right now, with my hair all in a mess and this horrible old robe.

"I'm fond of you, too," Martin said coolly. "The two of you have given me more than formal hospitality. You let me butt into your business and you bitch at me when I get out of line. It's a new experience for me to be part of a family. I like it."

Andrea felt herself flushing. She had been an egotistical fool to imagine even for a moment. . . . "I'm glad you feel that way," she said. "But I don't want to take advantage of you. I know you're busy. You don't have to worry about Jim. He's fine now."

"Do you think so?"

"Why, of course. It's obvious. He's happier, more cheerful—"

"Damn it," Martin said, slamming his fist down on the stair rail, "I don't know how a woman of your obvious good sense can be so blind. The kid is a prisoner here. He can't get away. Do you honestly believe a boy of nineteen is going to be happy with the company of two sedate adults like us, tied to four walls and a few acres of ground? He needs people his own age—he needs freedom, independence. . . ." He broke off. After a moment he said more quietly, "I have a real talent for screwing myself. Your turn now. Go ahead, let me have it."

"Oh, the hell with you," Andrea said, forgetting her resolution. "You drive me crazy with your gloom and doom. I'm going to bed."

"That wasn't so bad," Martin said. "I do believe you're mellowing, my dear."

II

The dream came again that night. She was certain of the date this time, for on this third occurrence she made a note on her calendar next day.

There was not a gleam of light in the room when she woke, battered and engulfed by the frantic flailing of invisible wings. Numbing cold sent waves of shivering through her body. Teeth clenched and fingers frozen on the coverlet, she stared up into the blackness. And after a while it was there—a small spark of light, dazzling against the dark. She reached out for it, and slowly it expanded, defeating the chill of the air. Spreading, it lost the intensity of its initial burning; a dim, faintly shining shape, it hovered for a time, then faded, leaving warmth and quiet behind.

III

The strangest thing about the dream—as Andrea preferred to call it—was the quickness with which the memory of it faded. As she lay quivering in the dark, she contemplated every possible means of relief—tranquilizers, a neurological examination, a psychiatrist. . . . If a self-proclaimed exorcist had turned up, she would have hired him on the spot. In the cold light of day the terror faded, like the memory of pain. She told herself it was probably an expression of some deep inner doubt, which would fade as success brought freedom from anxiety. Ignore it and it would go away.

She had no time next day to worry about it, for she woke to the drumbeat of pouring rain, the heaviest she had ever seen. The backlash of the season's final hurricane had moved inland, pouring tons of water on an already flooded countryside.

Before the power went out they heard of bridges washed away, highways under water, and streams overflowing. The telephone went out too, but Andrea did not need formal notification to know the guests she was expecting would not arrive. The bridge over the stream bounding her property was under water by midday, and the pasture looked like a brown lake. She spent most of the day frantically mopping up puddles. Water poured in under the doors and through hitherto unobserved cracks around windows and eaves.

To add to her exasperation the men found the storm exhilarating. They kept running out to watch the water rise, returning to drip on her polished floors. Tiring of this activity at last, they left Andrea to cope with her puddles. Chortling over his foresight in refusing to trade his antique typewriter for an electric model, Martin went back to work. Jim retired to the attic, where he spent the rest of the afternoon.

Andrea was sitting on the bottom step listlessly watching a puddle spread out across the hall when Martin's door opened.

The house was so dark he would have fallen over her if she had not growled a warning.

"What are you doing there?" he asked in surprise.

"Giving up. My hands are frozen, I've emptied twenty buckets of water out the door, and it just keeps coming back in. I've had it."

"You need a drink. And some food—those cold sandwiches we had for lunch weren't very sustaining."

"The stove is electric," Andrea pointed out, with forced calm. "I can't cook."

"Oh, you poor city slicker. How would you have managed in pioneer days?"

"I'd have cut my throat."

"Come on." He pulled her to her feet. "Let Uncle Martin demonstrate his skills."

Within ten minutes he had a fire going on the hearth in the library. Dry-shod and enveloped in her warmest robe, Andrea sipped sherry and watched as he coaxed the fire to a blaze.

"The worst is over, I think," Martin said, squinting knowledgeably at the hissing flames. "Clear skies by morning. . . . But God knows how long it will take to restore power. We'd better have something simple. Hot dogs. Have you got any? Never mind, I'll see what I can find."

Humming in an off-key tenor, he trotted out. Andrea knew he would make a mess of the kitchen, but she couldn't have cared less. The wine warmed her interior as the dancing flames cheered her soul. At that moment she would have voted for Martin Greenspan for President—or any other office to which he aspired.

He came back with a loaded tray, and distributed pans and pots around the hearth. "Good thing you filled the kettle," he said cheerfully. "We may be a little short on water before morning. Absurd, isn't it, with all that liquid pouring down outside?"

"There's bottled water in the pantry," Andrea said. "For emergencies."

"I'd call this an emergency, wouldn't you? I'll put a couple of buckets outside; but if worse comes to worst, we can haul water from the stream to flush the toilets. You are on well water, aren't you?"

"Oh, my God. I didn't even think of. . . . Yes, there's a well. With a pump. Run by electricity. . . ."

"You'll get used to it. You'll have to, if you live in the country."

"When did you—"

"Baked beans, hot dogs—I found some skewers we can use to toast them. I don't suppose you have any marshmallows?"

"You're crazy," Andrea said, laughing. "What do you think this is, a Girl Scout picnic?"

"A true philosopher makes the best of whatever comes," Martin said. "I could use an extra pair of hands here—no, don't get up. Where's Jim?"

"Upstairs. Lord knows what he's doing in the dark. He'll probably break his neck coming down the stairs." Andrea's tone was one of gloomy resignation.

Martin went into the hall. "Jim? Where the Hades are you?"

Andrea didn't hear a reply. When Martin returned he reported, "He's coming."

"He'll fall. He can't see—"

"He has a flashlight. What do you think he is, stupid?"

"Oh."

"More sherry?"

"Yes."

Before long Jim came clattering down. "What's for supper?" he asked hopefully.

"Nothing for you unless you get your carcass over here and help me," said Martin, squatting before the fire.

"Look what I found." Jim shook out the bundle he was holding. It proved to be a pair of white linen drawers, lavishly trimmed with lace and ribbons and large enough to encase the rear end of a baby elephant.

Martin sat down with a shout of laughter. "Beautiful. Why don't you model them, Jim?"

"No, don't," Andrea exclaimed, as Jim, grinning at the success of his joke, sat down and prepared to put his foot into the garment. "It's worth a lot of money. Linens and Laces, that new shop in town, sells petticoats and other clothes of that period with price tags of eighty and ninety dollars."

"I'll pay you eighty for that object if you promise to wear it to the supermarket," Martin offered.

The evening ended with laughter and charred hot dogs, and although the tickling sensation at the back of her throat warned Andrea that she was coming down with a cold, she dropped right off to sleep. The sherry might have had something to do with it.

IV

When the doorbell rang, early the following morning, Andrea looked up from her newspaper in surprise. She was pleased with herself, for she had managed to start a fire and heat water for coffee without assistance. The rain had stopped, the sky was blue, and the newspaper had arrived, which indicated that the road to town was open. It was the first Sunday morning she had had free for a long time, and she looked forward to a long lazy hour with the papers and a pot of coffee. The last thing she expected or wanted to see when she opened the door was the vacant face of Linnie Hochstrasser.

"There was no need for you to come, Linnie," she said, blocking the doorway. "I couldn't call you—the telephone isn't working—but surely you realized our guests wouldn't make it, in that storm."

109

"I just thought. . . ." Linnie shifted, trying to see past Andrea into the house.

"I appreciate your coming, but I really don't need you today."

"Well, I thought. . . ."

"Go home," Andrea said firmly.

"Yes, ma'am." Shoulders drooping, Linnie turned away.

Andrea closed the door. Then she gave a start. "Goodness, Jim, don't sneak up on a person like that. I thought you were still asleep."

"I heard the doorbell."

"It was that stupid Linnie. I'm just not in the mood to deal with her today. She should have known better than to come."

"Maybe she wanted to talk to you." Jim followed her into the kitchen.

"What about?"

"She's having problems with that boyfriend of hers. She wants to break up with him, but he's giving her a hard time."

He went on talking while Andrea immersed herself in the style section. She was not particularly interested in Paris fashions, but she was even less interested in the romantic problems of Linnie Hochstrasser.

"Free country, after all," Jim said. "If she doesn't want. . . ."

"Hems are going up again," Andrea said. "Just look at these clothes! They almost make a person believe male fashion designers do hate women."

Jim reached for the sports pages.

Telephone service was restored that afternoon. Reba was the first one to call, asking how they had weathered the storm. As Andrea described Martin's wilderness expertise, amid appreciative chuckles from Reba, it occurred to her that Martin was only one of the things for which she was indebted to the older woman. One of her guests had said, only half in jest, "Mrs. Miller said if we stayed at the Holiday Inn instead of your place, we couldn't eat at Peace and Plenty. Not that I'm sorry, Miss Torgesen; we've enjoyed it very much."

"Reba, you've got to come and visit us. Do you realize that you haven't even been inside the house?"

"I don't drop in on people unless I'm invited," Reba said.

"You don't need an invitation. Consider yourself invited, any time. I like you too much to offer you a meal—I'm a wretched cook—but why don't you come for a drink one evening?"

The alacrity with which Reba accepted told Andrea that her feelings had indeed been hurt, but that peace was now restored. "I've been meaning to ask you about Linnie," Reba went on. "How is she working out?"

"Fine." She would have been less enthusiastic if Reba had not been Linnie's sponsor. Eventually she meant to explore the possibility of a replacement, but the direct question caught her off guard.

"You may have to fire her."

"Why?"

"Because she's set her cap for Jim, that's why."

"I suspected as much." Andrea managed to conceal her amusement at the quaint phrase, which she had last encountered in the pages of Louisa May Alcott. "She has a crush on him, but he's not interested. He thinks she's a child."

"That's not how I heard it. Hell, it's none of my business what the two of them do or don't do. It's that crazy Gary Joe I'm worried about. He's threatening to beat Jim up."

"Gary Joe? Oh, yes—Linnie's fiancé."

"Fiancé is one word for it. Gary Joe Bloomquist is no damned good. Lazy, shiftless kid—he'll end up in the slammer sooner or later, for drunk driving if nothing worse. I was sorry to see Linnie get involved with him. She's not all that bad—dumb as a mule, but harmless. Gary Joe is sexy, if you like the type—dark, glowering, sullen—one of those barrel-chested, fat-lipped guys. Apparently Linnie has been needling him about Jim—how handsome he is, how gentlemanly. . . . Well, you can guess the rest.''

Andrea felt a twinge of pity for the unfortunate Linnie. If Reba's description of Gary Joe was accurate, Jim must seem like all the heroes of fiction rolled into one—courteous, sensitive—and a wounded hero at that. But Linnie would have to go. It was absurd to suppose that Jim, her fastidious, intelligent Jim, could succumb to the charms of a Linnie. Still. . . .

''Thanks for telling me,'' she said. ''I'll think about it. Would Thursday be a good day for you?''

They agreed on Thursday, subject to possible changes in Andrea's schedule, which had been disrupted by the rain, and Andrea hung up.

I mustn't neglect Reba again, she told herself. It's bad business, and bad manners. Besides, I rather like the old witch. Maybe I'll ask her for dinner sometime. She must get tired of the same food, even food as good as hers. I really must learn to cook. It can't be too hard. . . . Someday I may want to serve meals. I couldn't compete with Peace and Plenty—not now—but someday. . . . I wonder if the guests are as bloody sick of muffins as I am?

At five Martin left for the restaurant—planning, no doubt, to make use of some of its other amenities. The power had not been restored and probably would not be until later that evening, according to Potomac Power and Electric. Andrea spent half the afternoon trying to reach them and the rest of the time mopping up. There wasn't much more she could do until she had water.

The smell of broiling meat led her to the library, where she found Jim cooking hamburgers, one of his two specialties. She sneezed. Jim looked up. ''Catching cold?''

''I hope not.''

"Why don't you take some cold tablets and sack out? A good night's sleep might help you fight it off."

Touched by his concern and persuaded by his logic, Andrea agreed. The lights came on while they were carrying their dishes to the kitchen, but Andrea was in no mood for housework. She enjoyed having Jim fuss over her; he tucked her up in bed with a hot toddy and a mystery story and a box of tissues, and a lot of other items she didn't want, but which she received gratefully. The pills and the alcohol made her drowsy. She was staring at the book, watching the print dissolve into fuzzy nonsense, when the door opened and Jim looked in.

"You asleep?"

"Getting there."

"I just thought I'd tell you I'm going out for a while," Jim said rapidly. "A guy I met at the Historical Association called and asked if I wanted to go out for a few beers. I won't be late."

He was gone before she could question him.

If she hadn't felt so groggy she would have followed, asking, admonishing, suggesting. All of which, she acknowledged, would have been an error. Maybe her cold was a blessing in disguise.

But she left her light on and remained sitting up, drowsing off and waking to glance at the clock, and drowsing again, until Jim returned. He had kept his promise. It wasn't quite eleven-thirty when he looked in again to wish her good night.

"Did you have a good time?" Andrea asked.

"Oh, you know—the usual."

"Invite your friend to come here next time, why don't you?"

"Yeah, sure," Jim said. "Good night, Andy."

V

If her cold was no better next day, it was no worse, but after eight hours of scrubbing and wringing out mops, caulking windows and patching leaks, taking telephone calls and changing reservations, she was not displeased to find that Jim had again assumed the role of chef.

"Spaghetti for a change?" she said, smiling.

"We had hamburgers last night."

"So we did. Thanks, honey; I appreciate your helping."

"No problem," Jim muttered, his back to her.

"Don't put the spaghetti on just yet. Let's have a beer and talk for a while."

"I figured you would want to go to bed early."

"I don't want to go to bed. It's those damned pills that are making me so sleepy. I think I'll stop taking them."

"That's the trouble with you, Andy, you always quit taking medicine when you feel better and then you get sick again. You need lots of sleep."

Surprised at his vehemence, Andrea said mildly, "Maybe you're right. But I get bored lying in bed."

"I could move the TV into your room. There's a good movie on tonight."

The cold medicine must have dulled her wits. Any experienced guardian of the young should have been alerted by the clues Jim had dropped. But Andrea didn't catch on until after the movie had started. It was one of the car-crashing private-eye dramas she personally disliked, but which she thought might appeal to Jim, and she left her room to ask if he would join her. The utter silence of the house struck her at once. Jim was not in his room, or in the kitchen.

After climbing to the third floor and finding no sign of him, she knocked on Martin's door.

"Something wrong?" he asked, seeing her worried expression.

"Is Jim with you?"

Sensing that a simple denial would not satisfy her, Martin stepped back and opened the door wide. From the middle of the bed Satan blinked arrogant golden eyes. Jim was not there.

"Where could he have gone? He's not in the house."

"So he's gone out," Martin said. "What's the big deal? He's not six years old."

"But he's. . . ." She swallowed. "He's handicapped."

"That still doesn't make you his nursemaid."

"Oh, shut up. You don't understand."

"Yes, I do." Martin sighed. He was in his shirt sleeves, his collar open and his glasses riding high on his forehead. "Did you look to see if he left a note?"

"No. No, I didn't." Andrea ran toward the stairs.

Martin looked at Satan. The cat yawned. "You are undoubtedly right," Martin muttered. "But I haven't your sangfroid, more's the pity." He followed Andrea downstairs.

The note had been in plain sight on the kitchen table, weighted down by the sugar bowl. Andrea was reading it when Martin came in.

"He's gone out with that same boy," she said angrily. "Says he didn't want to disturb me. . . . Who is this person? Jim said he met him at the Historical Association."

Martin's eyebrows rose. "I can't remember anyone in particular," he said evasively.

"Jim said there wasn't anyone there under eighty."

"Why do you assume this newfound friend is his age?" Martin asked.

"He didn't exactly say that. . . . It must be someone completely unsuitable, or Jim wouldn't take such pains to keep me from meeting him. Goddamn it, how can he do this to me?"

Martin appeared to be debating with himself. One of him lost the argument; he shook his head morosely and said, "Can I give you some advice, or will you bite my head off?"

"I'll probably bite your head off." Andrea paced, crumpling the note in her hand.

"I'll give it anyway. Don't wait up for him."

"I'll do exactly as I please, thank you."

"I know." Martin sighed again. "I don't suppose you want me to keep you company?"

"No, thank you."

"All right. I'll be upstairs if you want me."

Andrea spent the next hour pacing the hall, drinking coffee, smoking, and talking to herself. The coffee made her sick and the cigarettes raked her raw throat. After a while she moved a chair into position by the parlor window and sat staring at the road. Cars passed, their headlights forming increasingly infrequent streaks of brightness as the night moved on toward morning. Once a car turned into the drive. Andrea started to her feet. But the driver had only wanted to turn; the lights retreated and retraced their path.

At one-thirty—she knew the time to the precise second— she rose stiffly from the chair and went to Jim's room. The door could only be bolted from the inside, but the bolt itself had been a warning she had heeded until that moment. She had punctiliously respected his privacy, never entering the room without telling him she intended to do so. And this was her reward! He had broken their mutual trust, and no longer deserved her consideration.

She was looking for an address book—or, more likely, in Jim's case, a scrap of paper with a name and telephone number. Any name she didn't recognize. And she wouldn't hesitate to call, even at this hour.

If she had not been so frantic with worry and rage, it might have struck her as pathetic that there were no such scraps. Jim's desk and dresser had always been littered with them, signs of the friends of both sexes he had once acquired so easily. After searching every drawer in every piece of furniture and finding nothing, she picked up a notebook and shook it. A sheet of paper fluttered to the floor.

A single glance told her it was not what she was looking

for. The paper was covered with writing—a letter, or, from the irregularity of the lines, a piece of verse. Angry as she was, she would not have deliberately pried into Jim's private correspondence, but a phrase caught her eye—something about fallen bridges. Before she could read on she heard the sound she had been waiting for. Thrusting the paper into her pocket, she ran to the front door, reaching it in time to see the headlights swing on around the house into the service drive leading to the garage and barn. By the time she reached the kitchen door, the car was retreating. In the dark of the moonless night she could not see it distinctly, but she knew the sound of the engine; she had heard it often enough.

A small enclosed porch separated the kitchen from the out-of-doors. Jim had just opened the door. His outline was unmistakable, but there was something odd about his stance; he was tilted at an angle, like a leaning tower. When he saw Andrea he giggled and said, "Ah, shit. Caught me, di'n' you?"

The smell of stale beer was so strong Andrea realized he must have spilled a considerable quantity on his clothes. "Come in," she said. "If you can walk."

"Shit, yes, I can walk." But the first step was a stagger, and Andrea darted forward bracing herself against his weight. She felt him shaking with laughter as she held him.

With very little assistance from Jim she got him into the kitchen. When the light fell on his face she cried out. His mouth was swollen and his chin was black with dried blood. Patches of red scraped skin marked cheekbone and temple.

"You oughta see th' other guy," Jim mumbled. Releasing the crutches, which fell with a crash, he swayed toward a chair.

"Did I hear a car—" Martin stopped. After a moment he said, "Good God." Then he started to laugh.

Jim joined him. "Oughta see th' other bastard," he told Martin.

Andrea looked from one grinning, flushed male face to the other and burst into tears.

Her sobs sobered Jim faster than an icy shower. "Hey, sis, don't do that. . . . I'm okay. I feel fine." His eyes widened ingenuously and his swollen lips parted in a look of consternation; he was just about to prove his last comment a lie when Martin grabbed him and hoisted him out of his chair.

"Come on, you can make it as far as the bathroom."

Their hasty departure was followed by a series of distressing sounds, interrupted only by acerbic comments from Martin. When the latter returned, Andrea had stopped crying and was sitting in stony silence.

"I put him to bed," Martin said, rolling his sleeves down. "He isn't hurt—just a few bruises and a loose tooth. He must have given a good account of himself. I've seen Gary Joe; he's a big lout, but he's flabby and out of—"

"You're crazy," Andrea said flatly. "Both of you. All of you. Men."

"Want a cup of coffee?"

"If I drink any more coffee I'll throw up."

"A nice hot cup of tea, then. The old-fashioned panacea for ladies in distress."

She didn't argue. Martin handed her a cup and sat down opposite her.

"Time for a lecture?" Andrea inquired.

"Can you believe I don't particularly want to lecture?"

"No."

"In that case I'll go on. I can see Jim's point of view, because I belong to the same vulgar sex. I suppose it's difficult for a woman to understand."

"Try me."

"Andrea, the accident crippled Jim in more ways than one. In a sense it emasculated him. Amputation, symbolizing castration—it sounds glib, I know, but think what he's lost. His prized athletic abilities, his car. . . . Hell, I can remember

118

how I felt about that beat-up wreck of mine, even though it was back in prehistoric times; to a modern kid his wheels are more than a means of transportation. Is it any wonder Jim has turned to the two classic methods of asserting his masculinity?''

''Fornication and fighting.''

''That's one way of putting it.''

''He was with Linnie, wasn't he? I recognized the sound of her father's truck.''

''She's the only nubile female he has available,'' Martin said.

There was a note of criticism in his voice which Andrea chose to ignore. ''But why can't they—do whatever they want to do here?''

''Did you just say what I thought you said?''

''I don't know what I'm saying.'' Andrea's head dropped onto her hands.

''You'll feel better in the morning.'' Martin pushed his chair back and rose. ''Jim won't, though. . . . Good night, Andrea.''

''Good night.'' She waited until he had opened the door. ''Thanks, Martin.''

''Any time.''

Andrea stayed where she was, elbows on the table, hands supporting her head. She had not tried to defend herself against Martin's implied criticism, but it wasn't altogether her fault that Jim had lost touch with his friends at school. Admittedly she sometimes forgot to pass on telephone messages; it wasn't deliberate, she just forgot. Jim was welcome to invite friends to the house, he knew that; she didn't have to tell him. He was the one who had cut himself off. Was it because he didn't want the girls he had dated to see him as he was now?

Martin had left Jim's door open. She could hear him snoring. He never snored unless he had had too much to drink. This wasn't the first time he had come home somewhat the worse for wear, but on the whole he had been relatively moderate in his drinking—or so she had believed. She'd had to work nights so often, and he had sometimes called to say he was spending the night with a friend. . . . Of course he got drunk. They all did. It was perfectly normal, an undesirable but unavoidable stage in growing up.

Jim sounded as if he were strangling. Andrea went to his door and looked in. Martin had left a night light on—a cracked, plastic Donald Duck that Jim had fished out of a box of old toys. Donald was campy and funny now. . . . Or perhaps Jim now felt the need of light in his darkness.

Andrea straightened the blanket, drawing it up over Jim's bare shoulders. Martin had washed the dried blood from his chin and swabbed iodine on the worst of the raw spots. Under the marks of battle Jim's face was as peaceful as a child's. A faint frown of concentration wrinkled his forehead, as if he were working hard to produce those gargantuan snores.

"I love you so much," Andrea whispered. "Jimmie. I love you."

Jim turned onto his side. The snores subsided into soft, regular breathing.

Leaving the door open, Andrea went to her room and started to undress. It was not until she heard the crackle of paper in the pocket of her robe that she remembered the letter she had found in Jim's notebook.

She tried to resist. She fought the temptation successfully until she was actually in bed. Then she switched on the light and took the crumpled page out of the wastebasket, where she had thrown it.

It was not a letter. As she read the scrawled lines, an icy hand closed over her heart.

> The map is here, before me. I traced the lines
> Heavy black ink, over the roads and rivers
> Showing the way I meant to go.

All useless now. Bridges fallen, roads washed out.
"Detour." Not that way. Find another route.
There are other lines. Other roads, other rivers.
They lead to pleasant places on the map.
Mountains to climb, heights I yet may reach.
Then why do I feel
Lost and worse than lost? A stranger in a strange
   old world.
Is there no map of the world where I belong?

Chapter Seven

"He thinks he's going to die," Andrea said.

"He is going to die. I'm going to die. You are going to die. It's the one sure fact in this uncertain world."

"Stop it. You know what I mean."

Martin tossed the paper onto the table and walked to the window. Papers crunched under his feet as he moved. The floor by his worktable was strewn with crumpled yellow sheets. A significantly small stack of finished pages lay on the table beside the typewriter, where Satan was playing paperweight.

Obviously Martin's work wasn't going well. Andrea felt a pang of guilt, but she was past caring. Jim came first, before anyone else in the world, and there was no one to whom she could turn for advice except Martin. She had knocked on his door as soon as she heard him stirring that morning.

"You understand what it means, don't you?" she asked urgently. "Or am I reading too much into it?"

"What are you reading into it?"

She forced the word past her reluctant lips. "Suicide."

"Maybe."

She stared at him in dismay. This was not the warm, comforting assurance she wanted: "Everything is going to be all right." She should have realized that that masterful untruth was something she would never get from Martin.

"I shouldn't have bothered you," she said, rising.

"What are friends for?" His smile warmed his face, smoothing out the lines of age and worry.

Andrea sank back in her chair. "Thank you for that. I don't think I deserve it. I haven't been friends with anyone for a long time. I'm not even sure what friendship is."

Martin struck a pose, like a bronze statue of an orator. "A friend," he intoned, "is someone who tries to pick you up when you fall down. And if he can't, he'll lie down beside you and listen."

"Who said that? Mark Twain?"

"Martin H. Greenspan. I just made it up. Andrea, I'll lie down and listen any time, but I'm out of my depth in this. I'll be damned if I want to take the responsibility."

"Just tell me what you think."

"I'm insane to commit myself," Martin muttered. "But I don't think this poem—not exactly great literature, is it?—is significant in itself. You know and I know that the suicide rate for Jim's age group is higher than that of any other; I won't deny that. But they're a morbid little lot; they like to play around with the idea of death. This strikes me as a fairly typical outpouring. Didn't you ever write mournful verse?"

"No."

"Really? I did. I remember one effusion that began, 'O grisly specter, clattering bare white bones. . . .' Mercifully I've forgotten the rest of it."

Andrea couldn't help smiling. "What had you been reading?"

"Lovecraft and Poe. Most of my early work was derivative."

"Much of your later work is going to die in the bud if I don't leave you alone," Andrea said. "Thanks. I feel better."

"Good." He put a casual hand on the smooth mound of

Satan's back. Satan spat. After Andrea had gone, Martin looked at the cat. "You wouldn't lie down and listen, would you? Well, there are different varieties of friendship, I suppose. Satan, I don't know whether I'm playing it cool or cutting my own throat."

Satan rose, kicked a few papers onto the floor, turned his back on Martin, and went to sleep. Martin began gathering up his manuscript.

Andrea didn't need to be warned to leave Jim alone. She could remember how a full-blown hangover felt; compounded by aching bruises and a massive sense of guilt, it was something she wouldn't wish on her worst enemy. One ear cocked for sounds of life from Jim's room, she washed the breakfast dishes. Linnie had not come to work. Andrea was not surprised; Linnie had an instinct for self-preservation common to rodents and other crawling creatures. She had been looking forward to firing Linnie.

Jim was still asleep when she finished in the kitchen and went to check the reservation book. It would be a busy week for her without help; she had a booking for midweek and a full house on Friday—and Reba coming on Thursday afternoon.

At least it had stopped raining. Sunlight streamed through the parlor windows and lay in a rainbow pool on the stairs, where the stained-glass window filtered the light. Steam rose from the lawn as the sun fought to dry out ground soaked by weeks of rain, but the air coming in the open door was fresh and crisp.

She looked up when she heard a car approaching. Almost immediately she recognized the distinctive wheezing of the engine. Jumping to her feet, she went to the door. That little bitch is in for a shock if she thinks she can stroll in two hours late and pretend nothing has happened, she thought angrily.

It was not Linnie who got out of the truck, but her father.

He appeared to be dressed for a formal call. His overalls were faded, but spanking clean, and his shirt collar was buttoned.

Prepared for battle with a whining girl, Andrea felt a qualm at the sight of what might well turn out to be an outraged father, metaphorical shotgun in hand.

At least she could count on Mr. Hochstrasser not to make a scene. He wasn't the yelling kind. In fact, he appeared to be more embarrassed than she; seeing her at the door he took off his worn cap and smiled stiffly.

"Morning, Miss Torgesen. Nice day, ain't it?"

Andrea gave the appropriate reply. "It's good to see the sun again. I hope the rain didn't ruin your crops."

"No, ma'am, I got my hay in long ago." He twisted the cap in his hands. "Could I speak with you a minute?"

"Come in." Mentally bracing herself, she held the door open.

"Maybe you wouldn't mind comin' out. I'm not dressed for your good furniture."

They sat down on the veranda, Andrea in the swing and Hochstrasser a respectful distance away, in one of the wicker chairs. He perched gingerly on the edge of the seat.

Andrea wouldn't give him the tactical advantage of speaking first, even though he was obviously having a hard time finding words. For him they were tools as difficult to handle as hammer and screwdriver had once been for her.

"This ain't easy to say," he began, after an interval of throat-clearing and coughing.

Andrea remained silent. After a further noisy interval Mr. Hochstrasser said, "I s'pose you heard about the fight."

"I saw some of the results," Andrea said, going on the offensive. "And how any man could be low enough to attack a person on crutches. . . . I'm thinking of swearing out a warrant for assault."

"Well, now, ma'am, I wouldn't do that." An expression that might have been the beginning of a smile creased

126

Hochstrasser's leathery cheeks. "From what I hear, Jim gave as good as he got. Maybe better."

"That has nothing to do with it."

"Well, now. . . ." Hochstrasser's jaws moved rhythmically as he groped for words. She felt sure he was not actually chewing tobacco; he would consider that rude in the presence of a lady. The movement was pure reflex, to help him think. "Well, now, it does, in a way. What I mean is, Jim's got respect now. The way he stood up to Gary Joe. I reckon Gary Joe would have licked him in the end, but the rest of the boys down to the Shamrock they wasn't going to stand for that. No, ma'am. Once they seen Jim was ready to fight, even though he's a cripple, they just piled in and threw Gary Joe out of there. If you was to go to law it would—that's to say, it wouldn't. . . . What I'm getting at is—"

"I think I understand," Andrea said.

Courage was something she could understand, courage and the respect it won. Thanks to Martin's lecture she had gained some insight into the unwritten laws of the male world—an archaic society where violence was not the last resort, but a declaration of worth. Yes, she could understand it, even if she thought it was imbecilic in the extreme.

"An' if you're worried about Gary Joe, well, don't worry. He won't do nothing to Jim, not now. He lost a lot of respect."

"He's a violent young man, Mr. Hochstrasser."

"He'll end up in jail some one of these days," Hochstrasser agreed. "But I didn't come up here to talk to you about that, ma'am. It's Linnie."

Here it comes, Andrea thought, stiffening.

Hochstrasser did not expect a response. His eyes fixed on the toes of his shabby boots, he went on mournfully, "It ain't easy for a daddy to raise a girl right. The good Lord knows I done my best. Prayed over it a lot, I have. Someplace or other I must of gone wrong. She ain't bad, Linnie ain't. No, ma'am. Get herself a nice young feller, settle down, with some babies, and she'll be jest fine.''

"What young feller did you have in mind?'' Andrea asked.

Hochstrasser's head jerked up. He stared at her, his eyes wide and his mouth ajar. Then he began to laugh. It was a creaking, rusty sound, as if he hadn't practiced it for a long time.

"You wasn't thinking I came to. . . . By Jimminy, you was!'' He shifted his weight and crossed one foot over the other knee. For the first time he seemed at ease; in fact, Andrea realized, he was now in control of the conversation. "No, ma'am,'' he went on, chuckling. "I left my shotgun at home, for sure. I wouldn't want my Linnie marrying the likes of Jim. Oh, not on account of his leg,'' he added hastily. "Known a lot of fellers make out fine with one leg, one arm. But he ain't Linnie's kind. They wouldn't be happy.'' A fresh explosion of laughter seized him. He slapped his knee. "No, ma'am, that's not what I come for. Just to tell you Linnie wouldn't be coming to work no more. I'm making her go back to school.''

"That sounds like a good idea,'' Andrea muttered, red-faced and chagrined.

"Yes'm, I shouldn't of let her quit when she was sixteen. Girl with not enough to do is gonna get in trouble, that's sure as sunrise. Then she gets the young fellers in trouble too. Like Delilah in the Scriptures.'' Mr. Hochstrasser considered the fate of Samson in pensive silence. Andrea could almost hear him insisting that if Delilah's daddy had just kept her busy sweeping the temple and washing his robes she never would have got in no trouble.

"Yep, I reckon it was mostly Linnie's fault.'' Hochstrasser rose. He had said what he had to say, and now he was going. "Good day, ma'am. I hope this won't be no inconvenience to you.''

"Good-bye,'' Andrea said.

She couldn't remember when she had last felt like such a fool. The farmer had put her firmly in her place—the place where women ought to be, too busy tending babies and husbands to get in trouble.

Her sense of humor finally fought free of the morass of chagrin that swamped her, and she began to laugh. The gulf that separated her from people like Hochstrasser was wider than she had even imagined; but he had cheered her—much more than Martin, with his windy aphorisms and cautious equivocations.

She went looking for Jim. She would tell him the story, even though the joke was on her. It would be a good way of breaking the ice, of assuring him that she was not going to condemn him for sowing a few wild oats.

He was not in his room. His trail led from the tumbled sheets of the bed to the dregs of a cup of black coffee on the kitchen table and out the back door, which stood ajar.

The sun was high overhead. The bland blue skies, spotted with whipped-cream clouds, innocently denied any memory of rain. Jim was nowhere in sight.

She knew where he had gone. How she knew she could not have explained, but she was certain of it. With the old feeling of shrinking reluctance, she walked toward the graveyard.

Seeing it, she stopped short and stared. How had he found the time to accomplish so much? The grass was so lush and green it was hard to believe it had grown from seed. Stones and bricks outlined the sunken rectangles of the graves; dark slate and gray granite, pale marble and red sandstone, the markers stood in neat alignment. Against the far wall, under the trailing rosebush, stood a bench, a piece of gray cement supported by carved slabs of stone. She had found it, fallen and forgotten and half hidden by weeds, under the big oak tree in front of the house, and had ordered it taken to the storage shed. Someone must have helped Jim move it; he could never have managed the weight alone.

There were no flowers now, not even wild flowers. The rain had beaten them down. Patches of newly dug earth, now muddy puddles, outlined the shapes of future flower beds. But there was a single spot of soft color amid the tangled green of the rosebush—one bud, unmarred by wet, awaiting the sunshine to unfold.

Jim had not seen her. He was sitting on the bench, his head bowed and his hands clasped; he might have been musing on the meaning of life, or regretting his excesses of the previous night. So deep was his contemplation and so quiet her approach that he was not aware of her presence until she stood before him. He glanced up, his bruised face empty of expression, and then returned to his former pose.

Andrea sat down beside him.

"If you feel as rotten as you look, you have my sympathy," she said, her tone deliberately light.

"I didn't look in the mirror. I wasn't up to it. But I can't look any worse than I feel."

She put her arm over his shoulders. He shrugged it off. "Go ahead. Get it over with."

"I wasn't going to yell at you."

"Then I will. I lied to you, caused you needless worry, and made a complete horse's ass of myself. And you know what?"

"What?"

He looked up, meeting her eyes squarely. "I'm not sorry."

There was nothing she could say to that. Even expressed understanding would have sounded hypocritical.

"Linnie didn't come to work today," she said. "But her father was just here."

"Oh, Christ," Jim exclaimed, his eyes widening apprehensively.

"It's not what you think." Andrea knew better than to laugh. She had had time to revise the version of the interview which she had meant to tell Jim. He wouldn't see the humor in it; given a choice, he would rather have had Linnie's father

130

come after him with a horsewhip than be patted on the head and told to go home and behave himself, like a good little boy. But there was no way she could gloss over Hochstrasser's basic attitudes, and Jim's face grew even gloomier as he listened.

"So Linnie gets the shaft," he said. "And I walk away clean. What kind of bastard is that father of hers?"

"He's not a bastard. He's a kind, bewildered man who wants to do what is best for his daughter. His opinions may be old-fashioned—I think he belongs to some fundamentalist religious sect—but let's face it, the idea that the woman is always to blame isn't restricted to people of his type. Most men, and a lot of women, still feel that way."

"Including you?"

At least he had made it a question, instead of a flat statement.

"You ought to know me better than that, Jim. I was going to fire Linnie anyway; she's no damn good at housework. And she ought to be back in school; that much good has come out of this mess, at any rate. No, you're just as much to blame as she is. Probably more. You're supposed to have better sense."

"Thanks, Andy." The humor of that did strike him, as he said it. Smiling lopsidedly, he reached for her hand. "Lecture me some more. I love it."

"You're probably saying harder things to yourself than I would."

"Yeah. It won't happen again, Andy. I swear to God."

"I believe you, darling." She didn't doubt that he was sincere. He wouldn't commit the same folly again; it would be something else next time. But she refused to worry about it now; on this bright morning of promise, with Jim's fingers warm on hers, she knew everything was going to be all right.

It was time to change the subject. Jim didn't like her to gush, and he had had about all the emotional unheaval a man with a queasy stomach and an aching head could handle. She glanced around the small enclosure.

"You've done wonders with this place, Jim."

"You like it?"

"It's pleasant," Andrea said in surprise. "I always hated the place, to be quite honest, but now. . . . I can see why you like to come here."

"I thought," Jim said tentatively, "that I would look up some of the history of this place, like Martin suggested. Keep me out of trouble, hm?"

"That would be an interesting project," Andrea said heartily. Jim wasn't deceived. His eyes shone with amusement.

"You haven't got any more imagination than a rock," he said. "Don't you feel it? The mystery, the challenge?"

"I must admit—"

"Look here." He swiveled around and pointed at the ground behind the bench. "Remember the stone we found, with that funny epitaph? Doesn't that rouse your curiosity? Who was Mary, and why were those words carved on her tombstone? Who planted the rose, and why? I've thought about it a lot. I'd like to know who she was, and what happened to her, and why she—" He stopped abruptly, a trifle embarrassed at his own vehemence.

"She?" Andrea repeated. "Mary, you mean?"

"Yeah," Jim said. "Anyhow, I thought I'd, you know, get into a little heavy research."

"How do you plan to go about it?"

"Well, I had a talk with some old codger I met at the Historical Association." Jim gave her a sidelong glance. "I did meet some people there—but they weren't the kind that go out for a few beers."

"Get on with it," Andrea said, laughing.

"This guy said something about the record room at the county courthouse. They've got land deeds and wills clear back to the early days. This guy said that's how you do it—you look up the original property records and find out who owned the place, and—like that. So I thought maybe some day . . .''

He hesitated. Andrea said without emphasis, ''You'll need the car if you plan to go to Frederick. Want to go this afternoon and find out whether we have to do anything special to get you a new license?''

The glow that lit his face would have rewarded her for a far greater sacrifice. After all, she told herself, it isn't letting him go. It's another way of keeping him safe, with me.

II

Later that day a macabre thought struck Andrea. Jim had placed the stone bench beside the rosebush. Perhaps she had actually been sitting over Mary's grave.

She hadn't given Mary's stone much thought before Jim pointed out its unusual features; now she began to wonder too. It was indeed a strange epitaph, and as Andrea considered the most obvious meaning she felt a certain admiration for the woman who had asserted her unorthodox opinions so unequivocally, at a time when sanctimonious piety was the only acceptable viewpoint.

However, Linnie's absence left her so busy she didn't have time to speculate about nonessentials, or even to worry about Jim. Handing over a set of car keys had been one of the hardest acts of her life; she fully expected to be frantic with apprehension every second he was gone. But as she dashed from parlor to library to guest room she forgot for minutes at a time that Jim was out on the highway, vulnerable, mortal.

She was not looking forward to entertaining Reba, for she knew that human information center would be fully informed about Jim's fight with Gary Joe and all the ramifications thereof. But the invitation was overdue and she could not in all conscience cancel it. Besides, she needed Reba's help in finding a replacement for Linnie.

Reba had no sympathy with reverse snobbism; her car was a Mercedes, the latest model, and she drove with a panache worthy of D'Artagnan. The car stopped with a grinding crunch directly in front of the porch steps. After a moment Reba fell out. Apparently she had caught her heel, for Andrea heard a muffled "Goddamn stupid shoes. . . ." before Reba reeled to her feet. Andrea remained discreetly out of sight, for fear her friend might be embarrassed, but Reba was not at all self-conscious. Greeting her hostess, she collapsed onto the nearest chair. "Fell flat on my ass," she said gaily. "Too bad you didn't see me. It would have made your day."

Torn between amusement and concern, Andrea studied Reba's crimson face. "Sit still and catch your breath," she said. "Why don't I bring our drinks out here?"

"Don't want to cause you any trouble," Reba wheezed.

"No trouble. It's too nice a day to stay inside anyway."

In the hall Andrea encountered Satan, who steered a wide path around her before proceeding on his stately progress kitchenward. A dire suspicion sent Andrea flying to the table where she had placed a plate of tidbits. She had learned from bitter experience that Satan was extremely fond of cheese.

The prettily arranged canapés were intact. She had arrived in time—barely in time, probably, for Satan's expression had been that of a cat who was feeling virtuous because he had not been given the opportunity to sin.

Carrying the canapés in one hand and the tray with wine bottle and glasses in the other, she elbowed her way out onto the porch. Reba was fanning herself with a magazine, but her color had subsided and she was breathing more easily.

"Hot," she said. "Wish the weather would break."

"We're due for a thunderstorm if the forecasters are right," Andrea said.

Weather was not, as she had once believed, a form of

meaningless social chitchat. It was a subject of vital concern to country people. Farmers worried about crops and harvests; telephone and power lines seemed to be increasingly vulnerable the farther one got from the city. For an innkeeper a power stoppage was not an inconvenience, it was a catastrophe. As she had learned, it meant no lights, no food, no heat or air-conditioning, and no water. Andrea scanned the southern sky and the fat white cumulus clouds that moved across it with interest as intense as Reba's.

Reba was visibly touched and pleased at the effort Andrea had made—the pretty canapés, the fragile wineglasses, and the excellent vintage. After they had talked idly for a while she said abruptly, "You want to talk about it now or later?"

"I'd rather not talk about it at all."

"Let me give you some advice, kid. Stop being so goddamn sensitive. We've all got secrets we'd rather keep to ourselves, but this isn't anything you need to be ashamed of."

"I should have seen it coming."

"I tried to warn you. But," Reba admitted, "you never can figure what kids will do. You can't ride herd on them every minute." She lowered her voice. "Where is Jim? I don't want him to hear me."

"It's all right. He's out. Gone to Frederick, I think."

"Good. What I was going to say was that the whole business might turn out for the best. Jim's reputation around town is pretty high right now."

"I don't care about that."

"You should. If you two are going to live here permanently, he has to make a niche for himself, gain acceptance. Course I suppose he'll be going back to college one of these days, getting married, starting his own family. . . ."

This was not a topic Andrea cared to consider or discuss. She filled Reba's empty glass and then said, "You know Linnie has quit. Do you have any suggestions for a replacement?''

"I'll ask around. I suppose you don't want another teenage cutie.''

"I'd prefer a homely middle-aged grandma. Someone who can cook. Not that I'm thinking of competing with you—''

"You couldn't, kiddo," Reba said, lowering heavy brows. "You're a good egg and I like your gumption, but you don't suppose I'd have helped you if you had proposed opening another restaurant, do you?''

It was the first time Andrea had seen the matriarch unveiled, though she had always known it was there. The image was a little unnerving. Reba would be a bad enemy.

"Not that it would matter," Reba went on, waving her glass. "I'm pretty well established here; it would take a slick operation to do me any harm. Got more business than I can handle, actually.''

Andrea filled the glass. "I was thinking of breakfast," she said meekly. "And eventually something like high tea—with crumpets and cucumber sandwiches and that sort of thing.''

"Hmmm. Yeah, that might be a nice touch. You could hike your prices. But if you're going into food preparation in a big way, you'll run into problems with the board of health. They can be real bastards about their regulations. You might consider. . . .''

The subject absorbed both of them. They were deep in professional plotting when a shadow fell over them and Andrea glanced up with an exclamation of alarm.

"Look at that cloud! It's going to pour. We'd better go in.''

"I'll take the wine," said Reba.

The first drops of rain were spattering on the steps by the time they had gathered up the remains of the food and drink. "I wonder where Jim is," Andrea said, with an anxious look at the livid sky.

"You fuss about that kid too much," Reba said, kicking the screen door open.

Lightning flickered through the black clouds and was

followed by a far-off mutter of thunder. The inside of the house was darkly shadowed. Following her guest, tray in hand, Andrea almost ran into Reba, who had come to a stop in the hall near the foot of the stairs.

"Wait a minute," Andrea said. "I'll turn on some lights."

She did not pause after doing so, but carried the tray into the red parlor. She expected Reba would follow, but when she straightened up after putting the tray on a table, she realized Reba had not moved. Her head was turned as if she were listening. The sole source of light, directly overhead, distorted her features in an unpleasant fashion; the sharp shadows under her heavy brows and jutting nose stripped the surrounding flesh of its healthy color.

"In here," Andrea said. Reba did not stir until she repeated the suggestion in a louder voice. When Reba moved, her footsteps were slow and reluctant.

Andrea switched on several lamps. She was eager to show Reba the house. Everyone congratulated her on its appearance, but only a person who had seen the place in its desolation could really appreciate her efforts.

The red parlor was less formal than its counterpart across the hall, and the color scheme was particularly warm and cheerful on a rainy day. The curtains, fringed and tasseled in gold, had set her back a pretty penny, but they were worth it; their rich garnet matched the velvet upholstery of the carved settee and chairs and echoed the predominant color of the twin Bokhara rugs. It was not the setting Andrea would have created for herself; her tastes ran to the simplicity of Scandinavian design—chrome and teak and uncluttered surfaces—but she had become increasingly attached to her creation. The lady's chair, one of a pair, might have been built for her; the depth of the seat and its distance from the floor exactly suited her height.

Reba plopped down into the matching chair, a little deeper and higher, intended for the gentleman of the family. Andrea decided to wait before suggesting a tour of the house. Reba looked tired. Let her finish her wine and relax a little while longer.

The rain had become a steady downpour. Before long, Martin came down the stairs. "It's raining," he announced.

"I noticed," Andrea said dryly. "Look who's here."

"Hey, Reba." Martin went to the door. "Wind's blowing from the south. Shall I bring in the cushions?"

He went out without waiting for an answer, returning with an armload of cushions which he dropped unceremoniously onto the floor.

"I see you two lushes have drunk all the wine," he said, slicking back his damp hair.

"Open another bottle." Andrea spoke promptly, hospitably, but with an internal whimper; the wine was expensive, and every bottle made another dent in the accounts over which she pored so anxiously.

"Not unless you want some. I'll stick to scotch." Martin went to the breakfront Andrea used as a bar. "How about you, Reba?"

"Make it a double."

Andrea thought nothing of it, even when Reba drained half the glass without a pause. Local gossips claimed that Reba could drink any man in town under the table, but Andrea had never seen her the worse for liquor. Nor did she notice at first that Reba's loquacity had deserted her. Martin had plenty to say; he was furious about the latest news from the disarmament conference in Geneva, which appeared to be in a permanent state of paralysis. His diatribes on the intransigence of the United States delegation roused Andrea to impassioned rebuttal. It was not until the thunder moved off and the rain slackened that she remembered her duties as hostess.

"Talk about closed minds," she said. "I might as well argue with that table. Reba, wouldn't you like to see the rest of the house?"

Reba started convulsively. "No. I've got to get back. It's late."

"You've got your staff so well trained they can run the place without you," Martin said. "Relax, Reba. How about another drink?"

"No." Reba put her glass down on the edge of the table. Martin caught it as it fell, and Reba pushed herself to her feet. Swaying, she pressed her hand to her mouth. Her eyes had a wild, trapped look, like those of a fox encircled by hounds.

"What's the matter?" Andrea asked in alarm.

"You shouldn't mix your booze," Martin said. But the glance he exchanged with Andrea mirrored her concern, and he put a steadying arm around Reba's quivering shoulders.

"Yeah. Guess you're right. Don't feel so hot. Gotta get out of here—"

Brushing him aside, she plunged toward the door. The prisms on the chandelier chimed musically with the reverberation of her footsteps.

The others ran after her, Martin in the lead. The rain had died to a soft drizzle; off to the east a patch of blue showed as the storm passed.

"Will you wait a minute, you bullheaded old goat?" Martin exclaimed, catching Reba by the arm. "Sit down. Or if you want to throw up, there's the railing."

"I have to get back." Reba drew a long, shuddering breath. "Sorry, Andy. I haven't been feeling so good all day. . . ."

"You look better," Andrea said hopefully.

"Sure, sure. I'll be all right. Thanks—I had a good time. . . ."

Seeing that persuasion was unavailing, Martin said, "I'll drive you home."

"You don't have to."

"I know I don't. Give me the keys."

139

He helped Reba into the car and ran back to where Andrea was standing. "I'll walk back," he said softly. "Don't expect me till after dinner. And don't worry—it's probably a touch of flu or something."

III

So far—twice, to be exact—Jim had repaid Andrea's trust by being punctiliously prompt when he had the car out. He raised his record to three for three that day, returning shortly after Reba had left with Martin. "I figured you wouldn't want me on the road when it was raining so hard, so I pulled over till it stopped," he said virtuously.

"That was a wise decision, darling. Anyway, you're not late."

"Hey, look at the fancy food." Jim popped a crab canapé into his mouth. "You didn't leave much for me. Who was here?"

"I told you Reba was coming."

"Oh, right. Sorry I missed her. I thought she'd stay longer."

"She got sick. I only hope there's nothing wrong with the food. Maybe you'd better not eat those canapés."

"They taste great," said Jim, who was in a position to know; he had eaten at least one of each variety. "Lighten up, Too-Small; if the food was bad, she wouldn't have got sick so fast."

"That's right, I guess." Andrea forced a smile. "What did you do today?"

"I went to the courthouse, like I said."

"Any luck?"

"Some. I'll tell you later. Where's Martin?"

He'd consider his audience incomplete without Martin, of course. Andrea suppressed the familiar twinge of jealousy and said, "He took Reba home. I don't think he'll be back until after dinner."

"You sound like you've still got a cold. Want me to cook tonight?"

"No offense intended, but I'm a little tired of hamburgers and spaghetti. There's a casserole in the fridge. We can eat any time."

Jim was always ready to eat. They had an early supper and then he went upstairs, "to get some work done." Andrea didn't inquire further. She had not been able to shake off her cold, probably because she had been working like a Victorian scullery maid; she felt discouraged and extremely sorry for herself. Six guests arriving next day, and no help. . . . She was also worried about Reba.

Because she was anxious, she was on the lookout for Martin; and because he knew she was anxious, she expected him to come directly to her and reassure her. She heard him come in, but instead of coming down the hall toward the kitchen, his footsteps stopped. After a few moments she went in search of him.

He was not in the hall. In order to save electricity, she had adopted the habit of leaving only one light burning, a small lamp on the desk where she kept the visitors' book and a pile of brochures about local sights of interest. Both parlors were dark, and there was no glow of light from the library. Thinking he must have gone upstairs, she was about to follow when she realized there was someone—or something—in the red parlor: a shadow, slightly darker than the dark of the room, a slight, almost imperceptible movement.

"It's only me," Martin said, as she caught her breath. He moved toward her.

"What the hell are you doing? You scared the wits out of me."

"Nothing. I—er—uh—"

"Great. Just great. First Reba takes a fit, and then you start creeping around like Fu Manchu. Give me a break, Martin."

"Sorry." Martin scratched his chin, a habit he had when

he was worried or involved in profound meditation. He had a heavy beard; the rasp of his nails across the stubble inflamed Andrea's nerves, and she might have said something regrettable if Jim had not appeared at the top of the stairs.

"Is that you, Martin? Are you busy? I've got something to tell you."

"Yes, no, I can hardly wait," Martin replied efficiently. His eyes returned to Andrea and he said, "Reba's fine, if that's what you're uptight about. She ate more dinner than I did."

"Thank God. Why didn't you tell me right away?"

Martin was saved the necessity of a reply by Jim. "Guess what I did today?" he demanded.

"The mind boggles," Martin said. "What?"

"I found out who she was. I found Mary."

Chapter Eight

"She was born in 1823, the eldest daughter and only surviving child of Franklin Broadhurst, Esquire. Broadhurst bought this place at a bankruptcy sale in 1854—two hundred and seventy acres, a house and outbuildings, and two mills on the stream. The old house must have been torn down when he built this one, which, as we know, he did in 1862. He owned a lot of other property around the county, almost a thousand acres at one time; but when he died, in 1866, he had nothing to leave his daughter except this house and thirty acres. All the rest had been sold. He also asked for her forgiveness. The will doesn't say whether he got it.

"Mary was forty-three years old. She had been married to a Colonel John Fairfax, C.S.A. He must have died during the war, because in 1866 she was a widow with a little girl, four years old. Her mother had died some years earlier, so she was all alone, and almost broke.

"She didn't look around for a man to take care of her. Instead she turned her home into a boardinghouse—Fairfax's Hotel. She made a living out of it; it was still a going concern when she died in 1900, leaving an even more peculiar will

than her father had. The house was to be sold with all its
contents. She left one dollar apiece to a long list of cousins so
they could buy mourning rings. The rest of the money was
divided between her lawyer, a Mr. Wilberforce, and various
charities. Leaving him a legacy was a smart move on her
part, because he would make damned good and sure the will
couldn't be overturned by her cousins, and he would have to
carry out the wishes she expressed with regard to her burial.
Her tombstone was all ready, except for the date of her death.
It, and no other, was to be placed over her grave. She was to
be buried in the old Springer cemetery. If those wishes weren't
carried out, the lawyer was to be cut out of the will and all
her money was to go to the charities. Among these was a
home for animals, and the contribution was dependent on the
home taking care of her cat, Beelzebub. The lawyer was
directed to check monthly to make sure the animal was being
well cared for.''

Jim looked up from his notes with the air of a winning
runner who expects and deserves the kudos of the crowd.
Martin applauded vigorously. Andrea exclaimed, ''How do
you know all that?''

''It's a long and rather boring story,'' Jim said modestly.

They were sitting around the kitchen table while Jim lectured.
Notebook open before him, he had delivered his statement
with the aplomb of a professional historian, pausing only to
refresh himself from the beer can in front of him.

''I want to know how much you made up,'' Andrea said.

''I didn't make any of it up,'' Jim said indignantly. ''You
don't make things up when you're doing research; you put the
pieces together into a meaningful whole.''

''And a splendid job you've done of it,'' Martin said, in an
effort to smooth Jim's ruffled pride. He was only partially
successful.

''It was damned hard work,'' Jim insisted. ''I never did
this kind of thing before.''

"Darling, I wasn't doubting your word," Andrea said. "I never did this kind of thing either, and I'm curious."

"Likewise," Martin said.

Jim only wanted to be urged. "It was more interesting than I thought," he admitted. "Like a puzzle—you find a couple of pieces and you think, maybe the next piece I need is shaped this way or that, and then you go looking for it. And sometimes it's shaped the way you figured—what a triumph that is!—but often it's another shape altogether, and then you've got to rearrange the first pieces to fit it."

"I do not believe I have ever heard a more illuminating description of original research," Martin said gravely.

Jim took the statement literally, and tried to look modest. "Well, see, I was interested in Mary because that setup was so weird—her epitaph and the grave off in the corner, and—well, the whole setup. The problem was, I didn't know her last name or when she was born or died. I couldn't figure out where to start till I talked to that guy at the Historical Association, who told me about the county records. He suggested I should trace the ownership of the house back in time and find out who owned it during the 1800's. Once I got some last names, I could look them up and see if there was a woman named Mary in the family.

"So that's what I did. Every time a piece of property changes hands, the transfer has to be recorded. The documents—wills, deeds, and so on—were copied into big books, which are in the records room at the courthouse. They go back to the seventeen hundreds. The books are called 'libers' and the page numbers are 'folios.' Now, let's say I buy a house from Martin. On the deed it will tell the liber and folio where the county clerk has copied the deed, and also the liber and folio number of the previous transaction. Like, it would say. . . ." He turned the pages of his notebook and read,

" 'The same property that was sold to Martin Greenspan on September 15, 1966, by Joe Smith, see liber 10, folio 10.'

Then you look at liber 10, folio 10, and get the number of the sale before that one. Do you understand so far?''

His audience nodded respectfully.

''It isn't as easy as it sounds,'' Jim continued. ''For one thing, the libers—the volumes—aren't numbered in order, one, two, three, and like that. They run in series, under the initials of the county clerk. So, depending on how long the guy held the job, there can be seventeen libers of the series ASL and three of the series BD, and so on. There's a master index that gives the chronological order of the series, so if you want a particular year, you check the index and find what series it's in.

''That takes time. Also, the farther back you go, the more casual the records are. They didn't always record the numbers for the previous sale. There are separate indexes for Wills, Deeds, Birth and Death Certificates, and a lot of other things, and the cross-references are hard to find.''

He paused for a well-deserved wetting of his whistle.

''Let me see if I have it straight,'' Martin said. ''If the property passed by deed—by a sale—each time, all you have to do is go back to the volume that contains the record of the previous transaction. But suppose the property passes by inheritance. That change of ownership wouldn't be recorded by a deed. Is there a cross-reference to Wills?''

''Sometimes, sometimes not. See, what I did was, I started with Cousin Bertha Webber's will. It was a long-winded piece of legal jargon, but it said she had inherited from her father, so I looked up his will. That was way back in 1937.''

Andrea glanced at Martin and saw his face twist in a sour grimace. He was probably in his forties, she thought; he might have been born in 1937, a date lost in the remote mists of time in Jim's view.

Unaware of the distress he had caused, Jim went on. ''Her father inherited from his father. Nineteen hundred and two was when he died. Then I was lucky. Not all the older wills tell where the deceased got the property originally, but this one did. Here it is: 'That property known as Springers' Grove, bounded by hmmm, hmmmm, purchased by him from the estate of Mrs. Mary Fairfax, deceased.'

"The name gave me quite a shock, I can tell you. But I couldn't be sure it was our Mary till I'd gone on a little farther. I was able to look up her will, since I now knew her last name, and then I found her dad's will, and then I was sure. Because the old man bought the place from the Springers, and since Mary wasn't a Springer—''

"How do you know that?" Andrea asked. "I thought you said you couldn't read the other name on the tombstone."

"I just. . . ." Jim stopped. "It would take too long to explain. There are some traces left on the stone. They don't fit Springer, but they do fit Fairfax."

"So you worked that long, detailed story up from a couple of wills?" Martin said. "Nice work."

"Death and birth certificates too. Some of it was deductive reasoning," Jim said proudly. "But it's logical. For instance, the fact that Mary's husband was killed during the war. I couldn't find a death certificate for him, but since he was a soldier and she was a widow in 1866—that's how her father's will described her: Mary Fairfax, widow of Colonel John Fairfax, C.S.A.—it's reasonable to assume he died in battle."

"I wonder if Franklin Broadhurst was a Confederate sympathizer," Martin mused. "That would explain how he lost his fortune—contributing to The Cause. He died of a broken heart and extreme frustration, like any honorable old Reb. Mary wouldn't have married a Southern soldier unless her father—''

"That," said Jim loftily, "is the sort of unsubstantiated conjecture we researchers do not allow."

Another aspect of Jim's discovery had fired Andrea's imagination. "Eighteen sixty-six, did you say? That's almost a hundred and twenty years ago. I couldn't say we had been in operation that long, I guess; but why not 'Founded in 1866,' or—''

"Everything is grist for your commercial instincts, isn't it," Martin said.

"Why not?"

"Aren't you even mildly interested in people? Don't you wonder about that woman, struggling to survive in a man's world? I suspect she must have been a lot like you."

Still intent on promotional possibilities, Andrea dismissed this sentimental speech with a shrug. "Jimmie, remember those drawings we found? The woman in black—I'll bet you that's a portrait of Mary! I could have it framed, hang it over the desk in the hall. . . ."

"What drawings are those?" Martin asked.

"Didn't Jim show you?"

"No."

"Where are they, Jimmie?"

"I put them back where we found them," Jim said.

"In that dirty hole? That was foolish; something that old is worth—''

"Money," Jim said. "I know. Do you want to see them, Martin?"

"Please."

"I'll go—'' Andrea dropped back into her chair, wincing from the pain of a hard kick on the calf. Jim got up and went out.

"A gentle nudge would have gotten your point across," Andrea said, rubbing her leg.

"Sorry." He didn't sound sorry. "Why is Jim so reluctant to show me those drawings?"

"He's not; why should he be? They're rather peculiar, but they have nothing to do with him. He found them under the floorboards in the tower room. He's got some nutty idea of moving up there."

"So he told me." Martin's face cleared. "Maybe that's the

explanation. It's his own private place and he doesn't want outsiders poking their noses into his things. . . . I wonder why Mary Fairfax didn't marry again.''

"She probably had better sense.''

Martin smiled. " 'If you're an old maid, everybody feels sorry for you. If you're married, your husband bosses you. The best thing is to be a widow.' Where did I read that?''

"It must be a common attitude.''

"What a cynic you are. Let's see. . . .'' Martin reached for Jim's notebook. "Born in 1823. She was thirty-nine when her child was born. She was an old maid for a long time, at that.''

"How do you know? She could have been a widow twice over when she married the soldier. . . .'' Andrea paused. Why did that word rouse a shadow of memory in her mind? Dismissing it, she went on, "And she might have had a dozen children. They died young in those days.''

"Yes, but. . . . Ah, Jim. Are those the famous drawings?''

If Jim had felt any misgivings about displaying the find, there was no trace of any such feeling now. He handed it over and resumed his chair.

Martin took his time examining the sketches. Watching him, Andrea saw that he was quicker than she had been to sense their strangeness. The first sketch, of the worm-riddled roses, sent a visible ripple of shock across his face.

When he reached the portrait of the woman in black, Andrea said, "There she is. The dress is the style they wore in the 1880's, and the unrelieved black, even her jewelry, indicates she was a widow. It has to be Mary.''

"And Beelzebub,'' Martin murmured.

"That's right. Her will actually mentions the cat.''

"You don't seem to realize the significance of the name,'' Martin said, staring at the drawing.

"What?'' Jim asked.

"Beelzebub is the name of the Prince of Darkness—Lucifer—the Devil. Satan."

"It's a logical, if rather unimaginative name for a black cat," Andrea said carelessly. "People are so superstitious."

"Uh-huh. Well, I'll treat my old buddy with a little more respect from now on. You know, these are remarkable sketches. I wonder who did them."

"There's no name on any of them," Andrea said. "I don't suppose Mary—"

"A self-portrait? Not likely." Martin didn't explain his reasoning. "Where are you going next in your research, Jim?"

"I've pretty well exhausted the records room," Jim said. "I don't know where to look next."

"You dare say that in my presence?" Martin exclaimed. "Newspapers, you young ignoramus—newspapers. And if you ask me if they had them back in those antediluvian days, I'll slug you."

Jim grinned. "I guess it wasn't that long ago, was it?"

"It was very long ago," Martin said with a sigh. "But the printing press had been invented. Suppose we check the library."

"You haven't got time to help Jim with his hobbies," Andrea objected. "You're behind schedule now."

"It looks as if I may be farther behind," Martin said placidly. "I know the symptoms. I am about to wander off onto a seductive byway of useless research. Damn, but the story has its intriguing aspects, doesn't it? I'd like to see that will of Mary's. It reeks of vindictiveness—cutting off her relatives with a pittance. And what about her daughter? You did say she had a daughter, Jim?"

"Her name was Alice," Jim said. "She died in 1879. When she was seventeen."

II

Seventeen years old.

The words kept recurring to Andrea all next day as she rushed around preparing for her weekend guests. Seventeen. Two years younger than Jim.

Reba had called to apologize for her precipitate departure and to assure Andrea she hadn't forgotten about the matter of a replacement for Linnie. She had located a woman—middle-aged and homely, as required—who would work on a temporary basis until a job opened up at the bottling plant, but she couldn't start until Monday. Andrea's expressions of gratitude were tempered by disappointment. She had a full house that weekend.

Yet often as she worked a face intruded itself between her and the object of her labors—the strongly marked features of Mary Fairfax. Mary's story had affected her more than she had been willing to admit to Martin. She and Mary did have much in common. They were both strong women fighting to survive—too strong for kindness, perhaps, or for love. Like herself, Mary had loved only one person. Why was she so sure of that? Because of Mary's will, she supposed; Martin was right about that document, it was a virulent expression of contempt for everyone she knew—except one old black cat. Mary hadn't loved anyone enough to marry again; she may have loved her husband, but he had left her nothing except their child. She would not have been forced to open her home to strangers if she had inherited anything else from her husband.

Andrea felt certain the sketchbook had belonged to Alice Fairfax. Who else could have portrayed Mary with that compelling blend of admiration and resentment? That mixture was, and probably always had been, the normal attitude of adolescents toward their parents.

Seventeen. They died young in those days. And, typically,

151

Victorian artists and dramatists dealt with that tragedy by turning it into a lace-paper Valentine. How they did wallow in deathbed scenes, especially the deaths of the young and beautiful! Little Eva, Little Nell, Beth in *Little Women*. . . . It was worse than sentimentality, it was hypocrisy; instead of fighting back or cursing God, they had folded their hands and rolled their eyes heavenward, and draped the skeleton in plushy platitudes. "God's will be done." "He has called her home." "So young, so pure, so unstained by the sins of this world. . . ." Theirs had been a sinful cruel world, especially for women. From such an existence death might indeed be viewed as escape.

Mary Fairfax had not tried to escape. She had tucked up her widow's veils and gone to work. Andrea's sympathies were not for the girl who had died young, they were for the bereaved mother. Alice had escaped, Mary had been left to bear another, harder burden.

The fatiguing household chores took on a new and poignant interest when she thought of Mary performing them too—scrubbing the same floors, washing the same windows, even polishing some of the same furniture. The walnut what-not and the mahogany breakfront were old enough to have belonged to her. Mary had directed that the contents of the house be sold; why not, she had no one left to inherit her treasures. Seventeen. . . . Alice must have died—Andrea couldn't remember the exact dates—somewhere around 1880. Mary had lived alone for twenty years.

Yes, her sympathies were with Mary, not with Little Alice, dying young. Somewhere, at some time, she must have known a girl named Alice, a girl she thoroughly disliked. The name had negative vibes, as Jim would have said. Back in the third or fourth grade—a flaxen-haired, smirking child whose pig-tails never dissolved into straggling wisps and who was the teacher's pet.

III

Andrea got through the weekend somehow, and staggered on into Monday. The promised helper arrived, but was not much help. Slow and reluctant, obviously regarding housework as a more demeaning occupation than bottling syrupy slop, Mrs. Shorb had to be shown how to do everything, even how to make a bed. Jim took one look at the woman's glum face and retreated to his aerie in the tower. During the course of the day ominous sounds of sawing and pounding reached Andrea's ears.

After Mrs. Shorb left she didn't even have the energy to go up and find out what he was doing. Martin found her drooping over the kitchen table with a bottle of sherry on one side and a box of tissues on the other.

"You ought to see the doctor about that cold," he said.

"It's my sinuses, I guess." Andrea blew. "Standard complaint in this area."

"I brought you a present." Martin tossed a bundle of papers on the table. "It may or may not cheer you up."

As she reached disinterestedly for the papers, she heard Jim come clattering down the stairs. Martin's presence drew him like a magnet.

"Hi, Martin. Did you—"

"You might say hello to your sister," Andrea said hoarsely.

"Why? You've been here all the time. Did you find what you were looking for, Martin?"

"Some of it." Martin sat down at the table. "You should have come with me."

"I had stuff to do." Jim gestured at the ceiling. "What's that you have?"

"Xeroxed copies of old newspapers," said Andrea, leafing through them. "I'm glad you have time to waste, Martin."

"It wasn't a waste of time. I can get a couple of columns out of this material—changes in journalistic styles, quaint quotes, that sort of thing.'' He picked up a pile of sheets and began arranging them. ''I didn't take the time to sort these, but they should be more or less in order. . . . Here we go. This is the Frederick *Examiner* of July 17, 1869. It was a weekly—ten whole pages. Not a bad effort for a small community, but one can't help being amused at the arrangement, which seems to have been typical of newspapers of that period. There is hardly any national news, not to mention international. Even local news is relegated to the back pages. The front page features a poem, ''Always Look on the Sunny Side''—probably written by the editor's mother, judging from the quality and the fact that it is modestly anonymous; a moral tale entitled ''Mrs. Wilkins' Duty''; and six paragraphs of what might be loosely termed humorous stories.''

''Also useful bits of information,'' said Jim, reading over his shoulder. ''Andy, did you know that 'tabby cat' comes from 'Atab, a street in Bagdad'?''

''Uh,'' said Andrea, blowing her nose.

''On page three we get to the news,'' Martin said. '''On Friday last Mrs. Jonathan Fried slipped and fell on the staves of a half-barrel. One of her ribs was fractured and she suffered acutely.' And here, Ms. Businessperson, are the advertisements. Dr. Robinson guarantees a cure in all diseases of the Urinary Organs, Nervous and Seminal Weakness, Impotency and Syphilis.''

He handed the sheets to Andrea, who found them entertaining enough to distract her from her aching nose. ''Confectioner and Ice Cream Saloon,'' she read.

''Saloon?'' Jim repeated.

''Saloon. Ladies and gentlemen's watches, Henry Miller's Cheap Shoe Store—I admire his honesty, don't you?—French Pattern Hats and Bonnets, Manhood Restored. . . . Oh! Here's an ad for Fairfax's Hotel. Is that why you copied this, Martin?''

''I thought it might interest you.''

'' 'Fairfax's Hotel, Ladiesburg, Maryland. Mrs. Mary W.

Fairfax, Proprietor. First class in all its appointments. Private parlor for ladies. Commercial gentlemen welcome.' Not very imaginative, is it? I hoped she would have something unusual I could reproduce in my brochure.''

"Try this.'' Martin handed her another page. It did not contain advertisements, only news items, but the boldly printed NOTICE caught her eye.

'' 'NOTICE to all citizens of Ladiesburg, and in particular to those unknown parties responsible for the recent series of reputed accidents in and around my establishment. This is to serve NOTICE that in future anyone trespassing on my property with or without intent to do damage will face the pistols once owned by my late father. Though but a ''weak woman,'' I have inherited my father's skill along with his weapons and will have no scruples in employing them against those cowards whose evident purpose it is to force me from my home. Here I have every right to be, and here I will stay. Mrs. Mary Fairfax, proprietor, Fairfax's Hotel.' ''

"Here I stay,'' Andrea repeated. "So that was why. . . .''

"That was how it started,'' Martin said. "But one wonders. . . .'' He caught Andrea's startled eyes and smiled faintly. "I was referring to her religious views, or the lack thereof, Andrea. What did you think I meant?''

Andrea preferred not to answer. "Was she paranoid, or did this harassment actually occur?''

"Oh, it occurred. I found a couple of references to it; there were probably others I missed, or that were not reported. Here, for example, in the column entitled, 'Ladiesburg News,' we have the following:

'' 'On the night of the 8th ulto., the meathouse of Mrs. Mary Fairfax of this place was consumed by fire, origin unknown. Mrs. Fairfax lost nearly all of her meat, since fire fighting equipment was unable to reach her home until the fire was under full sway.' ''

"What's the date?'' Andrea asked, reaching for the paper.

"August. . . . The roads should have been all right at that time of year; why couldn't the fire engine get to her?"

"There are a number of suspicious circumstances about it," Martin agreed. "Other items over a three-year period mention the destruction of farm equipment, rude mottoes painted on the gateposts, and so on. All by parties unknown."

"But why? Why was she so unpopular?"

Martin shrugged. "I don't suppose we'll ever know. I could make an educated guess, though."

"Like what?" Jim asked.

"She was a woman alone, running a business. 'Commercial gentlemen welcome.' She couldn't afford to be too fastidious about her clientele; this backwater wasn't a commercial center or a tourist haven; many of her guests must have been of the type we laughingly refer to as traveling salesmen. Who knows what 'appointments' she offered to draw in trade?"

"If you're implying she ran a brothel, I'll call you a liar," Andrea said angrily. "That portrait is the image of Victorian respectability. I never would have suspected you of being a male chauvinist, Martin Greenspan."

"Hey, wait a minute. I don't care what she did for a living. I doff my chapeau to the lady. In case you hadn't noticed, I admire fighters, male and female."

He smiled at her, personalizing the compliment. Mollified, Andrea said snuffily, "All right, we accept your apology. I guess the neighbors would assume the worst. Even so, their resentment seems exaggerated. I'll grant you this was one of the most sanctimonious, hypocritical periods in history, but the same old vices went on flourishing—pornography, child prostitution—"

"Ah, but this was a small town," Martin pointed out. "Villagers have long memories, and they are slow to forgive an injury or a mistake. Once you establish a reputation, it's yours for life. You can give millions to charity and found orphan asylums by the dozen, and the village will shake its collective head and recall the crimes of your youth.''

''That's true,'' Andrea said, thinking of Jim. A spot of casual fornication and an exchange of blows had established him as a man worthy of respect. On such shaky and superficial foundations a man's life might rest—or a woman's. She shivered, and as if he were reading her mind, Martin added,

''It works the other way too. Once the town is on your side, you have to commit more murders than Gilles de Rais before it turns against you. Mary must have done something to alienate her neighbors, but it's unlikely that the truth will ever be known. Countless numbers of ancient scandals must lie buried under the dust of time; it's only the rich and famous who have their lives laid bare, the respectable middle classes band together to conceal their sins.''

''I don't care what she did,'' Andrea said. ''I'm on her side.''

Knowing she faced another long day with the recalcitrance of Mrs. Shorb, Andrea took her sinuses and her box of tissues to bed early. But instead of climbing under the covers with the book she had been reading, she opened the top drawer of her desk.

The golden eyes of Beelzebub glared at her, but Mary was looking at something else. Present enemies or past injuries— the heavy brows and unsmiling mouth contemplated no pleasant view. How remarkably that resentful child had captured her mother's strength: ''Here I stay.''

Right on, Mary, Andrea thought. The same goes for me.

She had taken Mary's portrait from the sketchbook the night before. Jim had gone off with the rest of the drawings— she didn't know or care what he did with them, so long as he obeyed her injunction to keep them safe. But she wanted Mary. She planned to find an appropriate frame, something ornately carved and gilded, so that the drawing could occupy

157

a prominent place in the hallway. Under it, perhaps, an engraved plaque with Mary's name and a legend, "Proprietor of Fairfax's Hotel, founded 1866."

It would be excellent publicity—worthy of a story in a Washington newspaper, or in one of the magazines that specialized in country living. Finding an appropriate frame might take some time, but there was no reason why Mary should languish in a drawer until one was acquired. Holding the drawing, Andrea inspected the pictures she had hung on the walls.

None of them had any particular meaning for her now, though they had once been favorites—a photo, cut from a travel poster, of the fantastic fairy-tale spires of Neuschwanstein Castle in Bavaria; an old movie poster—Clark Gable crushing Vivien Leigh in his muscular arms; a framed photograph of the cast of Jim's senior play. . . . He had taken the part of the brother in *Arsenic and Old Lace*—the one who thought he was Teddy Roosevelt, and who kept dashing up the stairs waving a sword and bellowing, "Charge!"

The photograph, of course, was sacrosanct. But the others—she couldn't imagine why she had hung on to them all these years. Fairy-tale castles and dashing lovers—had she ever been that young? Neuschwanstein's frame appeared to be about the right size.

Shortly thereafter the fairy-tale castle was in the wastebasket and Mary Fairfax hung in its place. She seemed to be looking at the door, frowning slightly, as if in warning.

Chapter Nine

Toward the end of the week, still struggling with sinuses, Mrs. Shorb, and another rainy season, Andrea was cheered by a call from a woman who wanted to bring a party of ten for a two-day stay. She explained that she only had four rooms; and when a long pause followed this statement, she wondered whether she had made a mistake by letting Martin monopolize her best room during the height of the season. However, the caller seemed more than reasonable. She would bring eight people instead, and if Andrea couldn't take them that weekend, they would come the following week. What nights did she have open?

This abnormal agreeableness should have warned Andrea, but she was in no mood to be critical. Rosy visions floated through her head—the inn becoming so popular, so much the fad, that people would come whenever she could fit them in.

Mrs. De Grange's check duly arrived and was promptly deposited, though Andrea had no reason to think it would not be honored; the address was Foxhall Road, one of Washington's most fashionable neighborhoods.

Three weekend guests stuck grimly to their schedules,

despite the unseemly weather. By driving herself beyond the call of duty and strength, Andrea made their stay a success—lighting fires in the bedrooms, serving extra food, moving her own television set into the room of a grumpy old gentleman whose arthritis was acting up. On Monday Mrs. Shorb gave notice—forty-eight hours' notice—which Andrea received with mixed emotions. Mrs. Shorb wasn't worth much, but she was better than nothing. At least she would be there to help prepare for the De Grange party. Beyond that, Andrea was incapable of planning.

The sun came out on Monday. On Tuesday it went in again. Wednesday morning Andrea awoke to the all-too familiar drip and drizzle against the window. Mercifully the guests did not arrive until late afternoon, and by that time the house was in order.

They were an effusive lot, given to much smiling and nodding and shaking of hands—with one exception, a tall blond woman swathed in folds of mink, who stood aloof from the others. The tilt of her chin, tightening the sagging muscles in her throat, and the careful positioning of her hands gave the impression of a professional model posing for a photograph. She could not have followed that career recently, for though her face was cleverly made up, it showed the ravages of half a century; but she had a certain air of distinction that made Andrea assume she was the leader of the group.

She was not Mrs. De Grange, however. That lady, plump and bespectacled and inclined to giggle, introduced the blonde as Mrs. Jones. Andrea produced the guest book, and one by one they signed their names.

She was a little surprised at the mixed nature of the group. Thus far her larger parties had been women, antique buffs or escapees from family responsibilities. Mrs. De Grange's group included both men and women, of widely assorted ages. Mr. Abbott appeared to be in his early twenties; he had a frightful case of acne and watery blue eyes, magnified enormously by his thick glasses. Miss Gorman and Miss Wilkins were middle-aged, the former short and stout and gruff, the latter looking and sounding like a nervous gray rabbit. The oldest member of the party was a man, so withered and wizened that his very ability to move seemed mildly obscene—a reanimated mummy. Introduced as Professor Schott, he showed Andrea his ill-fitting dentures and gave her a surprisingly strong handclasp. His most unusual feature was his eyes. Andrea felt an almost physical shock as they met hers; violently alive, they were the eyes of a fanatic or an intensely angry man.

There was also a married couple, Mr. and Mrs. Nasmith. They took one room, and the others sorted themselves out with little jokes and merry laughter—Miss Gorman, Miss Wilkins and Mrs. De Grange in one room, the Professor and Mr. Abbott in another—May and December. Mrs. Jones had a room to herself. Andrea wondered at this arrangement, but decided it was none of her business. Perhaps Mrs. Jones snored.

When they trooped downstairs shortly thereafter, on their way to dinner, Andrea was on hand to wish them *bon appetit* and inquire whether the rooms were satisfactory. She was overwhelmed with compliments. Everything was wonderful, charming, delightful. And would she mind if they explored her beautiful house?

"I'll be happy to take you on a tour of the house, whenever you like," Andrea answered, her smile a little cooler. She had had this problem before, though not often; some people felt that a night's room rent gave them the right to walk through doors plainly marked "Private" or "No Admittance."

"How kind," Mrs. De Grange gushed. "And this evening— may we sit in the library, or will you be using it yourself?"

"All the public rooms are open to guests," Andrea said.

"Oh, yes. I see. I do hope you won't feel obliged to entertain us. You must be worn out, and I'm sure you would rather have a quiet evening by yourself without—"

Mrs. Jones coughed. Mrs. De Grange broke off with a nervous giggle. "How I do ramble on. Good night, Miss Torgesen."

At least their good spirits aren't dampened by the rain, Andrea thought, closing the door. But she couldn't help wondering what common interest or occupation could unite such disparate types, and why they had sought out her inn. Most people were only too ready to talk about their hobbies and show off their specialized knowledge. None of this lot had so much as dropped a hint. Could Martin be the attraction? Fans of Martin Greenspan, Washington branch. . . .

She was glad to follow Mrs. De Grange's suggestion, for she was dead tired and the cold she had fought off for days was now fighting back. Settling in the kitchen with her feet on a hassock, she was half asleep when Jim came in.

"You look pooped. Want me to get supper?"

"There's a casserole in the oven."

"And you make fun of my menus," Jim said, without rancor. "Is Martin eating with us?"

"He said he was going to Reba's. It's just the two of us, Jimmie."

She had gone through half a box of tissues by the time they finished eating, but resisted Jim's suggestion that she take to her bed. "Not until the guests are settled for the night. Someone might want something."

Jim didn't volunteer to substitute for her. Normally he wasn't self-conscious, but some guests, especially the older women, fussed over him in a manner he found embarrassing.

"I'll be upstairs if you want me," he said, pressing his fingers against his forehead.

"That's the third time you've rubbed your head, Jimmie. Do you have a headache?"

"Can't put anything over on you, can I?" He turned away. "It's not bad. I took a couple of aspirin."

"I wish you wouldn't work any more tonight. All that

162

plaster dust and paint remover—it's no wonder your head aches.''

"I wish to God you'd quit fussing at me all the time! I'm all right, I tell you!"

He was gone before she could reply.

Andrea didn't resent his outburst. She had known his angelic mood, born of guilt and repentance, couldn't last indefinitely. Now he'd be on the defensive for a while, overly sensitive and prone to interpret everything she said as evidence of mistrust. At least she didn't have to worry about him sneaking out to a rendezvous with Mrs. Shorb.

She returned to her book. After a while she heard voices and knew the guests had returned. They seemed more subdued, speaking softly, without laughter. When the sounds died away she fell into a doze, but came instantly alert when footsteps approached the kitchen door.

The newcomer was Martin. He took off his wet raincoat and threw it over a chair. "You awake?" he asked.

"I am now."

"Sorry. I thought you ought to know what's going on."

Andrea sat up. All her vague doubts about her guests coalesced into a heavy lump of worry. A gang of thieves, specializing in antiques, a weird cult, sacrificing white cocks in the library. . . .

"What?" she demanded. "Nudists? Orgies?"

Martin laughed, his face softening as he watched her rub her eyes. "Nothing that bad. Didn't you recognize that woman?"

"What woman?"

"I gather from the guest book that she is calling herself Jones," Martin said dryly. "Not too inventive. . . . That's Starflower Morningcloud, the psychic. She has a column in the *Post* a couple of times a week. You must have read it."

"Psychic? I don't read that trash." But the name was

163

familiar—small wonder, it was not the sort of name one easily forgot.

"Then you're one of the few," Martin said. "Starflower— her real name is Ruby Dowdy, by the way—do you wonder she changed it?—she's one of the most influential women in Washington. Congressmen sneak into her house by the back door to learn what the stars predict for them, and she has advised at least one President. Which may explain why the country's in its present mess. Rumor has it that the First Lady is one of her best customers."

Andrea slumped back in her chair. "Oh, for heaven's sake. How silly can people get? Does she believe in her own powers, I wonder?"

"Probably not. You don't care?"

"That a lot of nitwits fall for. . . ." Andrea sat up again. "My head feels as if it's stuffed with cotton. Maybe that's why I'm so slow tonight. . . . What are you trying to tell me, Martin?"

"Well, I don't know much about these things," Martin said, maddeningly deliberate. "Maybe you'd like the inn to acquire a reputation as a haunted house. But I would suppose—"

"You suppose right." Andrea jumped to her feet. "What are they doing?"

"Appears to me they are holding, or about to hold, a séance. I remember one well-publicized case, in which Star- flower investigated a presumed poltergeist; the owners of the house later sued her for destroying the value of their property and making it impossible for them to sell—Andrea! Andy, come back here—don't go off half-cocked—"

He made a grab for her as she shot past, but missed his hold. Swearing under his breath, he went after her.

Since the red parlor was the one most favored by guests who didn't care to watch television, Andrea had lit fires in that room and in the library, and left lights burning in the green parlor as well. The sliding doors separating the latter room from the library were closed now.

Andrea attacked the heavy oak panels with the strength of rage. The only light in the library came from the fire on the hearth. Shadows coiled and shivered, turning into hollow-mouthed masks the faces that gaped at the opening doors. "Mrs. Jones," ensconced in solitary dignity at the head of the long library table, was the first to recover from the surprise. She let out an unearthly shriek and began writhing.

Professor Schott pointed an accusing finger at Andrea. "Murderer—monster! Lady Starflower was in deep trance, vulnerable to the slightest shock. You have killed her—mutilated her, savaged her—"

Andrea, who prided herself on her self-control, found herself screaming like a fishwife. "Get out of my house! All of you. Pick up that hypocritical bitch and get her out before I really savage her!"

Starflower continued to squirm and scream. She managed to stay in her chair, however, until one of her acolytes lowered her gently to the floor. The din rose as other voices joined in. Miss Wilkins let out piercing, wordless hoots at spaced intervals, like a smoke alarm.

Hands closed over Andrea's arms, and Martin's voice said loudly, "Let's just calm down, everyone." Andrea, still intent on mayhem, tried to free herself. Martin gave her a little shake. "Let me handle this. Here, Jim, see if you can keep her quiet."

"Right. Cool it, Too-Small." Jim wrapped an arm around her rigid shoulders, half embrace, half restraint.

Martin turned on the lights. In the commonplace glow of electricity the scene lost its macabre intensity; the participants became ordinary people blinking owlishly in the glare and looking as foolish as they felt. Starflower stopped writhing and sat up.

"Ah," she gasped, clutching her heart. "Ah, the torment—

the agony of separation. . . . Where am I? What has happened?''

"Get up, Ruby, you'll get your fancy robe dirty." Martin pulled a crumpled pack of cigarettes from his pocket and lit one. Surveying the ensemble with mildly critical, mildly humorous eyes, he went on, "You've made an egregious ass of yourself this time. It will make an entertaining little paragraph in my column. Naturally, I won't mention names."

Rising, with some dignity, Ruby shook off her attendant's hands and glowered at Martin.

"My column may have a few paragraphs as well, Greenspan. And I will mention names. The shock to my system—"

"Is invisible to the naked eye. Come off it, Ruby, you couldn't convince any doctor in the country, much less any judge, that you have suffered damages. Miss Torgesen, on the other hand, could charge you with breach of contract, inciting to riot, malicious mischief. . . . Give me a minute and I'll think of some others."

Ruby drew herself up. "This is a house of evil," she said, in a low, thrilling voice. "I sensed it the moment I entered these accursed walls. Doom, death, possession await the dwellers in this house!"

"Threats, now," Martin murmured, blowing a perfect smoke ring. "Defamation. . . . I wonder if a house's character can be defamed? We'll find out. If the place is so nasty, dear, how can your sensitive psyche stand it?"

"I would have cleansed this house of its evil. Now, injured and rejected, I leave the dwellers to their fate."

Andrea was still furious, but the insane intensity of her rage had passed. Before she could comment, Martin said quickly, "Tit for tat, Ruby. You keep quiet and so will I. Whatever else your performance might have been, it was an outrageous violation of this lady's hospitality."

"She didn't say guests are not permitted to contact the spiritual world," squeaked Miss Wilkins. This innocent comment won the helpful spinster a glare from her mentor. Martin laughed.

"She didn't specify that you were not allowed to do aerobic dancing in the parlor, either, or play touch football. But anyone who had such intentions would have had the decency to inquire first. Then there's the fact that you registered under a false name, Ruby—"

"I am leaving this house at once," Ruby declared. "The vibrations are too painful."

"But it's raining," said Miss Wilkins.

"Obviously Miss Torgesen isn't going to throw you out into the night," Martin said. "But I suggest you cut your stay short."

Disdaining reply, Ruby swept toward the door. Her followers trailed after her. Martin saved the coup de grace until the medium had passed out of sight, but not out of hearing. "Since Miss Torgesen held the rooms for you, you won't expect a refund," he called.

The only reaction he got was a faint "Oh, dear," from Miss Wilkins.

The spiritualists left early next morning. Andrea carried their trays up at seven-thirty, the hour they had requested. When she went for the trays later she noticed that most of them, including Ruby, had gobbled every bite.

In the cold light of day—and a cool gray rainy day it was—she couldn't believe she had behaved so extravagantly. She'd had a right to be indignant. The last thing she wanted was to have the inn acquire a reputation as a haunted house. It might attract some business, but not the kind she wanted. An emotionally disturbed guest might have a heart attack or a stroke, and decide to sue. And, once the sensation had passed, the reputation would linger. "Oh, Harry, I wouldn't stay there, not for anything—something comes in the night and pulls the covers off the bed—and someone said someone she knew didn't get a wink of sleep because she saw a Woman in White on the stairs. . . . Or was it a friend of someone she knew?''

Legally Andrea was unsure of her ground. Her hotel experience was of little help; the unwritten rule in that business was that guests could do what they liked in their own rooms, so long as they didn't set the place on fire and no one complained. But because Ruby and her coterie had used one of the public rooms for their performance, she had a moral, if not a legal right to object.

However, Andrea had to admit that her reaction had been extreme. She could have handled the matter much more effectively if she had remained coolly dignified. The memory of her behavior made her squirm, but she was on hand next morning when her guests left. It was not possible to run a hotel without developing a certain thickness of skin.

Martin didn't appear, but Jim was on hand to give her moral support. With a wink and a grin and a ''thumbs up'' signal, he went to the door, ready to throw it open.

''Starflower'' swept regally down and out, without giving Andrea so much as a glance. The others straggled after her, dealing out dirty looks and indignant murmurs as they passed. Perhaps the sight of Jim, unsmiling and formidable despite his crutches, quelled any more vehement expressions of resentment.

Shoulder to shoulder at the door, Jim and Andrea watched the guests crowd into their cars. ''Starflower'' sat alone in the back seat of the Cadillac, which was chauffeured by Mr. Abbott. The others all got into the second car.

Then a tall, thin figure detached itself and trotted back toward the house. From the agitated manner in which Miss Wilkins fumbled in her pockets and her purse, Andrea assumed she had forgotten something. She opened the door and stood back so that Miss Wilkins could return to her room to search for the missing item.

Instead the woman turned to her and caught her hand. "I told them I forgot my gloves," she said in a mumbling undertone. "Dear Miss Torgesen—I know you didn't mean any harm—indeed, I can understand your attitude—my dear mother, who has now passed into the next world—and who has thus far refused to speak to me, despite Starflower's efforts. . . . What was I saying?"

"I have no idea," Andrea replied, trying to free her hand. Miss Wilkins' fingers were as cold and clammy as a bundle of dead herring. She hung on. "My dear mother. Yes—she would agree with you, I am sure—but, Miss Torgesen, I beg you will reconsider and ask Starflower to cleanse this house. She is the soul of charity, she will relent, I know. Oh, Miss Torgesen, believe me—there is something wrong here, so terribly wrong. . . . I have only a shadow of Starflower's gift, but even I can feel it—an aura of spiritual malaise, so strong, so troubling. . . ."

It was impossible to be angry with the woman. She was six or seven inches taller than Andrea, but her hunched posture and stooped shoulders, marks of a lifetime of shyness, made her seem as defenseless as a child. Andrea had the feeling that sarcasm or rudeness would reduce Miss Wilkins to a sniveling, squeaking mass of protoplasm.

Behind her, Jim said quietly, "It's okay, ma'am. We appreciate your concern, but it's okay."

Miss Wilkins dropped Andrea's hand and grasped Jim's. As she looked at him, her eyes overflowed. "Dear boy," she whispered. "So young—so unprepared . . ."

A hail from without made her start. Tears dripping off her chin, she scuttled out.

Andrea slammed the door. "Now you can see why I don't want people like that here. She'd turn any normal guest into a gibbering idiot."

"She's a good-hearted old soul," Jim said. "She meant well."

Andrea wiped her fingers on her skirt. "Her hands are cold enough. If that means a warm heart. . . . Good riddance, anyway. I only wish I knew who was responsible for that invasion."

"Responsible?" Jim looked at her in surprise. "What do you mean?"

"Starflower didn't latch on to this place by accident," Andrea said grimly. "And I don't believe she gets her information from the next world. Somebody dropped her a hint."

"It wasn't Martin."

"I didn't say it was."

"But that's what you were thinking. Why can't you give the guy a break, Andy. He's done so much for us—"

"I don't want to discuss it." Andrea sneezed violently.

"Okay, okay. How's your cold?"

"Coming along nicely, thank you."

"Why don't you—"

"If you suggest I should go to bed, I'll scream! I don't want to go to bed. I just want everyone to stop bugging me!"

The men avoided her the rest of the day, retreating like medieval peasants from a leper. Martin made a tentative sortie at lunchtime and was met with such curtness that he retreated to his room. He tried again about five, in time to see Andrea swathed in rain gear, heading for the door.

"Where are you going?"

"Who cares?"

Martin rolled his eyes at Jim. "We care," he said. "If you'll tell me what it is you need—"

"You," said Andrea thickly, "are a guest. A paying guest. Paying guests do not run errands for the proprietor."

"I said I'd go," Jim began.

Andrea slammed the door.

People who do not have colds cannot understand why sufferers from that affliction make such a fuss about it.

People who do have colds wonder how they could have forgotten how terrible they felt the last time. Their agony is intensified by the fact that nobody takes them seriously. "It's only a cold; take some aspirin and go to bed." People who have colds hate everyone else in the world, especially people who do not have colds.

Andrea hated everybody, including herself. Splashing through the puddles in the supermarket parking lot, she listed her grievances in a silent diatribe. She had to do everything herself. Nobody helped. Or, if they did do something, they made a mess of it and she had to do it all over again. Jim took hours to do the simplest errand; he probably cruised all over the county, trying to pick up girls. Martin was always lecturing. He treated her as if she didn't have an ounce of sense. Starflower Morningcloud. . . . "I should have slugged her," Andrea muttered.

The supermarket was crowded. Andrea stormed up and down the aisles bumping people with her cart and demanding, "*Would* you mind? *Excuse* me!" in tones that turned the smiles of greeting to puzzled frowns. When Mr. Bliss, the manager, said cheerfully, "Got quite a cold, haven't you?" she froze him with a look.

At the end of the aisle devoted to paper goods, where she had gone in search of more tissues, she saw a familiar form scuttle out of sight, like a large crab who has spotted a fisherman. Andrea wondered why Reba was trying to avoid her, but since she didn't want to see Reba either, she did not go in pursuit. It was pure misadventure that they met at the checkout counter.

"Poor kid, you look terrible," Reba said sympathetically. The sympathy softened Andrea a trifle, but she noticed Reba seemed to be in a hurry; she jerked her shopping cart back and forth, endangering the woman ahead of her in line.

"I'm in a bad mood," Andrea admitted. "I told you about the party I was expecting this week?"

"Yeah." Reba started piling oranges on top of the previous order. With a martyred look, the woman ahead of her put a divider in place.

"You can't imagine what happened," Andrea said.

"I heard."

"How? Martin! I'll bet it was Martin."

"Uh—well—"

"I didn't handle it too well," Andrea admitted. "But can you imagine the gall of that woman? This could be disastrous for me."

"Oh, now," Reba said uncomfortably. "I mean, I see why you're upset, but—"

"Upset? Can you imagine how my dear little grandmas and grandpas will react if they hear the inn is haunted? Peace and quiet is my stock-in-trade; they aren't going to patronize a place where shrieking specters are apt to pop out of the closet in the middle of the night. I just wish I could get my hands on the fink who told Starflower Crazyhorse to look me up."

Reba bent to retrieve a lone orange from the bottom of her basket, but Andrea saw her face. Guilt was written over every feature.

"Not you!" Andrea exclaimed.

Reba straightened. Her face was dull crimson. "I better tell you or you'll think it was somebody else. . . . God, I'm sorry, Andy. I never thought—"

"You told her?" Andrea's voice was very quiet.

"She's an old customer," Reba said wretchedly. "I didn't do it on purpose, honest to God. It was that night—when I got sick—I wasn't sick, not to my stomach, I. . . . It was the house. It just got me, I can't explain how I felt. . . ."

"An overpowering sense of spiritual malaise?"

"Yeah, that's it." Too late, Reba realized that the question had been ironical. "No—I mean—not exactly. Martin brought me home—you remember—well, I felt better once I was out of the house, but I was still queasy, and when I stopped by

Starflower's—Ruby's—table, like I always do, she asked me what was wrong, and I. . . . She claims to know about things like that. But I wouldn't have done it if I hadn't felt—''

"How many other psychic nuts have you told?" Andrea asked.

"None. I swear. Look, Andy, if there's anything I can do—''

"You've done plenty already." Andrea turned her shopping cart in a sharp curve and went to the end of another line. By the time she finished checking out, Reba had left the store.

She told Martin the story when he came to help her carry in the bags of groceries. She owed him an apology, implied if not explicit, for suspecting him. At least that was her excuse for dumping her troubles on him after she had vowed not to do it again. Her real reason was that she wanted a sympathetic ear.

She didn't get as much sympathy as she had hoped for. "Reba wasn't trying to make trouble," Martin said. "You didn't see her at her worst. She broke down while I was driving her home—shivered and gibbered and babbled. . . . I've never seen her like that."

"She told you how she felt? And you didn't tell me!"

"Tell you what? That our tough-minded, hardheaded friend has a hidden streak of. . . .'' He hesitated, and then said frankly, "I don't know what to call it. You'd say 'superstition,' I imagine.''

"What exactly did she say? Did she see something—hear a voice, or—''

"You want everything in black and white, don't you? It's not that simple. I asked her the same thing. She wasn't too coherent, but I gather the sensation was not a sensory impression. Rather, a growing awareness of something wrong—abnormal. . . .'' He shrugged helplessly.

173

"An aura of spiritual malaise," Andrea murmured.

"That's more specific than anything I got out of her."

Andrea didn't contradict his assumption that she had heard the phrase from Reba. Starflower and her disciples were all frauds, deliberate or self-deluded; their testimony didn't count. Yet the coincidence troubled her, and there was a note of appeal in her voice when she spoke.

"You wouldn't call it superstition. What would you call it?" Martin didn't answer at once. Andrea said, "If you tell me you have had the same feeling. . . ."

"No. Quite the reverse. When I got back that night, I gave it the old college try. I stood there in the dark trying to reach out with my spiritual pseudopods, or whatever one does—feeling, I might add, like a complete jackass. To me this house is friendly, homelike, welcoming. Professional psychics like Ruby give me a sharp pain in the derriere. But Reba is a woman I know and admire. What happened to her was real—for her. I can't deny that reality just because I haven't experienced it myself."

"I'm not interested in philosophy," Andrea said rudely. "If people have hallucinations, they ought to keep them to themselves."

"Well, the damage is done, and in my opinion—which you don't want but are going to get anyway—you are overreacting. Can't you forget it? You won't improve matters by picking fights with Reba."

The truth of this was so evident, Andrea didn't bother to answer. When she and Jim sat down to an early supper she heard the front door slam and said angrily, "There he goes, off to Peace and Plenty; I suppose he and Reba will sit around getting soused and talking about what a bitch I am."

Jim put a roughened hand on her forehead. "You feel hot."

"I don't have a fever, and I'm not going to bed! Jimmie, do you think I'm being unreasonable?"

"No. That's what you want me to say, isn't it?" He stood up, adjusting the crutches. His face was that of a stranger, remote, distant. "See you later."

If he had shouted at her she would have gone after him, explaining, defending herself, apologizing—for what, she wondered? She hadn't done anything. It was Martin's fault. Jim admired him and tried to emulate him. He was always on Martin's side, against her.

Wearily she cleaned the kitchen and began making muffins— loathsome things, she couldn't even stand the sight of the gooey gray batter, much less eat them. Tomorrow she must start looking for help. She couldn't go crawling to Reba now.

Jim had not come down when she finished her chores. Her body ached from the top of her head to the soles of her feet, and her nose felt like a raw wound. As she brushed her teeth and wincingly scrubbed her face, she realized she dreaded going to sleep. If there was a time for nightmares to attack, this was it, when she was worn out physically and emotionally.

When she opened the medicine cabinet to look for dental floss, her fingers found a small bottle on the top shelf. She had forgotten about the sleeping pills. The doctor had prescribed them for her—had virtually forced them upon her—during the weeks after the accident. The first one she'd taken had left her drowsy and depressed all next day and she'd decided not to take any more.

Her hand seemed to move of its own volition, opening the bottle, tipping out a single capsule, putting it to her lips.

She read for a while, and then the soothing drowsiness came. It felt wonderful. Mind and muscle alike unfroze, went limp and loose, floated in a soft, warm haze. The book fell from Andrea's hand. Her eyes went to the end of the room, where Mary's portrait watched the door.

"That's right," she murmured. "Keep a lookout. Don't let 'em in. And while you're at it, maybe you could make it stop raining."

II

The pill gave Andrea the first good night's sleep she had had since her cold began to bother her, and if she dreamed she had no memory of it the following morning. Nor did she remember her drug-induced speech to the portrait of Mary Fairfax. If she had remembered she would have been amused at the coincidence, for the rain ended and was followed by beautiful autumn weather. Her bookings increased as a result; cool crisp nights and sunny days turned the wooded hills into the brilliant panorama extolled by local travel agents. The big oaks in the front yard were a blaze of crimson and the dogwoods lined the driveway like scarlet ribbons. Their colors muted by distance, the farther hill slopes looked like paisley shawls flung down across the countryside—mauve and rose, burnt umber and soft yellow, patterned by the deep unchanging green of the pines.

A series of maids came and went. Most were incapable, few stayed more than two days. The men tried to help. Jim was willing, but limited in what he could do. He rigged up a backpack that enabled him to carry wood for the fires and supplies from the car, but it tore Andrea apart to see him limping through the house, his young shoulders bowed. It was easier to do it herself.

Martin was willing and far less limited; it was Andrea who was unwilling to let him help. She told him she appreciated the offer and then sent him about his business. After a few rebuffs Martin returned to his typewriter and the company of Satan, whose indifference to him, if just as great, was not so forcibly expressed.

Despite her growing exhaustion and shortening temper, Andrea stuck grimly to her intention of supervising her guests whenever they occupied the public rooms. There would be no more séances in her house! She flushed out one suspect, a little gray woman with staring blue eyes whom she found stretched out at full length on the leather couch in the library talking to the ceiling. And on the following Sunday Starflower's column was devoted to the psychic's thrilling encounter with "a house of evil, not fifty miles from the nation's capital, where ancient crime and modern skepticism fill the ancient walls with a grisly miasma of doom." Starflower wasn't stupid enough to mention names, but the hints she dropped would have enabled any interested parties to identify the house.

Andrea raged, but she knew it would be a mistake to challenge Starflower. Bland ignorance was her best course; eventually the interest would die down. She redoubled her efforts to weed out potential psychics. The task was made easier by their naiveté; one woman called and inquired, "Is this the haunted house Starflower mentioned in her column?" Andrea was pleased to inform the caller that she was fully booked for an indefinite period.

Such incidents didn't improve her disposition, already soured by overwork. One evening, as she drooped half asleep over Jim's inevitable hamburgers, the breaking point came. Jim jogged her elbow, saying, "You aren't listening. I said, I finished stripping the woodwork. I need—"

Andrea's elbow gave way, her chin slipped off her hand, her neck jerked back, and she bit her tongue. Her eyes filled with tears. Jim, who had been on the verge of laughing, exclaimed, "Jesus, Andy, I'm sorry—don't cry—"

"It's all right. I bit my tongue. It hurt."

"You're bushed, that's what's wrong with you. And I'm no goddamned use at all," Jim said bitterly.

"But you are! And you could do more if you—"

She bit her tongue again, on purpose this time; but Jim knew what she had been about to say.

"If I'd get an artificial leg."

"I'm thinking of you, Jimmie. You could do so many more things—"

"My knee is gone," Jim said quietly. "That makes it a lot harder. I'll never be able to do the things I wanted to do. Never. And I won't go back to that hospital. I'd rather be dead than go back there."

"Was it that bad? No—" She shook her head. "That was a stupid, stupid question. Forget I asked."

"I'd just as soon forget the whole thing."

"Me too." Andrea wiped her eyes and tried to smile. "What were you going to say before we got off the track? You need what?"

"I'm ready to start painting," Jim said. "Except for one thing—I have to replace one of the windowsills. I thought I'd go to town tomorrow, pick up some lumber, primer, and like that. I need some. . . ." He paused, and then went on smoothly, "Some advice. How about coming with me, and giving me your expert opinion?"

III

Next morning Andrea primped and fussed over her appearance as she would have done for a party. This was the first time in months that Jim had asked her to go anyplace with him. It was partly her fault; she had not taken enough interest in his work, or tried to encourage him to confide in her. She hadn't realized how he felt about the hospital. Absorbed in her own anguish, she had not been sufficiently aware of his.

But that was over and done with—forgotten. From now on she would try harder to help and to understand.

Jim drove. Andrea stared straight ahead and talked about the weather and the advantages of latex versus oil-based paint. It wasn't far, only a mile.

Jim didn't need her advice after all. He and Mr. Burton, the manager of the hardware store, were old friends; they greeted one another by name and retired to the back of the store, where they plunged into an animated discussion. Left to her own devices, Andrea wandered up and down the aisles inspecting the merchandise and pretending not to listen. "Yeah, well, old wood like that, you'll need two coats, unless you use a primer. . . . Probably softwood, a house that age, they only used hardwood on the main floor. . . ."

When their purchases had been loaded into the trunk of the car, Jim nudged Andrea. "Look there."

Framed by boxwood and cherry boughs, the facade of Peace and Plenty glowed pale gold in the sunlight. On the steps stood the most disconsolate figure Andrea had ever seen. Reba wore an ancient sealskin coat. Her arms hung limp at her sides and her shoulders sagged. She looked like a sad old black bear.

Jim waved one of his crutches. "Hey, Reba."

A furry arm lifted in a tentative greeting.

"Stop that," Andrea hissed.

"Oh, come on. It's time you two made up."

Reba was a motionless black blot of depression in the sunny fall landscape. A smile tugged at Andrea's mouth. "You set this up, didn't you?" she said.

"Holding a grudge is immature," Jim said.

"Well. . . ."

As they approached, Reba's shoulders straightened. She looked hopefully at them.

"Good morning," Andrea said.

Meaningless courtesies were not Reba's style. "Are you still mad?" she demanded.

"Of course not. I've forgotten all about it."

"Thank God! If it makes you feel any better, I've punished myself worse than you could. Come on in. Have a cup of coffee. You still need somebody to work for you? I've got a couple of ideas. . . ."

Grinning triumphantly at the success of his coup, Jim declined the invitation. "I haven't got time to listen to a couple of broads gossip. Call me when you're ready, Andy, and I'll come pick you up.''

It would have taken a heart of stone to be unmoved by Reba's pleasure at being back on good terms with a friend. Andrea's heart was not of stone, though it had acquired a fairly flinty covering over the years. A layer of it dissolved as Reba fussed over her, offering every delicacy the restaurant had available and putting into her coffee twice as much sugar as she wanted.

"You want one of the girls?" she asked, like a professional white slaver. "Any one of 'em—take your pick."

"No, thanks. Your girls are too young and pretty. I want a middle-aged broad with absolutely no sex appeal."

"Can't say I blame you." Reba chuckled. "Linnie's gone back to high school, you know. Her daddy keeps her closer than the plaster on the wall."

Andrea felt an unaccustomed blush warm her cheeks. Mr. Hochstrasser wasn't a talking man, but she was willing to bet the story of her faux pas had gotten around town. She changed the subject. After Reba had described the prospects she had scouted, they agreed that a Mrs. Horner might work out.

"She's a little slow," Reba said. "But once you show her how to do something, she'll do it right—and go on doing it till you tell her to stop. Only other thing wrong with her is that she doesn't talk much."

That struck Andrea as a distinct asset. She said Mrs. Horner sounded just fine.

"I'd better be getting back," she said, rising.

"I'll drive you home," Reba said. "No sense bothering Jim."

"You mean you'd enter that house of evil, filled with a foul miasma?" Andrea asked jokingly.

Reba sank back into her chair with a squashy thud. "I wanted to talk to you about that. I couldn't get up the nerve."

"About Starflower, or the house?"

"The house. I don't want you to think I'm a stupid ass."

"I don't—"

"Sure you do. Anybody who believes in that psychic crap is a stupid ass. I don't believe it . . . but it happens to me."

Andrea sat down again. "What does it feel like?"

"Oh, it's easy to describe." Reba gave a brusque bark of laughter. "Sick. I feel sick as a dog. My skin crawls, I get chills."

"But surely—"

"I've felt rotten other times, like with a flu? Sure. This is different. It isn't my insides acting up, it comes from outside— from some thing outside."

She made two words of "some thing," emphasizing the break; and the commonplace, almost imperceptible alteration sent a chill through Andrea.

"Do you see anything?" she asked.

"No. But I know it's there. Something wrong—not evil, nor malevolent, just . . . wrong. But that's why I run," Reba said simply. "I'm afraid that if I stick around I *will* see it."

"It's happened before, then?"

"Maybe half a dozen times. And in the damnedest places; one was a fancy hotel suite at the Mayflower, in the old days, when it was the classiest hotel in town. It was a political shindig, some congressman who was a customer of mine. That time it was a person, not a place, that set me off. I didn't even know the guy's name. Handsome, middle-aged man, with thick gray hair and a New England accent. He killed his wife, a couple of months later. Beat her to death with a shovel."

Reba raised her hand to wipe the perspiration from her broad forehead. More shaken than she cared to admit, Andrea said, "It must be terrible. I'm sorry; I didn't realize. Have you seen a doctor?"

"I figured you'd ask that," Reba said, with a humorless

smile. "I saw three doctors. They all told me to lose fifty pounds and stop smoking."

"I suppose the reason other people don't react as you do is because you are more sensitive—"

"Goddamn it!" Reba brought her fist down on the table. "I hate that word—it sounds like Ruby Starflower."

"I'm sorry—"

"I wasn't yelling at you. I'm not sensitive and I'm not psychic, and when I die—which will be in my prime, because I won't quit smoking or drinking or eating—they'll plant me in the Methodist cemetery and that will be it. I don't know what this is, or why it happens. After the first couple of times I stopped trying to understand, I just got my ass out of the place as fast as I could. Should have done the same at the inn. I was having a good time, and I hated to upset you. . . ."

"It's all right."

"Yeah." Reba took a long, shuddering breath. "I feel better. Thanks. We won't talk about it anymore. I don't like to talk about it."

"Could I ask just one question?"

"Shoot."

"You used to visit Cousin Bertha occasionally. Why didn't it happen then?"

"It wasn't there then," Reba said.

Chapter Ten

Andrea walked home, refusing Reba's reiterated offer of a ride on the grounds that she needed the exercise. What she really needed was time to think.

Now she understood why Martin had been reluctant to repeat what Reba had told him. "You had to be there." Reba was a tough old woman and an admitted skeptic; for that very reason her impressions carried more conviction than the calculated pronouncements of Starflower Morningcloud. Her sincerity could not be doubted. The world's finest actress could not have put on a performance like the one Andrea had just witnessed.

She left the houses of the town behind her and walked along the shoulder of the road, keeping an eye out for approaching traffic. What was it Martin had said? "I can't deny that reality just because I haven't experienced it myself." But that was just Martin's wishy-washy liberal refusal to take a positive stand on any issue. He would probably concede the small but finite possibility of actual flying saucers driven by actual green Martians.

If Reba's experience had been the only evidence of something strange, Andrea could have dismissed it as Scrooge dismissed Marley's ghost: "An undigested bit of beef, a crumb of cheese, a fragment of an underdone potato." There were other signs. Individually they were trivial, inconsequential; collectively they were hopelessly contradictory. Reba turned green with terror when she entered the house; Martin found it warm and welcoming. One guest heard the rustle of angels' wings; she herself cowered, frozen with fear, at a winged assault. And how could one possibly assess the relative weight of the various pieces of testimony? The claim of a Ruby Dowdy could be dismissed out of hand. Reba's story certainly had more validity—but how much?

Reaching her own driveway, Andrea stood studying the house with newly critical eyes. If I were Reba, she thought, I'd start seeing things. A shadowy figure on the widow's walk, leaning over the railing. A white, blind face at the window of an unoccupied room. Something—some *thing*—scuttling into concealment behind a tree, leaving a slimy trail of decomposition.

An architecturally minded guest had once used the phrase "wedding-cake Gothic" to describe the house. Rising tier on tier, floor upon floor, its white walls gleaming like spun-sugar frosting, it looked almost good enough to eat. The carved swags and moldings were the decorations on the cake, the emerald green of the lawn the velvet cloth on which it was displayed. It was a beautiful old house, and the images it suggested were those of turn-of-the-century nostalgia—children playing on the lawn, attended by nurserymaids in white aprons and frilled caps, Mama rocking placidly on the veranda as she did her needlework, Papa standing on the steps surveying his domain with proprietary pride, thumbs in his vest pockets.

Perhaps, Andrea thought, it was impossible for her to be dispassionate. It was her house, her creation; she had made it what it was and she loved it with the uncritical affection any artist feels for the work of his hands and heart. Her strength and energy, her hopes and dreams had gone into it, they were part of the fabric. She was part of it. If her project failed, if she had to give it up—leaving would be like tearing up a vital part of herself.

She wouldn't fail. "Here I stay," she said aloud, with the solemnity of a vow; and it seemed to her that the house heard, and was glad.

II

The long walk home had done what Andrea hoped it would; it had helped her get things in perspective, and allowed her to shake off the dark fantasies Reba had planted in her mind. That was probably Reba's trouble—too much food and drink, not enough exercise.

She was not tempted to discuss the matter with Martin. He had apparently broken through, or jumped over, his writer's block. He stayed in his room all day, not even emerging for lunch, and whenever Andrea passed his door she heard the rattle of his typewriter.

Jim had found a way around his block too—the physical limitations that might have prevented him from completing his remodeling. That afternoon a pickup truck stopped in front of the house. The driver, a bashful, towheaded youth, introduced himself as "Wayne—my dad owns the hardware store?" The rising inflection indicated a question to which Andrea could not think of an answer; but Jim, who had obviously been expecting him, appeared in time to rescue her. "Wayne's going to give me a hand," he explained.

"Yes, ma'am," said Wayne.

That was all he said to Andrea, but he was talkative enough after she had left them to themselves; she heard them laughing and chattering nonstop as they transported the things Wayne had brought upstairs. Some of the items—a power saw, pieces of scaffolding—roused the direst forebodings in

Andrea, but she refrained, with some difficulty, from comment and admonition. If this was what Jim needed to keep him happy, he could have it.

Bright and early next morning Mrs. Horner made her appearance. Andrea's first reaction was not enthusiastic. Mrs. Horner waddled when she walked and refused to look Andrea in the eye. She was even less articulate than Wayne; the latter was capable of coherent speech, he simply chose not to exercise that facility in Andrea's presence. But Mrs. Horner didn't speak three words during the first hour. In fact she only spoke one: "Morning." Her responses to direct questions were in dumb show—a nod for yes, a shake of the head for no, and a blank stare for everything else.

After pointing out the location of cleaning materials, Andrea retired, leaving Mrs. Horner at work in one of the upstairs bathrooms. She didn't care if Mrs. Horner ever said another word so long as the woman understood what was expected of her, and did it. Returning half an hour later to ascertain whether this goal had been achieved, she found that only half the bathroom had been cleaned, but that half shone with such dazzling purity that one might literally have eaten off the floor or out of the tub. Mrs. Horner had started at the wall and methodically cleaned everything in her way, including the cracks in the claws of the tub feet.

Andrea indulged in a little dance step as she ran downstairs to answer the telephone.

The caller was one of "my grandmas" as Andrea called them, wanting to know whether she and her husband could be accommodated over Thanksgiving.

"My daughter wants us to stay with them, of course," she explained, "and I suppose at Christmas we won't be able to get out of it, but I simply cannot face it more than once this year—you have no idea what it is like! I don't know which screams the louder, the cat when the baby pulls its tail or the baby when the cat scratches it—and the older ones play those noisy television games, all beeping and tooting and tweeting—and if one speaks to my son-in-law when a football game is in progress, he snarls—literally snarls and snaps, my dear!''

Andrea did know what visits to the children were like, because Mrs. Green had told her about them at length. She liked the garrulous, cheerful old woman and her amiable husband, so she assured her that their usual room would be ready for them.

After she had hung up she sat tapping her pencil thoughtfully on the reservation calendar. Thanksgiving was less than two weeks away. The balmy, unseasonable Indian summer weather made it seem impossible that Christmas would soon be here.

She had been so busy trying to get her enterprise afloat and solvent that she hadn't made plans for the holidays. Perhaps she ought to close down. It would be wonderful to have some time alone with Jim; they hadn't spent a leisurely day together for months—not since the day before the accident.

Frowning, she studied the calendar. Thanksgiving was now a lost cause, but it probably would have been in any case. Hadn't Jim said something about Kevin joining them? It was a safe bet that he would. His parents were divorced and living at opposite ends of the country, but three thousand miles had not mitigated the loathing they felt for one another and the intense jealousy they shared concerning Kevin. He was damned if he went to one parent and damned if he went to the other; Andrea couldn't really blame him for taking the easy way out and avoiding both.

Kevin—and Martin, the omnipresent guest, the man who came to dinner. Obviously he wasn't married, but he must have some kin—brothers and sisters, cousins—to whom he could turn at the time of year when family ties were closest and warmest. Odd that she knew so little about him. He knew only too much about the most intimate aspects of her life. But that was her own fault; she had succumbed to that insidious charm of his when she was tired and worried, yet she had never invited his confidences. She had never asked him about himself. She had never cared enough to ask.

Andrea made up her mind. No bookings for Christmas. She and Jim would have that day to themselves if she had to kill to get it. They would have a tree, and presents. . . . She could get Jim something really nice this year, thanks to Martin's payments.

Martin—always Martin. Impulsively Andrea reached for the telephone, but before she lifted the instrument she reconsidered. Martin had a habit of pacing disconsolately up and down the hall when he was at an impasse, and she certainly didn't want him to overhear her quizzing Reba about him. Maybe she could persuade him to go for a walk. That room of his must be a shambles, it hadn't been cleaned for. . . .

Andrea leaped to her feet. She had forgotten Mrs. Horner.

"She'll go on doing what you told her to do until you tell her to stop," Reba had said. Mrs. Horner must have finished the bathroom by now; would she then go back to the beginning and clean it all over again, or would she remain in the same spot, scrubbing it in mindless repetition like a mechanical toy whose works have jammed?

Neither of the above. Mrs. Horner stood outside the bathroom door, bucket and brushes in hand, staring vacantly at the floor.

"I'm so sorry," Andrea said. "I should have told you what to do next. Would you like to do one of the bedrooms?"

Mrs. Horner looked, if possible, even blanker. It was rather like operating a computer, Andrea thought, conquering an insane desire to laugh. You had to phrase the question correctly or there would be no answer.

"You can do one of the bedrooms," she amended.

Mrs. Horner brightened, and Andrea said, "Let me just see if. . . ." She knocked on Martin's door. She didn't hear the typewriter, so perhaps this would be a good time to interrupt him.

He flung the door open and faced her with such a formidable frown that she stepped back, treading heavily on the foot of Mrs. Horner, who had trailed her like an obedient dog. His shirt looked as if he had slept in it, his scanty hair stood straight up around his head like a rusty halo, and his face was smudged with ink.

"What's the matter?" she asked.

"I am changing the typewriter ribbon," said Martin. "I have been changing the typewriter ribbon. I will be changing the typewriter ribbon now and forever more, world without end, amen."

Mrs. Horner then spoke her second word. "Amen," she repeated devoutly.

Andrea caught her laugh in midcourse and turned it into a cough. "Surely you must have changed several million ribbons over your career," she said.

His eyes were narrowed with answering amusement; since the joke might reasonably appear to be on him, he smiled. "I have. And never in all those million cases have I done it without a struggle that makes Waterloo look like a skirmish."

"Why don't you get one of those new typewriters that use cartridges?"

"I can't type on them," Martin said sulkily.

Andrea was distracted from this exchange by the sight of Martin's bed, a tangled mass of blankets and sheets in the midst of which Satan reposed like a black inkspot. The floor was littered with the crumpled victims of Martin's creative efforts, and the wastebasket was overflowing.

"I'll change your ribbon for you if you'll get out of here for half an hour and let Mrs. Horner clean," she said. "Oh— Mrs. Horner, this is Mr. Greenspan."

Mrs. Horner was now flat up against the opposite wall. She shook her head violently.

"No, ma'am. Ah jest can't. Ah'm sorry. Ah'll do any kinda work you want, but Ah ain't goin' in there with that there critter."

So that was what it took to wring speech from Mrs. Horner—passionate emotion. There was no need to inquire as to the identity of the critter. Mrs. Horner's wide blue eyes were focused in horrified concentration on Satan.

Martin came into the hall and closed the door behind him. Mrs. Horner relaxed with an explosive gasp. "Thank you, sir. Ah forgot about that critter bein' here."

"I'll take him out," Martin offered. There was sincere goodwill in his voice, but there was also a certain reserve; and Mrs. Horner was quick to sense it.

"You can't take him out," she said flatly. "Not iffen he don't wanna go. No, sir, thank you, but Ah don' think Ah can clean that there room."

Horrified apprehension filled Andrea. She fully expected that Mrs. Horner's next pronouncement would be, "Ah can't work in this here house with that there critter."

"I'll take care of Mr. Greenspan's room," she said quickly. "Would you—you can clean the room at the other end of the hall."

To her relief, Mrs. Horner nodded. After explaining the routine, she hurried back to Martin. He watched admiringly as she dealt with the typewriter ribbon.

"Where did you find that remarkable woman?" he asked.

"Reba, of course. I was afraid for a minute there that I was going to find, and lose, her in the same morning. She's a little peculiar, but she cleans like a dream. I only hope Satan doesn't decide to move from room to room."

Satan showed no inclination to do so. When Andrea approached the bed he opened one eye the merest slit and closed it again.

"Maybe you should wait till he's ready to—" Martin began.

"Nonsense. This room is a disaster, and I'm going to clean it right now. Damn it, Martin, did you wipe your hands on the sheet after you tried to change the ribbon?"

"I'll buy you some new ones," Martin said guiltily.

"It will wash out. I hope. . . . Go away. I can't work with you looking over my shoulder."

"Leave you here alone with the critter? I'm prepared to join in the fray, or at least bind up your wounds afterwards."

"It's ridiculous, the way you all let that animal intimidate you," Andrea exclaimed. "Get up off there, Satan. Scat. Move your butt." She took hold of the blanket in which Satan was nested and gave it a sharp tug. Satan rolled onto his back, all four feet in the air. Martin laughed. Satan spat.

"Watch out," Martin said, as she reached for the cat.

"Don't be silly." Satan hung like a stuffed toy from her hands as she lifted him. Andrea staggered. "My God, he's heavy," she gasped.

"He does it on purpose," Martin said. "He can instantly double his weight when he wants to."

"You and Mrs. Horner. . . ." Andrea dumped the cat onto a chair. "Sit there till I'm through," she told him.

Satan glowered, but remained where she had put him.

"Now," Andrea said, glancing with poorly concealed triumph at Martin, "get out of here and let me work."

Martin shook his head and took his departure.

Not at all discomposed by the unwinking feline stare that followed every move she made, Andrea stripped the bed. When she went to fetch clean sheets, the vacuum cleaner, and a trash bag, she was careful to close the door behind her. A glance into the rear bedroom showed Mrs. Horner placidly at work. Martin had apparently joined her; Andrea couldn't see him but she heard his voice rambling on, in an unending monologue. They should get on beautifully, Andrea thought.

Satan was unperturbed by the vacuum cleaner, which most cats, she had been told, disliked intensely. He didn't blink, even when she vindictively vacuumed all around and under the chair in which he was sitting.

Martin came back just as she was finishing. He waited until she had turned off the machine, and then said, in tones of mild surprise, "It looks better."

"That's not a compliment. Anything would look better. How can you stand to work in such a mess?"

"I'm used to it."

"You should have taken a walk in the nice sunshine. Didn't you find conversation with Mrs. Horner a little one-sided?"

"Mrs. Horner," said Martin oratorically, "is like a gold mine. It takes a while to strike pay dirt, but once you hit the mother lode the nuggets of rare metal make the effort worthwhile. To put it another way—"

"I wish you would."

"Once you get her started, she talks," Martin explained. "I'm tempted to write a regional novel; she'd make a superb character. Do you know what she said about Satan? 'That there's a witchcritter, that is. He still got some o' his nine lives left. He was here in my granddaddy's time and he'll be here when you and me is dead and gone.' "

"That particular breed and color has apparently perpetuated itself in this area," Andrea said. "If it were white or calico, people wouldn't be so superstitious about it."

"I shouldn't make fun of her," Martin said repentantly. "She's a good soul. Promised to make me an apple pie."

"She can cook?" Andrea's eyes lit up. "Then she can believe in witches and familiars and all the devils in hell as far as I'm concerned."

Andrea was anxious to test Mrs. Horner's talent, so the following morning she produced an armful of magazines containing recipes and glossy, touched-up color photographs of coffee cakes and breakfast rolls. She didn't care what Mrs.

Horner made; any change from the loathsome muffins would be a blessing.

Mrs. Horner liked the pictures, but when she realized what Andrea wanted, her face blanked out. "Ah don't cook outta books," she said.

"You can use one of your own recipes," Andrea said encouragingly.

"Ah don't. . . . You want me to make one o' these?" She indicated a photo of a braided breakfast ring, shiny brown with egg white and bristling with glazed almonds.

"It doesn't have to be that one," Andrea said patiently. "Anything I can serve for breakfast. But," she added, with a sudden memory of the most popular fare available in local farmers' markets, "not sticky buns."

"Not sticky buns," Mrs. Horner repeated.

"They're too messy. Just do anything you like. Do you mind?"

Mrs. Horner shook her head. Taking this for the response she wanted, Andrea left her to it. Not until she had started straightening the parlor did it occur to her that perhaps Mrs. Horner didn't cook "outta books" because she couldn't read.

She was sweeping the veranda with the door left open to the balmy air when a series of seductive odors began to seep out. Her stomach responded before her brain did, with a hopeful lurch and mutter, but she forced herself to finish the job. In a way it was a pity to remove the leaves; they ranged through all the shades of red from scarlet to deep cinnamon brown, forming a multihued carpet lovelier than any man-made product. It took almost an hour to sweep the veranda, but it was one of Andrea's favorite jobs when the weather was fine. Cousin Bertha's mums were masses of bloom, sunshine-yellow and soft amber, rust and magenta and lavender. A group of sycamores down by the creek might have been composed by an oriental painter; the pale, dark-splotched trunks rose in symmetrical angles almost too perfect to have occurred naturally.

As she paused to catch her breath, Andrea experienced a moment of utter peace, one of those rare instants when everything seems too perfect to last. The year was dying, not in wild gusts of storm but in placid acceptance, and the brilliant colors of the fallen leaves were trophies of the past summer, and promises of spring to come.

And the smells from the kitchen were divine in quite another sense. Andrea bent to her task with renewed vigor, and then, shouldering her broom, went in search of the heavenly odors.

Jim was already there. She wasn't surprised; he had always been able to smell a chocolate bar, wrapped in two layers of paper, from sixty feet away. Elbows on the table, he was devouring cinnamon buns while Mrs. Horner watched him benevolently. Two pans of the delectable concoctions lay on the table, their surfaces laced with white frosting. On the counter was a bowl filled with dough rising to a pale hemisphere, and when Andrea entered Mrs. Horner turned to remove another pan of rolls from the oven. They had been shaped into bowknots, and Andrea watched in impressed silence as Mrs. Horner poured over them a pan of orange-gold liquid that spread and settled in a shimmering glaze.

"Have a bun," Jim said thickly. "This lady is the greatest cook in the entire world. We're engaged to be married."

Andrea had never heard Mrs. Horner laugh, but she deduced that the series of gurgles emerging from her parted lips fell into that category. "Gotta fat you up first, boy," she said. "Ah don't like skinny men."

She and Jim exploded with amusement.

Martin's head came around the corner of the door, his nose quivering. Between them, he and Jim ate a whole pan of cinnamon rolls, and in their presence Mrs. Horner became almost coquettish. When Andrea congratulated her on the rolls, she shook her head. "They's better with lard," she said. "Git me some lard next time."

"I'll get you ten pounds of lard," Martin said devoutly. "A chariot drawn by six white horses and a sable cloak. Will you marry me, Mrs. Horner?"

"No, sir, Ah can't. Ah'm already engaged."

She and Jim poked one another and exploded again.

When the pan of buns was empty, Andrea evicted the men by main force and left Mrs. Horner shaping her yeast dough into braids. Her fat, clumsy-looking hands moved with the sure skill of a craftsman. Andrea went meekly upstairs and cleaned the bathroom.

At one o'clock the kitchen counter was covered with pans of goodies which Andrea contemplated in a state close to awe. Mrs. Horner accepted congratulations with a bashful nod. She had relapsed into her customary taciturnity when the men left. Andrea accompanied her to the door.

"I'll see you tomorrow," she said happily.

"No, ma'am. Not tomorrow."

"What? Why not?" It was a cry of anguish.

"Snow," said Mrs. Horner. "Ah can't drive in the snow."

"Snow?" Andrea glanced at cerulean skies, soft sunlight, a balmy breeze stirring the leaves. "Oh, no, Mrs. Horner. The weather forecaster says—"

"Ah can't drive in the snow."

Too taken aback to argue, Andrea watched Mrs. Horner plod down the stairs and climb into her aged car. Its original color was a matter of speculation; it had faded to a dull tannish-gray, and from what Andrea could see of the tires she couldn't blame Mrs. Horner for refusing to drive in bad weather. That was a problem she would have to deal with eventually—but snow, tomorrow?

She sped back to the kitchen just in time to rescue the weekend's breakfast rolls from Jim and Martin.

* * *

When Jim had returned to the tower and Martin had reluctantly climbed the stairs to face his typewriter, Andrea got the car out and drove to town. Reba was delighted to see her. "Twice this week! You're getting to be a real gadabout, Andy. Sit down and have lunch."

"Thanks, I've eaten. But I'll join you in a cup of coffee if you can take the time."

"Sure, sure. Good to see you. Figured you'd be busy this fine weather. We don't usually have much snow till after Christmas, but this is the longest autumn I can remember in years."

"Mrs. Horner says it's going to snow," Andrea said.

"Oh, shit! I was going to drive to Baltimore tomorrow. Guess I better cancel."

"Reba, it isn't going to snow! But I can see I'll have problems getting Mrs. Horner to work this winter. Where does she live?"

They discussed possible solutions to Mrs. Horner's timidity about driving—she lived several miles out on a graveled country road which, according to Reba, was unreachable in bad weather except by jeep.

"By the way," Andrea said, "is Mrs. Horner illiterate?"

"She can write her name," Reba said shortly. "Never wondered about it, to tell you the truth."

The implication was clear—what did it matter? And Andrea was inclined to agree. "I just didn't want to put her in an embarrassing situation by assuming she could," she explained.

Reba's face cleared. "I see what you mean. That's nice of you."

"Oh, I'm so nice I can't stand myself."

"Why do you put yourself down all the time? You are a nice person. Or you could be, if you'd take the time."

"I've never had the time," Andrea admitted. " 'Being nice' is a luxury I can't afford."

"Bull," said Reba. " 'Nice' is a dirty word to you. You

think it's an admission of weakness. Hell's bells, girl, I've been there myself. But I was wrong and you're wrong. The quality we're discussing—and I admit 'nice' is a stupid, inaccurate word for it—is a sign of inner strength and peace of mind.''

"You sound like Martin," Andrea said. "Which reminds me—''

"Go ahead, change the subject," Reba jeered.

That was Andrea's intention, but she didn't want to admit it. "No, really. One of the reasons I came was to talk about Martin. I don't want to pry, but I realized yesterday I was facing a potentially awkward situation.''

She went on to explain her dilemma about the holidays. "I don't want him to feel he isn't welcome," she said mendaciously. "And to ask him point-blank might give that impression."

"He isn't figuring on going anywhere," Reba said. "He hasn't anywhere to go."

"No family? No friends?"

"He's got heaps of friends. Hell, he could stay with me anytime, he knows that, and there are others who feel the same way. But there's nobody close. At least. . . ." She hesitated, stirring the dregs of her coffee in an aimless fashion, and then said abruptly, "Contrary to what you may think, I don't usually blab about my friends' private affairs."

"Then don't tell me."

"I think I better. It's only fair to Martin. He has got kin. He's got a son. Twelve years old. Martin hasn't seen him for three years."

Andrea's jaw dropped, her mouth forming a perfect circle of surprise. Before she could comment, Reba raised a massive, admonishing hand. "See? That's what I mean. If you only knew those facts, which aren't hard to find out, you'd think the wrong thing. Martin is crazy about the kid. What happened was not his fault but his tragedy.

"He was crazy about his wife, too. She wasn't worth it—one of those overbred, undernourished little wisps of a girl with big baby-blue eyes and silvery-blond hair, and no brains to speak of—but Martin worshiped the ground she walked on. I knew 'em both back in those days, when he was still a starving young reporter. That was one of the reasons why her family objected to the marriage—that and the fact that he was a Jew. Oh, yeah, they made no bones about it; they were old Southern gentry, rotten with family pride. The one gutsy thing Marietta ever did was tell them to go to hell and elope with Martin.

"It never would have lasted. By the time they'd been married a year he was heavily in debt. She couldn't stop spending the way she always had, and when he'd try to explain that he couldn't afford to buy her fur coats and jewelry, she'd cry and have a tantrum. When she found out she was going to have a baby, all hell broke loose. I guess the poor little jerk had a few screws missing; she acted like she didn't know where babies come from and couldn't figure out how hers had got where it was. She tried to make up with her family, but they wouldn't have anything to do with her; she had made her bed, and now she could lie in it.

"She died having the baby. No stamina, no guts. . . . Once she was properly dead and gone, the family came down on Martin like a swarm of killer bees. He had murdered their darling, and they wanted her baby. Daddy was an ex-judge, one of the old-boy network that runs Virginia, and Martin didn't have a chance. The fact that he was drunk for six months after Marietta died didn't help. Unfit, that's what they called him. He didn't fight back. I guess he didn't care about anything."

"I had no idea," Andrea murmured. "You'd never think, to see him now. . . ."

"He's fine now," Reba said. "He's got the guts that poor little wife of his never had. Losing custody of the kid shocked him out of his misery, I guess; he stopped drinking and worked like a son of a bitch. Once his career was underway, he went back to court and was awarded visitation rights, but by that time the kid had been taught to fear and hate him. Finally he quit trying. Said it was too hard on the boy.''

"I'm glad you told me," Andrea said. "I won't say anything to him.''

"You better not. I don't want to lose another friend on account of my big mouth.''

"If you're talking about me, you haven't lost my friendship," Andrea said with a smile.

"No more spiritualists?''

"The sensation, such as it was, seems to have died down.'' Andrea rose. She felt an overpowering need to get out into the sunshine. Martin's unhappy history had cast a shadow over her spirits. No doubt Reba's account had been biased. Nevertheless, Andrea believed it.

"I'll make a point of asking him to have Thanksgiving with us," she said.

"That would be real. . . .'' Reba grinned, and finished the sentence. " . . . real nice. I haven't seen him as attached to anybody as he is to you and Jimmie. Andy—have you ever thought about—''

"About what?''

"Never mind," Reba mumbled. "I guess you haven't.''

"I can't imagine what you're talking about. Why don't you come for Thanksgiving dinner too? The food won't be up to your standards, but I'll cook a turkey—if Mrs. Horner can tell me how.''

"You come here.''

Reba's face had turned an odd shade of dirty gray. Her eyes shifted away from Andrea's, like those of a mass murderer caught with a bloody knife in hand. "I was going to ask you anyway," she said quickly. "It's easier for me, you know that, and you deserve a day off, and—''

"You still feel the same way," Andrea said, incredulously. "You are still terrified of the house."

Reba didn't answer.

III

The sun sank gloriously into a soft night filled with stars. Andrea awoke next morning to find her room as dark as twilight. Against the dull gray of the window snowflakes drifted like big white polka dots.

She threw the covers back and ran to the window. The landscape was muffled in white under a sky the color of dull pewter. Every bush had a peaked white cap and the azalea bushes were half buried in snow.

Andrea said, "Goddamn it to hell!" and stamped her foot. Mrs. Horner had a lot of nerve complaining about Satan. How the devil had she known it was going to snow? Not that her absence would matter; most of the guests would probably cancel if the rest of the area was equally affected.

The first call came soon after eight. It was from one of her more considerate grandmothers. "I wanted to let you know as soon as possible—my dear, we've got sleet and freezing rain mixed with snow; Jack simply refuses to drive, and I can't blame him."

By eleven the others had also canceled. Andrea sat down at the kitchen table and ate four of Mrs. Horner's orange biscuits while she read the paper backward, from the comic page to the front. It was impossible to face today's headlines straight on; one had to work up to them gradually, by way of B.C. and Heloise and the acrimonious debates of the District of Columbia school board.

This was her first true winter day in the house. The icy rains and sleet of March had not prepared her for this—a hiatus, a break in the frantic routine of living. The snow fell in great slow clumps, and in utter silence, without the hiss of sleet or the drum of rain. The birds had sought shelter, or huddled in stoic discomfort on branches and power lines.

When she went to call Jim to lunch, he said he didn't want any. He wanted to finish this part of the painting; Wayne was coming over later to help him move the scaffolding. Snowing? So what about it? Wayne's dad had a jeep, he'd be here one way or another.

Andrea would have lingered, but Jim's responses were short, almost brusque, and the sight of him balancing on one foot atop the scaffold made her nervous. She trudged back downstairs and made sandwiches, which she carried up to him, receiving in return an abstracted "Thanks, I'll eat 'em later."

Martin didn't come to lunch either. She let Wayne in when he arrived—how he had managed to get through the snow she didn't know and didn't want to know. Sometime later she heard him leave, but did not get up from her chair. She felt as lazy and unmotivated as the drifting snow. She was lying on the couch finishing the mystery story she had been reading for weeks when a streak of pale sunlight illumined the page.

The clouds had parted as if by design to frame the coppery orb of the setting sun in an aureole of molten light. The long slope of fallen snow on the south lawn shone with a shimmer of golden-rosy pink, against which the branches of shrubs and trees stood out in delicate outline. It was magical—a winter day in Fairyland. Pink snow, like the self-multiplying mounds the Cat in the Hat had tried vainly to clear away. . . . How Jim had loved that silly book! She thought of calling him, and suggesting that they go out to make pink snowballs and a rose-colored snowman; but just then the clouds drew a veil over the face of the sun and the enchantment vanished. Just as well, she thought, her face as shadowed as the soft gray snow. It would hurt her almost as much as it would Jim to know that he must limp, slowly and dangerously, where once he had run like Mercury with wings on his heels.

She put on her coat and boots and went out, taking a broom with her. The snow had stopped and the clouds were lifting. A lovely irregular line of soft lavender showed to the west, as the sky cleared to bare the shapes of the mountains. The sun had gone; a faint afterglow marked the place of its death. Andrea started sweeping the porch, but soon tossed the broom aside. It was too beautiful an evening to work. Every change in the light transformed the landscape, bringing subtle shadings of color to the snow, colors for which there were no words—not violet or silver or azure, but blends of all three. Her breath made white puffs in the darkening air as she walked slowly toward the gate, scuffling her feet in childish enjoyment. As dusk deepened, the shadows of the shrouded shrubs stood out against the eerie shimmer of the snow-covered ground.

When she reached the gate she turned, with a sense of almost breathless anticipation. The house rose up in all its solid perfection, its white walls reflecting the silvery glow of the snow. The tower windows formed concentric arcs of light. A shadow passed back and forth against the lower arc—Martin, pacing. The rest of the house was dark. The bulb in the hall lamp must have burned out. She distinctly remembered turning it on before she went out.

There was no traffic on the road. Darkness closed in around her, but she had no feeling of loneliness or isolation; a company of shadows surrounded her, the memories of all those who had lived in the old house, who had paused where she stood now to admire its beauty and anticipate the warmth of homecoming.

Not until the last afterglow died and stars sprang up in the night sky did she retrace her steps. Once she closed the door the hall was as black as pitch; the fanlight and the narrow strips of glass that bordered the door were shadowed by the overhang of the veranda. Surefooted and unconcerned, Andrea felt her way toward the light switch. As she moved with hands outstretched and eyes blind, something brushed past her and started up the stairs.

She felt it pass. She was about to call out a greeting, for it was something—someone—familiar, as unmistakable even in the darkness as Jim's presence would have been, or Martin's. Then she realized she had no name to give it. It was not Jim, nor Martin.

Her hand found the switch. The light made her blink. She knew, even before she looked, that there would be no one in sight.

From upstairs came the sound of a door opening and, after a moment, Martin's voice. "Andrea?"

"Here," she called, her voice steady.

"Where are you?" His footsteps sounded along the corridor.

"Down here. What do you want?"

Martin stopped on the landing and looked at her, shading his eyes with one hand. "What do *you* want?" he asked; then, seeing her snow-covered boots and coat: "Were you upstairs a minute ago?"

"I just came in."

He descended the rest of the stairs and stood beside her. "Didn't you knock on my door just now?"

"No."

"I must be losing my mind." He brushed his nonexistent hair back from his forehead in a puzzled fashion.

"Maybe it was Jim," Andrea suggested. She had no intention of telling him of her experience. He would speculate and question and turn it into something sinister, frightening. It had not been frightening. It had been . . . hers. Her own private encounter. No one else's business.

She heard Jim coming down the stairs. As he moved along the second-floor corridor, she met Martin's eyes and knew what he was thinking—no one could have mistaken Jim's walk for hers, or been unaware of his approach. Nevertheless, as soon as Jim was within earshot, Martin asked him.

Barbara Michaels

"Not me, I've been upstairs all afternoon. Maybe it was a burglar. A polite burglar, whose mum taught him to knock before entering."

Martin was not amused. "I don't know whether it knocked or not," he said slowly. "It was the cat that made me think someone was there. He bounded up and stood staring at the door. Then he jumped off the bed and ran to it and mewed to get out. He was excited. Purring and pacing back and forth, the way pets do when—"

"You are wasting your talents on nonfiction," Andrea jeered. "You ought to write ghost stories. For heaven's sake, Martin!"

"When they greet someone they know," Martin said.

Chapter Eleven

Mrs. Horner came to work the following morning. Andrea was not surprised; rising overnight temperatures had begun to melt the snow in her driveway, and a high of around fifty was predicted. Besides, Mrs. Horner had said she wouldn't be there "tomorrow," not "tomorrow and the next day." Andrea was prepared to accept any future predictions. There was nothing more uncanny about Mrs. Horner's nose for weather than there was about the other peculiar things that had happened to her since she came to live in the haunted hills of Maryland. Perhaps the whole region was haunted, and the inhabitants of Ladiesburg were descendants of a coven of devil-worshipers, or castaways from a lost flying saucer.

The guests who had canceled the day before called to say they would be coming after all. As was his custom when guests were expected, Martin went to Peace and Plenty for lunch, pausing only long enough to exchange pleasantries with Mrs. Horner and assure her that Satan was safely shut up in his room. He knew and Andrea knew that this was no guarantee Satan would stay there, but neither saw any reason to mention the cat's talent for teleportation to Mrs. Horner.

Jim didn't appear until after Mrs. Horner had left. He ate the lunch Andrea forced on him as fast as he could cram it into his mouth and announced he was going to town. He needed a couple of things. Could he have some money? Twenty bucks ought to do it.

Andrea handed it over without debate, but promised herself she must have a long talk with Jim soon. He was spending altogether too much time in the tower room, breathing in fumes and dust. He had lost much of the healthy color he had acquired earlier in the fall, and there were new lines on his forehead, marks of constant squinting or frowning. Perhaps he needed glasses, Andrea thought. He hadn't had his eyes checked for a long time. If only he would vary his interests, dividing his time between them instead of concentrating with fanatical intensity on one after the other. First the graveyard, then his research at the courthouse, now the tower room. . . . Hopefully he was almost finished with the last; then perhaps he would turn to something less taxing.

Having finished in the kitchen, she went upstairs for a final check of the guest rooms. The chill in the corridor struck her at once. There was a blast of cold air rushing down the stairs from the attic.

She had had to lecture Jim before about leaving windows open. Fresh air was essential when he was using some of the more powerful paint strippers, but he had been told to close the windows when he left the room. Andrea went up. As she had expected, the draft came from the tower. Either he had forgotten to close the door, or the wind had blown it open.

Like all the windows in the house, those in the tower were double-hung—two sections, one above the other—but since the tower windows were almost floor-to-ceiling in height, they had four panes in each section instead of the conventional two. Both sections of the north window were missing, as was the windowsill and part of the inner molding. The window sections lay on the floor, and an empty space four feet wide by eight feet high gaped in the wall.

It was obvious what had happened. Trying to replace the rotten sill, Jim had found the damage more extensive than he had expected. He had blithely removed the entire window—how, she could not imagine—and had been unable to get it back in place. He probably hoped he could get the advice or the help he needed at the hardware store and repair the damage before she found out about it.

She approached the gaping hole with extreme caution. The sill was only three feet from the floor; an unwary step, a slip or a trip, could propel a person straight out through the empty space to the ground forty feet below.

She had had some vague idea of putting up a makeshift covering, but it didn't take her long to realize it couldn't be done—not by her at any rate. There wasn't a damn thing she could do except close the door and refine the lecture she meant to give Jim.

She had every intention of stopping a safe distance away, but somehow she kept moving forward—slowly and carefully, but moving. The ground was a long way down. The rhododendrons below were big old bushes, but rhododendron wasn't a thick growth like boxwood or yew; it wouldn't break her fall, she would just crash through it, smashing the brittle stems and the brittle bones, the fragile flesh. . . . It would hurt, but not for long. It would be quick. Quicker and kinder than other ways of dying. . . .

One detached portion of her mind knew what was happening and screamed in silent terror. It tried to hold her back, but muscle and sinew pulled her forward. She stood in the opening, hands clutching the frame on either side; and the sweat poured down her face as she swayed, locked in a motionless struggle, fighting to jump and fighting not to jump.

Then she felt something touch her shoulder, touch and close tightly, like the firm grip of a warm, strong hand. It broke the paralysis that held her in the opening. Gasping, she stumbled back and fell in a huddled heap on the floor.

"Andrea? Where are you?" It was Martin's voice, Martin's footsteps approaching. "Do you know there's a hell of a cold blast blowing down the stairs? I think Jim must have. . . . Holy God! What happened? Did you fall?"

Warm firm hands lifted her to a sitting position. Not the hands that had saved her—not the same at all. "Where are you hurt?" Martin demanded. "Talk, damn it."

"I didn't fall. I'm all right. . . . I almost. . . . Martin—I wanted to jump. I stood there—in the window—and I wanted to let go and fall, all the way down. . . ."

"Jesus Christ." Martin's face grew visibly paler as he looked at the gap in the wall. "Damn that kid! I'll break his neck. Come on, Andy, let's get you out of here."

"It wasn't his fault. . . . Close the door, Martin."

"Yes, of course. Here, let me help you."

"I'm okay." His touch made her self-conscious. Collapsing onto the bottom step, she took a long, shuddering breath. "Wow. What an experience!"

"It's not uncommon," Martin said.

"Really?"

"Heights affect some people that way."

"You?"

"No. But I'm not wild about being high up with nothing between me and the ground. A railing, even a pane of glass, gives an illusion of protection."

"That must be it, then. I'm not afraid of flying; I've never had anything like this happen."

"Let's hope it doesn't happen again."

"It won't. Forewarned, forearmed."

"You okay now?"

"Yes, I'm fine." She got to her feet. "I'll speak to Jim. It wasn't his fault—I hardly ever go in that room, and no one could have anticipated that I'd react so—so neurotically."

"Suit yourself. Just don't go back in there. Promise?"

"Yes, of course."

Jim didn't get a lecture after all. When he came back, the towheaded Wayne and the latter's father, Mr. Burton from the hardware store, were with him. In some confusion of mind Andrea retreated into the kitchen before they could see her. She didn't want to humiliate Jim in front of his friends. In fact, now that she had had time to think the matter over, she would rather he didn't know about her bizarre experience. He would reproach himself—unnecessarily, it was her own fault—and he would worry, and get funny ideas. . . . She would warn Martin to say nothing. It was pure bad luck that he had found her before she had time to recover.

She waited for almost an hour before she went up to see what they were doing. The window was back in place; Burton was wielding a caulking gun while Jim looked on and the useful Wayne swept up debris.

"Why, Mr. Burton," Andrea exclaimed. "I didn't hear you come in. How nice of you and Wayne to come and help."

"No trouble at all, ma'am. Jim had most everything done; it was just a question of putting it all together. Some jobs need two pair of hands. Wasn't much going on at the store, so I figured I'd show the boys a couple of shortcuts."

The explanation was more elaborate than the situation required; Burton was covering up for Jim, helping him to maintain the image of male omniscience. Neither of them, nor Wayne, would ever admit he had run into a problem he couldn't handle. No, they were just pitching in, saving time with a few shortcuts.

"We're very grateful," she said.

"Least I can do for a good customer. Jim's pretty handy, but he's got plenty to do if you figure on getting this room in shape by Thanksgiving."

"Oh, I don't see how we can possibly—"

"No reason why not," Burton said. "There—that should do it. We'd best be getting back, Wayne. Just take that there bag of trash with you when you go down."

"Thanks again," Andrea said.

"Don't need no thanks for being neighborly. You got a smart boy here, Miss Andrea. Any time he wants a job I'll hire him."

"I may take you up on that," Jim said.

After the Burtons, junior and senior, had gone, Andrea gave the room a critical inspection. She had no sense of uneasiness now that the window was back in place; in fact, she found it hard to believe that she had been so affected.

The overall impression was one of utter chaos, but Andrea had now had enough experience to recognize that the greater part of the job was done. Preparing the surfaces by stripping and scraping, patching and sanding was the most time-consuming activity. Jim had finished these preliminaries. A few coats of paint and the room would be ready for occupancy.

Andrea turned to Jim, who stood with his back toward her. His shoulders were rigid, and the hands gripping the crutches were white-knuckled with tension. "What's the matter, Jimmie?" she asked.

He shied away from the hand she put on his shoulder, his face still averted. "Nothing. Why do you ask?"

"You weren't your usual chatty self."

"You talked for both of us. Just like the goddamned nurses at the hospital. 'Yes, Doctor, we're feeling much better today!' "

The sound of the doorbell gave her an excuse to retreat from a situation she didn't know how to handle. Glancing back over her shoulder, she saw that his pose was less tense and it hurt her to think that her very presence could arouse such inexplicable resentment.

The first guests had arrived; they bustled in, full of apologies for their cancellation the day before. They hoped they weren't too early. Andrea assured them their room was ready and escorted them upstairs.

Mrs. Hinckley, a bright-eyed, slender woman of sixty-odd, was the sort of guest Andrea found difficult—paradoxically so, for people of her type rarely complained and took minor inconveniences in their stride. But they wanted to talk all the time—to her. How old was the house? Where had she found the charming antiques? What made her decide to go into the innkeeping business? Andrea foresaw a long afternoon and evening with nice, amiable Mrs. Hinckley.

The family from Delaware who arrived a little later fell into another category with which Andrea was only too familiar from her former job. Mrs. Bascom had the nervous apologetic air common to women who spend a great deal of time being embarrassed by their husbands; Mr. Bascom's first words were a complaint about the length of the drive and the difficulty of finding the inn. Since Andrea's printed circular included directions designed for an illiterate eight-year-old, she was not inclined to feel guilty. There were also two teen-aged girls. Andrea's brochure made it clear that she did not accept children under sixteen; the junior Miss Bascom, though dressed in a style that was far too old for her, was obviously a year or two under the prescribed age, and she did not look like the sort of child who would find a weekend in the country to her taste. Her first question on viewing her room was "Where's the TV?"

The Hinckleys left for an early dinner, followed shortly thereafter by the Bascoms. Andrea hid, without compunction, when she heard Bascom's grumbling voice. As soon as the house was clear she went upstairs. Martin's door opened a crack. "What's the rating?" he asked.

It had become a standard inquiry. If the rating was high and if Martin was in the mood, he joined the guests in the library or the parlor after dinner. If negative conditions prevailed, he kept to his room.

"Three or four out of ten for the Hinckleys," Andrea said. "Inoffensive but dull. The Bascoms. . . ." She turned her thumb down.

"That bad, eh. Him or her?"

"Him. And junior her—one of the kids is a real loser."

"Hmmm." Martin scratched his chin. "I'm in the mood for a fight. Does he look like a Republican?"

"Well, it isn't stamped on his forehead."

Martin withdrew. Andrea went up to the tower.

Jim was perched on the stepladder painting the chair rail. He grinned at her. "What's the rating?"

"You feel better," Andrea said, smiling.

"I never felt bad. Sorry I yelled at you. What's the rating?"

She supposed that hero worship was a normal attribute, but sometimes she got tired of hearing him imitate Martin. She replied rather shortly.

"Don't join the crowd. One, possibly both, of the women will try to mother you, the daughters will make passes at you, and Martin is gearing up for a loud political argument."

"Sounds interesting."

Andrea did not pursue the matter. "What do you want for dinner?"

"Pizza," said Jim, painting busily.

"Again?"

"I thought it would save you cooking. How does this look?"

"It looks wonderful, darling. You really are doing a super job. I wish I had time to help you."

"It's okay."

"Maybe we can go to town Monday and pick out the paint for the walls. What color were you thinking of?"

"I'm going to paper. It's already ordered."

"You picked it out?"

"You don't mind, do you?" Jim looked at her, the corners of his mouth ready to smile or sag according to her reply.

What could she say but "Why should I mind? What is it like?"

"You'll see when it comes. Big surprise, okay?"

"Okay. When do you want to eat?"

"In about an hour. I want to finish this coat."

Andrea went downstairs, straight through the kitchen and into Jim's room. He would be occupied for quite some time.

It was not the first time she had stooped to an act which she herself considered contemptible, and repetition had not dulled her sense of shame, but she did not hesitate. The top of Jim's desk was covered by the miscellaneous debris he collected—copies of Martin's columns, clipped from the newspaper, letters, glasses coated with milk scum or beer, a crumb-covered plate, two screwdrivers, circulars, paint samples. . . . Andrea sat down at the desk. The second drawer was locked. Andrea unlocked it, using a nail file to press back the simple latch, and took out a blue spiral notebook.

She had started looking through Jim's papers after she found the poem. She had no choice. It was the only way she could find out what was bothering him, since he refused to confide in her. Even as a child he had had an annoying habit of reticence. She would never forget that terrible year after their father and stepmother were killed. Jim adored Helen; he was too young to remember their real mother or resent the woman who had taken her place. Andrea had been jealous of their mutual affection, she could admit that now; but by the time she left for college she had achieved a grudging recognition of Helen's worth. That first year away from home had been a revelation—new friends, exciting new ideas, and her first serious love affair. Johnny. . . . She had been desperately, wildly in love—and now she couldn't remember his last name or what he looked like.

She had been nineteen, about to begin her sophomore year, when the plane went down in mid-Atlantic during a storm. There were no survivors. Recognition of her new responsibilities had forced grief into the background, but Jim, only eight years old, had no such help. It had been a dreadful time, not because he was frantic with grief but because he couldn't or wouldn't let it out. His small pale closed-in face still haunted her.

But, she reminded herself, he had worked it out. He ran it out, fought it out, played it out, exorcising his private demons through physical outlets. He didn't have those now. But he could find other means. If he couldn't, she would find them for him.

Andrea opened the notebook. Jim's present outlet seemed to be poetry—or rather, verse, for his outpourings did not merit any loftier term. A smile softened her face as she read the scribbled lines. One verse was an imitation of the Song of Songs, with innumerable references to female anatomy. Another seemed to be an attempt at a sonnet. He was trying to find new worlds to conquer, bless him; a year ago he wouldn't have recognized a sonnet if it had bit him. "O fairest blossom of the dying year, Leave, if you go, some lingering smell. . . ." "Smell" had been crossed out—and rightly so, Andrea thought—but he had been unable to find a rhyme for "scent." The sonnet was unfinished.

One page was without revisions or crossed-out lines. Here Jim had copied quotations, evidently in the hope of stimulating his fainting Muse. "That undiscovered country from whose bourne No traveller returns. . . ." So he had found *Hamlet*—another confused adolescent. A long passage from *Romeo and Juliet*—"Death, that hath sucked the honey of thy breath. . . ." He might not be able to write poetry, but he could recognize the true metal when he saw it. "We are such stuff as dreams are made on. . . ."

Andrea closed the notebook and replaced it in the drawer. She reached instinctively for the dirty glasses, but remembered in time; everything must be left exactly as she had found it. She'd tell Jim this evening that she intended to clean his room. He would appreciate the effort she was making to respect his privacy.

II

Jim and Martin ignored her rating. Both came to the library after dinner and matters went exactly as Andrea had predicted, which for once gave her little satisfaction. Mr. Bascom complained about the lousy local restaurants and the lousy weather and the lousy, rude people he had met; then, goaded deliberately by Martin, he turned his ire on the lousy government, bellowing non sequiturs in lieu of argument, while the Bascom daughters rolled eyes, hips, and breasts at Jim. Jim tired before Martin did; after less than half an hour he excused himself and fled.

Mercifully the Bascoms stayed only one night. The Hinckleys remained until Monday. Before they left, Mrs. Hinckley asked about Satan. She had never seen him, but evidently his notoriety had spread. She doted on pussycats; her visit would not be complete without a glimpse of the inn's most famous resident; would it be too much trouble . . . ?

What she really wanted—Andrea suspected—was a glimpse of the private sanctum of the inn's most famous two-legged resident. Obviously she couldn't allow curiosity-seekers to intrude on Martin, so she went up and carried Satan down. She was the only one he allowed to handle him—even Martin bore the scars of ill-advised attempts to shift Satan off his papers or his bed—but he growled all the way downstairs. As always, Andrea was struck by his incredible weight. He lay in her arms like a lump of black granite, rumbling.

Mrs. Hinckley did not need to be warned not to touch the pussycat. Satan spat at her and she backed away, murmuring insincere compliments.

Jim had gone to the hardware store to pick up the wallpaper

he had ordered. When he got back, the Hinckleys were still leaving; they had been leaving for almost an hour, and Mrs. Hinckley was apparently prepared to go on leaving indefinitely. Mr. Hinckley, bored but resigned, turned when he saw Jim unloading the car.

"Here, son, let me help you with that," he said.

The offer was kindly meant, but Jim resented it. His face flushed with anger and for a moment Andrea was afraid he would say something rude. He controlled himself, mumbled a thank-you, and followed Hinckley up the stairs.

"What a pity," Mrs. Hinckley murmured. "An accident, I suppose?"

Andrea was tempted to snap, "No, it was self-inflicted," but she kept her temper. She had encountered more direct, impertinent questions than that. She nodded, lips pressed tightly together, and Mrs. Hinckley, more sensitive to nuances than some guests, dropped the subject.

Jim was usually more tolerant than Andrea, but Mr. Hinckley had apparently struck a nerve; when Andrea entered the tower room he scowled and let go of the roll of paper he was holding. It coiled up again, showing only the blank back surface.

"Let's see what you picked," Andrea said, determinedly cheerful.

He made no move to help her, watching sullenly as she pulled out a section. "Good heavens," she exclaimed.

"You hate it."

"No, I don't. It's—very pretty. It just isn't what I expected."

Roses—buds, half-opened and full-blown blossoms—bloomed on a silky cream damask background. Green leaves and coiling stems surrounded the flowers, which ranged from pale shell-pink to a vivid carnation.

Jim had long since passed the stage when he wanted his walls and his bed covered with huge reproductions of football players and NFL symbols in primary colors; but this dainty,

216

feminine paper was the last thing she would have expected him to select. It was, however, a perfect choice for the light, airy chamber with its delicate moldings and high ceiling. Andrea had a sudden vision of the room as it should look— white woodwork, roses climbing the wall, thin muslin curtains at the windows, and soft white draperies around the alcove where the bed would be. A narrow brass bed set with medallions of French enamel, piled with ruffled pillows. . . .

The room would look delightful furnished in that way, but it wasn't what Jim would want. The decorating scheme she had envisioned would only be appropriate for a woman—or a young girl.

"I like it very much," she said. "It's absolutely right for this room. When you're ready, I'll help you hang it."

"I can do it myself."

"But, darling, the ceiling is twelve feet high. You can't possibly—"

"I can do it myself! I don't want any help. I want," Jim said loudly, "to do the whole thing by myself. How many goddamned times do I have to tell you that? Why the hell can't you leave me alone?"

His eyes bulging, his cheeks stained with dark blood, he rose unsteadily. Andrea backed away.

"I'm sorry," she stammered. "If that's what you want—"

"I do want. Now get the hell out of here!"

Breathless and shaking, Andrea ran to her room and closed the door. He had been angry before, but she had never seen him look like that—insane with rage, almost threatening. She had done nothing to deserve it, and neither had poor well-intentioned Mr. Hinckley.

After a while she recovered enough to comfort herself with the now familiar platitudes. He was going through a difficult period. He had lost his temper with her before. He was always sorry afterward. This time was no different except in degree. Once he got over it, he would apologize.

But she had to get out of the house. She didn't want to see anyone, not even Jim—not yet. She would drive to town and do a little shopping. Several of the small baskets she used for breakfast rolls were missing—probably via the suitcases of guests like the Bascoms. Even the casual thieves among them, accustomed to carrying off souvenirs from motels and hotels, would hesitate before stealing her antiques; Haviland china and cut-glass vases were valuable, traceable, and not worth the risk. But the baskets were fair game.

Andrea drove through town. The crisp bright air and the greetings of people she knew made her feel better. By the time she parked in front of the basket shop, which sold a variety of other craft items as well, she had convinced herself there was nothing to worry about.

As she sorted through the piles of baskets Sue Vanderhoff, the proprietor, entered from the back of the shop. Sue was about Andrea's age, and an excellent businesswoman; her baskets and wreaths and pottery had a distinction that raised them above the run-of-the-mill crafts featured by most shops. Recently she had added a line of handmade clothing—woven, patchwork, embroidered—which she modeled herself, though the voluminous peasant skirts and baggy Russian blouses did not suit her short, heavy figure. Hung all around with silver chains, bangles, earrings, and belts, she jingled when she moved.

"Got in some patchwork vests," she said. "I'll let you have one at cost if you'll tell your customers where you bought it."

"I can't afford it, even at cost," Andrea said, with a glance at the price tag on the Texas star vest Sue was holding. "Is business that bad?"

"Business is pretty good, actually." Sue lit a cigarette and dropped her lighter into the pocket of her skirt. "Thanks in part to you. If I weren't so cheap, I'd give you the vest. Maybe if they don't sell. . . ."

218

"They'll sell." Like all Sue's merchandise, the vest was beautifully made, its colors a blend of mauve, rose, and lavender. "I'm doing fairly well myself. I thought trade would slacken in cold weather, but this seems to be the season when the hardcore antique buffs come out of their holes."

"That's what Al Wyckoff was saying at the meeting the other night. You ought to come, Andrea; you're a member, aren't you?"

"The Merchants' Association? Yes, I am. I keep meaning to come, but I'm so damned tired at night, and your last two meetings have been on Friday, which is one of my busiest days."

"I'll talk to Al about scheduling the next one for midweek. He wants to get you in on his latest scheme—a day-long open house, with all of us participating. We can't decide whether a harvest or Christmas theme would be best."

They discussed the plan for a while, and Sue said, "I knew you'd have some good ideas. You've got to come to the next meeting; the inn will be an important part of the deal. Listen, if you're tired that evening, I could come pick you up."

Andrea assured her that wouldn't be necessary, but she was flattered by the offer. She paid for her baskets—ten percent discount to a colleague—and left.

She still didn't want to go home. The weather was chilly but pleasant; hands in her pockets, she wandered down the street. The Thanksgiving decorations were up—cornstalks tied to the lampposts, bunches of Indian corn and brightly colored gourds hanging on the doors. Her steps slowed as she passed the restaurant, and when she saw Reba at the window, waving and gesticulating, she realized that she had hoped to see her. Not that she had any intention of discussing Jim's outburst; she just felt like chatting.

Reba lived above the restaurant, where her rooms included a prettily furnished parlor, but the shabby, overcrowded office was where she spent most of her time, and it was now comfortably familiar to Andrea. She sat down in her usual chair, shifting to avoid the broken spring, and put her feet on a hassock. She had stopped asking Reba to visit her.

"So how's Jim?" Reba asked.

She usually inquired after him, but on that occasion the question smacked of clairvoyance. Andrea replied almost too quickly.

"Fine, just fine. He's working on the house—painting, papering. . . . Doing a good job, too."

"So I hear " Seeing Andrea's expression, Reba chuckled fatly. "You might as well get used to it, Andy. Small towns will talk. It's just neighborly interest."

"Like hell it is."

"People are the most interesting things there are," Reba insisted. "Look at Jane Austen—all she ever wrote about were ordinary people doing ordinary dull things."

Andrea was not in the mood for a literary discussion. "How's business?" she asked.

"Always busy this time of year, through the holidays. Had any interesting suckers lately?"

From the gleam in her eye Andrea knew she had heard about the Bascoms. "I don't know why you ask me. Martin blabs everything to you."

"You don't get 'em like that often," Reba said consolingly.

"No, really I don't. I have someone coming this weekend who sounds interesting. He's supposed to be an authority on old houses. Says he's writing a book. I don't mind people looking the place over if they have a legitimate reason and admit it openly."

"What's his name?"

"Holderman. John William Holderman."

"Holderman?"

"Do you know him?"

"I know of him," Reba said slowly. "He's written several

books. About . . . about local history and architecture. Among other things.''

"He's legitimate, then. I meant to look him up in the library, but I haven't had time.''

"Oh, yeah. He's well known.''

"But you didn't know I was expecting him, did you? Your stool pigeon slipped up on that one.''

"You shouldn't talk about Martin that way,'' Reba said soberly. "He's damned fond of you, Andy.''

"I like him too. He can be a pain in the neck sometimes, but I owe him a lot. I'll be sorry to see him leave.''

"When will that be?''

"Spring, I suppose. He said something about March. Reba, do you know where I can get. . . . Oh, I'm sorry—did you start to say something?''

"I changed my mind,'' Reba said.

Andrea left the restaurant in a much improved mood. Reba had a number of irritating affectations, but her gusty good spirits were infectious. She was about to cross the street when a man passed her, shoving her so that she staggered a few steps before turning to stare indignantly at his retreating form. Something about the big, slouched body was familiar, but she didn't identify him until he reeled around the corner and she saw his face.

Gary Joe—Linnie's "fiancé.'' Andrea had heard, via Reba, that Mr. Hochstrasser had told Gary Joe he was no longer welcome at their house. He had had a couple of brushes with the law—driving while impaired, another fight at the Shamrock. And here he was, drunk and aimlessly wandering, on a work day.

"Are you all right, Andrea?''

The hand on her elbow was that of Al Wyckoff, owner of Past and Present. He was a retired Marine Corps colonel and carried himself with military rigidity. According to Martin, the same description could be applied to his political opinions.

"I saw that roughneck push you," Wyckoff went on. "If you want to lodge a complaint—"

"I'm not damaged. It was an accident. He seems to be a little unsteady on his feet."

"He's drunk," Wyckoff snapped. "Lost his job at the gas station—incompetent and unreliable—so of course his immediate reaction is to get drunk. I don't know what's the matter with these kids. No wonder the country is in such a mess."

"They aren't all like Gary Joe. And there are plenty of worthless bums in our generation, Al."

"Tactful woman." He smiled at her, then sobered. "Have you thought about getting a dog, Andrea?"

"What on earth for?"

"Protection. You're pretty isolated out there."

"Protection against what? Oh, for heaven's sake, Al—you aren't thinking of Gary Joe!"

"He resents you. Blames you and Jim for breaking up his affair with Linnie."

"I'd rather have a gun than a dog," Andrea said flippantly. "Pass the word, Al—I'm going to buy a gun, and if Gary Joe sets foot on my property I'll fill him full of holes."

"That's the spirit," Al said with an approving nod. "You'd do it, too."

"Well—"

"That's an even better idea. You'd have no trouble getting a permit, and I can find you a nice little handgun—a thirty-eight police special, for instance."

"I'll let you know," Andrea said.

When they parted, after discussing a date for the next Association meeting, Wyckoff added, "Don't put off getting that weapon, Andrea. Not that I think you've anything to worry about, but. . . ."

Damn him, Andrea thought as she turned the car and

headed homeward. He's just trying to scare me. She wasn't afraid of Gary Joe. She had dealt with the likes of him before; most were cowed by her resolute air and biting tongue, and she had not scrupled to employ any means necessary on the exceptions. While working at the Washington hotel, she had felled a foul-mouthed drunk who was annoying guests in the lobby by hitting him over the head with a vase when he lunged at her; her victim had required nine stitches, and she only wished it had been more. No, she wasn't afraid of a local yokel like Gary Joe.

Al had a point, though. The house was isolated, and some of her guests were well-to-do. Dog or gun, or both? Maybe Jim would like a dog. He hadn't had one since his adored old mutt had died, a few months after the plane crash. So far as she was concerned, a dog would be an unmitigated nuisance. She had no illusions as to who would feed, water, walk, and clean up after the animal. She would. And it made her shudder to think how Satan would react to a dog. Anything smaller than a Doberman would be torn to shreds.

Yet in some ways a dog was preferable to a gun. She didn't share Martin's silly liberal ideas about gun control, but she did recall reading that more householders were shot with their own weapons than were burglars. Accidents could happen. Boys were unreasonably fascinated by guns. . . . She was thinking, naturally, of the children of guests. If a sixteen-year-old boy found a gun lying around he wouldn't be able to resist handling it, and if he managed to shoot himself, the publicity could ruin her.

A dog might not be a bad idea. Maybe—oh, delightful thought!—maybe the dog would tear Satan to shreds. She would talk to Jim about a dog that evening.

Monday nights were the best in the week. The weekend guests had gone by then and the midweek crowd had not arrived; Peace and Plenty was closed on Mondays, so Martin had gotten into the habit of eating with her and Jim that night.

(He paid extra, of course.) Usually they spent the evening quietly, watching television and talking, nothing exciting—but Andrea looked forward to Mondays.

Mrs. Horner had baked one of her delicious apple pies. Jim loved apple pie. Andrea had planned a casserole, but instead she took a package of steaks from the freezer. A good, well-balanced meal, that was what Jim needed. All that pizza and spaghetti couldn't be good for him.

As twilight deepened, she was tempted to go and call him, but something held her back. When at last she heard the sound of his crutches she was absurdly tense; she had to force herself to relax.

Standing in the doorway, he surveyed the dinner preparations and let out a whistle. "That's quite a spread. What are we celebrating?"

"I couldn't face another of those damned casseroles," Andrea said, returning his smile with an unaccountable sense of danger eluded. He was as anxious to forget the incident as she; even an apology would have recalled a singularly unpleasant moment.

While they were eating Andrea brought up the subject of a dog. Jim's response was unenthusiastic.

"I don't know; it would mean a lot of work for you, wouldn't it?"

"It would be your dog, Jimmie."

"I don't know."

"Why don't you wait till spring?" Martin suggested. "Housebreaking a puppy is a lot easier when the weather is fine."

"That's a good idea," Jim said. "Maybe in the spring."

As soon as he'd finished eating Jim pushed his chair back and picked up his crutches. "That was great, Andy. Leave me a piece of pie, will you? I'll have it later."

"But. . . ." Andrea caught herself. Jim's expression, watchful, defiant, warned her of trouble ahead if she objected.

224

She couldn't stand another explosion like the last one. "I thought you wanted to see that special," she said tentatively.

"I changed my mind. A couple of things I want to finish . . ." He went quickly out.

"Has he always been like this?" Martin asked.

"Like what?" As always, his question put her on the defensive.

"So single-minded—so obsessed."

"That's a horrible word to use. He's finding new interests—"

Martin shook his head. "It's becoming more pronounced. He spends most of his time up there working like a navvy. What's so urgent about the job?"

"I'm not pushing him, if that's what you think."

"I'd rather think that. Then I could give you one of my much-loved lectures. I'm only too well aware of the fact that it was his idea from the start and that he is obsessive—sorry, but that's the only word for it—about getting it done."

"He wants to move into the room—"

"I know. I'm in favor of that."

"You would be."

Martin got up and began clearing the table. "I can also understand why he likes the tower room. It's charming. What I do not understand is why he can't think about anything else. Was that, by any chance, where you found those extremely curious sketches?"

"What are you getting at?"

Her voice was sharp with challenge, not only of what he had said, but what she feared he was about to say. Martin was not the man to avoid an argument; when he shrugged and went to put the dishes in the sink she knew he was not surrendering to her but acknowledging his own uncertainty.

"Nothing that makes any sense. Maybe I'm getting senile."

"You should be working, instead of inventing things to worry about, like a bored old lady." Andrea rose. "Let me do that. You're splashing water all over the floor."

"All right. With such a splendid example of industry before me, I can do no less than attempt to emulate it. Good night, Andrea."

If he hadn't splashed water she would have found some other excuse to interrupt him. She had a fairly good idea of the direction in which his thoughts were running. He dreaded them as much as she did; they contradicted the entire structure of assumptions and axioms on which his life was based. Broad-minded, skeptical, and tolerant, he had no faith, even in his own religion. She understood his quandary, for it was her own. Without fixed rules and prescribed guidelines there were no answers, only an infinite series of possibilities, unproved and unprovable.

Later, she crept up the back stairs, crawling on hands and knees in the dusty darkness, for fear that light might betray her presence. There were no sounds from the tower room, not at first. When she pressed her ear to the keyhole, a big old-fashioned aperture to which the key had never been found, she heard the murmur of Jim's voice.

He might have been reciting poetry or reading aloud. But he wasn't. He was talking to someone, pausing, and then responding. She could not make out the words, nor could she hear a second voice. Just Jim's, talking to someone who wasn't there.

After a while he stopped talking. There was silence for a time. Then she heard another sound—the soft, desolate weeping of a child lost in the dark.

Chapter Twelve

Long after Jim had come downstairs and gone to bed, Andrea lay awake staring at the ceiling. She had left a light burning, but the shadows it cast were almost worse than darkness. She was tired, but she was afraid to sleep—afraid of attack from the hidden enemy in her own mind. Wings, beating against invisible bars, trying to escape—it was a classic symbol whose meaning she could no longer deny. Breaking the bonds of the flesh, soaring into the sunset, releasing the spirit to seek the light; the literature of all the world's religions contained similar phrases. And that was all they were—empty phrases, wishful thinking, desperate hopes for which there was no substantiation. "That undiscovered country from whose bourne No traveller returns. . . ."

Ah, but what if some One had returned? Some One who passed like a shadow through the dark house, perceptible as a terror of the soul to those sensitive enough to feel it—who assailed her with guilt and fear and was luring Jim into the darkness it inhabited? Under all his recent acts lay a common obsession—death. The dead past, the long-dead women who lay in the old graveyard, but whose presences remained in the space where they had once lived.

Andrea's eyes turned to the picture on the opposite wall. She could barely see it, but Mary's features were as familiar to her now as her own, and as she concentrated on them her depression began to lift. There were reasonable explanations for all the things that troubled her, and they made a lot more sense than the fantastic theory she had been considering. Jim was going through a period of adjustment. The doctor had warned her it wouldn't be easy. Temporary setbacks were only to be expected. Leave him alone and let him work it out.

Mary would have understood and agreed. Mary was like her—pragmatic, skeptical—a fighter, a survivor.

Andrea yawned. Turning on her side, she slept, and did not dream.

II

The week before Thanksgiving Kevin called to say he couldn't come. His father had had a severe heart attack in early November, and he had decided to brave the maternal wrath and spend the holiday with his dad.

"Sooner or later you have to do what you think is right, even if it's inconvenient," he explained seriously to Andrea.

"You've made a very mature decision," she said, with equal gravity, and with a new compassion. She of all people knew the devastating shock of that first confrontation with the fact of mortality. She said a few more things—mere platitudes, but they seemed to comfort Kevin—and after she had passed him on to Jim she realized that she was actually disappointed. I must be mellowing in my old age, she thought, faintly amused. Or else Reba is getting to me with all that "nice" nonsense of hers.

Jim bore the disappointment with apparent equanimity. Enlisting the help of Wayne, Martin, and anyone else who could be coerced into carrying things, he moved his belongings to the tower. In Andrea's opinion the room looked odd—Jim's masculine, utilitarian old furniture in that bower of roses and virginal white paint—but he seemed satisfied.

The only comic note in an otherwise depressing week was the arrival of John William Holderman, author and authority on old houses. He came the Friday before Thanksgiving, the last of the four guests Andrea expected that day. The sun was setting in a satanic blaze of scarlet when she opened the door; baring artificially white teeth and enveloped in a long black cape, Holderman appeared to loom over her like Dracula looking for a jugular vein.

Once inside, he shrank to normal size—a dapper little man whose sleek black hair was as artificial as his teeth, and who walked on tiptoe trying to look taller. His manners were reminiscent of the court of Louis the Seventeenth; bowing, kissing Andrea's hand, he thanked her for her courtesy in receiving him and assured her that her lovely home would be prominently featured in his forthcoming book.

Martin took an instant dislike to him. "Pompous little jackass. Who the hell does he think he is, telling me smoking is bad for my health?" Jim was amused and interested. If Holderman had been twice as odd, Andrea would have welcomed him for distracting Jim. He joined them next morning when Andrea showed Holderman over the house and asked a number of questions about construction and materials. Holderman knew all the answers, or sounded as if he did. His admiration of the tower room pleased Jim.

"You did this, young man? Splendid! You have a real feeling for period restoration."

Later, as she made beds and emptied wastebaskets, Andrea caught glimpses of Holderman trotting around the grounds, weighted down with photographic equipment whose straps crisscrossed his slight body like bonds. If she had not known what he was doing she would have thought him an escaped lunatic; he lay flat on the lawn, skulked behind bushes, and climbed trees as nimbly as a monkey, to get a closer shot of a particular architectural feature.

The hope of being mentioned in Holderman's text—"Miss Torgesen, the lovely and gracious chatelaine. . . ." inspired Andrea to search her closet for something glamorous to wear that evening. To her dismay, most of her dressier garments, which she had not tried on for months, were now too big for her. She had lost more weight than she realized. Finally she selected, *faute de mieux*, a dark-green wool that hung loosely from the yoke and could be belted to any diameter required. Forcing her feet into pumps, she limped into the library.

The presence of not one but two celebrities brought the other guests out that evening. Even Jim was there. Martin was chainsmoking, and glaring at Holderman.

Later, Andrea could not recall which of the guests introduced the subject of ghosts. It had happened before; old houses of any era seemed to inspire speculation of that nature, and she had developed a stock response: "I hate to disappoint you, but we've never had anything of that sort here."

On this occasion, however, the question was not directed at her. "Now, Mr. Holderman, admit it—you are ghost-hunting. I read your book and absolutely loved it."

Holderman giggled self-consciously. "Oh, dear. I hoped that youthful effort was forgotten. I haven't dabbled in folklore for many years."

Wreathed in smoke like an evil genie, Martin said, "You're sure of that, Holderman? Miss Torgesen has a prejudice against psychic investigators."

"Dear lady!" Holderman turned to Andrea, his hands fluttering agitatedly. "I hope you don't suppose I would take such an advantage. You have seen my work on architectural history—"

"Of course." Andrea smiled stiffly. "We're honored to be

included in your next volume, Mr. Holderman. It's such an interesting subject.''

The sensation-seeking lady was not so easily distracted. "Oh, yes, but I do love ghost stories, Mr. Holderman. Please tell us about something absolutely terrifying!''

"I can only refer you to the classics, dear madam. Poe and James, Machen and Blackwood—''

"But those are stories. I'm talking about real ghosts.''

"That is a contradiction in terms," Holderman said flatly. "Ghosts are unreal; therefore there can be no such thing as a real ghost.''

Andrea gave him an approving smile. Preening himself, Holderman went on, "The stories I collected in my book, and others of the same nature, can be attributed for the most part to one of two causes: subjective hallucination, or misinterpretation of purely natural phenomena. They are entertaining, particularly on a windy winter night, but they are—stories. Nothing more.''

No one spoke for a moment. Holderman's manner was so dogmatic and so positive that no one wanted to contradict him.

No one except Martin. "For the most part, Mr. Holderman? You do make exceptions, then.''

"There is a third category," Holderman admitted. "A few cases only, reported by reliable witnesses and inexplicable in terms of hallucination or—forgive me—stupidity. I have a theory about them.''

"Naturally you do," Martin purred. "May we ask what it is?''

"Psychic impressions," Holderman said. "Violent emotions, passions, acts—might they not leave an impression, like a sound recording, in the places where they occurred? Pictures invisible to the eye as certain sounds are beyond the range of human hearing, but perceptible at certain times and to certain persons, who are attuned to that specific emotion.''

III

The warmth with which Andrea said good-bye to Holderman next morning gave the little man delusions he cherished for months and prompted one of his most fulsome literary pieces. After the book appeared Andrea wrote him a note of thanks, but he never knew the real reason for her affectionate leave-taking.

Impressions, impersonal as photograph recordings or photographic prints. . . . That must be it, Andrea thought. That explains everything. Reba's negative reaction and her own fondness for the house, shadows in a darkened hallway, dreams of desperate wings. The house had been a hotel; dozens, no, hundreds of people had walked its corridors and slept in its rooms, each with his own history of joy and sorrow. The old house had seen birth and death, love triumphant and love defeated. Some people could tune in to certain wavelengths, but not to all; others were "deaf" to all impressions.

The girl, Mary's daughter—for the moment Andrea couldn't remember her name—had died at seventeen. Jim and "the guys" made a show of toughness, but they were sentimental slobs at heart. They honestly believed that every love was the best and last; it was from their ranks that cynical old generals recruited the warrior children who felt honored to die for the fatherland, for Mom and apple pie. Bored and frustrated, Jim had developed a sentimental attachment to . . . whatever her name was. If he had lived in the nineteenth century, he would have grown Byronic sideburns and written bad verse about beautiful young maidens dying young. No doubt he pictured her as delicate and goldenhaired. Whereas she had probably been squat and sallow and homely as a mud fence.

IV

The inn was fully booked over Thanksgiving, which put a crimp in holiday celebrations. Andrea took a few hours off to dine with Reba at Peace and Plenty and Martin plied them with wine in an attempt to cheer things up, but the weather refused to cooperate, producing the gloomiest, drippingest fog of the year, and even Reba's spirits appeared to be dampened.

It was Monday morning before Andrea had a chance to deal with the minor breakdowns that always occur on a holiday weekend, when repairmen cannot be located. At breakfast she announced that she was going to one of the shopping malls in Frederick—news that was received with the same degree of apathy by Martin and Jim. Armed with a long list, which ranged from apples (stewed, with brown sugar, for breakfast) to a zipper (for the green dress), she tried for five minutes to start the car before she realized the gas tank was bone-dry.

Jim, of course. He had an uncanny knack of using up the last drop of gas just as he pulled into the garage. Andrea ran back to the house. Martin would have to give her enough gas to get to the Amoco station. She would have siphoned it off herself without bothering to ask if his tank had not been fitted with a lock.

Thinking of locks reminded her that he had mentioned there was something wrong with the latch of his door. It wouldn't stay closed. She decided to have a look at it while she was there; it might be something simple she could fix herself.

The door was slightly ajar. As she approached Andrea could hear him talking. He had had his own telephone installed. Reluctant to overhear or interrupt, she hesitated before knocking. Then she heard a phrase that made her forget her scruples: "I'm not happy about his move to the tower."

He was talking about Jim. But to whom? It didn't matter. He had no right to discuss Jim so familiarly with anyone. Andrea put her ear to the door. The next sentence she heard turned her beet-red with fury.

"No, on the contrary, I think he's coped well with his

233

handicap. That's what worries me. . . . What do you mean, why? You're the shrink, you're supposed to know these things. Because it's normal—if I may use that word—for a kid his age to be depressed about losing a leg. If he's not depressed about that, he's depressed about something I can't explain. . . . Not yet. I asked him pointblank the other night if he would see a psychiatrist; he gave me a big boyish smile and said there was no need, he felt fine. But I'll keep working on it. . . . I know you can't. You've already done more than I had any reason to expect. . . . Thanks, Tony. . . . Yes, I will.''

Andrea waited for a few seconds to make sure he was finished. Then she kicked the door open.

Satan was sitting on Martin's typewriter, shedding into the works. He growled. Martin jumped, swore, and dropped the phone. It began to buzz maniacally. Andrea stood waiting in deadly silence while Martin put the pieces back together.

"Damn," he said. "I thought you went shopping."

"Who were you talking to?"

Martin sat down on the unmade bed. He answered without hesitation. "A friend of mine."

"A psychiatrist?"

"One of the best."

"Well, that makes it all right. That justifies your unwarranted interference in our affairs!"

"Sit down," Martin said.

"I don't want to sit down. I want to slug you, you nosy bastard!"

Satan rumbled deep in his throat; the fur on his back stood up in a stiff ridge. Martin sat with folded hands, eyes meekly downcast—a totally inadequate target for the rage that boiled in Andrea. She turned on the cat.

"You shut up! How dare you growl at me? Get the hell out of here—get your big fat furry ass off there!"

Satan leaped off the table and trotted out, moving faster

than was his wont. If Martin had laughed Andrea would have pounded him with her fists. Instead he repeated, "Sit down. You have a right to be indignant, but you ought to listen to me first."

His unwavering calm drilled a hole in the molten shell of her anger; it rushed out, leaving her on the verge of tears.

"Martin, how could you? You had no right."

"He doesn't know Jim's name," Martin said. "He'll never know, unless Jim consents to see him."

"You're crazy. Jim doesn't need a psychiatrist. He's fine."

"He is miserable," Martin said flatly. "He is desperately unhappy. You have an enviable capacity for ignoring things you don't want to see, but even you must have realized that. There have been times when his eyes remind me. . . ."

"Say it. You couldn't offend me more than you have already."

"I once saw a couple of louts push a dog out of their car and take off," Martin said. "I suppose it had become a nuisance to them. It wasn't a particularly attractive animal—a mutt, middlesized, shaggy. . . . It stood there watching the car drive away. Its eyes had the same look Jim's have now. Bewildered, lost, uncomprehending."

After a moment Andrea regained control of her voice. "Damn you, Martin. Of all the low, underhanded rhetorical tricks—"

"It was tacky," Martin admitted. "But it's the truth."

"You're wrong. Jim has problems, I admit that—but he's coping with them."

"If it's any consolation to you, Tony Benson agrees," Martin said.

Her face lit up with surprise and joy. Martin swallowed, and went on reluctantly, "He's speculating in a vacuum, of course. He's never talked to Jim. But according to him, Jim seems to be adjusting to his handicap with remarkable maturity. He's exploring alternatives—reading, carpentry, gardening. . . . I told Tony that. He said, 'So what's the problem, buster?' "

"So what is it?"

"I don't know," Martin mumbled.

"I wish you'd keep your worries to yourself," Andrea said. "They get me upset, even when I don't believe them."

Martin resisted the temptation to point out that it was not his fault that she knew about his worries. "Tony also said," he went on, "that I was suffering from frustrated paternal instincts. You know about that, don't you? Reba told you?"

"Yes." Andrea didn't look at him.

"You never mentioned it."

"I didn't want to sound like—like a—"

"Nosy, interfering bastard? Tony may be right at that. I don't know what it's like to be a father. I wouldn't recognize the symptoms."

Andrea hesitated, but not for long. Friendship, she reminded herself, is the willingness to lie down and listen. Besides, Martin never held his tongue when he thought she was wrong.

"Why did you give up? He's your child, you have the right to—"

"Tear him to pieces?"

"Show him you love him," Andrea said.

"Now who's using tacky rhetorical tricks?" She had hit him where it hurt; his face was flushed and vulnerable, his voice rough with anger. "If that's your idea of love, then heaven help the man who. . . ."

"Go on."

"You know what I was going to say."

"Yes. Now the shoe is on the other foot, isn't it? And you don't like criticism any better than I do."

The angry color in Martin's face subsided. "Got me that time. All right. The agreement works both ways. You're entitled to give me your opinion and I'm entitled to blow up.

But you're wrong, Andrea. Terribly, fatally wrong. Love can't be forced or mastered. Sometimes the only way you can keep it is by letting go.''

V

It was the mildest December in almost twenty years. Three weeks before Christmas the temperature reached sixty, and Andrea spent an hour in the garden trying to push little green shoots back into the ground. Martin caught her at it, and laughed so hard his glasses fell off his forehead.

"What do you think you're doing?"

"They'll freeze," Andrea said anxiously. "They think it's April."

"It won't hurt them."

"Really?"

"Take my word for it."

Andrea straightened, lifting her face to the sun. The day was so warm she wore only a light sweater. "What are those big bushes by the shed?"

"Lilacs. You really are a city slicker, aren't you? Didn't you see them in bloom last year?"

"I don't remember. I guess they must have bloomed—and the others too, the dogwood and forsythia and cherry trees. I can't recall seeing them, though."

"You had other things on your mind."

"I've never done much gardening. We lived in an apartment for so long. . . . I remember years ago helping my mother plant bulbs. She loved flowers. There was one variety—they must have been hyacinths. Big, tall, fluffy things."

"Right." Martin's voice was very soft.

Andrea went on dreamily, "They were the prettiest shade of blue—distinct and yet pale, like a spring sky. I called them my flowers. We'd go out every year, in April, and make a big ceremony of finding the first green shoots."

"How old were you when she died?" Martin asked.

"Twelve. Jimmie was just a baby. Helen—my stepmother—poor thing, she really tried so hard; but I never told her about my flowers. I went by myself the next April. They didn't bloom that year. I thought spring would never come again."

> "Years on years I but half remember . . .
> Man is a torch, then ashes soon
> May and June, then dead December,
> Dead December, then again June. . . .
>
> "One thing I remember;
> Spring came on forever. . . ."

"Vachel Lindsay," Andrea said.

"That's right. I keep forgetting you were an English major."

"Is there anything you don't know about me?" Andrea's smile was rueful but unoffended. "I'm surprised I remember that. I haven't read poetry in years."

"How about a walk along the stream?" Martin suggested. "I'll talk poetry to you. I know lots of poetry."

"I've wasted enough time already," Andrea said.

Martin recognized the tone; with a smile and a shrug, he left her to return to her work.

VI

Always, after a disaster, there is that sense of outrage. Why didn't I know? How could it happen, and I be unaware, even happy? Andrea was happy that day. Jim was unusually gentle and affectionate. Instead of retreating to his room after supper, he spent the evening with her, sprawled on the couch watching television. He didn't say much, but whenever she looked up she found him watching her. It was still early when he rose and said he thought he'd turn in.

"Good night, darling. Sleep well."

Jim put his arm around her and kissed her. "Good night, Andy. I love you."

It had been a long time since he said those words. Andrea was so touched she was unable to respond.

Precisely when the vague uneasiness first started she could not have said. A nagging sense of something forgotten, something unobserved, it grew as time wore on; she ran down her mental list of chores and found no neglect, no omission. The sensation was still undefined when it rose to a violent pitch of alarm that lifted her from her chair, her sewing trampled underfoot as she ran out of the kitchen and up the stairs.

Martin heard her running feet pass his door. She was standing in the doorway of the tower room when he found her. Before he could ask what was wrong she spun around. Her eyes were wide with terror.

"He isn't here. He's gone."

"My dear girl, there are a dozen places and a dozen reasons—"

"No. No. This isn't like the last time. There's something wrong. I can feel it. Help me find him—please, Martin, we have to find him."

Martin trailed after her with the air of one humoring a harmless lunatic, but when Jim was not to be found in any of the obvious places, or in several that were not so obvious, he began to take the matter more seriously.

"Did anything happen tonight?"

"He told me he loved me," Andrea said, and caught her breath.

"Don't get yourself worked up. Think. It's a beautiful night—warm, full moon—maybe he went for a walk."

His voice and the casual touch of his hand on her arm steadied Andrea. "He said he was going to bed. If he decided to go out, on any normal errand, I'd have heard him. He

239

would have to make a deliberate, painful effort to avoid being heard.''

"He's not in the house," Martin said. "Unless he's hiding. I'll look."

"No. The front door—the chain is off. I put it on after supper."

"We'll need a flashlight."

"There's one in the table drawer."

The car was in the garage. The shed where Jim kept his weightlifting equipment was locked and dark. The interlaced branches of the lilacs wrapped them in a web of shadows as Martin moved the beam of light at random across the lawn. The wide acres of meadow and pasture lay silent under the moon.

Andrea shivered. "I know where he is."

Martin didn't argue, or warn her to watch her footing. He was close behind her when she reached the gate in the wall enclosing the graveyard.

Moonlight blanched the standing stones and the sunken rectangles they guarded. The shadows of the tall cedars hid the bench, by the rosebush; at first Andrea saw only a dark shape that seemed too bulky to be a single seated figure. Martin turned his flashlight in that direction. It was Jim. He blinked.

"I took some pills," he said. "It was a mistake. I thought. . . ."

He tried to stand, but lost his balance and fell forward, on hands and knee.

Martin pushed Andrea out of the way. Dropping down beside Jim, he raised the boy's drooping head. "When?"

Jim muttered something Andrea couldn't hear. Martin slapped him across the face, hard enough to rock his head. "How many?"

"It was a mistake," Jim said distinctly.

The light Martin held made a pool of paleness on the

ground, but Andrea could not see what he was doing. The frozen horror that had held her motionless broke; she ran to Jim and took his face between her hands. His eyes were closed.

"Get him to the house," Martin said. "Take that arm, I'll take this one."

They had to drag him, his arms over their shoulders, his foot trailing. When they reached the kitchen, Martin said brusquely, "Sit him up. That chair."

Jim fell into it like a straw scarecrow, arms and head flopping. Andrea reached for the telephone. Martin's hand closed over her wrist, hard enough to hurt.

"Who are you calling?"

"The rescue squad—a doctor—"

"Stop and think. Do you want the whole town talking about this tomorrow?"

"But he's—" Her stiff lips could not pronounce the word.

"He's not dying." Martin opened his clenched hand. The capsules were red on one end, white on the other, filled with tiny globules.

"My sleeping pills. Oh, my God, I forgot—"

"How many were there?"

She pressed her hands against her temples, trying to think. "He gave me a dozen. . . . I took one—no, two."

"There are five here," Martin said. "And I may not have found them all. They're hard to swallow without water. He didn't think of that. He hasn't had a fatal dose."

"You can't be sure."

"I'll make sure," Martin said grimly, and heaved Jim to his feet.

The process was unpleasant in the extreme for all the participants, but primarily for Jim. He didn't resist; in fact he tried, piteously, to cooperate. Andrea finally broke down when she saw him trying to obey Martin's demand that he walk by himself, the crutches slipping from his flaccid hands.

241

Finally Martin said, "You'll do. Sleep it off," and let Jim collapse onto the couch.

Jim's hair and face dripped with water and his naked body shook with involuntary spasms of retching. The cold towels Martin had slapped onto his chest and back had left red patches, like burns. As Andrea bent over him he opened one eye and looked directly at her.

"It was . . . mistake," he said clearly.

"I believe you," Andrea whispered. "It's going to be all right, Jimmie."

"Good," Jim said. Turning on his side, he curled up, wrapping his arms around his shivering body.

Martin spread a blanket over him and tucked it in. The gentleness of the gesture, after the rough handling he had given the boy, was too much for Andrea. Martin steered her to a chair as her knees buckled.

"You need a drink," he said. "Then off you go to beddy-bye."

"I'm going to sit up with him."

"So am I. Neither one of us will get any sleep. Does that make sense?"

She reached for the glass he handed her and observed, with vague surprise, that her fingers would not bend to hold it. Martin muttered under his breath, and held the glass to her lips. "Down the hatch."

It was straight bourbon and it exploded like a firebomb in her churning stomach. She wiped her eyes and tried to catch her breath.

"Better?" Martin asked.

"Yes. No. . . . I felt better when I didn't feel. If you know what I mean."

"I know exactly what you mean." Martin lifted his own glass in a sardonic salute. "Here's to better days."

"Oh, my God—"

"Drink up."

The next swallow wasn't explosive, only warming. Martin reached for the bottle and refilled his glass. The dark stubble on his cheeks blended into the purple stains under his sunken eyes.

"It was a mistake," Andrea said. "An accident."

"If you believe that, perhaps you'd like to buy my share of the Brooklyn Bridge."

"You heard him."

"Yeah," said Martin, pouring a third drink.

Andrea finished hers. "Are you calling my brother a liar?"

"You're drunk," Martin said. "Congratulations. Go to bed."

"I am not drunk. I will have more."

"Why not? The sooner you fall on your face, the sooner I can put you to bed."

"Bed, bed, is that all you can talk about? You saved Jimmie's life. You're wonnerful. An' I resent you like hell. Why are you doing this? Why are you always around, doing this and doing that?"

"You don't know?" Martin stared blearily at her over the rim of his glass. "You dunno. You're the only one in the whole goddamn town who doesn't. They laugh and nudge each other when I walk by—there's that lovesick jackass who hasn't even got the guts to tell the girl how he feels."

"Love," Andrea repeated. "Who? Me?"

"Son of a bitch," Martin said mournfully. "I never thought a couple of drinks would go to my head like that. . . . I'm tired. I'm tired, and I'm sick, and I'm still cold inside when I think how close he came. . . . Yes, love, you." He gave a short grating laugh. "My God, if this isn't the love scene of the century. Here I sit, looking like Wallace Beery and smelling like a cesspool, half soused, making my declaration of undying passion to a lady who is even drunker than I am. Are you sober enough to wonder why I haven't bothered to mention this tedious subject before? It's not because of my innate modesty, I assure you. I'm bald and overweight and fifteen years your senior, but that's not what held me back. I was afraid you'd kick me out if I told you how I felt. You don't want me. You don't want anybody. There isn't room in your mind or your heart for anyone except. . . . No, not Jim—the bloated, warped image of Jim you've set up to be your idol and your cross. Can't you see what you're doing to yourself—and to him?''

Andrea's eyes were as big as saucers. The only emotion left in her drained mind was surprise. Martin's speech was so out of character that she felt as if he had turned shape, like a werewolf. Not knowing what else to do, she finished her drink.

''Catharsis isn't all it's cracked up to be,'' Martin said, in his normal voice. ''What a night. Near tragedy succeeded by howling farce. . . . How do you feel?''

''I don't know.''

''That makes two of us.''

Jim began to snore. Andrea's head turned, as if drawn by a magnet, and Martin said, ''I'll watch him.''

''Maybe I better lie down,'' Andrea muttered. She put her glass on the edge of the table, watched it wobble, and pushed it with her finger. ''In my room. I'll be right there. You call me if—''

''I will.'' He sat poised, ready to go to her assistance if she fell, but she got to the door with only a few stumbles. She turned.

''I'll talk to you in the morning,'' she said ominously, and reeled through the door.

Martin covered his face with his hands. His shoulders shook, but it would have been hard to say whether he was laughing or crying.

Chapter Thirteen

"Sure, I'll go see the guy," Jim said. "If you want me to."

Andrea had never been so conscious of the twelve years' difference in their ages. After sleeping most of the day, Jim was back to normal, whereas she felt as if she had been put through a wringer. Watching him shovel in quantities of leftover casserole and half of Mrs. Horner's pie, her stomach heaved.

Martin had only picked at his food. A stranger comparing him and Jim would have unhesitatingly selected him as the one who had overindulged. He appeared to be suffering from a massive hangover, and although "tactful" was not a term Andrea would have applied to his conversational technique, he was normally a little more oblique than he had been on this occasion. Without introductory comments or any reference to Andrea's opinion, he had blurted out, "I want you to see a psychiatrist friend of mine, Jim. Will you go?"

Jim's ready response caught him unawares. He had geared himself up for an argument, and when his prepared speech became unnecessary he was at a loss for words. He averted his eyes as Jim polished off the pie and gulped down a glass of milk.

A look of amused affection narrowed Jim's eyes as he surveyed the silent, dissolute figures of his elders. "I'm sorry I put you through that crap last night," he said. "It was a stupid-ass thing to do. I won't ever try that again. I guess there's no reason why you should take my word for it, though. I'll do whatever you say."

"Why?" The word burst from Andrea. "Jimmie, why?"

"It was a mistake," Jim said. His eyes shifted momentarily and then returned, wide and candid, to meet Andrea's. "I only took a few of the pills. All of a sudden I knew . . . well, I knew I was doing a dumb thing. I tried to make myself throw up, but it didn't work, and I wanted to get back to the house, but I was getting so groggy I couldn't move. . . . Then I really got scared. I called you. Did you hear me?"

"Yes," Andrea said. "I heard you."

"That's enough bathos," Martin grumbled. "Jim, I'd like to kick your ass from here to Baltimore and back. I'm not the sucker your sister is. As far as I'm concerned, you're on probation."

"Can't blame you," Jim said amiably.

"You'll go with me to see Tony, as soon as he can take you?"

"Sure, Martin. Whatever you say." He reached in his pocket and tossed a jingling bundle onto the table. "Here, Andy. I'm grounding myself."

"Oh, honey, that isn't necessary—"

"I have to prove myself before you can trust me. Words aren't enough." He leaned forward, his eyes steady and shining. "But I'll say them anyway. *It's all right.* I was mixed up about a lot of things. I still don't know all the answers, but I'm sure of one thing. I'm a very lucky person. I love you, Andy. Martin, I love you too. Never thought I'd say that to another guy!"

"Hmph," said Martin, trying not to show how touched he was.

"So—well, I guess that's it. Can I have another piece of pie?"

Martin excused himself shortly thereafter, saying he had work to do. Leaving Jim lying on the couch watching a basketball game, Andrea went upstairs. Her feet dragged. She was no more anxious for a confrontation than was Martin, with his feeble excuses about working, but she knew she couldn't ignore this particular awkwardness in the hope that it would go away.

At first she didn't think he was going to let her in. He blocked the doorway, looking down at her with a determined lack of expression, until she said, "We have to talk."

Martin's lips twisted. "I've talked too goddamned much already. Oh, hell, I guess you're right. Come in."

Satan was sprawled in the middle of the bed. He gave Andrea a bored look and closed his eyes. Andrea was strongly tempted to boot him out; it was almost as bad as having a third party present during a private and delicate interview—not a sympathetic person either, but a cynical critic. Before she could yield to this weakness Martin said,

"I hoped you were too loaded last night to remember what I said."

"I thought maybe you were too loaded to mean what you said."

"No such luck, lady. There is unquestionably *veritas in vino*. What are you going to do about it?"

She had not been able to look at him at first. Now she could face him, for his mocking voice and half-smile contradicted the declaration whose truth he had just confirmed. "That depends on you," she said uncertainly.

"Me? I'm not going to do anything. You're safe from my lecherous advances, if that's what is worrying you."

"I'm not worried."

It might have been taken the wrong way, but she knew Martin would understand. "Thanks," he said soberly. "Andrea, what I said last night doesn't really concern you. It's my problem. All you have to do—if you can—is forget I said it. If I had any dignity I'd get the hell out of here, but I'm not going to do that unless you tell me to go. I want to stay."

"Because of Jim?"

"That's part of it. I care for him a great deal. Even if I didn't—care—for you, I'd want to do what I can for Jim."

Andrea sat down on the bed, her hands clasped. "I want you to stay."

He understood that too—the promise, and the limitations. Eyes shuttered, he watched her without speaking until she could go on. "I want you to stay as a friend. I didn't fully realize until last night how much I depend on you. It's a little late to say thank you, but it's never been easy for me to say thanks, or ask help from other people."

"You didn't ask for it, it was thrust upon you. What's bothering you, Andrea?"

"It's so unfair," she burst out. "I take so much from you and I can't give you anything in return—"

Martin's laughter was free and uninhibited. "You've been wallowing in romantic novels, dear. I thought you were too intelligent to believe that tripe. 'The pale rose of friendship does not satisfy a heart yearning for the crimson rose of love.' Friendship is rarer than love, Andrea. Coming from you, it means a great deal."

"Then it's all right?" she asked hopefully.

"Yes, you poor little thing, it's all right. Just leave it to Uncle Martin."

II

By the time Martin was through with him, Jim had been examined by half a dozen different medical specialists. The only thing Jim protested about was the physical.

"Oh, shit, Martin, do I have to? I've had so many needles stuck in me over the past year, I leak like a sieve. And I hate walking through the waiting room carrying that goddamn little bottle."

Martin looked sympathetic but did not yield.

"I may faint," Jim said darkly.

The form he had to fill out resembled one of the IRS's more diabolic inventions. He worked on it the night before he was to see the doctor, muttering and grumbling. "How the hell am I supposed to know if I had chicken pox?"

"You did," Andrea said, from across the table. "Not measles; you were inoculated against that."

"Urinary infections? Fainting spells?" Jim's pen moved smoothly down the list, checking off negative answers. "Holy God, I never knew so many things could go wrong with the human body. Double vision, epilepsy, high blood pressure, headaches. . . . I'm healthier than I thought."

He was, said the internist, in excellent health. By the end of the week he had checked out one hundred percent with everyone except the psychiatrist. Benson had agreed to see Jim three times, for diagnostic purposes. Andrea knew they owed this consideration to Martin's influence. A psychiatrist of Benson's reputation did not take new patients on such short notice.

The results of the medical examination encouraged her, but the change in Jim's behavior was the most conclusive proof of his return to normalcy. Cheerful and buoyant, affable, cooperative, he showed not the slightest sign of the moodiness that had affected him earlier. He had said that taking the pills was a mistake. Andrea believed him. The sleeping capsules were labeled, but Jim might not have read the label or recognized the name; he could have mistaken them for tranquilizers or amphetamines. His generation used drugs as panaceas for all their troubles, looking for highs, lows, increased perception, augmented sexual potency, and God knew what else. The only surprising thing was that he had not resorted to them before.

She was on pins and needles the day Jim and Martin went for the third and final visit to the psychiatrist. Not that she was afraid Benson would say Jim still had suicidal tendencies; if he said that, he was wrong. What she dreaded was Benson's interpretation of her relationship with Jim. He was bound to find something nasty and Freudian lurking in the woodshed, especially with Martin instilling his own prejudices. Martin's criticism wasn't based on Freud, but it was equally unpalatable: "Smother love, tied to his sister's apron strings. . . ."

What she resented most was the fact that she might never know what Benson said. She had been outraged when Martin told her the psychiatrist was not going to report his findings to her. "You are not entitled to know," he said flatly. "You're not Tony's patient, Jim is."

Jimmie will tell me, Andrea assured herself. I'll get it out of him somehow.

She had no intention of trying to pump Jim when Martin was present. They would have a casual, companionable evening, as they did every Monday. She put a bottle of wine on ice and made Jim's favorite canapés—cocktail sausages stuffed with cheese and wrapped in bacon, ready to put under the broiler.

They were even later than usual, and by the time they arrived Andrea was talking to herself. "He knows how worried I am. . . . Inconsiderate, thoughtless. . . ." When the kitchen door opened, the bright smile she had fixed on her face two hours earlier started to slip. Hastily she turned to put the canapés in the oven.

They didn't say hi, how are you, sorry we're late. Instead

they continued with their argument about raising the legal drinking age.

"Statistics prove you're wrong," Martin insisted. "The eighteen-to-twenty-five age group has the highest fatalities from drunk driving—"

"Statistics don't count with individuals. What that law does, it punishes me for somebody else's crime."

Andrea swung around. "Hello, there," she said.

"Hi," Jim said, throwing his jacket on the floor. "My point, Martin, is that—"

"You're late."

"Sorry. Reba flagged us down while we were passing the restaurant. She wants to know if we can have Christmas dinner with her."

"I can't plan that far in advance. I want to know what we'll be doing next week."

"Same as usual, I guess," said Jim.

Andrea abandoned subterfuge. "When is your next appointment?"

Jim looked blank. "Oh, you mean the shrink. I'm through."

"I know you're through with Dr. Benson," Andrea said tightly. "What does he want you to do next?"

"I think something's burning," Jim said.

Andrea turned with a shriek. The canapés were a sorry wreck. The bacon was charred black and most of the cheese had oozed out onto the broiler.

"Hey, that's the way I like 'em," Jim said, as she mourned over the corpses.

Martin caught Andrea's furious eye and said quickly, "Tony suggested Jim might join an encounter group. Young people his age."

"Well?" Andrea turned on Jim, hands on her hips. "Are you going to?"

"Whatever you say." Jim blew moistly on a blackened hot dog and popped it into his mouth.

"What do you want to do?"

"I thought maybe if you guys were through taking me apart you might let me go back to what I really want to do," Jim said mildly.

"And what is that?" Martin asked.

"Enjoy life " Jim said, reaching for another canapé.

III

Andrea was so impatient to talk to Martin that he was barely out of the room before she started after him. "I want to ask him about Christmas," she explained.

Jim rolled his eyes and grinned. "Oh yeah?"

"You're disgusting."

"I don't think it's disgusting, I think it's cute."

Andrea fled.

Martin was expecting her. The door opened before she could knock. Ushering her in, he said, "We've got to stop meeting like this."

"I could kill you—both of you. You deliberately stalled—"

"I was preparing my stomach for a large helping of crow," Martin said with a wry face.

It took her a moment to understand. "You mean—"

"Mmm-hmmm. Tony wouldn't go into detail; he said he was violating all his professional instincts by telling me as much as he did. To put it in a nutshell, he's bought Jim's explanation of the pills. Says it is absolutely impossible, in his opinion, that Jim intended to commit suicide."

Andrea's relief was so profound she couldn't speak. Martin proved he was no saint by adding maliciously, "He also recommended, strongly, that Jim get away from you."

Andrea was too happy to take the suggestion seriously. "I knew he'd say something like that. Psychiatrists are such cynics; they don't believe in normal, loving family relationships."

"Come down off your cloud," Martin snapped. "You don't really believe Jim is going to spend the rest of his life here, do you? He's not seriously handicapped; people with far worse disabilities have made careers for themselves, married, had families. I swear, Andrea, I can see the picture in your mind—you and Jim fifty years from now, spinster sister and bachelor brother, running this place and puttering around with your harmless hobbies, sterile and withered and dried up—"

"You're the rudest man I have ever known," Andrea exclaimed. "I don't know why I listen to you."

"Because you know I'm right. Jim ought to be going back to college. It's probably too late now; his application should have been in months ago."

"That is an unreasonable attitude, Martin. The time to submit applications was last fall. Jim was just out of the hospital. He needed a period of recuperation."

Martin lifted his shoulders and threw his hands out. "Why do I bother?" he asked Satan.

Andrea answered for him. "I don't know. All I want you to do is admit you were wrong about—"

"Oh, no." Martin pushed a pile of books off a chair and sat down. "I don't give a damn what Tony says, I still don't buy the accident theory. Jim meant to kill himself that night. Something made him change his mind. I don't know what it was, and he isn't about to tell me. I don't doubt, however, that he has changed. For one thing, he has lost interest in the most morbid of his obsessions—the ghost of Alice Fairfax."

"What are you talking about?"

"You know what I'm talking about. You were the first to notice his macabre interest in the graveyard. You were right there and I was wrong, three cheers for you and another helping of raw crow for me. Come on, Andy, you must have realized it wasn't Mary Jim was interested in. It was Alice. Her room in the tower, her grave in the cemetery—"

"Alice's grave?"

"You haven't a spark of imagination, have you?" Martin asked disagreeably. "That's Alice's grave, next to her mother's. Why else would Mary choose to lie there, instead of being properly planted in the Episcopal cemetery where her father is buried? Why would she have that epitaph carved on her tombstone unless it was a warning to posterity: Don't move my bones, this is where I want to remain. And the flower, the damask, the Rose of Castile—"

"You told me yourself it was impossible for a rose to live that long. You're making that story up."

"I didn't say 'impossible,' I said 'unusual.' And I can't prove Mary planted the rose on her daughter's grave. It doesn't matter. Maybe your cousin Bertha planted it, in her youth, after she noticed the stone and felt sorry for the girl who died at seventeen. It's a romantic age—sloppy and sentimental, you would say. But I think that may be the explanation for Jim's fantasies about Alice. Today's youth hasn't lost that romanticism, they have only learned to hide it. Jim was at loose ends and his secret fantasies turned sick on him."

Andrea had come to similar conclusions. Perhaps it was Martin's air of smug certainty that prevented her from admitting it.

"I still don't understand why you're so sure Alice is buried there. It's all surmise—"

"It's fact, my dear. And Jim knew it for a fact. That book he borrowed from Reba has the details."

"What book?"

Martin looked at her pityingly. "If you'd take the time to dream a little and laugh a little and pay a little attention to what other people are thinking. . . . But I guess it's not your fault. You've never had the time, have you?

"The book I'm talking about is the one that contains records of local cemeteries. When the author copied the stones in the Springer graveyard in 1938, many of them were still standing. Mary's was not among them, but Alice's was intact. He copied the name and the dates. That's all there was on the stone.''

"He knew all along? Why didn't he tell me?''

"You'd have laughed at him,'' Martin said.

"I would not!'' Andrea jumped to her feet. "I've taken all the insults I'm going to take from you, Martin Greenspan. In case it's slipped your mind, I was right this time and you were dead wrong. Eat your crow, and I hope it chokes you!''

IV

Martin put his head around the kitchen door. "Busy?''

"Yes.'' Andrea did not look up.

Martin edged in and sat down on the sofa, like a patient in a doctor's waiting room. Andrea went on with what she was doing. He was such an exasperating man. . . . However, his refusal to hold a grudge was one of his more attractive qualities. You could have a knock-down, drag-out screaming match with Martin one day, and he'd be smiling and affable the next time you saw him.

She took a little longer than she would ordinarily have done over the accounts, and then said, with a resigned look, "Yes?''

"What are you doing? The monthly accounts?''

"Yes.''

"You seem extraordinarily cheerful. Doing my accounts always puts me in a terrible mood.''

"I feel cheerful.'' Euphoria rose like a fountain from her feet to her smiling face; she threw her arms in the air. "Martin, I'm going to make it! We've done even better than I dared hope. I took such an awful risk when I poured every penny we had into this place; sometimes I'd lie awake all night adding up those endless bills and thinking I must have been crazy—but now I'm sure. It's going to be all right.''

"That's great. You deserve it, Andy.''

Barbara Michaels

"You helped a lot." Andrea hugged herself in sheer exuberance. "This is going to be the best Christmas of all time. And I haven't even started my shopping! What would you like for Christmas, Martin?"

She heard him catch his breath, and her smile faded. "Sorry. I keep feeding you straight lines, don't I?"

"You have a deplorable weakness for clichés. I wasn't thinking what you thought I was thinking. You looked like a little girl counting the days till Santa Claus comes. I think it's the first time since I've known you that you appeared to be completely, gloriously happy."

"It's the first time I've had reasons to be happy." She counted, solemnly, on her fingers. "I'm solvent—what a drab word for that marvelous condition! Jim is completely recovered. I own a beautiful, charming home; I have friends. . . ."

"I think I prefer you in your caustic mood," Martin said judiciously. "This sweetness-and-light routine is out of character."

"You're an old grouch." Andrea propped her chin on her hand. "We'll have a huge Christmas tree," she murmured. "I kept mother's ornaments, and there are boxes and boxes of Bertha's in the attic. . . . A twenty-pound turkey and all the trimmings. . . . Holly and pine boughs and wreaths all over the house. . . . Church on Christmas Eve, carols, and the organ playing . . . You are going to spend Christmas with us, aren't you? Or—I'm sorry, I didn't think. Is Christmas against your principles?"

"I'm extremely ecumenical," Martin said gravely. "I don't find any harmless celebration offensive. I'd be honored to spend the day with you. I'll even go to church. What do you want for Christmas, Andrea?"

"You don't have to—"

"Forget I asked. You'd only mention something useful and dull, like a new broom. I'll use my imagination."

Andrea pulled a pad of paper toward her. "I've got to start

256

my shopping. I want to get something really nice for Jim. Some parts for his hi-fi, or even a video tape recorder. . . ." She turned back to Martin. "Did you come in here for some reason?"

"I brought you the mail. There's a package from John William Holderman."

"He said he'd send me copies of the photographs." She took it eagerly.

"I thought as much. I'm curious to see how they came out."

The parcel had been packed with the finicky care she might have expected from Holderman. Inside the brown paper, painstakingly sealed with yards of tape, was a heavy cardboard box to which a white envelope had been affixed.

"Cheating the U.S. mails," Martin said, with satisfaction. "Personal letters are supposed to go first class. What's he say?"

Andrea handed him the note. Martin read it aloud; like many lecturers and speakers, he loved the sound of his own voice.

" 'Dear Miss Torgesen, I cannot thank you enough for your charming blah, blah and so on. . . . Greatly enjoyed . . . hmm hmmm. . . . The incisive wit of Mr. Greenspan. . . .' " He gave Andrea a sheepish grin. "It was more incisive than witty, wasn't it?"

"You were rather churlish," Andrea replied, picking at the tape around the box.

"Whereas you were 'a fitting hostess for a home of distinctive elegance.' Then he says, 'It is curious how the camera can bring out features unseen by the human eye.' What does he mean by that?"

"We'll soon see." Andrea finally succeeded in wrenching the lid off the box. The photographs were five-by-seven glossies, and there were almost a hundred of them. "They are superb," Andrea said admiringly. "Look at this detail of the parlor mantel. I never realized this part of the carving was meant to be a sea horse; I always thought it was just a meaningless ornamental curve. That must be what he meant, about the camera showing things the eye doesn't see.''

"No," Martin said. "I think he was referring to this.''

His voice was so odd that Andrea looked at him in surprise. Silently he handed her the photograph he had been examining.

It was a shot of the exterior of the tower, not from ground level, but from a point about halfway up. She couldn't imagine how Holderman had taken it from that height until she remembered the apple tree. He must have climbed practically to the top and leaned out at a perilous angle, for the camera had been aimed straight up at the roof of the tower. It was an unusual and rather frightening viewpoint; the entire structure appeared to be toppling slowly toward the photographer, who seemed in imminent danger of being crushed.

Two windows of the tower room were visible. In one of them—the north window—was a pale shape, like a featureless human figure.

"Jim must have been standing at the window," she said.

"It isn't Jim.''

"A reflection, then. A cloud.''

"There were no clouds in the sky that day. It was perfectly clear.''

"What is it, then?''

"Dunno.''

Andrea looked again. The closer she looked, the less distinct the shape became. "It could be anything. A trick of the light—''

"It's hard to make out," Martin admitted.

"All right, Martin." Andrea leaned back and folded her hands with an air of exaggerated patience. "I know that tone. What do you think it is?''

"That's how she died. Alice Fairfax. She fell, or jumped, from that window.''

After a moment Andrea said, "How do you know?"

"The newspaper, of course. The font of all knowledge. It took me a while to find the paragraph. There's no index, and I didn't know the month."

"Fell, or jumped?"

"That's what it said in the paper. In a case of that sort no one could be certain, unless she left a note. Which apparently she did not."

"But you, of course, think she jumped," Andrea said. "Are you inventing a new plot, or what?"

"I'm evaluating the evidence," Martin said, refusing to take offense. "Your experience at that same window—and now this."

"This isn't evidence." Andrea pushed the photograph away. "It's a light streak. You said yourself that a lot of people have an impulse to jump when they stand in a high place."

"Oh, right. I said a number of things, most of them stupid."

"So you're becoming a believer—in ghoulies and ghosties and Reba's upset stomach?"

"I'd be happier if I did believe," Martin said plaintively. "Anything would be better than the state of amorphous indecision in which I exist these days."

"That's your problem, not mine. I'm perfectly satisfied, and I don't intend to think about it again. I'm going Christmas shopping."

"Fine with me. What can I do to contribute to the jollity of the season? I'd make a pretty fair Santa Claus, don't you think?" He patted his stomach.

"You've lost weight, haven't you? I'm afraid you'd need a pillow to fit the part."

"Flattery will get you anything you want," Martin said off-handedly. He looked pleased, though, and Andrea smothered a smile. Men accused women of being vain, but they were just as bad.

"We're all a little too old for Santa Claus, more's the pity. I'm going to insist that Reba come here for dinner. It's time she got over those absurd notions of hers."

"You don't cure people of irrational ideas by pointing out that they are irrational," Martin protested.

"Maybe they weren't completely irrational." Martin's eyebrows rose, and Andrea laughed. "No, I'm not a believer either. But I was impressed by what Mr. Holderman said the other evening, about strong emotions leaving a sort of psychic imprint. That would account for Reba's experience. Once she understands that it is impersonal and harmless, she won't be afraid of it."

"It's possible," Martin said, without conviction.

"Well, when you talk to her about it, don't sound so doubtful. We've got to make her believe that's all it is. Half the battle is believing something is true."

"Oh, dear, it must be wonderful to know all the answers," Martin said.

V

Jim entered into Andrea's plans for Christmas with charming enthusiasm.

"He's too charming," Martin muttered. "I don't like it."

Andrea had nagged him into helping her cut greens for the house. The wind blew chill across their faces as they crossed the frozen meadow toward the trees; the dried weeds crunched under Martin's galoshes, which were new, and a little too big for him. He kept tripping over his feet.

"You're never satisfied," Andrea retorted. "First you say he looks like a lost puppy and now you're worried because he's too happy. Make up your mind."

"The normal human state is somewhere between misery and bliss. The kid is euphoric. He acts like someone who has fallen in love—or found Jesus."

"Bitch, bitch. Watch out for the rabbit hole."

Martin tripped, staggered, and recovered himself. "He's not on drugs, is he?"

"Who, Jim? Are you still harping on him?"

"If he is, I'd like the name of his supplier," Martin muttered. "He's on a permanent high. It's as if he—"

"This tree is nice and thick," Andrea interrupted. "Do you want to pick up pine cones or cut boughs?"

"My knees don't give so good, as Mrs. Horner might say. I'll cut."

"You poor old codger."

"I'm forty-six," Martin said. He clipped industriously for a few minutes and then added, "Old enough to be Jim's father."

Andrea did not reply, so Martin increased the intensity of his provocation. "Found any more poems in his desk?"

"Damn it, Martin." Andrea threw a handful of pine cones into the basket and stood up, pushing her hair back under her knit cap. "Have you been spying on me?"

"People who live in glass houses—"

"You don't think I wanted to pry, do you? I had to. I never did it before—well, not very often. There was all that drug business when he was in high school, and I felt it was my duty—"

"Don't defend yourself so vehemently." Martin dropped the secateurs and lowered himself, grunting, onto a fallen log. "Did you find any drugs?"

"He was growing a marijuana plant. In the closet, with a plant light."

"Ingenious," Martin said with a grin. "You still haven't answered my first question."

He touched the log beside him and after a moment Andrea shrugged and sat down. The woods were very quiet. In summer the paths were almost impenetrable, a jungle-thick interlacing of honeysuckle and waist-high weeds, grown wild and exuberant in the damp, hot climate. Now the frail skeletons of stem and leaf lay flattened underfoot and the pine needles gave off a faint spicy scent. The globe of the declining sun hung like a giant crimson fruit in the network of branches west of them.

"I haven't looked since he moved to the tower," Andrea said.

"Why not?"

"I told you. I hated doing it. . . ."

"You don't like that room, do you?"

"That has nothing to do with it. The main reason is that I don't feel any longer that it is necessary. You said it—he's happy."

"I keep thinking of that first little masterpiece you showed me."

"I've forgotten it," Andrea said.

"The hell you have. It was a rotten poem, but the images continue to haunt me. The road map and the bridges fallen. . . . That figure of speech describes his behavior these last months. He was searching for something. One frantic attempt after another—one road after another found to be impassable. . . ."

"And now he's found what he was looking for."

She expected Martin to disagree. Instead he nodded. "Yes, he's found it. I only wish I knew what it was."

VI

A few days before Christmas Andrea sat in her room wrapping presents. The door was closed. On it hung a sheet of paper on which she had scrawled: "No Admittance. Knock Before Entering. This Means You!" Jim was sequestered in his room, presumably engaged in the same activity. The sign on his door was even more emphatic.

Coils of ribbon, crimson and green and gold, strewed the bed. The crisp bright paper made soft crackling sounds as she folded it around her parcels. The radio was tuned to a local station that had promised an afternoon of Christmas music. Andrea's spirits were so high that even gems such as "Jingle Bell Rock" and "I Saw Mommy Kissing Santa Claus" only made her smile. The sole traditional item missing was snow; there was little chance of that, according to the weather forecast, although the low-hanging gray clouds looked threatening and a sharp wind rattled the branches of the trees outside the window.

Business had been slow the past week, but she was fully booked from the nineteenth to the twenty-fourth. Many of the nearby communities sponsored Christmas open houses and walks and celebrations; next year, perhaps, Ladiesburg would have a festival of its own. Andrea had formulated plans which she meant to present at the next Merchants' Association meeting; the inn would, of course, play a large part. Her Christmas decorations were intended to show the town what she could do along that line—a traditional Victorian Christmas, with wreaths and greenery, big red velvet bows, and Cousin Bertha's spun-glass ornaments. Everything was done except for the tree itself and the ropes of boxwood and pine boughs that would frame doorways, mantels, and mirrors. Greens dried out so quickly in the house; they couldn't be arranged until the last minute. It would be an all day job, but it would be fun, with Jim and Martin helping.

Poor Martin. He was trying hard to simulate a festive spirit, but she knew his heart wasn't in it. His religious scruples were not the problem; he would strip and paint himself blue and join in the ritual observances of the ancient Druids with perfect equanimity if he were so inclined. Andrea knew what was bothering him. She wished she could convince him there was no cause.

Her busy fingers stopped as she glanced from the bow she had just tied to the picture hanging by the door. She couldn't imagine why she had once found it disturbing. It was really

263

quite lovely, combining the charm of primitive portraiture with the skill of an untrained but talented artist. And what a face it was—not beautiful, the struggles of life had left their scars on cheeks and brow. But the strength, the resolution. . . .

Andrea raised her hand in salute. Then she gave a soft, self-conscious little laugh. No, Martin would never understand; he thought of her as narrow and unimaginative, yet his was the truly narrow mind. Like all self-proclaimed skeptics, he had a buried streak of primitive superstition running through him; when faced with something out of the ordinary, his first reaction was apprehension and alarm.

She reminded herself she must be fair. She had felt alarm too, in the beginning. Yet from the beginning she had been conscious of a force, sustaining and supportive. How else could she have survived the back-breaking work and terrible anxieties that would have crushed most people? It had always been with her—not a ghost or a restless spirit, that was nonsense—but the imprint of a will so strong it had survived for half a century to reinforce a woman with similar strengths and similar needs. She was able to draw on that strength because she and Mary were so much alike. A mind of another pattern would not feel or receive it, just as a body would reject an organ from a donor who was of the wrong type.

Why shouldn't it be true? And if it was not true, what was the harm in believing it? Many people had private superstitions. Mary was hers—a talisman, a good-luck charm, a guardian angel.

Poor Martin. . . . Her invitation to spend Christmas with them had been a sudden, spontaneous impulse, but she didn't regret it. She was very fond of Martin. He could be maddening at times, but he was sweet and funny and utterly dependable. She owed him a great deal. Hopefully they could go on being friends after he left. Anything else was out of the question, naturally. Not for the insulting reasons he had suggested; she just wasn't attracted to him, sexually or romantically. She felt sure he didn't care for her in that way either. A man in love wouldn't remain so detached—never touching, never seeking closeness. He was ripe for marriage, that was his trouble—lonely, dreading old age. He had imagined he was in love with her because she was there. Any woman would do as well. If he were married, with a family of his own, he would stop interfering in her life and Jim's.

That business of Jim's interest in the girl who had died young—it was typical of Martin to read all the wrong things into it. He thought of it as morbid, a sick fantasy. It was nothing of the kind, only a sensitive boy's daydream, a passing crush no more dangerous than her own youthful passion for movie stars and heroes of swashbuckling novels.

She could enjoy Martin so much if he would just stop bugging her about Jim. That was the source of almost all their arguments. Naturally she wanted Jim to lead a normal life. He would go back to college eventually—when he felt well enough—there were several excellent little schools nearby. If he chose to live on campus, that was his decision; but if he had a car of his own. . . . She could afford to buy him one next fall, assuming that business continued to improve.

If he wanted to leave, she wouldn't stop him. But why shouldn't his vision of the future coincide with hers? Together they could make the inn a success. A Christmas festival as famous and popular as that at Williamsburg, a gift shop, a restaurant—there were lots of possibilities. Not many young men had a career handed to them on a silver platter, a chance to be employer instead of wage slave. . . .

Andrea tied a bright red ribbon around her package and added it to the pile on the bed. Poor Martin. She would have to find a nice wife for him.

VII

Andrea had her assistants up at dawn the next morning. Having observed Martin's struggles with his typewriter ribbon, she was not surprised to discover that he was hopelessly clumsy at manual labor; he fell off the stepladder twice, hit his thumb with the hammer, and got tangled up in the ropes of greenery.

Mrs. Horner accomplished very little that day, since she kept coming to the door every ten minutes to admire the latest decoration and mutter, "My, that sure is pretty." However, she had appeared that morning with a big box of homemade cookies, and as Jim said, her cookies were worth a multitude of sins.

By midafternoon the downstairs rooms looked beautiful, and even Martin, absently sucking his bruised thumb, admitted that the results justified the effort. Sprawled on the stairs, Jim said, "We've forgotten something. No mistletoe."

"It is not, thank God, a plant indigenous to this region," said Martin, around his thumb. "If it were, your sister would have demanded that I climb a tree to get it."

"We've got to have mistletoe," Jim insisted. "We can probably get some in town. Hadn't we better get started?"

"If your heart is set on mistletoe, go and get some," said Andrea, folding the stepladder.

"We're supposed to go to Sue's open house," Jim reminded her.

"Oh, damn. I completely forgot. I can't go. We haven't even started on the tree yet."

"We'll decorate the tree tonight." Jim stood up and put his arm around Andrea. "With all the trimmings—carols, hot buttered rum—the works. Come on, Andy."

"I've got two people coming tomorrow and four the day after," Andrea began.

"We'll help you tomorrow. Won't we, Martin?"

"Sure," Martin said, a smile softening his face as he watched them.

"I know what that's worth," Andrea scoffed. But she couldn't resist the appeal or Jim's embrace. Like all boys he had objected to hugs and kisses, but recently his demonstrations of affection had become more frequent. She stood on tiptoe to kiss his cheek. A few years ago he would have squirmed and made faces. Now he returned her kiss with a hearty smack.

"It'll be fun. You don't have to dress up; Sue said it was come as you are."

Naturally Andrea paid no attention to this absurd remark— just like a man! She knew every woman at the party would be dressed to the hilt. She burrowed in the back of her closet, hoping, illogically, to discover some forgotten garment that would suit the holiday spirit, but of course found nothing; she hadn't bought new clothes for a year, and her best had been less than glamorous. Finally she slipped into the old green wool, scowling as she belted it tightly around her waist. At least it was the right color.

They had to park some distance from the basket shop. Most of the cars must belong to Sue's guests; the other shops in town were closing when they got there. As they walked along the street, the door of Past and Present opened, and Al Wyckoff called to them.

"On your way to Sue's party?"

"That's right. Aren't you going?"

"I was just closing when I saw you. I found a frame for you, Andy—I think it's exactly what you wanted. Come in and have a look."

Once inside they scattered, Martin to examine the old books, Jim to admire Wyckoff's collection of antique tools. The frame was perfect—not too wide nor heavy nor ornate, like so many of the ones Andrea had seen. It was also in good

267

condition. Some of the gilt had rubbed off but the delicate papier-mâché molding was intact.

Andrea looked dubious, as a matter of principle. Wyckoff said, "Hard to find one this size, you know. And it's in excellent condition."

"Not too bad. . . . How much do you want for it, Al?"

"Let you have it at cost." He named a figure that struck Andrea as reasonable, though far from cheap. She reached into her purse.

"What's that for?" Jim asked curiously.

"Mary's picture. I told you I intended to hang it in the hall. Do you think this frame will suit it?"

"It's okay, I guess. How do you know it will fit?"

"I measured it, silly." She handed over the money and Wyckoff began wrapping the frame. "By the way, Andy, have you decided about that weapon?"

"I don't want to think about guns at Christmas, Al."

"Who are you going to shoot?" Jim asked.

"Nobody. Al thinks—"

"I don't think, I know. It's a jungle out there, and every property owner has the right to defend himself."

From Martin, seemingly deeply engrossed in a book, came a raucous and uncouth raspberry.

"Now don't fight," Andrea said firmly. "You two disagree about practically every subject I can think of, but this is no time for a debate."

"I don't like guns either," Jim said. "Anyhow, you don't know my sister, Mr. Wyckoff. She doesn't need bullets. God help the poor sucker that gets in her way."

"You won't think it's so funny if Gary Joe Bloomquist breaks in there some night and—"

"Oh, for God's sake, I'm sick of hearing about Gary Joe," Jim said, losing his patience. "You people are trying to make him into a local Jack the Ripper. He's not so bad."

"How can you say that?" Andrea demanded. "You, of all people."

"He gets mad and he gets frustrated and the only thing he can think of is to punch somebody out," Jim said. "Haven't you ever felt that way? And you're a lot smarter than poor old Gary."

"I admire your charitable attitude," Wyckoff said grumpily.

"That doesn't mean I won't beat the shit out of him if I catch him hanging around," Jim said with a grin. "Assuming I can, that is."

"I don't want to hear any more about guns or beating people up or any more four-letter words," Andrea said forcibly. "This is Christmas, damn it."

The whole town was at Sue's, and as Andrea had expected, the women were resplendent in their best. Sue jingled like Santa Claus's sleigh, and rather resembled that hearty old gentleman in her scarlet caftan embroidered with white doves of peace. She hailed them from across the room and gestured hospitably at the punch bowl.

Martin was prompt to follow the suggestion, but Andrea remained standing in the doorway with Jim beside her, on the fringes of the crowd but part of it. Smiles and greetings and calls of "Merry Christmas" came at them from every direction. Someone was playing a guitar and a few determined souls were bellowing "God Rest You Merry, Gentlemen," their voices almost drowned by the general uproar of laughter and conversation. One of the singers broke off to mime an invitation to Jim. He waved back, but stayed at Andrea's side.

"It's like we've been here for years instead of only a few months," he said.

Andrea nodded, remembering last year's office party—a typical production of its kind, when they all got drunk as soon as they possibly could and people who ordinarily didn't have a civil word for one another paired off in dark corners for a spot of adultery. If Reba's tales were to be believed, Ladiesburg was not immune to either failing. But there was a difference; she couldn't put it into words. . . .

"Like we belong here," Jim said. "Like family."

After leaving the open house they drove to the highway for a hamburger at one of the fast-food places, and then went home and got to work on the tree. The night was crisp and cold, crackling with stars. Jim started a fire and Martin opened a bottle of his favorite hock, then a second bottle. That was his major contribution; Andrea refused to let him handle the fragile old ornaments or climb the ladder. She did the upper section of the tree herself, topping it with a tinseled star eight inches across that had once belonged to Bertha. Then they all collapsed onto the sofa to admire their work and finish the wine.

Ropes of cranberries and popcorn, tinsel tarnished to antique softness draped the green boughs. Andrea had found a box of old cards among Bertha's treasures and had interspersed them with gleaming glass balls. Candles would have completed the period look, but she was afraid to risk them; multicolored lights flickered on and off, sending gleams of crimson and blue, green and gold around the curved surfaces of the ornaments.

"What a lot of work for something that will only last a week," Martin said.

"Don't play Scrooge. Admit it's beautiful."

"There's magic in it," Martin agreed. "Peace and joy, the innocence of childhood. More wine?"

"Why not?" Andrea held out her glass.

"Not for me, thanks." Jim stood up. "I'll leave you two alcoholics to finish the booze."

"Good night, darling. Sleep well."

She didn't see what happened; she only heard a soft thud and a muffled exclamation from Jim. Martin, who was facing the door, laughed. "What was that about alcoholics, buster?

Anybody who misses a doorway that size has got to be a little looped.''

"Jimmie, are you all right?" Andrea shifted position. The overhead lights went out and Jim said, "There. You can see the tree better now. And I don't want to hear any cracks from you, Martin, till you've made it upstairs on your own feet."

"I've no intention of moving," Martin said comfortably. "Good night, Jim."

Jim moved slowly, cautiously up the stairs. When the sound of his footsteps had died away, Martin chuckled. "Subtle, isn't he? He thinks I wouldn't have nerve enough to make a pass with the lights on."

"Are you going to?" Andrea asked drowsily.

"Sure. Why do you suppose I've been plying you with liquor? And I'd hate to disappoint Jim."

She wasn't prepared for what happened. She had no intention of objecting to something so trivial; it didn't matter, one way or the other. When his arm went around her she leaned against it, relaxed and content. The gentle touch of his hand stroking her cheek and throat, brushing the hair back from her forehead, made her feel like a contented kitten. She yielded readily when he tilted her face toward his, and giggled a little as the stubble of beard pricked her cheek. A breath of soft answering laughter warmed her parted lips before his lips found them.

Gentle at first, then more demanding, his kiss roused feelings so long denied that their presence filled her with a vast astonishment. Turning, she strained against him, holding him. Long—so long, so cold in the outer darkness, starved and forgotten. . . . How was it possible to forget? Or had it ever happened? Not like this, not this way.

Martin was the first to pull away. He had to free her clinging hands; raising them to his lips, he held them clasped in his for a moment before returning them to her in a grave, almost ritual gesture of relinquishment.

Crimson and gold, silver and blue, the lights flashed in the darkness like fallen stars. Breathless and dazzled, Andrea reached for Martin. He had moved back to the far end of the sofa, leaving an empty space between them.

"Why did you stop?" she whispered. "Why don't you. . . ."

Martin was silent for a moment. Then he said quietly, "It must be your decision, reasoned and deliberate. You know I love you. Maybe now you know how much. Too much to tumble you on the couch when you're in a mellow mood, and have you regret it next day."

She recognized the quality of his caring but denied its wisdom. The dictates of the mind and the demands of the body were irresolvable; reasoned passion was a contradiction in terms.

Martin took her hand and held it lightly, at arm's length. "I'm too old to make love on the couch," he said mockingly. "It gives backaches in the morning. Besides, I don't do myself justice that way. Invite me to your room, Andrea, and see what happens."

If he had taken her in his arms or even stroked her hand in a certain way, she would have spoken. His withdrawal was deliberate, his casual tone a calculated move in a game she had already lost. She felt chilled and bewildered. But he had been as aroused as she; she could not be mistaken about that.

"I don't believe you," she said.

He didn't ask her what she meant. "There are too many of us here," he said. "It has to be just you and me."

Chapter Fourteen

As usual, Andrea was the first one up the following morning. She was glad to have a little time to herself before she faced Martin; she had been in no state to think clearly the night before. Her mental condition wasn't much better now. The more she thought about what had happened, the more incomprehensible it became. If she hadn't known Martin so well, she would have suspected him of deliberately stirring her up, just to prove he could, and then pulling back to watch her stew in her own frustration. She didn't believe it. Such petty malice was completely out of character for him.

So what was the point of that too-brief encounter? She had been ready and more than willing. If it had been up to her, they would have made love, on the couch or the floor or anywhere else he chose. It could still happen, anytime he wanted it. He had proved that, if he had proved nothing else; never, with any other man, had she felt such a total commitment of feeling and senses.

It couldn't be the practical difficulties he was concerned about, though they definitely concerned her. Somehow she couldn't see herself carrying on an affair in her own home, with guests coming and going, and right under Jim's nose. That might have been what Martin meant by his enigmatic reference to "too many of us." He couldn't make a simple statement, he had to dress it up in flowery literary language. He had always been critical of her love for Jim; was he jealous, or, despite his apparent sophistication, inhibited by the presence of a younger man, who was also her brother?

It wouldn't bother Jim. His manner made that clear; he greeted her with his usual smacking kiss and casual "good morning," but there was a gleam in his eye and a meaningful smile on his lips that spoke louder than words. Obviously he assumed that she and Martin had—what would his generation have said? Made out? Had sex? Whatever he called it, Jim was in favor of it. His air of pleased complacency made her want to slap him.

He was still at the table when Martin appeared, and although Andrea was grateful for the presence of a third party, Jim's sidelong glances didn't relieve the tension. However, Martin seemed unaware of nuances. There was no change in his treatment of Andrea, not even a tender look behind Jim's back. Gradually Andrea's self-consciousness was replaced by annoyance. Martin was acting as if nothing had happened. Well—nothing had happened. She had made too much of it. Apparently it had meant nothing to Martin.

She dismissed it from her mind, or tried to. The effort was made easier by Martin himself, who had resumed his old manner, friendly and casual and mildly sardonic.

The arrival of guests left Andrea too busy to brood until the morning of the twenty-fourth when the last of them left. She and Mrs. Horner spent the day cleaning up. She had a card for Mrs. Horner, enclosing an extra day's pay, but somehow that seemed inadequate after she found three parcels under the tree; the tags were printed in large round letters such as a child might have used.

It was Jim who made the gracious gesture she had neglected.

He came downstairs as Mrs. Horner was preparing to leave. "Merry Christmas," he said, handing her a package and kissing her on the cheek.

"What was it?" Andrea asked after Mrs. Horner had taken her leave, speechless with emotion and clutching the parcel to her ample bosom.

"Just a little shelf I made. I copied the one in the kitchen, with the curved sides and the cup hooks. She said once she liked it."

"Jimmie, that was sweet."

"I made all my presents," Jim said proudly.

"So that's what you've been doing up there."

Jim lowered his voice conspiratorially. "I made a box for Martin, out of a piece of walnut Wayne found for me. Do you think he'll like it?"

"He'll love anything you made, darling."

"I better get back to work. I haven't finished Reba's present, and I want to give it to her tonight. She is coming, isn't she?"

"Unless she chickens out."

Andrea had been forced to revise her plans for Christmas Day. Reba had pointed out, with some justice, that she had to be on hand to greet old customers, some of whom had been coming to her for years.

"Christmas Eve, then," Andrea said firmly. "I'll ask Sue and Al and some of the others. Come late if you must, but come. You have to, Reba. You'll never get over this if you give in to it."

Reba had listened glumly to Andrea's facile diagnosis of what ailed her. Convinced she was not, but she obviously wanted to please her friend.

"Oh, all right. I'll give it the old college try. But if I bolt don't be surprised."

"You just have to keep trying," Andrea said.

Reba rolled her eyes and groaned.

Later that afternoon Andrea opened the leaves of the mahogany table in the green parlor and began setting out plates and napkins for the buffet she had planned. The food could not be set out until the last minute, for Satan would browse among the sandwiches if they were left unguarded. Satan took a dim view of Christmas. Andrea had caught him backing up to a basket of boughs, tail raised and quivering, and had sent him flying out of the room with a smack on the behind. However, his greed was stronger than his fear of her and she didn't trust him an inch.

Martin found her there. "Here's your Christmas present," he said, offering a large box.

"You shouldn't have," Andrea said formally.

"Open it now."

"We agreed we wouldn't open presents until tomorrow."

"I want you to open this one first."

Curiosity got the better of her. The package was beautifully wrapped, undoubtedly by the store at which it had been purchased. Neat corners and dainty gold bells in a nest of green ribbon were beyond Martin's skill.

She unwrapped it carefully, taking her time and reminding herself not to thank him too effusively. If he wanted to play it cool, she could be cool too. But when she saw the contents she could not hold back a cry of delight.

It was a long hostess gown of sherry-brown velvet. Intricate scrolls of gold braid and beads trimmed the wide neckline and trailing sleeves. She had never owned a dress so extravagant and so obviously expensive, and as she stroked the soft velvet her spontaneous smile faded.

"Martin, I can't accept anything like this."

"Don't you like it?"

"It's gorgeous. But you'll have to take it back."

"I can't. It was on sale."

"Liar."

"I won't take it back. Throw it out, cut it up for dust

276

cloths, give it to Mrs. Horner. I don't care what you do with it. But I had hoped you would wear it tonight."

"I can't possibly."

"At least try it on."

She knew what he was thinking—that once she put the dress on she would be unable to resist keeping it. She would show him she wasn't that weak. She would tell him the dress didn't fit. Then he would have to return it.

But when the soft fabric slid caressingly over her body and she turned to look at herself in the mirror, her resolutions went up in a puff of simple vanity. The color brought out the creaminess of her skin and the hidden highlights in her brown hair. The fit was perfect, clinging to her shoulders and breasts, falling in graceful folds from the waist. The face that looked back at her from the mirror couldn't refrain from smiling; flushed cheeks and shining eyes completed the flattering, irresistible image.

Before the glow faded, while she stood posturing and turning, there was a knock on the door. It opened a crack; Jim peeked in.

"Hey, wow," he exclaimed, and flung the door open so that Martin, immediately behind him, could see too.

"I couldn't put it better myself," Martin said. "Hey, wow!"

Trying not to smile, and failing conspicuously, Andrea shooed them away and changed back to her working clothes. Martin knew he had won; she couldn't give the dress up, it was the most becoming thing she had ever owned. There was something almost diabolical about his awareness of her weak points; she had not realized herself until she saw the shimmering image in the mirror how much she had longed for a pretty dress. The fit was perfect, even to the length, and she could not help but be moved by the grace and subtlety of that demonstration of caring. He knew her so well he saw desires she herself was barely conscious of. He knew the very shape of her body.

He also knew how to undermine her independence. The gift was the sort of thing a husband might give a wife, or a lover his beloved—costly, intimate. When people admired the gown, as they were sure to do, she would have to explain that it was Martin's gift, and they would draw the obvious conclusion.

Probably they had already drawn it. Strange that that had not occurred to her before. . . . Ladiesburg loved its gossip, and the townspeople would assume as a matter of course that an adult male and an adult female sharing the same house were sleeping together. They might gossip about it, but they wouldn't really care; times and morality had changed since the days of Mary Fairfax.

Martin's gift would remove any remaining doubts. It was the crowning irony that the assumption should be false. Utterly bewildered, Andrea gave the gown a last, loving look and shook her head. She couldn't figure out what Martin had in mind. She wondered if he knew himself.

II

Andrea stood in the open doorway greeting her guests. Light and warmth poured out to welcome them; the smell of wood smoke from the open fires blended with the aroma of dying fir and cedar. Robed in velvet and gold, she was the perfect picture of a gracious hostess—chatelaine of a distinguished and beautiful mansion, as J. W. Holderman might have put it. As she pressed the hands of friends and returned their salutations she was struck, not once but over and over again, with the contrast between her present position and the one that had prevailed the preceding Christmas. The exhausting, hireling's job, the cramped little apartment—too small for entertaining, even if she had had friends she cared to invite—the shabby, cheap furniture and spartan existence. . . . Only a year ago. It had not been the easiest year of her life but the end result was worth the struggle—almost worth the suffering.

Her dress attracted the attention she had expected. Several of the wives favored her with knowing smiles, but the only one to comment directly was Sue, who had evidently had a nip or two before she came. "If you ever get tired of him," she said, pointing at Martin, who was mercifully not within earshot, "throw him my way, will you?"

Reba was the last to arrive. Andrea thought it might take her a while to work up the necessary courage; she had stationed Jim at the door to watch for Reba and head her off in case she got a last-minute attack of cold feet. Calling, "Here she is," he went out to meet her. When Andrea got to the door he was herding her up the steps, rather like a dog nipping at the heels of a shambling, reluctant black sheep.

"Well, I'm here," she grunted. "But I don't know for how long. My God, Andy, you look gorgeous. Never knew you had it in you."

Andrea took her hands and drew her in. She had made up her mind that she would not refer, even obliquely, to Reba's fears. Acknowledging their existence was tantamount to admitting their reality. "Aren't you going to ask where I got the dress?" she asked gaily.

Reba gave her a reluctant smile. "So I know. You gotta give the guy credit for good taste."

"Go and tell him." She took Reba's coat and handed her over to Jim, who was hovering helpfully. She had felt it necessary to explain to him why it was necessary to keep an eye on Reba, but of course she had played it down. "Some people have funny ideas sometimes." Surely one of the understatements of the year.

As she went about her duties as hostess, she glanced at Reba from time to time. No ominous signs so far, she was glad to observe; Reba was eating and drinking and talking with her usual verve, and Martin, who had been appointed number-two watchdog, had taken over from Jim. He and Reba were the focus of a good-sized group. Sue was among them, leaning familiarly against Martin; catching Andrea's eye, she grinned and winked.

Hostessing this group wasn't difficult. Most of them knew one another and had a lot to talk about. Avoiding Al Wyckoff, who was bearing down on her with the evident intention of discussing guns, she was captured by another antique dealer who wanted to know if she intended to sell any of her furniture. As she moved from one person to another, and ran out to the kitchen to replenish plates of sandwiches and cookies, she forgot about Reba for a while.

The crowd around the buffet table finally began to thin out. Some people had moved across the hall, into the red parlor, and others had migrated to the library. Andrea congratulated herself. The party was going well. The noise level was still high, always a sign of social success. Jim and Wayne and a few other young people were sitting on the floor talking. Al Wyckoff had literally buttonholed Martin, his hand firmly grasping the other's lapel. Martin was trying tactfully to free himself, without success.

He caught Andrea's eye and grimaced at her, in a signal she had learned to recognize. What was he trying to tell her? Reba, of course. He was supposed to watch out for Reba, and now the old woman was nowhere to be seen.

Andrea made her way through the room, nodding and smiling but managing to avoid being stopped. Reba was not in the library. She retraced her steps, meaning to look in the red parlor.

Crossing the hall, she happened to glance to her right. There was her quarry, standing motionless in front of the desk. Her immobility and the long brown garment she wore, rather like a monk's robe, made her hard to see in the shadows.

"What are you doing here all by yourself?" Andrea asked cheerfully. "Come and give me a hand. I'm going to serve coffee."

Reba's head turned like that of an aged turtle, the rest of her body remaining motionless. Her brow was furrowed, but with puzzlement rather than distress.

"Where'd you get this?" She indicated the picture over the desk.

"I found it." Andrea saw no reason to go into detail. "She was the owner of the house a century ago, when it was a hotel. It's a nice touch, don't you think?"

"Uh-huh."

The portrait looked as if it had always been there, in the place where it was meant to hang. Again Mary watched the door, alert and in command, her cat at her feet.

Reba rubbed her forehead. "Where's the bathroom?"

"This way. Are you. . . ." She didn't want to say it.

"I'm drunk," Reba said. "Did it on purpose. Got drunk as I could fast as I could. Now I've got to pee."

"All right," Andrea said soothingly. "Come on. Lean on me."

"Ha! If I really leaned on you, kiddo, you'd be flat on the floor."

Reba appeared to be perfectly steady on her feet, but Andrea decided not to risk the stairs. She led Reba to her own bathroom, behind the kitchen, and then started the coffee maker. The sandwiches needed replenishing too. She took a plate out of the refrigerator and removed the plastic wrap that covered them.

Satan was asleep—or pretending to be asleep—in the big wingback chair. "Don't bother hanging around, buster," Andrea said vindictively. "You're out of luck this time."

"Who're you talking to?" Reba came in, brushing vaguely at the front of her dress. Crumbs flew up and resettled.

"That damned cat. He's taken to hanging around the kitchen lately. I suppose he thinks I'll forget and leave food out."

Reba looked at Satan. The cat stretched and sat up. Curling his tail neatly around his haunches, he stared intently at Reba. Reba stared back. Then she walked toward the chair, pausing between each step like a participant in a state funeral procession.

"Bertha's cat," she said thickly.

"That's right. He seems to have—"

"Mary's cat."

"What?" Andrea turned. She was just in time to see Reba's body topple. She didn't bend at the knees, but fell stiffly sideways like a felled tree. Lunging, Andrea got a shoulder under her, and tipped her onto the couch.

"What is going on here?" Martin asked, from the doorway.

"She just. . . ." Andrea gestured helplessly. "I guess she passed out."

"I couldn't get away from that stupid ass Wyckoff." Martin bent over Reba, feeling for a pulse, lifting her eyelid. "She's out cold, all right. Pulse is a little slow, but within normal range."

"Where did you go to med school?"

"I was on the police beat in Boston for a year. You pick up quite a lot of useful information watching the ambulance crews. . . . Did she say anything?"

"No, she did not. She was fine. I told you it was all in her head."

"Got any ammonia handy?"

"Why don't you just let her sleep it off?"

"I don't like the way she's breathing," Martin said. "I've seen a lot of drunks, but this. . . . Get me that ammonia."

Andrea went to the sink, pausing on the way to swat Satan off the table, interrupting a slow but determined progress toward the sandwiches. She handed Martin the bottle. Uncapping it, he waved it under Reba's nose.

At first there was no reaction, and Andrea began to get

worried. She had had a few inadvertent whiffs of ammonia over the years, while cleaning with it, and she knew its effects. If Reba was that far gone. . . . Then Reba lifted a big hand and pushed the bottle away. Her eyes were still closed.

"Don't," she said, quietly but distinctly.

"Okay," Martin said, visibly relieved. "Are you—"

"Don't cut it. It's so pretty. Nice flower . . . oh, damn. I told you. . . . No, don't hold it. Let it go. Can't you feel the thorns? There's blood all over your. . . . Let it go, I tell you!"

Her breathing was definitely abnormal now—a series of harsh, quick gasps. Andrea started forward in alarm. "Try the ammonia again," she urged.

"No. Wait." Martin waved her back. "Reba—can you hear me?"

"I can hear you."

"What do you see now?"

"It's growing," Reba said. Her voice sounded as if it were coming from a great distance. It echoed, hollowly. "Green tendrils, twining, twisting. Oh, my God—it's got him. He's caught, he can't. . . . Why don't you try to get away?"

Her voice rose to a wail. "Who?" Martin demanded. "Who is it, Reba?"

A violent shudder ran through her body. If Martin had not caught hold of her, she would have fallen off the sofa. "Who is it? Who do you see?" he asked.

Reba's eyes opened. "I see a bald, middle-aged reporter," she said. "What the hell are you doing to me, Martin?"

Martin sat back on his heels. "What are you doing to me? You scared the living daylights out of me, you old bat."

Andrea pushed past him and bent over the sofa. "Reba, are you all right?"

"Sure. You better get that cat off the table, Andy. He's after the sandwiches again."

The change of subject and of manner was so startling,

Andrea could only stare. Satan took a crab sandwich and left, unmolested.

"I'd better be going now," Reba said. "Tomorrow is a busy day for me. I had a very nice time. Thank you. I hope I didn't spoil the party. I shouldn't drink so much."

Martin steadied her as she got to her feet. "I'll drive you home."

"No. I can drive myself. Look. Steady as a rock." She held out her hand.

"But you just said you—"

"I just said I'd drive myself. Hell, the car can drive that road all by itself. Thanks again, Andy. See you tomorrow?"

"Yes, of course," Andrea said, still staring.

Martin went out with Reba. He was trying to convince her she should let him take her home. He'll lose, Andrea thought; Reba is even more bullheaded than he is.

She appeared to be fully recovered, but she must have had too much to drink; it was the only possible explanation. She had displayed none of the symptoms that had afflicted her on that first disastrous visit.

There was only one thing. . . . Andrea frowned, trying to remember.

Reba had seen the picture. She had observed the cat crouched at its mistress's feet. There was no inscription on or under the portrait; Andrea had not found time as yet to have a plaque engraved. So far as she could recall, she had not told Reba anything except that the subject of the portrait had once owned Springers' Grove Farm.

How had Reba known Mary's name?

III

Christmas Day was something of an anticlimax. Everyone was tired and mildly hung over, and inclined to wince at the sight of food. The high point of the day was the ceremony of opening the presents. Andrea had spent a lot of time and effort selecting exactly the right components for Jim's hi-fi. She had even called Kevin to ask his advice.

As she expected, he knew precisely what Jim wanted and where to get it. "Tell the old bum I'll see him sometime in January," he added. "Got to go to my mother at Christmas—turnabout is fair play—but I've got a long break midsemester, and I'll be out thataway sooner or later."

Jim seemed pleased at his gifts, but he was more interested in seeing what Andrea and Martin thought of his presents. Martin's response was all he could have wished; stroking the satiny finish of the box, Martin insisted on a step-by-step description of the construction process, and promised to keep the box for his most valued treasures.

"Love letters?" Jim asked, with a glance at Andrea.

"Checks," Martin said.

Andrea's gift was a frame of carved and polished walnut. The photograph it enclosed was an enlargement of a snapshot Kevin had taken in the fall—she and Jim standing side by side in front of the house. She had protested when Kevin asked her to pose; she was wearing an old shirt and faded jeans, and her hair was a mess. . . . But the picture had turned out to be one of her favorites. Jim was smiling, and at the last minute he had reached for her hand. Tears came to her eyes as she looked at it, and Jim said, with satisfaction, "I like people to cry over my presents."

They were engaged to have dinner at Peace and Plenty; but even Jim confessed he didn't think he could do justice to one of Reba's six-course meals and Martin made a sour face when Andrea insisted they would have to eat, hungry or not. Reba was as busy as she had claimed. The dining room was still full when they arrived, and people were waiting for tables. When Reba joined them in her office, where a table had been set for four, she was visibly unsteady on her feet.

"Everybody wants to buy me a drink," she grunted, falling into a chair. "Helluva way to celebrate Christmas, getting poor old Reba bombed."

The only reference made to Andrea's party was a rather grim one. "Al's place got broken into last night," Reba said. "Must have been when he was at your open house."

"Was anything taken?" Andrea asked.

"Cleaned out the cash box. Told Al he should have taken it to the bank, but he said he didn't have time. They figure it must have been an amateur. He didn't touch the stock, not even the silver."

"Any suspects?" Jim asked.

"Somebody saw Gary Joe hanging around—"

"I knew they'd try to pin it on him," Jim said in disgust. "That poor bastard hasn't got a chance."

"Maybe," Reba said. "But he isn't doing anything to help himself. I offered him a job a couple of weeks ago—"

"You would, you old softie," Martin said, smiling. "What did he say?"

"He told me to do something I suspect is physically impossible," Reba said with a chuckle. "Stupid damned kid. . . . Have some more stuffing, Jim."

Andrea, whose chair faced the bookcase, had noticed a new acquisition—a pair of bookends, solid pieces of wood simply but beautifully finished. She assumed they must be Jim's gift to Reba, but the latter said nothing about them until her guests were ready to leave.

"Did you guys see these?" she asked, pointing.

"I think I recognize the craftsmanship," Martin said with a smile. "They're beautiful."

"Place of honor," Reba said gruffly.

"Do you like them?" Jim asked.

"It's the best present I ever got. I'll treasure it, Jim."

Jim put out his hand and Reba took it. Her face contorted in a desperate effort at self-control, but without success; the tears poured down her face, turning the thick layer of powder into paste and washing tracks through her wrinkles.

"Hey," Jim said. "There's nothing to cry about, Reba. This isn't a wake. It's a celebration."

"Right. Oh, damn it to hell. . . . Merry Christmas, you guys."

IV

After the holidays Ladiesburg closed its doors to the public. Many of the antique dealers went off to warmer climes, and the others retired to the living quarters over their shops, opening only by appointment. Andrea didn't feel she could afford to close, but bookings for January dropped to almost nothing. She gave Mrs. Horner the month off, a gesture which the latter accepted phlegmatically, remarking, "Gonna be lots of snow this month."

Reba left town too. Andrea was not aware of this until she called the restaurant one day and learned of her friend's departure from the assistant manager. Surprised and a little hurt, she passed the news on to Martin.

"It's the first time in years I've known her to take a vacation," he said, frowning. "I hope she's all right."

"Paula said she had gone to visit friends in Arizona."

"Strange that she didn't mention it to either of us. . . . Well, you'll be left in peace for a while. I'm going away for a few days myself."

"Where?"

"Why, darling, I didn't know you cared."

Under the circumstances, the remark was doubly insulting. Andrea stalked out of the room. She assumed he was going to New York; his publisher probably needed buttering up, for Martin appeared to be making very little progress with his book. Not that she cared. At long last she and Jim would be alone together.

Somehow it wasn't the way she had expected it would be.

Jim was wonderful—much more companionable than he would have been a few months earlier, or even a year ago, before the accident. He didn't seem disappointed or distressed when Kevin called to postpone his visit until the end of the month. He wasn't upset or disappointed about anything. Nor was his amiability merely negative, the absence of ill will. His enjoyment of the things they did together was positive and joyful, infecting Andrea with the same pleasure. He had regained his old interest in sports, including football; he and Andrea made a big occasion of the Super Bowl, drinking beer and eating hot dogs, criticizing the plays and having a fine time.

Andrea knew she should have been blissfully happy. How often in life does one attain a long-desired, seemingly unattainable goal, and find it all one hoped it would be? The sensation she felt was so slight it was hardly discernible—too vague to be called dissatisfaction or disappointment or concern. When she was with Jim she was not conscious of it. But Jim wasn't always with her; he seemed to have plenty to do by himself, and to be perfectly content with his own company. Andrea found herself with time on her hands, and it was then, when she sat reading or sewing or just relaxing, that the dim, almost invisible shadow tiptoed into the edge of her consciousness.

It was Martin's fault, of course. She had grown accustomed to the strange state of existence he had created, and to the paradoxes implicit in it and in him—the skilled, passionate lover who had lost all interest in taking her to bed, the man who told her one day he adored her and the next day called her a selfish egocentric brat, the admirer who had given her the most subtly flattering gift she had ever received, and who didn't care to claim so much as a kiss as his reward. His behavior made no sense at all; she had given up trying to understand it. Her own feelings were another matter, one she could, hopefully, analyze. She admitted to herself now that she did love Martin, but the word that had once seemed so easy to define had lost its meaning. She didn't know what love was. Physical desire, affection, respect—all those she felt. Whether that was all she ought to feel she did not know. Martin had turned her world upside down; she was living in a room that no longer had a floor or ceiling or walls.

Martin's quibbles and criticisms had even contaminated her relationship with Jim. She didn't agree with him—but he might have a point when he said Jim needed companions his own age. She had never thought she would see the day when she missed "the guys." But that day had come; not only did she regret their loss on Jim's account, she missed them herself—big, noisy, amiable consumers of other peoples' food, joking and kidding with her, filling the apartment with laughter and mud and dirty clothes and love. It was perhaps not surprising that Jim should have let them drift away. The interests they had shared were no longer Jim's interests. But surely he needed someone. . . . I'll talk to Kevin, she promised herself. If he says he can't make it I'll ask him to change his mind. I'll beg him, if I have to.

Another unexpected development during the days of Martin's absence was her growing reluctance to look at Mary's picture. It came on so gradually she was scarcely aware of it until one day as she passed through the hall, preoccupied with details of a business letter she was about to write, she found herself standing in front of the picture with both hands on the frame, preparing to lift it down. When she realized what she was doing she pulled her hands away. "What's the matter with me?" she asked aloud. But no one answered.

She was sitting on the sofa in the kitchen, staring off into space, when Jim came in. Satan was curled up next to her. He never sat on anyone's lap, but occasionally he condescended to be stroked, slowly and gently.

"Well, now, if that don't beat all," Jim exclaimed, in a deplorable imitation of the local accent. "You sure do make a purty picture a-settin' there with your pussycat next to you, purrin' his little heart out."

"That cat doesn't know how to purr," Andrea said, with a disparaging look at Satan. "As a lap cat he's a failure."

"He's been hanging around the kitchen a lot lately. Funny—he never came in here when Mrs. Horner was around."

"Takes a witch to know a witch's critter," Andrea said with a smile. "No doubt they had come to an understanding."

"He always did like you."

" 'Like' is a word that is not in Satan's vocabulary. I'm sure the attraction is proximity to food."

"Maybe he misses Martin." Jim looked at her slyly. "I miss him. Don't you?"

"Not desperately, no."

"You don't have to kid me, Andy. He's crazy about you."

"Now, Jim—"

"He told me so, a couple of months ago."

Andrea didn't know whether to laugh or be angry. "Asking your permission, was he?"

"We're friends," Jim said. "It would make me feel good if you. . . . You need someone, Andy."

Just what she had thought about him. "We have each other, Jimmie."

"Right. Only. . . . Are you going to marry him?"

"He hasn't asked me," Andrea said sourly.

Chapter Fifteen

When Martin had been gone for a week Andrea gave up pretending to herself. She missed him. For several days she had developed a habit of stopping in the middle of her work, her head tilted, listening for a sound that never came. When the telephone did ring, which was not often, her reaction to the voice on the other end was always disappointment. There was no reason why he should call, except to announce his return. He didn't owe her a daily report, but he did owe her that much.

Instead of calling, he simply turned up one gray afternoon and let himself in the front door.

Andrea was in the kitchen trying for the second time to reproduce Mrs. Horner's cinnamon rolls. The first attempt had been such a disaster that even Jim the omnivorous had been unable to eat them. Struggling with the dough, which had developed a macabre life of its own, Andrea swore at it and at herself. It was humiliating that she couldn't duplicate the efforts of a fat middle-aged woman who couldn't even read a magazine.

She heard the sound of the key in the lock, and her heart

gave an unwelcome leap. It had to be Martin. Jim was in his room, and no one else had a key. And she might have known he would return, without warning, at a time when she looked her worst—hair uncombed, face bare of makeup, hands smeared with recalcitrant dough.

Wiping them on a towel, she ventured into the hall.

"It's not a burglar," Martin said.

"You might have let me know you were coming."

"I guess I might have. Hello."

"Did you have a good trip?"

"Hey, Martin!" Jim's greeting was much more enthusiastic, and Martin's dour look turned to a smile.

"Hey, Jim! Everything all right?"

"Sure. It's good to have you back, though." He glanced out the door. "What happened to the bug?"

"It finally breathed its last," Martin said morosely. "I had to rent a car. Want to help me look for a replacement?"

"Great. Now?"

"No, I have to work up to it. It's been a shock to me, after all these years. Besides, I'm taking your sister to dinner tonight."

"Swell," Jim said.

"Wait a minute," Andrea said.

"Oh, sorry. Would you care to dine with me this evening, Andrea?"

"Sure, she'd love to," said Jim.

II

Jim saw them off, beaming like a proud father, but his attempt to suggest that the occasion constituted a normal social engagement was not helped by the protagonists. Andrea had weakened at the last moment and put on a new dress she had bought the week before; expecting at the least an admiring look, she relapsed into sullen silence when Martin only glanced at her and made no comment. Martin behaved like a man who was carrying out an unavoidable obligation—entertaining an aged aunt or homely sister. Conversation was nonexistent until Martin turned onto the road; then Andrea said, "Aren't we going to Peace and Plenty?"

"Obviously not."

"Where are we going?"

"I haven't decided."

Several minutes elapsed before Martin spoke again. "Is that a new dress?"

"There was a sale last week—"

"That's what it looks like. A sale, last week."

"Damn it, Martin—"

"It's not an inherent lack of taste," Martin mused. "You did a fine job on the house. Don't you think you deserve as much consideration as a pile of wood and plaster?"

The silence that succeeded this question was not broken again until they reached the outskirts of Frederick, the nearest town of any size. Martin turned abruptly into a parking lot. "This looks as if it would do."

If what he wanted was privacy, the restaurant he selected fit the bill; it was only half full and they were given a table in a corner, away from the door and the kitchen. When the waiter had taken their order for cocktails, Martin leaned back in his chair.

"Heard anything from Reba?"

"No."

"Anything happen while I was gone?"

"No."

"What would you like to eat?"

"I don't care."

The waiter brought their drinks and Martin ordered for both of them.

"That takes care of that," he said. "Hello, Andy. Have I mentioned lately that I love you?"

"Don't try to sweet-talk me!"

"That is a sin I've seldom if ever been accused of. I missed you."

"I'm sure you were rarely vexed by the thought of me. Did you have a good time in New York?"

"I wasn't in New York. I was in, among other equally tedious places, Mobile, Alabama."

"Oh?"

"Mobile, Alabama," Martin said, "was the home town of Colonel John Fairfax, C.S.A."

For a moment she couldn't think what he meant. Then— "Mary's husband," she exclaimed.

Martin shook his head. "Not Mary's husband. She never had a husband. Her child was illegitimate."

III

"Don't ask me if I'm sure. I'm sure. Don't suggest alternative possibilities. I've eliminated them. Don't interrupt me. I want to get this over with. For once in my life I am not looking forward to lecturing.

"The man from Mobile was the only John Fairfax who had the rank of colonel. That's why I investigated him first. He was married twice, to local Mobile belles. Neither was named Mary Broadhurst.

"So maybe Mary's John wasn't a colonel. One must allow for the normal human tendency to exaggerate. It's not an uncommon name. I checked out two lieutenants and a captain as well. Nothing.

"It was a clever move on her part. It would have been hard to prove she had not been married, at some time, to a man of that name; by selecting one of the enemy, from a distant area, she lessened the chance that a local nosy parker could trace him. There were Confederate troops in and out of Maryland during the first years of the war.

"Her lover may have been one of them. We'll never know who he was, or why she was still an old maid at the age of thirty-nine. The local boys weren't good enough for a Broadhurst? Her father must have had something to do with it; he wouldn't have made a point of asking her forgiveness if he hadn't felt guilty.

"At any rate, he backed her up when she told him she was pregnant. They picked a name out of the casualty lists and got their story ready. While the old man was alive no one dared challenge them. But when he died, leaving her alone and broke, tongues began to wag. She probably was not very popular anyway; I can't see her sucking up to the local gentry. Someone found out—not all the truth, that would have been difficult to prove—but enough to make her the town pariah. If she had crawled humbly off in a corner, wrapped in her widow's weeds, they might have forgiven her in time. But that wasn't Mary's style. She stood up to all of them and she won. But she paid a heavy price."

Martin stopped talking and picked up his glass. "Here's to her," he said.

Andrea had listened with a singular lack of surprise, as if someone were narrating a story she had heard before. It only increased her admiration for Mary Fairfax—she had earned the name, let her keep it. Faced with the same situation, under the same circumstances, she would have done the same, if she had had the wits to think of it.

"Here's to her," she echoed. "But what does it matter, after all?"

Martin countered with another question. "To whom? It mattered a hell of a lot to Mary, and even more to her daughter. Do you know what the word bastard meant back then? It was a label that barred a person from all the desirable things in life—a career, a place in society, a good marriage. I'd like to think Alice never knew the truth, but I'm afraid she did. That drawing of the soldier—the idealized face of the father she never knew—was something she didn't want her mother to see. She must have had some suspicion or she wouldn't have hidden it.''

There was a pause, while the waiter brought their food. Then Martin said, ''I haven't finished the saga. I started where Jim did, at the county courthouse. I was looking for Mary's wedding license, in case Jim overlooked something. I didn't find it, of course. But I did find a license for Alice Fairfax.''

That piece of news did surprise Andrea. ''But Alice was never married. Are you sure?''

''It was our Alice, all right. The dates and place of residence fit. The license was never used. And, as we know, the tombstone gives her maiden name.

''Now,'' Martin said, forestalling her next question, ''you are about to ask me why. I'll tell you why. Or at least, what I think happened.

''The license application was dated three months before Alice died. It was not her death, then, that prevented the marriage. She jilted him, or he jilted her, or someone else broke it up. The boy's family may have interfered, because of her illegitimacy. But I rather suspect history repeated itself; Mary decided the young man wasn't good enough for her daughter. Three months later Alice fell, or jumped, from the tower window. The coincidence of time is not conclusive, I grant you, but it is certainly suggestive.''

''Do you suppose she could have been pregnant?''

''That would be ironic, wouldn't it? The timing is right. It doesn't really affect the case, however.

''And now,'' Martin went on, poking distastefully at his cooling food, ''you will again ask why. Why have I wasted ten days tracking down this tragic but long-gone history? Since you ask, I will tell you.

''There are two ways of interpreting the things that have happened over the past four or five months. First there is the rational, commonsense explanation. I needn't go over it in detail, because I'm sure it is as familiar to you as it is to me. Like me, you've spent a lot of time and effort trying to convince yourself that it's true.

"The second explanation is far simpler and far less acceptable. It is that Mary Fairfax, or some part of her, still exists. It is her presence, tormented and guilt-ridden, that Reba feels. Her influence has guided you from the start. The rose she planted over her daughter's grave still lives, by supernatural means. When she comes to my door, her cat greets her. Oh, yes,'' he smiled, without humor, at Andrea's look of astonishment. "I know she's there. She's been back since. I look up, feeling her presence. I see that infernal animal preening himself and rubbing against an invisible skirt. Have you ever heard Satan purr? He purrs when Mary enters the room. And she was in the parlor that night. . . .''

"You mean that's why you didn't—''

"I don't perform well before an audience.''

"I never heard anything so incredible in my life,'' Andrea said sincerely.

"Oh, yeah? How many other incidents have there been, that you neglected to mention to me? We've both concealed things from one another, and for the same reason—we haven't the guts to admit we're facing something we don't understand. Or do we?'' Martin threw out his hands. "I just don't know. This is the first time I've been faced with a situation that can be explained in two entirely different, mutually contradictory ways. When I went looking for the rest of Mary's story I hoped I'd find something that would settle the matter, one way or the other. What I came up with is a perfectly valid motive for a restless ghost, but it's no solution to the problem.''

"What precisely is the problem?'' Andrea demanded. "If you're afraid of your own fantasies—''

"I could learn to live with Mary,'' Martin said seriously. "For a restless spirit she's quite well behaved—she doesn't

297

throw dishes around or pull the covers off the bed or howl in the night.''

Andrea laughed. "You're joking. It's all a joke—isn't it?''

"Making fun of myself is an old habit—Tony would call it a defense mechanism. I'd probably try out one-liners on the hangman while he was fitting the rope around my neck. That doesn't mean I would be indifferent to the gravity of my situation.

"You still don't understand the basic issue here. It's not Mary—guilty ghost, or figment of my imagination. It's not you. Mary hasn't injured or affected you. You're the same person you always were—if not more so.

"It took me some time to see it myself. Reba told me there was nothing wrong with the house before you came to live there. What she forgot was that Jim came too. He was the catalyst, the moving force, not you. Think what has happened to him. Admittedly much of his behavior can be accounted for in rational terms, like all the rest of this damned mess—but aren't the rationalizations wearing a little thin, Andrea? You can discount my fantasies if you like, but the fact can't be denied: The house isn't good for Jim. He's got to get out.''

"There's a rational, commonsense explanation for your feelings about that, too, Martin.''

"I'm only too well aware of it. And I'm sure Tony Benson would agree with you. But it isn't true. I'm not asking you to choose between me and Jim. I love Jim. Never thought I'd say that about another guy. . . .''

She was unable to return his smile. "I won't deny I'm troubled about Jim. But this is too—too amorphous. I need something solid, something I can get my hands on.''

"My God, so do I! When the medical reports came back, I was in a deep depression for days. It would have been so easy if they had found a physical problem—or a mental one. We could have dealt with that. But how do you cure a haunting?''

Andrea shook her head. "I might buy one ghost. But I draw the line at two."

"Let one in and the door is open; you can't keep the others out. The evidence for Alice's presence is even stronger than it is for Mary's. You've got better sense than to stand in an open window forty feet from the ground. What else happened that time? You didn't tell me everything, did you?"

"I felt a hand on my arm," Andrea said. "Holding me back—pulling me back. I think I'd have jumped if it hadn't been for that."

"There we are again," Martin said helplessly. "Subjective hallucination, or Alice, trying to save you from her fate?"

"Or Mary."

"Mary." Martin considered it. "That's even neater, isn't it? Alice is the destructive force; her despair still permeates the house. Mary is the good guy, earning her passage out of Purgatory by helping others as she failed to help her child. No, damn it, it's too Dickensian. Too carefully plotted."

"Perhaps the basic error we're both committing is attributing human characteristics, motives and feelings, to these—these—"

"Why shouldn't they have human feelings? They were human."

"Martin, I'll play this game as long as you like, and I'll play fair. But it's as you said—for every occurrence there are two explanations. I can't buy yours."

"Even after what happened to Jim?"

"What happened? He was on the verge of a nervous breakdown after a traumatic mental and physical experience. I'll even admit you may have been right about his intention of committing suicide. There were other things I didn't tell you about—things I refused to admit even to myself. . . . But when he found himself actually in danger of dying, when the reality hit him, he knew he had made a mistake. He didn't want to die."

"He didn't want to come back," Martin said softly.

"That was a long time ago. He was in pain, confused. . . . It's different now."

"The night we found him in the graveyard, after he'd taken the pills, did you have the impression that he was not alone? That someone was sitting there beside him?"

He waited for her to answer. When she remained silent he shrugged. "All right. Believe what you like, but admit that it would be better for Jim if he went away. Not for ever, just long enough to build a normal life for himself."

"If he wants to go, I won't stand in his way."

"That isn't good enough. He doesn't want to go. Don't you see that that is what worries me? You must make him go. Kick him out. Set him free."

Andrea shivered. "I'll try."

He reached for her hand. "It's going to be all right, Andy. . . . What do you say we stop and get some hamburgers to take home? I can't eat this disgusting slop."

IV

The great search for a car to replace Martin's beloved Beetle began next day. He and Jim left early in the morning and did not return until suppertime. They had had no success, and, according to Jim, they never would if Martin didn't change his attitude.

"He compares every car we see to the VW," he said, half in disgust, half in amusement. "He's in deep mourning. When I point out some neat job, he looks at me like his wife has just died and I'm trying to drag him to the altar."

"Today's automobiles are heaps of junk," Martin argued. "Now the VW—"

"Is dead and gone," Jim shouted. "Now you listen—"

"And the prices!" Martin raised his eyes heavenward.

"Cars today cost as much as a house used to. I paid six hundred bucks for—"

"Don't say it," Jim warned.

"There's something obscene about shelling out thirty thousand dollars for a heap of chrome and tin."

"So who said you had to get a Mercedes? That was the salesman, not me. That red Corvette, now—"

"I refuse to buy a car I have to drive lying down."

The argument raged most of the evening. They finally agreed to have another go at it next day. Andrea, who had refrained from giving her opinion even when appealed to by both sides, firmly refused an invitation to join them.

If the matter of a car had been left to Martin, he probably would have gone out and bought the first thing he saw that had four wheels and a drive shaft. Involving Jim was part of a campaign that would include subtle suggestions about colleges and summer jobs and the like. Andrea had no objection. Yet, as always when Jim was with her, her forebodings seemed utterly absurd. He was so happy.

For months she had been sleeping soundly, without dreaming, but that night she was a trifle uneasy. There had been several burglaries recently, one at the gas station and another at a farmhouse whose deaf, elderly owner had a reputation as a miser. Al Wyckoff had called to tell her about them and to repeat his offer to find her "a nice little handgun." She had told him flatly that she didn't want a gun. But for the first time since she had moved into the house she was on edge. Her room was on the ground floor, and so far from the rooms where the men slept that she doubted they would hear if she called.

Like all homeowners she had developed a sensitivity to night sounds. The ones she had become accustomed to, like the murmur of the stream and the passing of cars on the highway, didn't disturb her slumber, but any unusual noise woke her at once. According to the illuminated dial of the clock on her bedside table it was three-twenty when the crackle of dried frost-stiffened grass outside roused her from deep sleep.

Listening intently, she identified the sounds as furtive footsteps. She felt more anger than fear. Her window was open a few inches. She could tell that the intruder had stopped some distance away—perhaps at the window of the room that had been Jim's, now unoccupied. Careful not to let the bedclothes rustle, she slid out of bed. The sneakers she had worn that day were on the floor. She slipped her feet into them, and reached under the bed.

Neither Jim nor Martin knew about the poker. They would have laughed themselves sick if they had known, and then lectured her about rushing in where angels and sensible people feared to tread. Andrea would have been the first to admit that the poker's usefulness as an offensive weapon was limited, particularly for her. It just made her feel better. Gripping the heavy metal tool, she crept into Jim's old room.

She had barely entered when the furtive noises exploded into cacophonous discord—howls and human cries of pain, the hasty retreat of a heavy body now more concerned with speed than silence. She reached the window in time to see a dark bulk disappear behind the barn.

No need for caution now; she ran to the kitchen and snatched up a flashlight. It took her several minutes to unbar the back door. There were double locks, in addition to a bolt. Poker in one hand, flashlight in the other, she threw the door open.

A blast of cold air made her shiver. The night was still until she heard a car engine start up. It rose to a roar and faded into the distance.

He had made his escape. She considered going out to look for footprints, but a combination of cold and common sense restrained her; though she was fairly certain the car she had heard belonged to the trespasser, she wasn't absolutely sure, and it would have been foolhardy in the extreme to risk an encounter. She was about to retreat when the flashlight beam disclosed a moving figure. Tail bristling and switching, Satan swaggered up the steps and into the house.

Andrea locked the door. Satan sat down in front of the stove. Without deigning to look at Andrea he began grooming himself, licking his paw and passing it over his ears and nose. When he started worrying at one paw, Andrea realized there was something caught in a claw. She stooped and removed a shred of cloth.

Relieved of this impediment, Satan went on washing himself. Andrea looked at her find. It was the smallest possible fragment, only a few threads—dark blue, like the fabric used for jeans.

She watched Satan for a few minutes. Then she went to the refrigerator. There were a few pieces of chicken left from supper. Stripping the meat off a thigh, she put the dish in front of the cat.

Not until then did she hear footsteps thumping down the stairs. Martin was a heavy sleeper; if aroused in the middle of the night he was inclined to be bumbling and incoherent. When he appeared in the doorway, yawning and rubbing his eyes, she allowed herself to be sarcastic.

"Never mind, hero. It's all over."

His half-closed eyes moved from her to the poker on the table and then to Satan, noisily chewing chicken. "There was somebody out there, then. I thought I heard a noise. . . ."

"It's a good thing I wasn't counting on you or Jim to defend my honor," Andrea said.

"Jim is sleeping the sleep of the just." The full meaning of what he had observed finally penetrated and Martin's eyes opened all the way. "You didn't go charging after him with that poker, did you?"

"I have better sense than that. What you heard was Satan—and a scratched, bitten burglar."

"Oh."

"I think I'd better get a dog," Andrea said thoughtfully. "I'll do it first thing tomorrow."

Martin dropped heavily into a chair. "Why bother? You've got him." He indicated the cat, who looked back contemptuously.

"The man probably stepped on his tail. I can't count on that happening twice in a row. A dog is more dependable."

"There's another alternative," Martin murmured.

"I'm not going to sleep in your room, if that's what you're suggesting. I may as well hand out keys to all the local hoodlums as leave this part of the house empty at night."

"I could sleep in your room."

"Sleep is the word. It would probably take me ten minutes to get you up and on your feet."

"The world's most alert bodyguard I am not," Martin admitted. "But I have other qualifications you might take into consideration."

"Another time, perhaps," Andrea said, surveying his rumpled face and drooping eyelids with unconcealed amusement. Yet she felt a slight pang of disappointment when he nodded sleepily.

"I'm not at my best right now. You aren't nervous, are you? If you'd like me to sleep on the couch—"

"Oh, go to bed," Andrea exclaimed. "Luckily I've got Satan to protect me."

She was looking through the advertisements in the newspaper next morning when Jim and Martin joined her. "I really don't know much about dogs," she confessed, after explaining to Jim what had happened and cutting short his exclamations of distress and concern. "What's a good kind?"

Martin laughed. "It depends on what you want."

"Well, obviously."

"Do you want a guard dog, an attack dog, or just a mutt that will bark on demand? You can pay up to a thousand dollars for a Doberman that has been taught to pursue and hold a suspect, or you can go to the pound and pick out a cheap barking machine.''

"Oh. I don't think I want a Doberman. They look mean.''

Jim didn't join in the discussion, but when Andrea asked if he would go with her to the Humane Society, he was not unwilling. "Martin and I planned to look for a car today,'' he said. "Martin, how about if we go to the pound with Andy first?''

"Not me,'' Martin said. "I can't stand animal shelters. All those big sad eyes begging me to take them. . . . Most of them are on their way to quick extermination.''

"It's a lot more merciful than being abandoned or mangled by a car,'' Andrea said.

"I know, I know. I kick in a few bucks to the Humane Society every year, and I admire the job they do. But I'm a gutless coward and I don't mind admitting it. You go, Jim. When you get back we'll head out.''

The animal shelter was more of a trial than Andrea had expected. Martin's fault again; he was sensitizing her to a lot of things she had never thought much about. She finally settled on a large shaggy brown specimen of indeterminate breed that was, the shelter assistant assured her, "just a pup,'' although he was already the size of a sheep and almost as woolly. He acted like a puppy, though, falling over his own large feet in his frantic attempt to get out of the cage and into her grasp, licking her hands furiously, and wagging his tail so hard it stung her calves. He also proved his ability to bark.

"What do you think, Jim?'' she asked.

There was no answer. Jim was sitting on the floor getting his face washed. "We'll take that one,'' Andrea said.

She found she would have to wait a few days until the dog got its shots. Even then she had a dog before Martin had a car. Ragmop had been installed, with all his accoutrements—

feeding dish, water dish, doghouse, collar and leash, and a huge stack of newspapers—while Martin and Jim were still looking.

Andrea was firm about keeping the dog outside most of the time. "He's going to be as big as an elephant. I can't have an animal that size underfoot all the time, especially during the busy season. He's unsanitary—"

"I have to concede that," said Martin, examining his shoe.

"He'll stop doing that eventually," Andrea said hopefully. "I was referring to his other, permanent disabilities—shedding, fleas and so forth. He has a perfectly good doghouse, for which I paid a small fortune. I don't know what you two bleeding hearts are complaining about; I'm the one he keeps up half the night with his howling."

"What are you talking about?" Jim demanded. "I can hear him too. Anybody within a ten-mile radius can hear him. If you'd let him sleep in my room—"

Ragmop liked Jim's room. He preferred any room in the house to his kennel, but he liked Jim's room the best, partly because Jim was there and partly because Satan wasn't. The first meeting between the two animals had been almost as violent as Andrea expected, but she had to admit it wasn't Satan's fault. After one incredulous look at the panting, palpitating bundle of brown fur, Satan would have preferred to ignore the vulgarity; but Ragmop, impervious to snubs, wanted to play. Satan sat unmoving until the dog got within six inches of him and then neatly bisected Ragmop's nose with one casual swipe. The first encounter should have been enough, but Ragmop was either dim-witted or incurably absentminded; he couldn't resist Satan, even though he knew better.

Ragmop was only allowed inside under supervision and he wasn't allowed in the library or the parlors under any conditions. Martin's room was out of bounds because of Satan, so Jim's was almost his only refuge. The first time Jim took him there,

Andrea and Martin trailed along. Neither would have admitted it, but both wanted to see how the dog would react. When he settled down beside Jim's bed, tail wagging and tongue hanging out, the conspirators exchanged a long look, hers triumphant, Martin's noncommittal. Either there was nothing wrong with the tower room, or the well-advertized sensitivity of canines to supernatural entities was a fraud.

Martin had not referred again to his theories. He succeeded in nagging Jim into sending away for college catalogs, but they interested him more than they did Jim; as Martin pored over them, reading excerpts aloud, Jim listened politely but did not commit himself.

The house was quiet. It was as if Martin's admission of his fears had exorcised them; for weeks there had not been the slightest manifestation of anything abnormal. Yet Andrea was conscious of a mounting sense of expectation—not apprehension or alarm, just a feeling that something was going to happen. She was looking forward to Kevin's visit, as was Martin, who had approved highly of the idea after she told him about it. Perhaps that accounted for the way she felt.

She was alone in the house one afternoon when the doorbell rang. She wasn't expecting a visitor. When she saw who it was, her eyes opened wide in surprise.

"Reba! I didn't know you were back."

"I got back yesterday."

"Come in. I'm so glad to see you. Jim and Martin are out—"

"I know. I saw them in town just now. That's why I came."

She let Andrea draw her into the house but when the latter tried to take her coat she shook her head.

"I can't stay. I came because there's something I have to tell you. Once you've heard it, you probably won't want me to stay anyhow."

"Why, Reba—"

Barbara Michaels

"We've been friends, haven't we?"

"We are friends. Though I'm miffed at you for running off without telling me."

Reba shook her head. Her face was pale but controlled, and Andrea noticed that she spoke without her usual affectations of careless grammar and vulgarity.

"Let me talk, Andy. It's taken all the courage I possess to make myself come here. I wasn't going to say anything. I ran away. But I finally realized I had to. It may end our friendship, and that means a good deal more to me than you know. But if I failed to speak, and something happened, I'd always feel guilty.

"I let you talk me into coming here Christmas Eve because I had decided I had to stop running away from it. I hoped you were right—that it was only an impersonal impression of something long-past and harmless. I didn't really believe that. But I had to take the chance because of you. If there was something wrong, something dangerous, I had to find out about it and warn you."

She stopped, breathing heavily. Andrea was too dumbfounded to speak.

"It wasn't so bad at first," Reba went on. "Not until I saw that picture. If I'd been a dog, I'd have put my tail between my legs and howled. But you came—and I thought, This is it, this time I'll see it through. The cat's eyes were like gold coins, like the shining objects hypnotists use to put people under. I let myself go.

"I don't remember what I said. But I remember what I saw.

"The first thing was a flower—a rose, I guess. A pair of scissors cut through the stem. The flower started to fall, but a hand caught it, and held it, in spite of the thorns. Blood ran down its fingers, but it held on. Then the rosebush started to grow. It shot out long tendrils stretching and writhing. Jim was there. The stems wound around him like ropes, holding

308

him. He didn't try to free himself. He just stood there, and the thorns tore him.

"I couldn't tell you. It would have sounded like Ruby Starflower playing psychic, and I knew how much you hate that sort of thing. . . . Then, the next day, when Jim and I shook hands. . . . It's going to happen soon, Andy. Very soon. I don't know what you can do to stop it, but you have to try."

"Something is going to happen—to Jim?"

"I'm going now," Reba said. "Good-bye, Andy."

Andrea made no attempt to stop her. Reba walked like a sick old woman, shoulders bowed and feet dragging. She didn't look back.

Andrea knew she ought to run after her and tell her it was all right. She recognized the courage Reba's visit had required; friendship of that quality was worth preserving. She should reassure her friend that the danger she feared but could not define had passed. The symbolism of Reba's dream was so direct she felt sure Martin must have told her of his beliefs.

A small silent voice in her mind jeered, "Aren't these rationalizations becoming a little strained?" but she refused to listen to it. She ought to go after Reba. . . . But she stood still, scarcely feeling the cold wind that numbed her arms and face, watching the Mercedes pull away.

The air was so thick she could hardly breathe; it clogged her straining lungs like heavy liquid. Her heart was pounding and her hands were sticky with perspiration, despite the cold. Then into the deathly silence came a sound that lifted the hair on her arms and neck—the sound of a dog howling.

Ragmop had resigned himself to the kennel after a few noisy nights, but even at his worst he had never sounded as he did now. The quivering lamentation rose and fell in a wordless litany of despair.

Andrea ran, stumbling in her haste, and threw open the back door. She had chained the dog that morning; he would

309

have followed the men, demanding to be taken with them, if she had not. He sat in front of the doghouse, his muzzle raised, pouring out his grief to the indifferent sky. Andrea pressed her hands to her ears. "Stop it!" she shouted hysterically. "Stop it, stop it!"

Instead of running to greet her as he always did, even when she was scolding him for some misadventure, the dog dropped flat, head between his paws. His tail dragging, he crawled into the kennel.

Andrea was shivering violently, but not from the cold. No wonder the howling of a dog had become the classic portent of death; there was no more poignant expression of hopeless grief than that terrible lament. Jim and Martin. . . . Why didn't they come home? They had been gone a long time.

The dog was silent now. She went back into the house, to the telephone. But that was no use; she didn't know where they were; she could hardly call every automobile dealer in the county. Mary's picture looked down at her from above the desk. Not Mary; Mary still watched the door. Strange that she had never observed before how tense and expectant was the pose of the stiff body, the tilted head.

Andrea started up the stairs, slowly at first, then running faster and faster. She was panting when she reached the steps that led to the tower room. The door was unlocked. Jim never locked his door now. He knew she seldom went there. He cleaned it himself, with a little help from Mrs. Horner. He had been hard at it the past week, carrying down bag after bag of discarded belongings. An early spring cleaning, he had called it. Getting rid of a lot of old junk. . . .

The room was as neat and impersonal as a hotel room before a guest arrives. Andrea went to the desk. Its top was bare—not a scrap of paper, nor an empty beer can. She started to open the drawer but her hand refused to move; she was afraid of what she might see. Emptiness. All gone, discarded.

She could hardly breathe. The air felt even thicker here, dense as oil. She went back to the door. A small mat covered the floor inside the threshold. Andrea kicked it aside.

The loose board came up in her hands. The sketches were there, in the old hiding place. Something else was there too, on top of the book. An envelope with her name on it, in Jim's writing.

She left the board lying aside, the door open. When she reached the second floor she knew she couldn't go any farther. Her legs wouldn't hold her up. She opened Martin's door. His clothes, tossed carelessly over the foot of the bed, his papers littering table and chairs, the smell of his tobacco and shaving lotion. . . . Feeling a little stronger, she sat down on the bed and opened the envelope.

V

Dear Andy,

You won't read this till after I'm gone. At least you better not—if you do, I'll know you've been snooping again!

You're going to feel bad, I know that, and I'm just writing this because I hope maybe it will help. I'm happy, really, and I want you to be glad for me.

It sure is hard to write stuff like this without sounding stupid! I guess I better start at the beginning—which for me was after the accident. I think I was supposed to die in that accident, Andy. I told you I didn't want to come back. What I didn't tell you was that I blamed you, at first. I was pretty shitty to you for a while. I'm sorry about that. It took me a while to realize that there was some reason for me to be here, and it wasn't your fault.

I don't understand all of it yet, but I know it has something to do with this house and her—Alice, the girl who used to live here. I had a lot of stupid ideas about her once; you know, that she was my long-lost lover, or

311

something. It isn't anything like that. Although I think I've known her before.

I took those pills on purpose, Andy. I just couldn't stand it any longer. While I was sitting there in the dark, waiting, something happened. It was like a voice telling me I was making a dumb mistake. That this wasn't the way to get what I wanted. That I had to wait. And that I wouldn't have to wait long.

So it will happen pretty soon, I guess. I don't know when and I don't know how, but soon. I'm not where I'm supposed to be. Neither is Alice. She's like me—a little farther along the way, but held back for some reason. I think maybe the reason I'm here is so I can help her find her way home.

I can just hear you laughing when you read this, it sounds so corny. But I guess you won't be laughing, will you. I hope you won't feel bad too long. Martin will help. I'm glad he'll be with you. This year has had a lot of good things in it. I'd have hated not knowing Martin.

Do you remember how you felt when you went back to college that first year, after Christmas vacation? You were sorry to leave me and Dad, but you were anxious to get back to your friends and everything. That's how I feel, only more so. I love you, sis. Be happy.

Jim

VI

Andrea was standing at the window in the parlor when they came back. At first she didn't know who it was. The car was a gleaming low-slung object, so new the marks of the sales sticker still showed on the windshield, its bright scarlet paint like a trumpet blast in the gray landscape. It paused in front of the house and she saw their faces—Jim behind the wheel, grinning from ear to ear, Martin beside him, his lips moving in anxious expostulation. After a moment they drove on toward the garage. Of course—it looked like snow. Martin might not care, but Jim wouldn't want a spot of damp to mar the new darling.

Their safe arrival, canceling her forebodings, should have relieved the heaviness that clouded her mind. But the web of rationalizations had finally given way. She had tried to mend the break—the letter didn't mean anything, it might be weeks old, it only confirmed what she already knew and had taken steps to combat. . . . The strands snapped and failed even as she wove them.

She was stiff from standing so long in the same position. Slowly she walked through the house, to the back door. Martin came out of the garage carrying a brown paper bag. She had asked them to pick up bread and milk and a few other groceries. Seeing Andrea, he waved. "Did you see it?" he called.

She nodded. "Jim will probably want to sleep in the garage tonight," Martin said cheerfully. "I can't get him out from behind the wheel. What are you doing here without a coat on? It's freezing. Put something around you and we'll go inspect the car. Jim will insist on showing you every gear in the damned thing."

He didn't give her a chance to reply, but she couldn't have spoken anyway. Every motor function in her body seemed to have halted—speech, movement, hearing. She let him nudge her back into the kitchen. He went on talking, his face flushed with cold, his lips moving, smiling. She couldn't hear what he said. He didn't seem to notice that she had stopped, like a watch someone had forgotten to wind. He draped a coat over her shoulders and led her to the door.

Jim had come out of the garage. He wasn't looking at them; head turned and hands tightly gripping the crutches, he was staring at the woodshed that adjoined the garage. He started toward it, moving quickly, avoiding the patches of ice that spotted the ground. He had almost reached the shed when the door burst open and a man staggered out.

As they learned later, Gary Joe had planned another attempt to break into the house. Hiding in the woodshed waiting for darkness to fall, he had whiled away the time with the help of the bottle he had brought with him. The sight of the car, gleaming symbol of the success and affluence he so desperately resented, brought him to the shed door, but he would have remained in concealment if Jim had not seen him.

The paralysis that had held her broke, Andrea cried out. Martin started down the steps, but he didn't hurry. Gary Joe was more of a danger to himself than anyone else; one nudge would topple him, if he didn't fall flat of his own accord. He stumbled toward Jim, but it was unlikely he realized who stood in his way; he saw only an impediment to flight and acted to remove it.

The clumsy, ill-directed blow didn't even touch Jim. But as he sidestepped, smiling and contemptuous, the crutch slipped on the frost-hardened ground. He stumbled back, his head and shoulder hitting the wall of the garage.

The sound was so soft it was scarcely audible. Jim went rigid, arms and body pressed against the wood. Suddenly blind and unfocused, his eyes tried to move, searching, but the effort was too much. He managed to mumble three words— "Not his fault . . ." before he fell.

Martin reached him first. Kneeling beside him, her hands clamped over his, Andrea was scarcely aware of Martin's frantic movements, or of how much time elapsed before he raised his head. Tears slid down his face, mingling with the icy drizzle that had begun to fall.

"It's no use. It must have been an embolism—massive brain hemorrhage. . . . I should have seen it coming. If I had paid attention to the symptoms instead of wallowing in my stupid fantasies. . . . He was dead before he fell, Andy. He didn't feel anything. . . ."

Andrea's fingers tightened. Heavy as earth, cold as stone, Jim's hand lay in hers. "He's not dead," she said. "He can't be. I won't let him die."

"It was quick and easy, Andy. He didn't suffer."

Andrea shook off the hand he placed on her shoulder, focusing every atom of her will on the fading, elusive shadow of identity. She had done it before. She could do it now.

"We can't let him lie here in the rain," Martin said.

She made no effort to prevent him when he lifted the limp body, only kept her grip on Jim's hand. Martin turned blindly toward the nearest room, which happened to be Andrea's, and laid his burden on the bed before dropping to his knees, gasping with strain and grief.

"Call the rescue squad," Andrea said. "A doctor."

"It's too late."

"Call them."

Martin struggled to his feet and went out, closing the door.

The distraction of speech had cost her. It was more distant now, that flickering thread of consciousness. She flung all the force of her will after it, insistent, untiring. Come back. Come back. . . .

Suddenly they filled the room with the soundless beat of their desperation—the frantic, flailing wings. Andrea cowered, hiding her face against the side of the bed, but never losing her hold on Jim's hand.

Help me.

Had she spoken the words or heard them spoken? No matter; the help was there. She felt its presence though her eyes were closed—a source of warmth perceived though not beheld. Her strength fed on it and fed it in return.

She raised her head. The room was dark with twilight, but she saw it plainly—the features now as familiar to her as her own, the somber widow's weeds, the small rough hands clasped over the ring of keys dangling from its waist. In its

315

presence the desperate wings retreated, weakening now and fainter.

It was Mary's face and form—no image, no imprint, no impersonal memory of the dead past, but Mary herself. Mary was dead and rotting under the stone in the graveyard, but Mary moved. Her tight mouth curved in a smile of welcome and fellowship. Her hands reached out.

Then, in a dazzling flash of revelation, Andrea knew what had happened to Mary Fairfax and the true nature of the bond between them. Not strength but its opposite, cowardly selfishness. For strength was renunciation and relinquishment, and only weakness would attempt to keep something limitless and free behind bars formed not by malice but by adamantine love.

There was no conscious moment of decision, only an instinctive revulsion that snapped the contact of body and mind alike. She found herself on her feet, hands empty, as she tried to communicate her denial, and her pity, to the fading shape who was no less a prisoner than the love she had tried to cage.

And they were gone—all of them—if they had ever existed except in the recesses of her own mind. The room was cold and dim and empty. She felt as if she had awakened from a long illness and endless fever-ridden nightmares.

Slowly she turned to the bed.

He was gone. For the first time she realized that the phrase was a simple statement of fact, not, as she had once believed, a euphemism concealing an unbearable truth. The form on the bed was as empty of identity as a photograph or a tinted, lifesized statue. Jim was gone. He was not there.

The long dusk deepened. Rain wept at the window, but her eyes were dry. She felt nothing. Not grief, not resignation, not even the poor comfort of self-sacrifice. That final fantasy had only been another illusion. It would have been better than nothing, but she could not even cling to that.

The sound of sleet at the window was more than she could bear. She raised her hand to close the curtains.

Sunlight gilded the world. The dogwoods along the drive were in full bloom, white star shapes tossing in a warm breeze. Jim was running down the driveway. He wore tattered old jeans and the T-shirt that said, "Where the hell is Ladiesburg, Maryland?" The gravel spurted up under his flying feet and his hair blew back with the speed of his running.

She was waiting for him by the bench beside the stone gatepost. Andrea had always pictured her as fair, but the hair cupping her small bent head had the iridescent shimmer of a blackbird's wing. She rose to meet him, hands held out and head thrown back, laughing. Before they passed out through the gate, into the road, Jim looked back. He raised one hand. Then they were gone.

At the sound of a soft knock Andrea turned from the window into the cold, winter-darkened room. The door swung open. Silhouetted against the square of light was Martin, hesitant, his shoulders sagging. She felt his grief and marveled at it; and as she went unhesitatingly into his arms she knew that finally she was capable of giving as well as receiving what they were meant to share.

He loved Jim too. One day she would tell him; he deserved that. It was of no consequence whether he believed her or not. She knew that what she had seen was not reality, but neither was it illusion. It was a symbol of a truth too profound to be comprehended by creatures with only five limited senses, but of that ultimate truth she had no doubt at all. Wherever Jim was now, he ran free in the sunlight.

THE BEST IN SUSPENSE

<table>
<tr><td>☐</td><td>50159-4</td><td>THE MILLION DOLLAR WOUND</td><td>$3.95</td></tr>
<tr><td>☐</td><td>50160-8</td><td>by Max Allan Collins</td><td>Canada $4.95</td></tr>
<tr><td>☐</td><td>50152-7</td><td>TRUE CRIME by Max Allan Collins</td><td>$3.95</td></tr>
<tr><td>☐</td><td>50153-5</td><td></td><td>Canada $4.95</td></tr>
<tr><td>☐</td><td>50150-0</td><td>TRUE DETECTIVE by Max Allan Collins</td><td>$3.95</td></tr>
<tr><td>☐</td><td>50151-9</td><td></td><td>Canada $4.95</td></tr>
<tr><td>☐</td><td>50461-5</td><td>ONE OF US IS WRONG by Samuel Holt</td><td>$3.95</td></tr>
<tr><td>☐</td><td>50462-3</td><td></td><td>Canada $4.95</td></tr>
<tr><td>☐</td><td>50614-6</td><td>THE BRANDYWINE EXCHANGE</td><td>$3.95</td></tr>
<tr><td>☐</td><td>50615-4</td><td>by Robert A. Liston</td><td>Canada $4.95</td></tr>
<tr><td>☐</td><td>50764-9</td><td>LION IN THE VALLEY by Elizabeth Peters</td><td>$3.95</td></tr>
<tr><td>☐</td><td>50765-7</td><td></td><td>Canada $4.95</td></tr>
<tr><td>☐</td><td>50762-2</td><td>DIE FOR LOVE by Elizabeth Peters</td><td>$3.50</td></tr>
<tr><td>☐</td><td>50763-0</td><td></td><td>Canada $4.50</td></tr>
<tr><td>☐</td><td>50775-4</td><td>THE AMBER EFFECT by Richard S. Prather</td><td>$3.95</td></tr>
<tr><td>☐</td><td>50776-2</td><td></td><td>Canada $4.95</td></tr>
<tr><td>☐</td><td>51060-7</td><td>GOOD BEHAVIOR by Donald E. Westlake</td><td>$3.95</td></tr>
<tr><td>☐</td><td>51061-5</td><td></td><td>Canada $4.95</td></tr>
</table>

Buy them at your local bookstore or use this handy coupon:

Clip and mail this page with your order.

Publishers Book and Audio Mailing Service
P.O. Box 120159, Staten Island, NY 10312-0004

Please send me the book(s) I have checked above. I am enclosing $_____
(please add $1.25 for the first book, and $.25 for each additional book to
cover postage and handling. Send check or money order only — no CODs.)

Name _____

Address _____

City _____ State/Zip _____

Please allow six weeks for delivery. Prices subject to change without notice.

HEATHCLIFF

AMERICA'S CRAZIEST CAT

☐ 56804-4   HEATHCLIFF AND THE GOOD LIFE $1.95
☐ 56805-2   Canada $2.50

☐ 56802-8   HEATHCLIFF AT HOME $1.95
☐ 56803-6   Canada $2.50

☐ 56806-0   HEATHCLIFF: ONE, TWO, THREE AND YOU'RE OUT $1.95
☐ 56807-9   Canada $2.50

☐ 56816-8   HEATHCLIFF: SPECIALTIES, ON THE HOUSE $2.50
☐ 56817-X   Canada $3.50

☐ 56808-7   HEATHCLIFF: THE BEST OF FRIENDS $1.95
☐ 56809-5   Canada $2.50

Buy them at your local bookstore or use this handy coupon:
Clip and mail this page with your order.

Publishers Book and Audio Mailing Service
P.O. Box 120159, Staten Island, NY 10312-0004

Please send me the book(s) I have checked above. I am enclosing $_____
(please add $1.25 for the first book, and $.25 for each additional book to
cover postage and handling. Send check or money order only — no CODs.)

Name _____

Address _____

City _____ State/Zip _____

Please allow six weeks for delivery. Prices subject to change without notice.